WITHIN

Edited by Stewart Wieck
Art by Timothy Bradstreet

Table of Illustrations

Contents

THE SCARLET LETTERS

by Scott H. Urban

The fog was just beginning to roll in as Corrinda found Café Prague. Thin white wisps crept around corners like sentries for an invading army of oblivion. Emerging from the mouth of an alley, like something born of the mist, came a huge dog of uncertain breed. Surely he's too big to be someone's pet in the city? she wondered. The canine ran across the road with an easy lope, not even giving a sniff in her direction, and was swallowed back up by the enveloping shadows of a narrow side-street.

Over her head, a sputtering neon sign caused the fog to glow in a blue nimbus. She could still see where someone, many years ago, had painted the name of the coffee house on the tall front window, using varicolored daisies and asters to give shape to the letters. Only in Haight-Ashbury, thought Corrinda, where the flower is in power. A handwritten sign taped to the window's lower left corner read "Open Mike Poetry Reading — 9 PM Until ???"

Corrinda brought herself close to the glass. As she did, another face approached her. She gave a start, then realized it was her own reflection. The bruise under her right eye was only now beginning to lose some of its purplish bloom. She winced and wished she had learned to use make-up somewhere along the line.

A plywood stage rose on the other side of the window. Two interior spotlights mounted on the ceiling were aimed at the stage. Someone was onstage speaking, but the glare prevented her from determining whether the person was male or female. She took another step and pushed open the door.

In all her 15 years she had never been to San Francisco, but she immediately felt more at home here than she ever had in Homily, some 500 miles to the north. The atmosphere was thick with smoke. It hung in spiraling coils like the thin ghosts of snakes. Her nose detected not only tobacco, but also cloves and pot. Ten circular tables, each with five or six chairs and most of them occupied, filled the center of the room. Ten additional chairs were lined up against the left hand wall. The patrons seemed divided equally between gray-haired day-trippers who had somehow missed the word that the '60s were over, and khaki-shorted out-of-towners who wanted a safe brush with the counter-culture. The bar was to the right, and a chalkboard hanging behind it proclaimed, "The Perk of the Day." Irregularly spaced around the walls were vintage Peter Maxx posters and psychedelically lettered broadsides announcing concerts by Jefferson Airplane and The Grateful Dead.

A lanky man with hair to the small of his back was shouting onstage. In his left hand he held a sheaf of wrinkled, stained papers. His right hand fluttered as if trying to work itself free of the confining wrist. He was saying something about government atrocities in Central America, but it was somehow mixed up with what his older brother had done to him when they were young.

She followed a roundabout course to the bar. Behind it stood a woman with thick, curly red hair, fair skin, and freckles the color and size of pennies. Corrinda ordered coffee, black, and watched it poured, thick and steaming, from a waiting pot. She passed a five-dollar bill over the counter, wincing as she realized she was now down to ones. She blew across the top of the mug while waiting for her change. She turned slightly, looking back at the stage, trying to get into the flow of the poet's declamations.

"Are you going to read tonight?"

The voice, right behind her ear, was unexpected. She gave a start, nearly slopping scalding coffee on her fingers. Cursing, she set down the mug and turned. She could have sworn there was no one behind her when she walked up to the bar, but a man now stood only inches away.

He was swarthy, stocky, and of medium height. He wore a black turtleneck sweater and loose-fitting black slacks. His hair, also black, was swept straight back from his forehead. She could see little of his eyes. They were set deep amidst his other features, whereas his nose was just a touch too prominent. He frowned with concern.

"I'm sorry. I didn't mean to frighten you."

"It's all right. I just didn't see you there." She began to ask him where he had come from when she caught a warning. Her palm was resting on the smooth, oak top of the bar, and she felt the message travel up her fingers, through her arms, and into her brain. Her pupils and nostrils flared wide.

She looked up at the newcomer. "Brace yourself against something," she said breathlessly.

His brows drew together in question, but before he could ask her what she meant, a rumble — at first distant — seemed to approach at supersonic speed. The floor beneath them rippled, as if they somehow stood on the surface of a wave. Glasses and plates beneath the bar shimmied against one another, trying to see how violently they could shake without shattering, though many fell and burst. A couple of the cafe patrons screamed, but by the time their cries faded so had the tremor, the faultline agitation flowing back into the mantle to be absorbed. Most of the audience was laughing now, releasing nervous tension. The bartender was standing up toppled bottles.

"It wasn't the Big One, folks," the lanky poet onstage announced, "so God must be telling me it's all right to finish my poem."

The man in black focused his attention on Corrinda. "You knew that was coming. You knew it before it happened."

She nodded, using a wad of napkins to mop up coffee that had spilled from her mug. "Sometimes I. . . catch things. I think of it as catching because I know there are messages flying around us all the time, out here" — she used her finger to point in 10 different directions — "and sometimes I just happen to be in a position to pick them up. It's like catching a baseball blindfolded. Most of the time you'll miss. But if you hold your mitt just right, you might catch one pitch out of a thousand. Sometimes I learn things about the past. Sometimes I learn about the future. Sometimes I know what another person is thinking right at that moment."

"What a gift to possess." The stranger smiled. "You have been blessed."

Suddenly she looked down and bit her lip. "You wouldn't think so. Not if you'd caught. . . some of the thoughts I have."

He nodded, accepting that without question. "So. As I was asking you before San Andreas interrupted, are you going to read tonight?"

She felt the blush rising on her cheeks. "I wanted to. Is it so obvious? It's the reason I came, I guess. But now I'm not sure. I don't know if my stuff is good enough. I don't know if it. . . sings."

"Ah." His eyebrows rose slightly. "Are you the new Belle of Amherst?"

She quickly shook her head. "No. Nothing like that. I write more about. . . the darker side of life."

"Emily understood that as well. She knew Death would stop for her and take her to the Narrow House. But that's beside the point. I would like to hear you read."

"I'm afraid I'll make a fool of myself. . ."

He nodded at the stage. "You couldn't do any worse than that one. You may get some applause. You may even feel like doing it again." He looked her up and down appraisingly, and she discovered, much to her surprise, she didn't mind. "What's your name?"

She hesitated. She had no idea who he was — for all she knew, he could have been a mugger, a psycho, a serial killer. She could lie, make up a name — but then she realized she would never see him again after tonight anyway.

"Corrinda. What's yours?"

He repeated her name in a low whisper. It had always seemed awkward before, but in his voice her name became something exotic and glamorous.

"That's different. Very beautiful." He glanced at the stage. "Go on up there. Before you can talk yourself out of it." The audience was clapping, seemingly with relief, as the lanky poet stepped from the stage.

She made her way between the tables, feeling as if she were walking toward a sacrificial altar. She had to keep swallowing. Stepping onstage, she turned toward the audience. The spotlights in her eyes jarred her, but she felt relieved she didn't have to look into any faces.

"Ummm." She brought her hands up nervously, brushed her hair back, then laced her fingers in front of her. "My name is Corrinda, and. . . I write poetry." Someone over to the right coughed. "OK." She didn't put her poetry on paper. The 20 or so pieces she had composed that she was satisfied with she had committed to memory. Now she almost wished she had then written down so that her hands would have something to do while she recited.

The words came, tremulous at first. Sweat dotted her forehead, prickled under her arms, but she gained confidence with each minute, her voice becoming increasingly stronger and firmer. She spoke of a mother's love turned into something venomous when the mother abandoned the family. She was able to take a stepfather's abusive and incestuous advances and turn them into something tragic, while they yet remained repulsive. She sang of an anger frustrated because there was nothing at which to strike. She mourned for dreams that were bittersweet to begin with because they could never come true. The lights, the audience, Café Prague itself evaporated; she spoke in a void, a place white yet without illumination, where words were the only things to console her. She was surprised when she reached her last word; it brought her back to the mundane. She blinked, now seeing patrons hunched forward in their seats, silent — waiting for her to continue.

"Ummm. That's it. Thank you."

She stepped from the stage and was taken aback at the applause that erupted around her. She was certain it was a mistake; they must have been clapping for someone who just entered. She headed for the door. Well, you did it, she told herself. You shared your poetry with the world. Now you have to figure out what to do with no money and no place to go home to.

She was just about to slip outside when an arm shot across her path — not touching her, but barring her exit.

"That was incredible!" It was the dark-haired man from the bar. "Please don't leave just yet." Flecks of purple and black swirled in his eyes, now revealed in better light.

"I. . . I really have to go."

"At least come finish your cup of coffee. I was saving it for you." He removed his arm, ushering her back to the bar.

She blinked several times, clearing her eyes, then nodded and preceded him to the back of the cafe. Now on the platform a woman sporting Marine-cropped hair, tattered T-shirt, and camouflage pants avowed she was a "feminist-revolutionary-lesbian," and she began to stomp on the plywood in time with her poetry.

"I could almost believe the Muse had descended and spoken through you." He picked up her mug and handed it to her.

She shook her head. "Please. It wasn't that good." She accepted the coffee and took a long sip.

"You underestimate yourself. Your poems are emotional and touching, but not maudlin. You can trust what I say. I've been. . . condemned to follow beauty." He leaned forward, peering intently at her face. "Your poems. Some of them come from life, don't they?"

She couldn't meet his unflinching gaze. "All of them." She dabbed at the hated tears with the already-soiled cuff of her military-surplus jacket. "When no one would listen to me, hold me, I found poetry. For the first time I had a world that accepted me and made me feel safe. The Romantics, the Symbolists, the Beat poets. . . . They seemed to understand the hurt I felt. They had fought against the unfairness of the world, and although they may not have won any battles, they did leave some beauty behind."

"It never ceases to amaze me. Humans' ability to hurt each other. . ." He brought his hand up near her cheek but refrained from actually touching her. "'Monster I must be. . .'"

"'Lest monster I become,'" Corrinda finished.

For the first time, the man seemed rattled. "Where did you hear that?" he demanded.

Corrinda's eyes darted left and right, as if she had done something wrong and now sought an exit. "It's a line from a poem," she said hastily. She reached into her jacket and pulled a thin book from an interior pocket. "In this book." It was smaller than a hardback, with an ash-gray cover and the title in a bold, red typeface:

The Scarlet Letters
by
Virgil

At the sight of it the man's eyes narrowed, almost as if it were a poisonous snake suddenly discovered too close. "By the blood!" His voice was nearly a hiss. "Where did you find this?"

She didn't know whether to drop the book, put it back in her pocket, or give it to him. "I — I bought it in a used bookstore. They usually only carry trashy romance novels, but one time I found this. . . . It was only two bucks, and I really liked the poetry. Have — have you read it, too?"

He ignored her question, as he had all her others. "Would you consider selling this to me?" His voice, up until now calm and resonant, quivered, as if its possessor were an alcoholic suddenly denied the bottle.

"I — I don't know." She looked at the chapbook uncomprehendingly. "It's my favorite. They're poems in the form of letters from a vampire to a mortal. They talk about the horrible Embrace of darkness. . . the uncontrollable thirst for blood. . . and the eternal longing for a final release. It depicts a world of night and shadows and death — more beautiful and more terrifying than our own world. It's a world I wanted to enter. . . I felt like the poet had read what was written in my soul. . ."

The stranger was so focused on the chapbook it seemed he had forgotten her presence. "Damnation! I thought I had rounded up and destroyed all of these years ago. . ." As if the volume were a fragile find at an archaeological dig, he lightly stroked the cover. As he did so, his fingers, thin and cool, brushed against her.

And she caught another of her messages.

Her jaw dropped, causing her to appear more frightened than when the tremor had struck. "Oh my God." Her voice was no more than a whisper. "How can you be standing here — when you're —"

She couldn't complete her question. He gripped her wrist and cinched. She gasped, cutting off her own words. His eyes bore into hers. "You've got to come with me." He was speaking — so softly she was certain no one else could hear him. "To a place where we can talk in private. You mustn't make a sound, understand?"

He began pulling her from the bar. She looked frantically around the cafe; no one seemed to be taking notice of them. She considered making a sound — plenty of loud, shrill screaming sounds — but she had no idea what he would do to her wrist, let alone the rest of her form, if she didn't cooperate.

He led her to a door in the rear wall. The red-haired bartender, who had gone into the back to load up on silverware, came through and almost walked into them. At the last moment he pulled Corrinda back out of the way. It was like she couldn't see us! Corrinda thought, nearly crying out. He squeezed her wrist sharply: Stay quiet.

They pushed through the door and found themselves in a small kitchen. The gleaming, stainless steel surfaces of an oven, refrigerator, sink, and preparation table ran along the walls. He led her to a second door in the far right corner. He looked back over his shoulder and was apparently satisfied with what he saw, or didn't see. "You caught something about me when we touched, didn't you?" He spoke quietly and earnestly, yet she could make out each of his words. He opened the door: wooden steps with peeling paint made a right angle turn as they led to a basement below.

As they made their descent, Corrinda spoke as if in a drug-induced stupor. "I saw — everything that is the opposite of light — shadows, darkness, night, the Void. . . . And I saw blood — an ocean of blood — and you — floating on its surface — not breathing — not even alive."

They stepped onto the floor of a stone-lined basement. The air was much cooler down here than it had been in the stuffy cafe upstairs. The chamber was illuminated by a single bare bulb of low wattage hanging from the middle of the ceiling. The center of the floor was taken up by tables and chairs, all in need of repair. Boxes with indeterminate contents were piled against one wall.

Only now were connections falling together in Corrinda's mind to link words, messages, and omissions.

It was not that she was naive or incapable of inductive reasoning. It was simply that, even with her unfocused prescience, the image she arrived at ran counter to all she had been taught to expect from a blind, heedless universe.

He bent to the floor and found a fingerhold that had been undetectable to Corrinda. He pulled up what looked like a solid stone slab and held it while motioning her over. "Sit down and swing your feet inside. You'll feel rungs. Climb down carefully. You'll be all right. This used to be a rum-runner's storage room during Prohibition."

She thought once more about bolting for the stairs but knew the time for that was long gone. She sat on the trapdoor's lip. "You wrote those poems, didn't you?" She peered at him so intently her gaze might have seared the flesh from his skull. "You're Virgil. The one who led Dante into Hell." She looked down into the dimly lit opening. "Should I abandon all hope?"

He wouldn't turn from her stare. "Haven't you already?"

She had no answer for that, and began to climb down.

● ● ●

At the bottom, she hugged her arms to her chest and waited for him to lower the trapdoor and descend. The chamber in which she stood was a mixture of the contemporary and the archaic. It was slightly larger than the main room upstairs. There was soft track lighting around the perimeter of the ceiling, but the primary source of illumination came from a pair of elaborate candelabra on a heavy oaken trestle table perhaps ten feet long. Aside from the candles, the table supported teetering piles of books, scattered papers, and a bottle or two of wine. In a far corner stood a huge bed with Mediterranean-style headboard and footboard. There were four or five photographs to either side of the bed. Corrinda stepped closer and examined them, her eyes growing wide with disbelief as she did so. The photographs all depicted Virgil with other people, some of whom she thought she recognized. "God! That's Jack London! And that's you and Kerouac — outside City Lights bookshop!"

Virgil nodded. "Can I get you something to drink? I keep some wine down here for my infrequent. . . guests."

"No thanks." She sat on the edge of the mattress and looked up at him. "London died in 1916. *The Scarlet Letters* was published in 1955. But you can't be any older than 35 or so. How can that be? How can you walk — when I can't feel any pulse of life inside you?"

He had turned away from her so that she was addressing his back. "Corrinda, you are not the only one who writes from personal experience." His words came haltingly, as if it pained him even to say them out loud. "You must understand that those poems describe my life — if what I wake to each evening can be called a life." He whirled on his heel toward her once more, hands outstretched as if imploring her to believe him, and she shrank back on the bed reflexively.

"There are those who live only by night. I don't just mean thieves and gang-bangers. There are things most people don't believe in. . . things they laugh at, because their laughter conceals the fear they feel in their hearts."

"So the Kindred — the vampires you wrote about in the *Letters* — they do exist."

She shook her head in wonder. "Have you. . . been here. . . since the Roman Empire?"

He couldn't hold back a self-mocking chuckle. "No, I am not the Virgil of the *Aeneid*. I had another name once, but I haven't used it in decades. I was born in Sicily in. . . well, the year wasn't in this century; let's leave it at that. I traveled across the States and wound up in San Francisco. I became a correspondent, sending stories to various European newspapers."

"How did you get like this?"

He stood by one of the photographs, running his fingers over the smooth glass. "In 1914 the Old Gringo, Ambrose Bierce, decided he wanted to cover the Mexican Revolution. The cynical bastard joined Pancho Villa's band. He didn't know what he was getting into. He was Embraced by a south-of-the-border Cainite — he never knew his Sire. It seems fitting that the author of *The Devil's Dictionary* was transformed into one of the Damned.

"He made his way back to San Francisco, the only home he had ever known. We knew each other from our newspaper days in the 1890s. He found me and made me one of his Progeny." Virgil rapped his knuckles against the grainy black-and-white image of a seated man with salt-and-pepper sideburns and mustache. The man's expression indicated he didn't think much of sitting still for the camera.

"Bierce was as bitter in death as he was in life. He said, 'All of life is a rehearsal for death and I must have made a poor understudy, for I have died, and yet here I walk.' It wasn't for long, though. He just couldn't help making enemies. He enraged one of his own Brood, who slew him some 60 years ago."

"This is incredible." Corrinda had absently knotted the fingers of her free hand in the bedsheets. "You're telling me some of the most famous people in America have become vampires?"

Virgil arched one of his eyebrows. "I'm only giving you a hint of the truth. I don't know it all myself. I try to stay out of Clan maneuvering. I don't want to run afoul of Prince Vannevar and his politics. I once got myself in enough trouble, over this." He tapped the little book Corrinda still held.

"What happened?"

"I am of the Kindred Clan Toreadors. We are. . . drawn to the aesthetic arts. I have always watched over Bay area writers and poets. During the '50s, I began keeping company with some writers who were determined to express themselves in innovative styles no one had used before. Lawrence Ferlinghetti, Jack Kerouac, Gary Snyder. They resisted what authority told them. They experimented, both with their bodies and their minds. They held readings that captivated me as nothing I had ever heard before. I spent time with them, spoke with them, read their work — never revealing my true nature, of course.

"They inspired me. I had written poems and stories before, but only for my own amusement. But I decided I wanted to capture the essence of what I had become. I wanted to portray both the wonder and the grotesqueness of the Masquerade — immortals doomed to feed off others to satisfy the cravings burning inside. I wrote them in the form of a series of letters to a mortal. I had the poems published privately and distributed in bookstores around town. I couldn't see them purchased during the day, but I understand they were quite popular at the time." He looked at Corrinda's book as if he couldn't quite believe he had produced such a thing.

"But of course, I had gone too far. I had broken the facade of the Masquerade. The Prince was outraged, and nearly called a Lextalionis — a Blood Hunt — upon me for making public secrets of the Kindred. Crawling on my belly, I swore that no human would ever take my poems as truth. I had to promise to retrieve and destroy all copies of *The Scarlet Letters*. I've been tracking them down for three decades. . . . Yours must be one of the few remaining."

Tears glinted in the corners of Corrinda's eyes. "I'm only human. . . but I know what you feel. Your poems are too lovely to destroy. They described exactly what I felt when I wanted to. . . damn it, kill my fuckin' stepfather!" She reached out suddenly and grabbed Virgil's sweater. "Please! Make me one of you! Take me too! Embrace me — do whatever it takes. . ."

With an animalistic growl he stepped back, freeing himself. "No!" he snapped. "You don't know what you're asking! Only now is Vannevar close to forgiving me. He's even attending a party here tonight."

She slid from the bed to her knees on the floor. "I do. I understand. . ."

"Fool! If you had the slightest notion what it is like to stalk your own kind, feed off their blood, you would run screaming from me! I've only told you as much as I have because I need your book and I owe you an explanation for what I'm about to do. I'm going to. . . touch your mind. It won't hurt you. You'll forget we ever spoke, and you'll forget you ever read a book called *The Scarlet Letters*. You can go back home and —"

It was her turn to shout defiantly. "No! I don't have a home anymore! My mom left us three months ago. Last weekend my stepfather came into my room in the middle of the night. He was walking in a cloud of sweat and smoke and beer. He. . . slipped into bed with me. He said. . . it wouldn't be wrong because we weren't really related. When he touched me, I caught a warning from him. He was going to rape me until he tired of me, then he was going to kill me. I pushed him away, and he slapped me, hard."

She gestured at the bruise under her eye. "I shoved him again, and he fell back, smacking his head on my nightstand. While he was unconscious, I grabbed his money and whatever I could stuff in my pockets. I ran into town and waited until I could hop the bus."

"Surely you have some other family to turn to —"

"There's nobody! I picked San Francisco because I knew there were poetry readings here, and I wanted to share what I had written with other people. But now I don't know what I'm going to do. I can only sleep in the bus terminal and wash up in the public restroom so long. There's no way I'm gonna turn tricks for some crack-freak pimp." Her words were distorted, catching in her throat. "I could wait on tables, but where am I going to live? I mean. . . . I'd be better off jumping from the goddamned Golden Gate Bridge!"

Virgil scowled. "What a typically adolescent thing to say."

"Please." She dropped the book and folded her hands. "I caught something else from you, when we touched. I know why you left home — why you traveled to America."

"Stop it!" He almost seemed frightened of the girl at his feet. "You're not to speak of —"

"You were beaten too, weren't you?" She brought her hands to her neck. "See, we're two of a kind. We understand each other." She undid the top three buttons of her blouse. "Here. I won't cry. I won't back out. Write me into your lines. Make me part of your poem. I want you to. Put your teeth in me. Kill me." She arched her head back, waiting for the strike.

His lips were pulled back. His incisors had descended instinctively, involuntarily. His hands came toward her as if rising through tar. Then he spun away, tearing himself from the sight of her pale, exposed flesh. "I can't! It's forbidden! If I Embraced you, Prince Vannevar would have me staked for the dawn!"

"Fine." She sprang to her feet and bolted toward the table. "There's nothing left for me anymore." She grasped one of the wine bottles by the neck and smashed it against the edge of the table. The crystalline shatter shredded their eardrums. "If you won't take me, I'll do it myself."

"Stupid bitch!" Virgil cried, starting for the table, but even with his preternatural celerity she was too quick for him. She brought the jagged point of turquoise glass up underneath her jaw and jabbed —

Both of them were screaming. Their positions from just a few minutes ago were reversed: Corrinda was now wavering on her feet; Virgil was on his knees, his arms outspread, looking up at her in shock. The sight of blood gently pulsing from her neck brought the Beast close to the surface. He felt himself hovering at the edge, a fraction of an inch from lunging at the thick red wash flowing down her shoulder.

"I love you. . . for helping me read tonight," she managed to say. "I want to. . . give you part of me. . ."

Eyes blinking rapidly, she walked behind the table and slumped against the wall. She bent forward from the shoulders and cupped her left hand between her small breasts. A warm rich flow coursed down her neck, spilled down her chest, and pooled in her palm. She brought up her right hand and dipped her forefinger in the deepening well. She then put her finger to the wall and began to write — her finger the pen, her blood the ink, a poem her message.

If I die, let it be with you.

The words were not as beautiful as she wanted them to be. Some of the letters ran, and some were difficult to make out. She had a hard time keeping on a horizontal line, and the words near the end of the line began to slope downwards.

Hold me close while the world falls in on me.

"Corrinda!" Virgil's mouth drew down at the corners. "There's a way for me to stop the bleeding! You can still return to the world where you belong —"

Whisper my name as the darkness rises

She didn't know if she could keep going now. The blood was overflowing her cupped palm and dripping to the floor below with heavy wet splashes. She had to consciously focus her eyes in order to see. "Shhh. It's all right." Her words were slurred. Her tongue felt thick and unresponsive.

And I fall into the dream that never ends

Her legs wouldn't stay straight any longer; it felt as if her bones were dissolving, leaving only the cold stone to support her. Some of her hair caught in the still-damp letters and trailed downward, red, as she slid to the floor. "Damn it! Damn it!" Virgil violently brushed away crimson tears. "You're going to cost me. . ."

He scrambled to her side as her eyelids met a final time. He took her hair in his left hand and lifted her head. He brought his right wrist up to his mouth and savaged it — taking out his frustration on his own flesh rather than hers. Thin drops of deoxygenated blood welled up from the inside of his arm. He wiped them across her lips.

"Drink. Drink well and come back from death, knowing you've cursed me."

There was a flutter against his skin. Her lips, like an infant's, smacked pleasurably. A small pink tongue darted into the red stains and licked. He felt suction as she began to actively nurse his arm, and the feeling that flowed through him was the closest to sexual ecstasy he was capable of experiencing anymore.

"They will make me pay for you," he said aloud, more to himself than the small form curled embryonically at his knees. "Oh, how they will make me pay." ⚲

INTERESTING TIMES

by Matt Forbeck

When he arrived at the Hyatt Regency, Paul got out of the cab, slipped the driver two twenties, and told him to keep the change.

The cabby thanked him and handed Paul a worn business card. "If you ever need a ride, give me a call. I work nights."

"So do I," said Paul.

While checking into the hotel, Paul explained to the clerk that he was extremely jet-lagged and did not wish to be disturbed for any reason. Once in his 14th-floor room, Paul hung the "Do Not Disturb" sign on the doorknob outside. Then he bolted the door from the inside and fastened the security chain. He jammed a chair under the doorknob for good measure.

Then he sat on the bed and watched TV for a while. *Chinatown* was playing on the late show. When it was over, he realized he was getting tired. His room faced east, out over the bay, and he could see dawn was coming. With a yawn, he gathered up the bedclothes and brought them into the bathroom. Soon he'd fashioned a comfortable enough bed in the tub. Before lying in it, he locked the bathroom door and turned out the lights.

The earthquake woke him. He'd never felt the world shake like that before, and it was disconcerting, particularly considering how high up he was. For a moment, he thought how ironic it was he'd come to California just in time to die. He wasn't sure his immortality would be any good if he was crushed to death, and he didn't want to find out.

Fortunately, the quake didn't last long. When he was absolutely sure the world had stopped wobbling, Paul pressed the button that lit up his watch. He had overslept. Perhaps he was a bit jet-lagged after all.

He climbed out of the tub and looked at himself in the mirror. A young man of about 30 looked back at him with old eyes. His curly blond hair fell forward over his dark blue irises. It was long on the top and short in the back and sides, very modern and just the right length. It never grew unless he cut it, and then it would grow like a weed until it reached its original length. The same with his fingernails. He perpetually showed a five o'clock shadow, but he tried to convince himself that it made him look rugged rather than sloppy.

He gathered up the blankets and pillows once again and returned them to the bed. Then he drew the cabby's card from his pocket and made a phone call. Before leaving for the lobby, he changed into a black polo shirt and a pair of blue jeans. San Francisco nights were especially chilly toward the end of October, so he wore his leather jacket. Such things meant little to him, but he knew that lack of attention to these kinds of details might make other people suspicious. Also, the jacket had an inside breast pocket in which he could stow his cross, which he did.

While removing the fresh clothes from the bag, Paul's eyes fell on his shirt and collar. He hadn't worn them in a long time, and he wondered if he ever would again. The rosary his mother had given him was there as well. He picked it up and thought about it for a second, then stuffed it into his pocket.

When the taxi showed up, Paul climbed into the back seat. Then he drew another card out of his jacket's breast pocket and read off the address. "It's a bookstore," he said.

Soon, the cab pulled up in front of a Haight-Ashbury storefront. The place looked like it hadn't changed since that infamous Summer of Love back in 1967. Paul had been too young for the hippie movement the first time around, but it was alive and well in the Haight today.

The store's wide, tall windows were festooned with tie-dyed T-shirts of every color. Some were embroidered with peace symbols, others with dancing bears. Dozens of rare and antique books sat beneath the shirts, rubbing shoulders with the latest best-sellers. The centerpiece in one display was H.R. Giger's *Necronomicon*, and Paul's eyes seemed drawn into the cover's seductive, alien curves. He shook his head to break the trance and then turned to back to tell the cabby to wait.

It was warm inside the store, and the strong must of old books assaulted him as the door swung closed behind him. There were several customers in the place, but no one was behind the cash register. Inside, the place looked just like the windows. T-shirts of all styles hung high on the walls, overlooking row after row of shelves crammed full of books. New books were to the right, old ones on the left. A display case in the middle of the long, tall room featured a number of rare books. One of them caught Paul's eye. It was a signed, first edition of *The Picture of Dorian Gray*.

"May I help you?" Paul looked up and met eyes with a beautiful young woman with long auburn hair. She wore a tight, long-sleeved shirt with thin, colorful vertical stripes and bell-bottomed blue jeans. Her eyes were bright and brown.

"Um, yes. I'm looking for a Marty Chin. Does he work here?"

"For sure," she smiled, "but he's in the back right now. Can I let him know who's calling?"

"Paul Able," he said. "Father Paul Able."

She smiled again and then turned and walked through a wooden door in the back of the store. She returned a minute later. "Mister Chin's pretty busy, but he's going to make some time for you. Just walk straight back through that door," she pointed, indicating one she'd come through.

Paul thanked her and followed her directions. The door was closed, so he knocked. A muffled voice beckoned him in.

Marty Chin was a short, clean-cut man with impeccable taste. His short dark hair was cut in a modern, European style which contrasted suavely with his Asian features. He wore a navy blue blazer over a crisp, white shirt and nicely pressed khaki pants. His cool brown eyes stared out at Paul from behind thin, round lenses set in rimless frames that hooked behind his ears. He wore a ready smile on his dark face. It showed all of his clean, white, even teeth.

Chin stuck out his hand, and Paul shook it. "Hello, Father, hello," he said motioning Paul to take the chair across the desk from him, which Paul did. The room was small but handsomely decorated. The walls were paneled in polished wood that matched the desk and chairs. The window behind Chin's desk looked out upon a private courtyard lit by dim footlights. Paul imagined it would look fantastic by the light of the sun, but knew that he would never see it that way.

"I am pleased to make your acquaintance." Chin's English was flawless, although obviously not his native tongue. He spoke with a Chinese accent, but Paul couldn't place its specific dialect. Chin walked around behind the desk and sat down. His smile faded softly to be replaced by a more businesslike look. "So, what is it that you want?"

"I'm looking for a certain man. A friend of mine gave me your name as a person to contact. He says nothing goes on around here without your knowledge."

"Your friend is very kind." Chin smiled again, briefly and easily. "Can I ask who you are looking for?"

"His name is Randy Elwood." Chin's eyes showed nothing. He sat back, though, a pensive look on his face.

Chin swept his right hand out wide and asked expansively, "And why are you looking for this person?"

"Do you know him?"

Chin cleared his throat softly. "I do not know him. I know *of* him, however, but I would like to know what is your interest in him."

"He and I have some unfinished business. It's a matter I need to take up with him personally." Chin looked as if he was going to interrupt. "And privately," Paul finished.

Chin's demeanor turned thoughtful again, and he steepled his fingers in front of him. "Ah, well, yes," he muttered and then fell quiet.

"I believe I can help you, Father. However," Chin looked as if something distasteful had crept into his mouth, "there is the small matter of the price."

Paul gave Chin a shocked look. He had known this was coming, but he wanted to drive the price down as far as it would go. If he didn't at least try, he was sure Chin would become suspicious.

"Come now, Father," said Chin. "I am taking a risk here, and I think it only fair that I should be rewarded for doing so. Mister Elwood is a dangerous man. Would you ask me to risk my life for nothing?"

"How much then?" Paul asked carefully.

Chin seemed to think about it for a moment, then named a figure. Paul halved it.

"Done. You are getting yourself a bargain here, Father, but because you are an honorable man, I feel certain I can trust you to keep our arrangement a secret. Confidentiality is important to a man in my position, Father, as I am sure you can see it would be."

Chin scribbled something on the back of a business card and handed it to Paul. "Elwood owns a tavern at this address; it's called the Bird of Paradise. It caters to meaner tastes than yours, I am afraid. I am sorry to have to send a priest into such a place, but it is, as you have said, a private matter, one in which I am sure I do not care to become involved."

Paul thanked him and got up to leave. Chin's eyes flew wide and he cleared his throat loudly. "I am sure you understand, Father, that payment is due immediately. You do have the funds upon you, do you not?"

"Of course," said Paul. He fished a wad of bills out of his pants pocket and peeled off enough large ones and let them fall to the desk. He stuffed the rest back into his pocket. "A pleasure doing business with you," he said as he turned to leave.

As the door swung shut behind Paul, Chin smiled viciously and tossed an old Chinese curse after him: "May you live in interesting times." Then he picked up the phone and started to dial. "And good luck, Father," he chuckled to himself. "You are going to need it."

• • •

The Bird of Paradise was located in the Tenderloin district, San Francisco's lame-duck excuse for Times Square. Although the area was slowly becoming gentrified, the streets were still crawling with all kinds of streetwalkers, pimps, and pushers. It was as if someone had decided to clean up the barnyard, but forgotten to move the animals out first.

Paul got out of the cab and paid his fare. It was dark inside the bar, but there were several stages which were brightly lit, and Paul could see to walk by their light. People in various stages of undress danced on each of the stages. Paul ignored them as best he could and checked the place out.

There were five different stages, three for women along the left wall of the large room and two along the right for men. The crowd seemed pretty well split along heterosexual lines, peppered with the occasional gay or bisexual or the simply curious. The lights on the stage made the darkness Paul was in stand out starkly. All the better for the patrons to not see each other.

Security seemed incredibly light. There was only the bouncer at the door. Paul guessed that the Bird was lucky to have clientele who behaved. He walked up to the bar, and when he finally got the bartender's attention, he asked her if she knew Randy Elwood. She pointed him toward a door in the back.

Paul made his way to the door. He tried the knob quietly, but it was locked, so he knocked. There was no answer, so he knocked again, harder. He was about to knock a third time when the door swung inward, spilling light into the back of the lounge.

"Whaddaya want?" grunted the swarthy, little man standing in the doorway. His hair and clothes were dirty and unkempt, and he smelled like he hadn't bathed in weeks. His breath was even worse. He was unshaven and fat and in a foul mood.

"I'm sorry, sir. I'm looking for a man named Randy Elwood." Paul tried to be as polite as possible. This was going to be a touchy situation, and he didn't need to blow it right away.

"That's me. Whaddaya want?"

"I was wondering if I could have a word with you." Paul glanced about cautiously. "In private."

"What for?"

"I need to talk to you about a girl in Milwaukee." Paul motioned past the man. "Could we?"

Randy appeared to wrestle with himself for a moment. Then the decision was made. "Yeah, sure. Come on in." He stepped back and waved Paul into the room.

Paul sat on the edge of a folding chair that had seen better days. Randy shut and bolted the door, wandered around to the other side of his desk and sat in a stained and torn executive's chair that squeaked when he fidgeted in it, which was often. The room's single window was blackened with dirt. A single 100-watt bulb in an unshaded ceiling fixture highlighted the dirt on the walls and the holes in the red carpet which was wearing toward black. It made Randy look even more haggard than before.

"So, what is it?"

Paul coughed once. "Do you know a young lady named Gabrielle Allende?" He looked at Randy for some sign of recognition, but found none. "She was found dead in Milwaukee last week."

Randy's indifference was starting to look more feigned. "Get to the point."

"She was killed by two men. I've already located one of them. He gave me your name."

Randy's slack face drew into a grimace. "That's a lie. Al woulda died first."

Or just after, thought Paul. "So you admit you killed her?"

The man's face started to snarl, but then cracked into a cold laugh. "Admit it? You're goddamn right I admit it. I'm fucking proud of it. She was a slut, and I did her a favor. She deserved to die."

Paul sat there agape. "And you don't feel the slightest remorse?"

"I'd do it again, given half a chance. In fact, maybe I'll find another whore and do it tonight. Whaddaya think of that, Priest?"

Paul shuddered. "No one deserves to die like that. Not a prostitute — no one. We're all equal in God's eyes. All deserving of mercy."

"Then God is blind, buddy — or dead. And if you're looking for mercy, you came to the wrong place." Randy bared his fangs. "Speaking of going like that," Randy growled, "you're about to find out what it's like."

Paul knocked his chair over as he scrambled to his feet. He backed toward the door while Randy skirted the desk and walked after him like he had all the time in the world. Paul tried the door. It was locked, of course. He wasn't planning on leaving anyway, but he had to make this look good.

"Time to die, Priest."

Randy was almost on top of him when Paul pulled his cross out of his jacket and shoved it in his face. It was a full foot long and made of wood. Its bottom tip had been hardened in fire and sharpened to a point. It scared the hell out of the vampire.

Randy yelled and dropped to the floor. Then he scrambled back toward his desk and climbed up and sat down on it. "What was that?" the squeaky voice cried. Randy stared Paul up and down until his eyes lit on the cross in Paul's hand.

"Son of a bitch! You've got a cross!" Randy slapped his forehead and started to laugh. "You know, for a minute there, I was worried. I thought you had — well I don't know what I thought you had, but I thought it was something else."

Randy gave Paul a hard, evil look. "It won't work, you know."

It was Paul's turn to laugh now. "I know the power of my faith." With that, Paul raised the cross before him again and started walking toward the killer.

Randy slid down off the desk, a smile on his face as well. For a long moment, the two of them squared off, neither able to make a step forward, each straining with all his might. Suddenly, Randy screamed in frustration and broke off the battle of wills and fell back behind his desk.

He was not beaten yet, though. He reached under his desk and brought out a snub-nosed revolver. He aimed it at Paul and fired off three quick shots. The first one caught Paul in the side and spun him back toward the door. He slammed into it and fell to the ground. The other two went wide.

Randy waited for a moment to see if Paul was still alive and then knelt beside Paul. As Randy bent over Paul's neck to suck out his life's blood before it all spilled out onto the crimson rug, Paul swept the tip of his cross up and plunged it into Randy's chest. Unerringly, the wooden stake found Randy's heart, immobilizing him instantly.

The bullets had injured Paul, but he knew he'd heal quickly. He got to his knees and examined Randy. He'd gotten him good. He licked his lips and extended his fangs. Now it was time to feed.

Paul hated what he was, but he had come to accept it. One of the basic tenets of his new life was that he had to feed, and food simply wouldn't do it. He needed blood, so despite his distaste for Randy personally, he bent to drink.

He had vowed never to feed on a human being, but he had no such scruples concerning vampires. Vampiric blood was strong and intense, much more so than mortal blood, or so he'd been told. Plus, by drinking the life essence of older vampires, he was able to absorb their power. Randy had been at least a few generations older than Paul, and it showed in the richness of his blood.

What shamed Paul most about his feedings were that they felt so good. They were more pleasurable than anything he'd ever felt. He was almost positive that once he started a feeding there was no way to stop. He didn't know for sure, though. He'd never tried.

Suddenly, thinking became impossible. The sensations were too intense. Everything else was shoved away. The only thing in the world was his wet and hungry mouth sucking harder and harder upon that vile man's hot, red blood.

When it was over, Paul collapsed across Randy's corpse. He just wanted to lie there, to regather his strength. He was disgusted by the cadaver, convinced he could smell it starting to putrefy, but he couldn't find the strength to move.

Someone was knocking on the door. Several people were pounding on it, actually. And they'd been doing so for some time, Paul slowly realized as he struggled to his knees. The door was made of reinforced steel, but was starting to show dents.

An ax head suddenly appeared in the wall next to the door.

Paul retrieved his cross from Randy's body and slipped it into his jacket. Then he struggled to his feet and stumbled toward the window. His strength was returning quickly now. Hopefully, it would come back soon enough.

The window wasn't just dirty. It had been painted over black. Paul grabbed a chair and tossed it through the window. The glass shattered, but the chair bounced back. Iron bars had blocked its way.

Paul grunted in frustration and threw himself at the bars. They were obviously meant to keep humans out, not vampires — at least not this vampire. One by one, he managed to wrest them free.

By the time he finished, the hole near the door had grown much larger. As he was climbing out the window, a shaggy head poked its way through the widened hole. "Hey, stop!" it yelled.

Paul turned to look. It was a mistake. The head snarled at him, its fangs showing prominently. It was a man's head, a man with dark eyes, bushy eyebrows, and long, dark hair. Death shone wetly in his pitch black eyes.

Their eyes locked. "I command you to *stop*!" the man screamed. Paul hesitated for a moment, feeling a mind searching for his own, but he sloughed it off. He stuck his tongue out between his fangs, then turned and slipped out the window.

Paul hit the ground running and took off for his hotel. When he found a populated street, he slowed to what he guessed was top human speed. Although it chafed to have to move so slowly, he didn't want to attract too much attention. A man running down the street in the middle of the night, not dressed as a jogger, was bound to make some people suspicious, but he could handle that. It would be hard to explain being able to dash past a sprinter, so he kept it slow.

He made a dozen different turns, back and forth across the city, always working in the direction of his hotel. He knew he was a mess, but that couldn't be helped. It was late, and there weren't too many people about. He still had a nagging feeling that someone was watching him, but when he ducked in an alley and looked behind, the street was empty except for a mangy stray dog.

He slowed to a walk as he reached the hotel and glanced about to make sure no one had followed him. Satisfied, he walked around to the rear of the building and found a dumpster.

His jacket had been trashed by the bullet, so he removed it. He took the cross out of the jacket and stuffed it up the back of his shirt, tucking the point in the waist of his pants. Then he ripped the lining out of the coat and used it to clean himself up as best he could. When he was finished, he wadded the destroyed jacket up and tossed it into the dumpster.

Then he found a service entrance. The door was locked, but he wrenched it open. Once inside, he found the stairs and took them to the 14th floor.

Paul stripped and jumped into the shower immediately upon entering his room. He used only hot water — the hottest. The searing heat could have boiled an egg, but it wasn't enough. He needed the blood off: his blood and Randy's. Its scent nauseated him. He needed to be clean, clean, clean!

He scrubbed and scrubbed until his skin shone like a baby's. The bullet had gone through him and both wounds were already gone. He scoured himself until the last drop of the vile stuff was gone. Then he stood under the shower head and wept, his bloody red tears mixing with the water and swirling thinly down the silver drain. He cried in great heaving, body-wracking sobs until he was out of tears, and then he scrubbed his face again.

Paul started to cry after he shut off the water, but managed to stop himself. He washed his face in the sink.

When he was through, Paul dried out the tub and set up his makeshift bed again, showing the same concern for security he had the night before. It was still several hours before dawn, but he was entirely spent. He fell asleep quickly enough, but just before he drifted off, a single burning question crossed his mind: How did that man know I was a priest?

By the time, Paul awoke the next morning, he had the answer: Marty Chin.

Chin had contacted Randy before Paul had arrived and let him know he was coming. If either Chin or Elwood had realized Paul was a vampire, it might have been all for him.

Paul was mad. He was going to get even.

He got up and replaced the bed clothes. Today he dressed in black jeans and a white T-shirt underneath a button-down, blue denim work shirt. He transferred his cash and his rosary from his blood-stained jeans into his pants pocket. Then he cleaned off his cross and tucked it into the back of his waistband, like a pistol. He wore the shirt untucked to help cover it. The bit of the T-shirt that showed behind the open collar of the denim shirt reminded him of his collar, and that made him feel a little better. He called for a taxi and went downstairs to wait.

When the taxi arrived, Paul climbed in and sent it to Chin's bookstore. When the cab arrived, he got out and told the cabby to wait. Inside, he saw the young woman behind the counter, but didn't stop to chat. He barreled through the shop and into the office, slamming the door shut behind him.

"Mister Chin, you and I need to talk!"

Chin was sitting behind his desk. He looked at Paul, then folded up a newspaper and said, "Ah, Father Able. I've been expecting you. Come in and have a seat."

"I prefer to stand."

Chin shrugged. "As you wish. I suppose you are here about last night. I assure you, Father, that I bear you no ill will, nor did I yesterday evening. I simply —" Chin stopped dead in mid-sentence, his eyes fluttered wider a grin creased his cheeks.

"What is it? Cat got your tongue?" demanded Paul. "I want some answers, Mister Chin, and I want them now."

Chin pointed to Paul's face. Was something wrong with his face? Paul didn't think so, but — oh, no. He ran his tongue across his upper teeth. His fangs were showing. Abashedly, he reached up and shoved them back in with his right index finger and thumb. He was taken aback momentarily, embarrassed by his loss of control. In an instant of anger, he had let his feeders fall into place, and from the look on Chin's face, he knew exactly what that meant.

"My apologies, Mister Chin. You have me at a disadvantage." Paul was quite contrite. He'd never blown his cover before, and he'd done it badly. He'd kick himself later, though. He had to get out of this situation first.

"No, Father," Chin said, "I believe it is you who has the advantage over me."

"I think I'll take that seat after all," said Paul as he slipped into the chair.

Chin drew a breath and then blew it out, long and slow. His eyes wandered up and down Paul's body. Eventually, he looked up and met Paul's pensive gaze with a tentative smile. "So," he said, "you are a vampire."

Paul nodded.

"I take it you are new to town. I have never heard of a vampire priest before. That is, of course, assuming you are a priest." Paul nodded again, more grimly this time.

Chin steepled his fingers in front of himself . "It seems to me we have a situation on our hands. You, obviously, do not want anyone to know that you are a vampire." Paul nodded once again. "Just as obviously, I do not want to die. So, how can we make each other happy?"

"I don't want to kill you."

"Well, that is good to hear. Can I get that in writing?"

"I — I mean I won't kill you."

"Come again?"

It was Paul's turn to blow out a frustrated breath. "I've taken a vow against killing human beings. I am a priest. I believe in the Ten Commandments, the Beatitudes and, most particularly, the Golden Rule. I won't kill you."

"Well," said Chin, "that is good." He smiled. "And how did this come to pass, if that would not be prying?"

Paul opened his mouth, then closed it. He still didn't trust Chin, but he needed help from someone. If he was to remain in San Francisco, he was going to have to infiltrate the city's vampire society. As much as the thought currently revolted him, eventually he would have to feed. "How much do you know about vampires? I mean, particularly the ones here in San Francisco?"

Chin's eyebrows raised appreciatively. "Ah, I see that we each have something that the other wants: information. Perhaps we can come to some sort of arrangement, then?" Chin's brow furrowed over his glasses. "Let us say that I will tell you everything you wish to know about the vampires of this fair city, with the exception of anything I have sworn to hold confidential, of course. In exchange, you tell me your story —" Paul started to nod, "— and you swear not only to not kill me, but to prevent me from coming to harm in any way, either actively or through your own negligence."

Paul scowled. "I won't be your bodyguard."

"That is not what I am asking. I merely wish you to guarantee that you will in no way be personally responsible for harm to come to me or mine."

Paul thought about it for a minute. Keeping the promise to make sure Chin would not be hurt by any actions he took would be easy. He had intended to do just this all along. But to talk about his new life, that would be difficult. "Why do you want to know about me? What good could it possibly do you?"

Chin gave Paul his ready smile. "Father, as you know, I am in the business of information. If there is anything about anybody in this town that needs to be known, I make a point of knowing it. Sometimes that information comes to me legally, and other times it reaches my ears through. . . less formal channels.

"I have become important to a great many people. They rely on my expertise and my advice, advice I can only give to them if I am well informed."

"I'm sorry. I can't have you telling everyone you know about my past."

"Yes, Father, I understand that. At your request, I will keep my knowledge of your history a secret. Your information is like a piece of a puzzle. It will help fill the gaps in my knowledge of the big picture. I need not show anyone else your past. It will simply be a single thread in the grand tapestry. A part of the background, if you will. For my purposes, that is sufficient."

Paul thought about it for a moment. Chin's words had made a great impression upon him. He still didn't trust the man, but he could see that they were both taking a risk by sharing their information. The agreement would be in their mutual interests, as would be its confidentiality. Paul realized how alone he was in this city. At some point he was going to have to trust someone, to take that leap of faith. It looked like that time was now.

"It's a deal."

Chin grinned from ear to ear, then spat on the palm of his hand and offered it to seal the pact. Paul followed his lead, spitting in his own palm and then shaking hands.

Chin wiped his hand clean with a handkerchief and then offered it to Paul. As Paul used it, he noticed the blood in his spittle had stained the white cloth a bright, rich red.

"So," Paul said, "who's to go first?"

"Well, since after you hear my information, you may very well want to leave, and I have no way of stopping you, I think you should begin."

"All right." Paul inhaled deeply and exhaled slowly. "Where to start? Let's see.

"It all began, I guess, in World Theologies 201 at Marquette University in Milwaukee. I was, and I believe I still am, a Jesuit priest, and I had recently earned my doctorate in Theology at Marquette. It was my first year as an associate professor at the school, and I was learning more than I was teaching.

"One thing I was learning was that I wasn't so sure I believed in God, at least not in the Judeo-Christian sense. This weakening of my faith is, to my mind, what allowed her to get close to me in the first place.

"I'm sorry, I'm jumping ahead of myself. She was a student in my evening class, and her name was Jesse Nicht.

"She was the most gorgeous woman I'd ever seen in my life. She had long, jet black hair and matching deep, dark eyes. Before I met her, I had no idea what alabaster skin might have looked like — it was just a phrase in a book — but she had it. It was the creamiest, softest, most flawless skin I'd ever seen. She almost seemed to glow from within.

"As a priest, I'm embarrassed to say I was extremely attracted to her. I started dreaming about her at night, and I was sure that she was interested in me as well. She started staying after class, debating theology with me. She was a staunch atheist, and I found our conversations incredibly engaging. There was a brilliant mind in that beautiful body, behind that flawless face, and I started to fall in love.

"One night I decided to confess my passion to Jesse. To my delight, she returned it. I immediately decided that I would renounce the priesthood and run away with her, if she would have me.

"She became ecstatic. She started kissing me deeply, all over my face and neck. Then suddenly, she bit me.

"It was the oddest feeling. Horror mingled with lust. Wanting it to stop, but never wanting it to end. Realizing, eventually, that it would only cease with my mortal life. And to tell the truth, I didn't care.

"I wanted it. I wanted it more than anything. As afraid as I was of death, I couldn't have imagined a more pleasurable way to die.

"But she didn't let me die. She pulled open her shirt and opened a vein in her chest. I was weak as a newborn child, but she pulled my mouth to her, and I drank. I drank deep and long, but it wasn't enough, couldn't be enough. Finally, she pulled me from her and looked deep into my eyes. I had become hers, forever. Or so she thought, as did I.

"The worst part of the whole experience wasn't the Hunger. Oh, yes, I was hungry. More hungry than I'd ever been for food. I craved blood, and that realization almost drove me insane.

"But as I said, this was not the worst. The most horrible part was that I was absolutely sure there was no God in this world. How could a benevolent deity allow such depravity in a world of His making? This evil creature had come in and seduced me — me, a priest! Where had God been in my hour of darkness? If He couldn't come through for me then, how could I believe He existed at all?

"Quickly enough, such issues fell by the wayside, eclipsed by my growing Hunger. I needed to drink soon, and Jesse had just the victim in mind.

"She brought me to my apartment building, to the second-floor rooms I shared with Father Steve Singer. Steve had been my best friend all the way through our schooling, both at the seminary and Marquette. Jesse wanted me to kill Steve, knowing full well that such an act would seal my fate, forever divorcing me from my mortal life.

"She shoved me into his room, and there he was, lying asleep in the light of the streetlight, looking like an innocent lamb. At this point, I started to cry, and my sobs awoke him. By the light streaming in the window, he could see my face and that of the woman behind me. And he could see our fangs.

"Steve realized what was happening. He grabbed the crucifix hanging over his bed and held it out before him like an iron shield. I hesitated, but Jesse pushed me forward again.

"Suddenly, I found I could go no further. The Hunger was, at this point, overwhelming. I could smell Steve's blood, hear it pounding in his veins, and more than anything else in the world, I wanted to rip my friend's throat out and gorge myself on his steaming blood.

"But the crucifix stayed my hand. I couldn't move forward. In fact, I was being pushed back. Suddenly, Jesse swept me aside and went for Steve herself. Steve's faith only intensified, forcing her even further away.

"It was then I had my epiphany. If Steve could do this, if he could actually ward off these two evil creatures by faith in God alone, then I had the kind of proof of which every theologian dreams. There was a God. There had to be. All that had been missing was my faith.

"Jesse was still trying to shake Steve's resolve when I attacked her. With strength I didn't know I had, I grabbed her and tossed her back against the far wall. She was surprised and stunned. I pressed my advantage and beat her until neither of us could move.

"Tired as I was, my eyes fell on her blood, on the blood I had spilled, and I was drawn to it like a moth to a flame. I grabbed her and sunk my teeth into her deeply and drank and drank and drank. I squeezed every last drop out of her, and then I drank some more. I absorbed the totality of her power and made it my own.

"When I was finished, I was so exhausted I could barely move, but my strength returned to me quickly, amplified by Jesse's blood in my veins. Eventually, I found the energy to lift my head.

"Steve was watching me, and suddenly what had happened hit home. He said my name once, in a voice choked with horror and disbelief. The shame was too much. I stood up and staggered into the hallway. At one end, I could see the new moon framed in the window. I ran for it and dove through the glass, landing on the pavement below.

"I barely felt the impact. I just kept running. By the time Steve made it to the window, I was long gone."

Paul fell silent at last. He felt spent, but at the same time relieved. He had only ever told Steve that much of his story, and it felt good to share it with someone, even a stranger. Perhaps especially a stranger.

Chin was relaxed in his seat and nodded when the tale was over. "And then?"

Paul looked at him with a weak grin. "I think that's enough for now. If you want to know about the rest of my life, we can discuss that at a later date. First, why don't you hold up your end of the bargain?"

"Of course. You wanted to know how to get in touch with the other vampires in the area."

"Correct."

"Well," said Chin, his eyes flashing, "there are a number of ways, but the best is the Alexandrian Club, a social club in the Marina District. It is a beautiful, private clubhouse which is frequented by humans of all sorts, and by some vampires as well, but it is simply a facade."

As he was talking, Chin took a blank piece of note paper from his desk and began scribbling on it. "I am writing the address of the club on this paper. Now, you might say that this tidbit alone is nice and juicy, but I have more. The Alexandrian Club is only the tip of a more sinister iceberg.

"Behind the main building, a large luxury yacht lies run aground upon the beach where it has been since the Earthquake of 1906. In 1917, the yacht was converted into a club with a very exclusive clientele. Only vampires are allowed in. Since its opening, no human has been allowed inside its walls." Chin handed the slip of paper to Paul.

"This club, known as the Vampire Club, caters to vampires of all types. As you may not know, considering your unique position, the vampire society is a fragmented one. Newly made creatures constantly rebel against the rules of the ancients, and within the ranks of the elders, there is constant infighting and jockeying for power. It is said that it is hard to get two vampires to agree upon anything but blood.

"This place is different. It is a kind of safe harbor for these creatures. Within the yacht's hull, differences are set aside, at least temporarily, and for a short time the vampires can relax in the company of their own kind. From what little I know about such things, this sort of establishment is unique in the world. It is there you will find others of your kind, and in a place where you will be relatively safe."

Chin smiled, and Paul smiled back. "I take it then that you are satisfied?" Chin asked.

"Yes," said Paul. "This conversation has proven. . . enlightening." He checked his watch. It was early yet. He still had plenty of time to check this place out.

"You must be going, then?" asked Chin.

"Yes. I'd like to investigate this Vampire Club as soon as possible."

Chin nodded. "I understand. You are a man of action." He stood and offered his hand. "I have truly enjoyed talking with you, Father Able. I hope we will have the opportunity again sometime."

Paul shook Chin's hand firmly. For a human, Chin had a good grip. "So do I, Mister Chin," he said as he walked out of the office. "So do I."

The cab was waiting right where Paul had left it. As he jumped into the back seat of the cab, he read the address off of the sheet of paper he was still holding and then stuffed it into his shirt pocket.

They drove in silence for a while until the cab pulled into a driveway. There was a plaque on the high brick wall next to the main gate, which was closed. It read, "The Alexandrian Club. Founded 1917. Private. Members Only."

A guard stepped out of a booth behind the gate and shone his flashlight into the cabby's face. "Who've you got in there?" he asked.

Paul stuck his head out of his window and spoke up. "My name is Paul Able. I'm here to join the club."

The guard raised an eyebrow and pointed the light at Paul. "Do you have an invitation?"

"Lodin recommended me." The guard looked puzzled, but he pointed the light away from Paul and disappeared back inside his booth for a moment. Paul was nervous. He hadn't known what to say, so he'd simply dropped the name of the most powerful vampire of which he knew: Lodin, the prince of Chicago. He'd never met Lodin personally, and sincerely doubted he would've recommended him for anything but a coffin, but the guard didn't know that. Paul just hoped Lodin's name would carry some weight this far west.

Apparently it did. The gate opened slowly, and the guard stepped out of his booth and waved them on in. They drove through the immaculately kept grounds and up to the front entryway. An apartment building lay off to one side, the name "Westminster" engraved above its entrance. The stretch of land between it and the Alexandrian Club was spotted with benches, tables, statues, and even a small flower garden. The area was lit by tastefully planted floodlights that gave an aura of liveliness to the area, even in the middle of the night.

When the cab stopped at the Alexandrian's front door, Paul got out and paid the cabby off, adding a hefty tip. As the cab drove away, Paul turned around to see the doorman holding the door open for him. Steeling himself for whatever might come, he walked in.

The foyer's walls were paneled in rich, warm oak and covered with paintings and photos. Comfortable looking sofas and chairs were scattered across a huge Persian rug. A pair of huge oaken doors lay directly in front of him.

"May I help you?" came a voice from off to the right. Paul snapped about, caught off guard. The voice's owner was a pretty, older woman dressed all in black. Her hair was dyed black, and she wore sunglasses, despite the fact the room was dimly lit. Her lips were painted red. "May I help you?" She asked again. She was standing behind a low counter recessed into the foyer's right wall. The words "Courtesy Desk" were engraved above the alcove.

Paul walked over and stood in front of the desk. "Um, yes. I'm here to join the club."

"Would you care to sign the register, sir?" She nodded to a leather-bound notebook sitting to her right. It was open, and the pages showing were half-full of mostly illegible signatures.

"Of course," said Paul. He grabbed the plumed ball-point pen in the stand next to the book and autographed a blank space. In the address section, he wrote "Milwaukee."

The woman handed him a card. "Temporary Member" was printed along the top of it. She had printed his name along the middle of it and signed the bottom left. "Just sign there in the bottom right, and you're all set." Paul did as he was instructed.

He looked up at her, and she smiled. She pointed to the double doors and said, "The main lounge is that way. Our night manager knows you're here and will be waiting for you. I hope your enjoy our time with us."

"I'm sure I will."

The walls of the main lounge were paneled in teak. Dozens of coffee tables and large, overstuffed leather couches and chairs dotted the wall-to-wall carpeting. The high ceiling took up the second floor, too, where a balcony ran the length of the walls. It was all very normal, except for the clientele. The people were an eclectic bunch, hailing from all walks of life. A biker gang hung out in a circle of chairs to the left, while a group of business people sat chatting about the stock market to the right.

A door in the rear opened and a cowboy walked out. He was an average-sized man, and wore brown cowboy boots, dark blue jeans, a brown, fringed leather jacket, a white work shirt, and a bolo tie with a bit of turquoise in it that matched the larger piece in his huge belt buckle. The only thing missing was a hat. His hair was short and sandy, as was his big, bushy mustache. His eyes were old and sad, but he wore a steady, half-sad smile. He came right at Paul with an outstretched hand. Paul met him halfway.

"Howdy, there. Name's Tex R. Cainen. Call me Tex." He had an inhumanly strong grip. Any doubt Paul had about the man being a vampire instantly vanished.

"I'm Paul Able." Paul decided to keep his priesthood to himself. "Pleased to meet you."

"Pleasure's mine, I'm sure. So, what brings you to these parts, Mister Able?"

"Call me Paul. I'm. . . vacationing. Things got a little hectic in Milwaukee, so I decided a change of scenery might be good."

"Well then, Paul, you came to the right place. There's no place more hospitable than the Alexandrian Club —" his voice suddenly lowered conspiratorially, "— especially to men like you and me. Know what I mean?" He gave Paul a strong, knowing wink.

"Yes, Tex," Paul said with a grin, "I believe I do."

Tex's voice raised again. "So, what say I give you the nickel tour of this shack, eh? There's a lot to see."

Paul was about to accept Tex's invitation when a distinctly Irish voice interrupted them. "I'm afraid that won't be necessary, old friend."

Tex turned and Paul looked up to see a man descending the stairs at the rear of the room. He was handsome with shoulder-length black hair which he wore swept back like a lion's mane. He was heavyset, but stopped short of being fat, and his eyes and smile sparkled constantly as if he were enjoying a private joke he was sharing with only you. He was dressed in a button-down mustard shirt and an olive-colored wool suit tailored to fit him flawlessly. He wore a brilliant tie with a bright yellow floral print and a handkerchief to match.

"Well, there you are, Sebastian. Where in tarnation have you been?" Tex turned back to Paul with his arms swept wide between his old friend and his new. "Paul Able, meet Sebastian Melmoth, owner of this dive. Sebastian, Paul's just gotten in from Milwaukee, and he's looking to take a load off for a while."

Sebastian shook hands with Paul, saying, "Well, I daresay we can manage to help him with that." He turned to Tex. "What say I take Paul off your hands for a while? I think you're busy enough here, and I'd like to have a few words with him if I might."

Tex broke into a wide smile and shrugged. A hint of sadness still hung at the corner of his mouth. "Why, sure. Like you said, I've got plenty around here to keep me busy. You two run along, and I'll see y'all later. Paul, it was good to meet you." Tex tipped an imaginary hat to them and was off.

Sebastian turned to Paul and smiled broadly, a gleam in his eyes. "So, how about that tour?"

"Sounds fine to me."

"Right. Now, let's see. That room over there — the one that Tex just disappeared into — is the bar and billiards room. Occasionally, I like to 'shoot a little stick' there myself, but tonight it's full of chaps best for a new visitor to avoid.

"On the other side is our spacious dining room. Meals are served cattle-car style at the typical hours. You can usually gag the food down if you're into that sort of thing.

"Back behind the stairs are storage rooms, bathrooms, kitchens, and other trappings of those still on the mortal coil. Upstairs, there's a map room, a video room, an art studio, a music room, some conference rooms, and, of course, a library. Plus, there's the room that few of us will make use of in the way it was originally intended: the solarium."

Paul laughed, and Sebastian favored him with a sidelong smile. As he rambled on, he constantly waved his arms around, pointing here and there in the general direction of the places he was talking about. Gradually, he and Paul meandered through the furniture, toward the back of the lounge.

"Well that's just about it for the Alexandrian Club. It's all very wealthy and oh-so ordinary and occasionally blah, and none of it is, of course, the reason that you've graced us with your presence." They had reached the back of the room and were standing before an alcove hidden under the stairs.

Sebastian beckoned Paul into the alcove, a knowing look in his eyes. A large oaken door stood hidden in the darkness. A small sign upon it declared it "Private."

Sebastian's voice turned low and full of intrigue. "In the over 75 years since I founded this club, few mortals have passed through this door. None returned alive."

His smile grew sardonic, as he flung the door wide, revealing a stone stairway leading down.

Sebastian led the way. The stairs were dimly lit by electric candles. A mural on the right hand wall depicted a man's descent into the Greek underworld. Paul recognized him as Orpheus, headed down to make an ill-fated bargain for his wife's life. The mural on the left showed a number of different vampires, each becoming more and more powerful as they descended. There were 13 steps. Why?

"The 13 steps are a tribute to the 13 vampiric tribes," Sebastian explained. Paul started, shocked at the answer to his unspoken question. How had he. . . ?

"And no," Sebastian continued, "although the power is within my means, I didn't read your mind. I just noticed you counting. I find mind reading extremely rude, don't you? I prefer to delve into a person's mind the old fashioned way: through conversation." They stopped at the lower landing. A large, three-headed dog was carved into the door's face in bas-relief: Cerberus, the guardian of the gates of Hades. The middle jaw carried a large brass knocker.

Sebastian flashed Paul another insider's smile, and then grabbed the brass ring and knocked three times. The sound resonated like thunder in the narrow stone passage. As the door swung open, he flung his arms wide and said, "Welcome, my friend, to the Vampire Club!"

Paul followed Sebastian into a large room decorated like a Victorian cruise ship. By the portholes in two of the walls, Paul realized they'd entered the luxury yacht Chin had talked about. Couches and chairs were scattered about the place, and a large crystal chandelier hung from the center of the ceiling. Tasteful paintings covered the walls, all with nautical themes. In one corner, the Titanic slipped into an icy sea, and in another the *Flying Dutch-*

man sailed over the Golden Gate Bridge. The portholes were all dark, and when Paul got close enough to inspect one, he realized they'd been painted over.

Eventually, he realized he was being watched, and when he turned around, there was Sebastian grinning at him. "You seem suitably impressed. Thank you for humoring an old man's hopelessly outdated sense of style." He gave Paul a shallow bow.

"It's very impressive," said Paul. "Is the whole ship like this?"

A sparkle entered Sebastian's eyes and glittered in his laugh. "No, not at all. There's quite a lot in store here for you." He turned and led Paul towards a door in the wall to their left. As he opened it, Sebastian looked back at his guest and said, "Gracious sir, may I present the Da Vinci Salon."

Paul was drawn in by the room's perverse magnetism. The decorator had gone entirely Renaissance here, from the furniture down to the small sculptures lining the walls. The only bits to break the illusion were the electric candles and the room's occupants, which were most definitely modern.

Tapestries covered parts of the walls, leaving three murals bare. In the first, a baby vampire lay in a manger surrounded by his vampiric parents. Three demons stood where there should have been magi, and the "cattle" in the background were human beings. In the second, a Christ-like vampire hung nailed to a cross while a centurion drove a stake into his chest as an achingly beautiful Mary Magdalene looked on. The third depicted a monster bursting from the ground before a sealed cave while a choir of bat-winged angels and demonic vampires sang in delight.

Paul was aghast. He turned to say something to Sebastian, but the Irishman was quietly admiring the ceiling. Paul looked up to see a portrait of Satan reaching out to touch an outstretched vampire's hand in a grotesque parody of Michelangelo's mural in the Sistine Chapel.

"I like to bring innocent young things as yourself into these places and despoil them. It's rewarding to know that you've been a part of one's education." Sebastian chuckled as Paul turned to face him.

"It's not all Satanic here, of course. Satan is a myth that humans use to rationalize evil in their world. After all, if someone else is to blame, they can hardly bear any personal responsibility, now can they?" Sebastian walked Paul around the room, pointing out life-sized statues of Dante — "A great myth-maker. Probably set humanity back 200 years." — and Machiavelli. "The man who set them back on track. Evil is a real and personal thing, you see, not a bedtime story with which to scare children."

He looked Paul in the eyes. "Am I boring you?"

"No, not at all."

"Sometimes I have a tendency to prattle, but once one has become a part of the myth, as have you and I, somehow the fantastic becomes so much less so."

They continued their tour, and Sebastian pointed out paintings of the Borgias and the De Medicis. He stopped for a moment before an ancient portrait of a dark, mustachioed East European nobleman which bore no name. Paul stared at it for a moment before he recognized it. "Is that. . . ?"

Sebastian grinned broadly. "That is a tale for another time. First, I think, we should finish our tour."

Paul followed his guide through a classical Greek doorway at the far end of the room. "This," said Sebastian, "is the Parthenon Room."

They had come to the prow of the ship. A Greek stairway sat in the far end of the room, providing the occupants a suitable setting in which to expound upon philosophical matters. The walls were covered with mosaics depicting the siege of Troy and the fall of Rome, as well as scenes from the *Aeneid* and the *Odyssey*. There were no chairs, only couches for reclining. The room was lit by electric braziers.

"This place attracts a different segment of our clientele," Sebastian noted. "Unfortunately, it's not nearly as popular as some other sections of the Club. The younger generations aren't too concerned with high thoughts anymore. And who can blame them? We live in a world gone mad, my friend. And when one is trapped in an asylum, one must be insane to survive. Devils like us don't seem to fit in places like this." He looked around him with a smile tinged with sadness.

"Anyhow, let's continue our little tour. I'm afraid this is a dead end, so we shall have to backtrack a bit. If you will follow me."

They left the Parthenon, and on their way to the main salon, Sebastian asked Paul what brought him to San Francisco. His nonchalant tone indicated that he was only interested in making chit-chat, but Paul became wary.

"I'm a little lost actually. I don't know a lot about vampire ways, and I came to San Francisco to learn."

"Oh. And what happened to your Sire?"

"She was killed in a fire soon after I was created."

Sebastian gave Paul an approving look. "It takes a strong mind to lead oneself through utter darkness to the light. I'm impressed you survived the experience. Most simply go mad."

"At first, I thought I would. I guess I don't know myself as well as I thought."

"A wise man once said, 'Only the shallow know themselves.'" Sebastian grinned at his little joke.

"Well, then, I must be pretty deep," Paul laughed. He was enjoying Sebastian's company and was despising himself for it. He had come to this city to kill vampires, not befriend them. Still, Paul had already seen dozens of vampires in the Club tonight and memorized their faces. Sebastian could wait until later.

"Who did you say recommended us to you?"

Paul knew his story was thin, but he opted to stick with it. "I didn't. It was Lodin, the prince of Chicago."

Sebastian cocked his head to one side and stuck out his lower lip. "Is that so?" Paul nodded hesitantly. Sebastian drew close and lowered his voice. "I happen to know that's a lie my friend, albeit a decently good one. First, as you couldn't possibly know, Lodin despised this club. He swore never to set foot in it. As such, I find it terribly unlikely that he sent you here. Second, he's dead."

Paul started to speak, but Sebastian waved him quiet. His voice returned to normal. "To be honest, I don't give a damn why you're here or who sent you. Keep your secrets if you like. You'll be a wonderful mystery. It'll make our time in this world much more interesting, and that's something neither money nor immortality can buy."

Paul stared silently at Sebastian for a moment, then nodded his thanks. Sebastian smiled and slapped Paul's back. "We've got eternity ahead of us, my friend. There's no need to hurry."

As they reached the door on the other side of the main salon, Sebastian opened it and said, "*Voila!* The Voltaire Salon."

This room was decorated in the classic Louis XIV style. The lights were brighter here but had less to show. Busts and portraits of period figures lined the walls, the largest being a fabulous portrait of Lord Byron. A gigantic mural of the signing of the Declaration of Independence occupied the right wall. A bust of Thomas Jefferson sat next to it. A harpsichord stood in the far left corner, surrounded by music stands. Portraits of Beethoven, Mozart, and Bach hung above it.

"Quite a lot to absorb, isn't it?" asked Sebastian. "Well, that's what the next room's for. It's kind of a sitting and thinking room. Very subdued." He opened the next door. "We call it the After Room."

Just as Sebastian had claimed, this room was by far the most calming of them all. A few tastefully done Impressionist paintings decorated walls which were painted in a smooth off-white. The lights were set low, the chairs and couches were deep and comfortable, and the few occupants were quiet and reflective.

"Well, that's just about it for this deck. What say we forge onward to the lower?"

"Sounds fine to me," Paul said.

Sebastian opened the door at the rear of the room, revealing nothing but darkness. He quickly ushered Paul in and closed the door behind them. "This is the upper end of the ship. It's mostly used for storage, but some of our less socially adept brethren, *i.e.*, the Nosferatu, sometimes use it as a bedroom. There's a stairway in here, if I can just find it. Hold on to my shoulder so you don't lose yourself and go tumbling down the stairs. Ah, here it is."

Paul let Sebastian lead him down through the darkness until he felt him stop. As they reached the lower end, Sebastian said, "Mind the cushions scattered on the floor. It's easy to stumble over them. Couples like to use this part of the ship to engage in *tête-á-têtes*." Suddenly, they hauled up short.

"The area we're about to enter is known as the Black Hole."

"Blacker than this?"

"No," Sebastian laughed. Paul almost swore he could see the gleam in the man's eyes, even in the pitch darkness. "It used to be the engine room back when this beached beast could move. Boiler crews used to be known as the 'Black Hole Gang.' Perhaps they still are, I don't know. But the name appealed to me, so I used it." He laughed again.

"It always struck me funny that the only place in the world where vampires of all sorts can rub shoulders is a ship out of water — a dry and barren vessel that goes nowhere, in fact, cannot go anywhere. I find that terribly apropos, don't you?

"I'll take your silence as agreement. Well, onward ho."

Sebastian opened the door, and they walked into a large room laid out as a posh night club. Black soundproofing lined the ceiling and walls. The steel floor, which echoed to the beat of the dancers' feet and reverberated to the rhythm of the blaring music, had been painted the color of dried blood. Or so Paul hoped. Private booths lined the walls. On a stage in the rear right, a man in a black suit worked a light and sound board and a bank of CD players. The lighting was confusing at best, swinging randomly around one moment and strobing desperately the next. The only steady light shone on a sign behind the disk jockey. It read, "Please Do Not Shoot the DJ. He is Doing His Best."

Paul turned to Sebastian, who had noticed him looking at the sign. "It's a tough crowd," he grinned. "Come on. There's just a little more left."

As they were walking along one side of the dance floor, someone started shouting. Sebastian craned his neck to locate what was causing the disturbance, and Paul followed suit. He couldn't see a thing. Without warning, a man leapt out of the crowd and knocked Paul to the floor. Paul struggled violently with his assailant for a few moments before the two of them were finally dragged apart. It was the vampire who had seen him in the Bird of Paradise.

The lights and music had stopped, and all eyes were upon Paul and his foe. The vampire from the Bird — someone called him Tony — was cursing a blue streak, but two other vampires had his arms pinned, and they weren't letting go. Paul was being held, too, but wasn't struggling. At a nod from Sebastian, the man and woman holding Paul released him. He shook his arms to loosen them up and took a long, hard look at Tony.

The man was beside himself, almost incoherent. He kept growling and whining, "He killed Randy. He killed Randy."

Sebastian gave Paul a hard, appraising look and then turned to Tony. "I don't care who killed who. I don't even care if anyone was killed. No one is getting killed in the Club.

"I have made this place a haven for us outcasts, us leeches upon human society. It's a place where we can be not just a shattered reflection of another place, but a world all our own. Above all, it's a place where we can let down our guard and be who we are. It's a place where we can feel safe, even if only for a little while.

"I don't care if you bust this place up, Tony. Everyone knows how much I enjoy a chance to remodel. I'll just send you a bill. But you've got killing on your mind, and that's not allowed here. Since this is not the first time this has happened, young sir, I'm going to have to ask you to leave."

Sebastian's eyes were practically glowing. Tony mumbled a half-hearted apology, saying he'd leave right away. With a nod from Sebastian, the two vampires holding Tony let him drop. The impact of his knees echoed on the steel floor. Tony stood up slowly, turned, and walked away.

Sebastian watched him leave, then turned to Paul. "Are you all right?" he asked. His voice was weighted with genuine concern.

"Yes. I'll be fine."

As Paul brushed himself off, Sebastian motioned to the DJ, who started his show up where it had left off. The crowd was soon abuzz again. "He'll return in a few days, once things have cooled off," said Sebastian. "He should be out of our hair until then, I should think."

Without a word about Tony's accusations, Sebastian led Paul into the next room. "We call this the Eternal Pageant."

The entire room was lit by blood-red lights. Several vampires sat around engaged in conversations, some serious, others light. All were giving their discourses their full, undying attention.

Paul turned his attention to the room, lest anyone feel he was staring at them. Thirteen paintings lined one wall. "The 13 vampire tribes," breathed Paul.

"Very good," said Sebastian. "You're a quick learner. The mural on the opposite wall depicts the various stages on a vampire's journey to inner peace."

"Even vampires have a religion? What's it called, this journey?"

"It's called *Golconda*. Not everyone believes in it, of course. To quote another wise man, 'If God did not exist, it would be necessary to invent him.'"

Paul spotted a stairway which led to the upper deck, but they walked past it and a door to their left without comment. The door in front of them opened onto a tremendous library decorated in the French Provincial style. The shelves were well stocked, mostly with horror novels concentrating upon vampires. A large, nude portrait of a young Mary Shelly dominated one wall, and photos of several famous horror authors lined whatever sections of wall weren't covered by shelves. Paul saw that some of them had even been autographed, including a photo of Bram Stoker.

Non-fiction books concerning the supernatural comprised one shelf. It included the diaries of several vampires, according to Sebastian, both living and dead. The largest volume was entitled *History of the Camarilla*. The Camarilla was the largest society of vampires in North America. With the information in that book, Paul could do a lot of damage.

"It's not quite as impressive as the title might lead you to believe," Sebastian commented, "but then few books are. It's full of unverifiable 'facts' and rather incomplete. Still, it's a work in progress.

"That will have to conclude our tour, I'm afraid. I hope you found it as enlightening as I did. Now, if you don't mind, I'd like to have a few words with you. In private." Sebastian motioned for Paul to follow him and led him back into the Eternal Pageant. Then he unlocked the door they had passed by before and steered Paul through it.

Once inside, Sebastian closed and locked the door behind them and offered Paul a chair. Paul thanked him and sat down. Sebastian tossed himself down on the edge of a luxurious four-poster bed and sat staring at Paul for a moment as if he had stumbled across a lost child and couldn't figure out what to do with him.

Paul looked around him. This was a bedroom, all right — Sebastian's, unless he missed his guess. The decor was late Victorian, and Paul found that Sebastian looked right at home in it.

Sebastian clasped his hands in front of him and said, "I'll be brief and to the point. I like you, Paul, but you're obviously new to this game. Let me give you a couple of pointers that will help keep your blood in your veins.

"First, I know you haven't presented yourself to the Prince yet, and you must do so immediately. San Francisco belongs to the Camarilla, and like any other society, they have certain protocols. Whether you follow most of them is of no great import, but if you fail to report to the 'head honcho,' as Tex so fondly refers to him, he'll become annoyed. He is a powerful vampire, and take my word on this: you would do well not to annoy him. At least not directly.

"His name's Vannevar Thomas, and he's a reasonable man. If you'd like, I can set up an interview with him for you. Yes? Good. By the middle of next week, I'll have a time and a place.

"Second, watch your back. This fledgling who accosted you on the dance floor may not be a real danger within these walls, but once you get outside, take care. At best, he'll corner you one night with a bunch of his friends and beat you within an inch of your life. At worst … well, let's just say he'll cross that inch.

"Last, if you want to stay here for a while, you're welcome to. No, I'm not inviting you to share my bed. We don't quite know each other that well yet, but the upper and lower ends of the ship are open to you. Although I'm sure I'm not acquainted with all your enemies, I don't believe anyone will threaten you there. If they do, there'll be Hell to pay."

Sebastian stopped there, apparently having said his piece.

"Thanks for the advice, Sebastian, but don't worry about me. I can take care of myself."

"Those are famous last words, my friend, but I'm glad we had this conversation. Now, we should rejoin the party, or people will start to talk." Sebastian got up off his bed and unlocked the door.

"I'm afraid I won't be staying," said Paul.

"But the night is still young, my friend," Sebastian protested, checking his watch. "It's barely 10:00."

"My apologies. I have some unfinished business I have to attend to."

Sebastian's eyebrows shot up as he opened the door and led Paul out. "Ah, I see. Well, we are all men of business in the end." He locked the door behind him and pocketed the key. "Can you find your way out? I have some matters here which your mention of business has reminded me of." He extended his hand, and Paul shook it.

"I hope you can manage to conclude your business satisfactorily."

"So do I, Sebastian. So do I."

With that, Paul turned and made his way over to and up the stairs that led into the Alexandrian Club. The door marked "Private" closed quietly behind him. He strolled through the main lounge and turned into the dining room. Dinner was still being served. Paul spotted a door to the rear of the room and went for it.

The kitchen was full and busy. A prep boy looked up and said, "Hey, mister, you're not allowed back here." Paul ignored him and walked straight through to the back door. He opened it quietly and slipped outside into the cool night air, closing the door silently behind him.

The ship lay directly in front of him down a steep drop from the lawn to a rocky beach. Someone's hopes and dreams had run aground along with that ship, he was sure. He stared at it until he could read the faded name stenciled across the bow: The *Royal Phoenix*.

Eventually, he heard some voices from around to his left. Carefully, he stole along the side of the building until he could make out what they were saying. The first voice was Tony's.

"Look, he's gotta come out sooner or later. There's no way Sebastian's gonna let him crash there after that fight."

"Look, Tone, I don't know. If this guy could kill Randy, maybe we should just let him be." This voice was broad and deep.

"Shut up, Jasper, you pansy-ass. You and Mikey there, you wanna live forever?"

A whiny little voice spoke up. "Well, yeah, Tony. I thought that's what this was all about."

Paul heard someone get smacked. He assumed it was Mikey. "You stupid bastard!" yelled Tony. "You're missing the whole point. It's not the immortality, man, it's the power. Who'd want to spend eternity as a wimp?" Jasper and Mikey started to protest.

These guys were just dumb. They were talking so loud, Paul was surprised the doorman didn't come around to see what was going on. Considering the clientele, he'd probably already had some bad experiences with this sort of thing, the kind that tell you to stay where you are and keep your mouth shut, even when you hear fools mumbling too loudly around the corner.

"OK, OK, just shut up. We're wasting time here," Tony growled. "You guys remember the plan? Mikey, you get up front and lure him over. Jasper and me'll be waiting right here."

Paul heard Mikey's footsteps receding into the distance. For vampires, these guys were idiots. He just hoped they stayed stupid long enough for him to kill them.

Paul silently made his way around to the other corner of the house. Then he walked cautiously through the courtyard between the Alexandrian and the Westminster. It was well lit and deserted. He peeked around the front corner of the brick building to see a weasely man in black pants, a white T-shirt and a black leather jacket that was too big for him making nervous conversation with the doorman. He wore glasses with thick black frames.

Paul stepped out from around the corner of the building and whistled at Mikey. When he looked up, Paul waved at him and ducked back out of sight. Then he drew his cross from his waistband and waited.

Soon, he heard Mikey walking through the grass towards him, saying, "Hey, excuse me. Excuse me, mister, I gotta talk to you about something."

As Mikey turned the corner, Paul grabbed him by his shirt collar with his left hand and hauled him down and out of sight. At the same time, he brought up the cross-stake in his right hand and drove it through Mikey's heart. Mikey barely had time to gag.

Paul dropped Mikey's body and examined his handiwork. Blood was everywhere, and he felt a twinge of Hunger, although he had just fed the night before. Mikey's eyes pleaded for Paul to let him free. Paul did what he considered the merciful thing and ended Mikey's damned existence.

Once he was finished, Paul retrieved his cross and wiped it on Mikey's jeans. Then he hid the body under a bush and slipped back around to the rear of the building.

He heard nothing, but remained patient. Ten minutes later, Jasper spoke up. "Geez, Tony, what's taking him so long? Maybe I should go check."

"Keep quiet, you moron. What if Mikey brought him around the corner right now? Huh? You'd have blown it, that's what. Stay here and keep quiet. I'll go check things out."

Paul waited until he was sure Tony had made it around to the front of the building. Then he crept up behind Jasper as quietly as he could. Jasper was a tall, bald black man with broad shoulders and a narrow waist. He looked like he could've been a boxer in his mortal life. He seemed oblivious to Paul's presence.

Just as Paul was about to strike, he stepped upon a small twig. It was inevitable, he supposed. Things had been going far too perfectly up until now.

Jasper snapped around to face Paul. Paul froze for a moment, just a second too long. He saw everything in perfect clarity, but couldn't move fast enough. Jasper was dressed all in black, similar to Tony, except for a white T-shirt with the words "Born to Kill" on it in dripping red. He had a gold ring in the right side of his nose. His dark brown eyes were wide with fear, and he had just enough time to scream before Paul shoved the stake through his heart.

Paul grabbed Jasper and ran and tossed him over the embankment. Suddenly, shots rang out from behind. Paul dove for the embankment, but a bullet caught him in the back of his left thigh.

The impact spun him around in mid-air, but he still managed to clear the bank. It hurt when he hit the ground, but not too bad. That was one of the benefits of vampirehood: no danger of shock.

Paul glanced about for something to save him. His eyes fell on Jasper, and a plan formed in his mind. He grabbed Jasper's body and hoisted it up toward the top of the bank.

People started appearing on the yacht's deck, but Paul ignored them. Then, a floodlight atop the ship came on, illuminating the entire beach. Squirming himself between Tony and the light, Paul grasped Jasper by his waist, and thrust him halfway up over the embankment.

Tony saw Jasper's silhouette and emptied his pistol at it. The bullets knocked Jasper from Paul's hands. Paul waited. He heard the pistol click on empty chambers three times before it was tossed aside. No more bullets. Paul grinned.

He still needed some sort of weapon to give him the edge, but he didn't dare haul the stake out of Jasper's chest. He had to kill him first, and that would take time. Then it hit him. He patted down his pockets and found it: the rosary.

Paul took the rosary from his pocket and held its tiny cross before him. The bullet in his thigh was forgotten. When Tony came over the embankment, he'd be ready for him.

Suddenly, Tony leapt over Paul's head and landed on the beach behind him. Paul spun around, but not quickly enough. Tony gored him across the chest with his claws, drawing blood. While Paul was still reeling, Tony struck twice more, scoring him across his cheek and tearing open his left side and knocking him to the rocky ground.

Tony stopped for a second to gloat. That was his fatal mistake.

"I've got you now, Mister High-and-Goddamn Mighty. You killed Randy, fucker, and for that, you're gonna die. I'm gonna rip your heart out and swallow it whole. I'm gonna drink you dry. I'm gonna —"

Tony's ranting gave Paul time enough to hold up his rosary's cross. Tony took one look at it and started to laugh. But when he tried to close in for the kill, he found he couldn't. He wasn't laughing anymore.

Tony pushed harder and harder, with all his supernatural might, but he couldn't get one inch closer. He made a last-ditch effort, his eyes tearing in frustration, screaming loud enough to wake the dead, but Paul's faith was unshakable and strong, and it held.

Spent, Tony staggered away from the cross, with tears of blood in his eyes. He stumbled over Jasper's body and fell sprawled upon the ground.

Paul was on him in a second, his knees planted in Tony's back. He wound the ends of the rosary around his fists and wrapped its length around Tony's throat. Nothing in vampire lore had ever mentioned strangling a vampire with a rosary, but Paul believed it would work. He needed it to work, and so it was going to work. And God be praised, it did.

Paul rolled off Tony's back and collapsed. After a few deep breaths, he remembered his job wasn't quite over yet.

He rolled back onto his knees and crawled over to Jasper's body. Tony had partially dislodged the stake when he stumbled over him, and Jasper was starting to become free. He could move his eyes a bit and talk a little, but only in a low, raspy voice as if his lungs were filled with fluid, which they probably were.

Red tears were running down the sides of his dark, sweaty cheeks. "Please, man, I ain't got nothing against you," he whispered.

"Not yet," Paul whispered back. "Not yet."

"Oh, God," Jasper begged. "Oh, God, please save me. Show me some mercy, man. Please, man, mercy."

"As you wish," Paul whispered as he shoved the cross in further. Tears ran down Paul's cheeks and fell onto Jasper's face, their blood mingling together before spilling onto the stony beach. "Go in peace, my son," Paul whispered, his voice raw and broken. "Go in peace." With that, he tore out Jasper's throat and watched his life flow into the sand.

For what seemed like an eternity, all was quiet. Then Tex was there, helping Paul to his feet. "I ain't never seen anything like it," he told Paul as he slung the priest's right arm over his shoulders. "You're one hell of a scrapper, kid. Good thing I managed to get the living folks barricaded in the Alexandrian before I left. Something like this could've blown our collective cover real bad." Then Tex called up to the ship, "What should I do with him now, Sebastian?"

Paul looked up to see Sebastian standing next to the light. His face was full of disbelief, and it took him a moment to compose himself. Slowly but surely, that same soft, yet wry grin crept across his face, and although he was too far away, Paul could've sworn he saw a mischievous twinkle in his eyes. Then Sebastian began to nod knowingly and to clap. Soon one person joined in, and then another and another, one by one, until the entire beach resounded with their applause.

"Return him to the ship, Tex," Sebastian called over the clapping. "I believe we can find it in our hearts to patch up our wondrous new hero."

As Tex helped the wounded priest up away from the sea, Paul turned to look back at the crowd one last time. Just then, Sebastian caught his eye and, in a voice it seemed only they two could hear, said, "Yes, times will be much more interesting with you around, my friend." ✝

THE VOICE OF THE HUMMINGBIRD

by S.P. Somtow

Huitzilopotchtli.

It was the will of the god named Hummingbird that our people should cease to be a wandering people, a desert people, an impoverished and simpleminded people, that we should journey down into the rich green valley at the world's heart and claim its lakes and forests for our own, and rule over all the nations of the earth. We were a people with a grand and glorious destiny; we had been called to a special covenant with our god; and if there were things that our god commanded us to do which, to those who did not share our special relationship with him, appeared brutal, cruel, uncompassionate, it was only that we alone could see the higher purpose; that we alone were charged with the guardianship of the knowledge of the secret workings of the universe.

It was the will of the god named Hummingbird that I should be the one to hear his voice and bear his message to my people; that I should lead them from the wasteland into the place where they would build the greatest of all cities, set in the center of the world as a turquoise in a circlet of gold. And it came to pass that I spoke, and the people obeyed, and we sealed our covenant with our own blood and the blood of the countless conquered. This was as it should be. Our people had been chosen.

Later I would come to understand that there were others, people no less proud than our people, no less confident of their moral rectitude, no less certain that the salvation of the entire universe lay in the application of secret knowledge that only their tribe possessed; there was even, across the great ocean to the east, a people whose god had called them to cross a great desert and seal a covenant and conquer and build a great temple. We Mexica were not, after all, unique; we were merely a repeating pattern in the wheel of history; and our history was not even the only wheel that was in motion at the time.

We didn't even have wheels then, anyway. After a dozen centuries I suppose one might be forgiven a few anachronistic metaphors. I learned about wheels a long time after the covenant was broken, in San Francisco.

I learned about the other chosen people from Julia Epstein.

• • •

There is a gap of about 500 years in my existence. One moment, the fire was raging in the streets of Tenochtitlan, and I was watching the stars fall from the sky, and cursing the silver-clad man-beasts called Spaniards who had blundered into shattering the equilibrium of the universe. Then, in a blink's breadth, it seemed, I was lying in a glass case, an exhibit in the San Francisco Museum, being pointed at by a petulant youth.

That I might have slept for a time — a century or two even — would not have been surprising. I had done that before, though only of my own volition. I had slept all the way through the conquest of the people of Tlatztelhuatec; I knew it would be dull; they were little better than cattle. But there were no signs that I had been in suspended animation. No cognitive disjunction. No sensation of falling, falling, falling into the bottomless abyss.

The room was gloomy; it had been designed to simulate the rocky chamber in which I had been found. There was no daylight. Torches flickered, yet they did not burn; the fire in them was cold and artificial.

Even lying under the glass, unable as yet to move more than the twitch of an eyelash, fighting the inertia of the dreamless sleep, I was aware that the world had become far stranger than I could have imagined. The youth who stared down at me was a mongrel; he had the flat nose and dark skin of the Mexica, but there was also something about him that resembled the man-beasts from across the sea. He had no hair save for a crest that stood unnaturally tall and was dyed the color of quetzal feathers. His robes were of animal hide, but black and polished to an almost reflective smoothness. He was not utterly inhuman — his ears were pierced at least — but from them hung, upside-down, a pair of those silver crucifixes that symbolize the man-beasts' god, whom they call Hesuskristos, who is in reality Xipe Totec, the flayed god, as Hummingbird once revealed to me in a dream.

He called out to a companion; this one's tufted hair was the color of fresh blood, and he wore a silver thorn through his left cheek. The language, at least, I knew, though the accent was strange and there were unfamiliar words; I had taken the trouble to learn the language of the man-beasts. There are two dialects; one, spoken by the black robes, is called Espanol; the other is the language of their enemies, known as English. It was the second of these I heard, in a boyish voice muffled by glass.

"Dude! It says he's been dead for 500 years."

"Pulled him out of the foundation of a 50-story office building after that big Mexico City quake. Yeah, perfectly preserved and shit. A hollow in the rock, a natural vacuum."

"Yeah, I saw it on *20/20*."

"Did you see that? He moved, dude!"

"Yeah. Right."

Five hundred years, but that was impossible! Hummingbird himself had told me that in a few short years the world would end in an apocalypse of blood and fire. How could 500 years have gone by? Unless, of course, the world had already ended.

That would explain the surpassing alienness of my surroundings. Even the air smelled strange. Even the blood of the two boys, which sang to me as it pumped through their arteries, exuded an unaccustomed odor, as though infused with the pulped essences of the hemp and coca plants.

The one with the crimson hair said, "No, dude, I ain't joking. Look at him, man, I swear his eyelids are like, flickering."

"You shouldn't have dropped acid at the Cure concert last night. You're still blazing, dude."

I turned my head to get a better view.

"Jesus Christ!" they screamed.

So the world had ended after all. The time of Huitzilopotchtli was over. There had been a fiery apocalypse — my memories had not deceived me — and we were now well into the World of the Fifth Sun, foretold to me by the god, and a new god was in power, the hanged god whose name those boys evoked, Hesuskristos.

I was full of despair. I did not belong here. Why had I been suffered to remain alive? Surely I should have been destroyed, along with the city of Tenochtitlan, along with the great pyramids and temples and palaces of my people. Could the gods not have been more thorough? But then that was just like them; come up with the grand concepts, leave their execution to imperfect mortals. I raged. My heart gave a little flutter, trying to bestir itself from its age-old immobility. My fury fueled me. I could feel my blood begin, sluggishly, to liquefy, to funnel upward through my veins like the magma through the twisty tunnels of Popocatapetl.

Soon I would erupt.

I lashed out. I heard shattering glass. The smells of the strange new world burst upon my senses. Then came the Hunger, swooping down on me as an owl on a mouse in the dead of night. No longer muffled, the rushing of young blood roared in my ears. The odor was sour and pungent. I seized the first creature by the arm, the one with the quetzal-feathered hair; the second, screaming, ran; I transfixed the prey with my eyes and filled him with the certainty of his own death; then, drawing him down to me, I fed.

I do not know how long we lay together, locked in that predatory embrace. His blood was youthful; it spurted; it permeated my pores; I drank it and I breathed it into my lungs; for a fleeting moment it brought back to mind those nights of furtive, unfulfilled encounters in the chill desert night; the burning curve of a young girl's thigh, the aroma of her liquidescing pubes. Those were the times before the god called me, when I was mortal and barely man.

At length I realized that I had completely drained him. I let go and he thudded on the polished floor like a terra-cotta doll. It was then that I became aware of a noisome clanging sound, a whirling, flashing red light, and men in strange blue clothing who brandished muskets of a sleekly futuristic design as they surrounded the plinth on which I lay. The boy who had fled stood beneath an archway, babbling and shivering and pointing at me and at his friend's desiccated corpse.

Perhaps, I decided, it would be more prudent to play dead for a little while longer.

• • •

I awakened in another chamber. It was lined with leatherbound codices of the kind the black robes favored. The room was lit by candlelight, and I sitting on a wooden chair. I tried to move, but I had been bound with ropes — metal ropes, artfully strung, and padlocked, the way the Spaniards keep their gold. Across an immense desk, cluttered with the artifacts of my people, jeweled skulls and jade statuettes and blood-cups, sat a woman.

She was of man-beast extraction, but not unattractive. I had never seen a woman of their kind before; they had brought none with them from their country, which was perhaps why they had become so ferocious. She was sharp-nosed, and had long brown hair. When she spoke to me, it was, to my amazement, in Nahuatl, the language of the Mexica people.

"I'm Julia Epstein," she said. "I'm the curator of our Latin American collection. Would you care for a little blood?"

"I'm quite full, thank you," I said.

"In that case, you might want to start telling me what the hell is going on. It's not every day that a museum exhibit gets up and starts attacking the public. Who are you?"

"It's not proper for me to give my name to you, a man-beast."

She laughed. "Man-beast! I know you Aztecs used to think that the Spaniards and their horses were some kind of hybrid monster, but times have changed. We drive automobiles now. I think it's safe for you to tell me your name. I'm not going to acquire any mystical power over you. Besides, you're just going to have to trust me; I'm the one who talked the cops into believing that that punk's story was just some kind of acid-trip fantasy; they have him under wraps now, the poor child, deciding whether to get him on murder one."

"Very well," I said, "I am Nezahualcoyotl."

"And I'm Santa Claus," said Julia Epstein, frowning. "So you say you're the Nezahualcoyotl, who claimed descent from the great gods of Teotihuactn, the greatest poet, musician and prophet of the Aztecs, their first great ruler, a man who was an ancient memory when Moctezuma was king and the Conquistadores swept over Mexico?"

"You are well informed," I said.

"Well, why not? It's no harder to believe that than to believe that an exceptionally well-preserved mummy, just dug up from the newly discovered catacombs in Mexico City, and my museum's prize exhibit, would get up, walk around, attack a few punks, and drink their blood. And to think that I dug you up with my own hands."

"So it is to you that owe my continued existence."

"If you want to call it living."

"What else would you call it?"

"You're a vampire."

"I'm unfamiliar with that word."

"Oh, don't give me that bullshit, Nezzy. I know everything about you guys. I can't get anyone to believe me, but I've gathered a shitload of information. Yeah, I'm an archaeologist, sure, but vampires are kind of a hobby with me, know what I mean? And this city's crawling with them. I know. I've got tons of evidence: clippings, photographs, police files. Tried to sell this shit to the *Enquirer*, and you know what? They rejected it. Said it wasn't, ah, convincing. Convincing! From the people who did the "Alien Endorses Clinton" story and the piece about the four-headed baby! Let me tell you what really happened. They found out about it. They're everywhere. Big cities mainly, but even the smallest town has one or two. They're running everything. Your worst nightmare about the Mafia, the CIA, the Illuminati, all rolled into one. They read my submission and they squelched it! Sounds pretty damn paranoid, doesn't it? Welcome to the quackpot world of academia."

"But what is a vampire?" I said. I was beginning to feel the Hunger again; just a prickle in my veins. Normally the blood of a whole young male would have kept me going for days, but it had been so long. I glanced down at myself, saw my papery skin, knew it would take a few more feedings to restore me to the semblance of life.

"A vampire?" said Julia. "Why, you're a vampire. You drink blood. You live for a long, long time. You are a child of the shadows, a creature of the night."

"True, but — are you saying that there are others?"

"Are you saying that there aren't others?"

"There was one other." It pained me to think of my young protégé, the one who had betrayed King Moctezuma to the man-beasts, the one whom the black robes called Hortator, which signifies, in their language, the man who beats the drum to drive the galley-slaves who row in the Spaniards' men-o'-war, because of the drum he stole from me, made from the flayed skin of the god Xipe Totec himself, the one I thought would succeed me, but who instead had destroyed my whole world. "There was the god at first. He called me to his service. I had thought to hand on the power to another, but. . ."

"That's where you're wrong, my friend," said Julia. "There's a whole network of you people. You have your tentacles in everything. You run this whole planet. You're in Congress. In the U.N. In the damn White House, for all I know. And all top secret. Don't worry. I won't give you away. They have a certificate on file that says I'm a paranoid schizophrenic; so who'd believe me anyway?"

"Even among the white men, people such as I?" It was hard to grasp.

"The New World was a universe unto itself in 1453. Maybe you were the only one here. Maybe your god came over the Bering Strait, nurtured his secret alone for 20,000 years. Perhaps he forgot, even, that there was a race of creatures like himself. Perhaps, after millennia, he became lonely; who knows? Or he needed another cowherd. He made you. You, Nezahualcoyotl, coming of age with an entire continent for your domain, completely ignorant of the customs, traditions, laws, identities of your Kindred — a law unto yourself. They're not going to like you."

"I think I'll have that drink now."

Julia Epstein rose and went to a white rectangular cabinet. She opened it. A searing cold emanated from it, as though winter had been trapped within its confines. She drew out a skin of chilled blood; not a natural skin, surely, for it was clear as water. "It's my own," she said. "I have a rare blood type, so I keep some around in case something happens to me and I need a quick transfusion. Yeah, more evidence of paranoia."

She tossed the skin to me. I sank my teeth into the artificial skin. The blood was sweet, a little cloying, and freezing cold; then I remembered, from my childhood, how much I had enjoyed the snow cones flavored with berry juice that the vendors used to bring down from the mountains; I savored the nostalgia. Twice today I'd had a remembrance of the distant past, before my changing. It is strange how one's childhood haunts one.

Julia herself drank coffee, which she poured from a metal pot and blended with bleached sugar. She shook back her hair. I was taken aback at the immodest way she stared at me; truly my god had no more power in this world, or she would have been trembling with awe. There was a faint odor of attraction about her; this woman desired me. And that was strange, for no Aztec woman would have dared think sexual thoughts about one who spoke directly to the gods.

"You need me," she said. "You'll be flung into a cutthroat society of dozens of your kind, with bizarre hierarchies, internecine politics, games of control and domination. You've been asleep for 500 years, and since then there's been a mass emigration. They like it better in the New World; fewer preconceptions, the American dream and all that, and the prey are a lot less careful than back in old Wallachia. Where everyone believes in vampires, it's hard for one to catch a decent meal."

"What? They do not give their blood willingly?" For that was the hardest new concept to grasp. Was it not the duty of humans to give freely of their flesh and blood that their gods might live? Was blood not the lifeforce that kept the sun and the stars in their courses?

"Willingly!" said Julia. "You do have a lot to learn."

"You'll help me."

She smiled. "Of course. But only if you help me."

"How?"

"By telling me all about yourself."

She unchained me, and I told her about the coming of the white men, and about Hortator's betrayal. And she in turn told me of her own people, who had once been nomads, who had crossed a tremendous desert to find a land flowing with milk and honey; who had made a covenant with a great and terrible deity who spoke in the voices of wind and fire; and I came to know of the vastness of the earth, and of how my people had been but one of many; how nations had risen and fallen, how even mankind itself had not always been the pinnacle of creation; how the great globe had formed out of the cold dust of the cosmos, and would one day return to dust.

In time, I came to love her; and that in itself was a strange thing, for our kind do not feel love as mortals feel it.

• • •

The man who came to be called Hortator belonged to me. I had captured him in the Flower Wars, which we hold each year when there are not enough captives from normal wars to feed the altars of the gods.

This year the war was held in a plain not far from the city. Moctezuma himself had come to watch; on a knoll overlooking the battlefield, he and the enemy king, Cozcatl, picnicked on tortillas stuffed with ground iguana, braised in a sauce of pulped cocoa beans, which the man-beasts call chocolate. I, as the mouthpiece of the god, sat above Moctezuma on a ledge lined with jaguar skin and feathers. It was a pleasant afternoon; the courtiers were wolfing down their packed lunch while I sipped, from a sacred onyx cup, the blood of a young Mayan girl who had been sacrificed only that morning; yes, the blood had been cooled with snow from the slopes of the volcano.

"It's not going well," said the king. "Look — the jaguar team has only snared about a hundred, and the quetzal team less than half that."

Once touched by the sacred flower-wand which was the only weapon used in these artificial wars, a soldier was sent to the sacrificial pen. It was a great honor, of course, to be sacrificed, and a thing of beauty to behold those hordes of young men, oiled and gleaming, rushing across the grass to embrace their several destinies. "They seem more reluctant than usual, Your Majesty," I said.

"Yes," said the king darkly. "I wonder why."

"I think," I said, trying to put it to him delicately, "it has something to do with the man-beasts from the sea."

"You'd think they'd be all the more anxious to get sacrificed, what with the present danger to the empire."

"Yes, but they've been spreading sedition, Your Majesty. I've just come from the prison; they've been interrogating that black robe they captured — a high priest of sorts. He says that our sacrifices are ignorant superstition; that the sun will rise each morning with our without them; and he's been babbling about Hesuskristos, their god, who seems to be a garbled version of Xipe Totec."

"You shouldn't say bad things about the man-beasts. Last night I dreamed that the Plumed Serpent was returning to claim his kingdom." He was speaking of Quetzalcoatl, the god-king who left our shores 500 years before, vowing to come back.

"Quetzalcoatl will not come back, Your Majesty."

"How do you know? Am I not the king? Don't my dreams have the force of prophecy?"

"You may have dreamt of him, Your Majesty; I, on the other hand, was his friend." It was because he lost the land in a wager that he had been forced to cross the ocean to look for a new kingdom, though that part of the story never made it into our mythology.

"So you say, Nezahualcoyotl. You say that you're a thousand years old, and that you personally led our people out of the wilderness. That sort of thing is all very well for the peasants, Nezahualcoyotl. But I'm a modern king, and I know that you often use the language of metaphor in order to enhance the grandeur of the gods. No, no, I'm not blaming you; I'm a mean hand at propaganda myself. It's just that, well, you shouldn't believe your own —"

It would not do to argue. I finished my blood in silence.

"Anyhow, I think we should have a bit of propaganda right now, Nezahualcoyotl. Why don't you go down there and lead the jaguar team personally? Give them a bit of that old-time religion. Stir up their juices."

"Sire, at my age —"

"Nonsense. Guard, give him one of those flower-wands."

I sighed, took the wand, and went down the hill.

The war was being conducted in an orderly fashion. Seeing me, members of the jaguar team made a space for me. I gave a brief and cliché-ridden harangue about the cycles of the cosmos; then it was time to charge. Boys banged on humanskin drums; musicians began a noisy caterwauling of flutes, cymbals, and shrilling voices that sang of the coming of Huitzilopochtli to the Mexica. The armies ran toward each other, chanting their war-songs, each soldier seeking out a good quarry. I too ran; not with supernatural swiftness, but like a man, my bare feet pounding the ground. Above us, the whistle of the atl-atl and the whine of flower-tipped arrows. The armies met. I searched for a suitable captive that would honor the god. I saw a man in the farthest rank of the enemy, more child than man, his limbs perfectly formed, his eyes darting fearfully from side to side. There was someone who saw no honor in dying for the god! I elbowed aside three pairs of combatants and came upon him suddenly, looming above him as he ducked behind a tree.

"I am your death," I said. "Give yourself up; give honor to the gods."

I touched him with the flower-wand. He glanced at it, took it, stared me defiantly in the eye.

"I won't do it," he said.

I knew then that he had been polluted by the preachings of the man-beasts. A fury erupted in me. I said, "Why have you been listening to them? Don't you know that they're only human beings? That they bleed and die like ordinary men?"

But he began to run. I was surprised by his speed. He leaped over a bush, sprinted away from the mass of warriors toward a field of maize that bordered the battleground. My first impulse was to let him go — for there was no honor in sacrificing so abject a creature to Hummingbird — but my anger grew and grew as I watched him shrinking into the distance. I could stand it no longer. I called upon the strength of the jaguar and the swiftness of the rabbit; I funneled into the very wind; soon I was upon him again. He turned, saw me running beside him, matching him pace for pace. I could smell his terror; terror was only natural; what I could not smell was the joy, equally natural, that a man should feel when he is about to embrace the source of all joy, to die that the sun might live. He was less than a man. Only an animal could feel this terror of dying without also feeling the exhilaration. I decided to kill him as he ran. I reached out. He struggled, but I drew on my inner strength; I pinned him to the ground. The corn encircled us. Only the gods heard what we said to one another.

"I won't go," he said again. "Kill me now, but I won't die to feed a god that doesn't even exist."

"Doesn't exist!" My anger rose up, naked and terrible. I started to throttle him. The odor of his fear filled my nostrils. It was intoxicating. I wanted to feed on him right then and there. I could feel his jugular throbbing against my fingers. I knew that his blood was clean and unpolluted with alcohol or coca leaf. His blood was pure as the waters of the mountain; but I could not kill him. "How long were you among the man-beasts?"

"Three years."

I had to let him live. He knew about the foreigners, their languages, their savage ways. I could not kill him until he had divulged all he knew. With a fingernail I scratched his arm, sucked out a few droplets to assuage my Hunger. I had to bind him to me. He could become a secret weapon; perhaps I could stave off the end of the world after all.

If only I had listened to the voice of Hummingbird! But I wanted to halt the wheel of time, and though I was a thousand years old I was still too young to understand that there is no stopping time.

"Who are you?" I said.

"I don't know. I don't have a name anymore; I've forgotten it. The Spanish called me Hortator. It pleased them to let me beat the drum on one of their galley ships. I've even been to Spain — that part of Spain that they call Cuba."

"Why aren't you still with them?"

"Pirates, Lord High Priest. I escaped; the others are dead, every one of them."

"And the man-beast who is called Cortez, who the king thinks is the god Quetzalcoatl, returned to reclaim his inheritance?"

"I don't know of him. The man-beasts are many — dozens of nations and languages. And all of them are coming here. They want gold."

I laughed; what was so valuable about gold, that would make these creatures come across the ocean in their islands made of wood? Was gold then their god?

"No, my Lord. They worship Xipe Totec; their name for him is Hesuskristos."

When I escorted my prisoner back to the pen, it was getting late. Moctezuma was bored and listless; Cozcatl was annoyed at having lost the war, though it would hardly have been good manners for him to be victorious over his sovereign lord. The two kings applauded as I approached them, and bade me eat with them; they had a fresh haunch roasting. "Excellent meat," said the king. "She was good in bed, too."

"You did her great honor, Sire, to inseminate her, sacrifice her, and eat her, all with your own hands."

"It was the Queen's idea, actually; she had been getting uppity. But what have we here?" He eyed my captive with interest. "A powerful-looking fellow; I didn't know you had it in you to bring in so fine a specimen."

He cast his eye about for his obsidian knife; when the king particularly favored someone, he was apt to sacrifice him on the spot. I had to think quickly to protect my source of information. "Your Majesty," I said, "the god has told me that this man is to be the next Unblemished Youth."

"Oh," said the king, disappointed, "we'll have to wait until the big ceremony, then." To Hortator he said, "You're a very lucky young man; you'll have the best in food, drink, and women, including four holy brides; until you're sacrificed, a year from now, you'll be worshipped as a god. Even I will have to bow to you, though you mustn't get any grand ideas."

"Yes, Sire," said Hortator. I could tell he was grateful for his reprieve. Perhaps, in time, I would be able to wash away the silly notions the man-beasts had planted in his mind. A year was time enough, surely, to persuade him to look forward to being sacrificed properly.

• • •

"You were planning to deprogram him!" Julia said, having by then become somewhat drunk. I myself was on my second skin of blood; my appearance was far less corpselike than it had been in the exhibit hall.

"I'd better take you home with me," she went on. "At least until you figure out what you're going to do with yourself. I mean — no credit cards, no social security number, no car — you could be in for some culture shock."

I was not sure what she was talking about, but a few hours later I was numb from confusion. I had ridden in a thing called BART, which is a cylindrical metal wagon that runs through tubes under the earth; I had been driven in a horseless chariot across a bridge that seemed to hang on wires above the ocean; I had seen buildings shaped like phalluses, strutting up into the sky; and the people! Tenochtitlan at its most crowded had not been like this. San Francisco — named, so Julia told me, after a nature god of the Spaniards — was a hundred times as crowded. There were people of many colors, and their costumes beggared description. In my feathers, leggings, and pendulous jade earrings, I must have looked a little odd; yet no one stared at me. This was a people accustomed to strangeness.

At length we reached Julia's home, an apartment within one of those tall buildings, reached by means of a little chamber on pulleys which seemed much more efficient that stairs; I could see that I was going to enjoy the many conveniences of this alien world.

Her home was an odd little place; she lived alone, without parents or children, without even any servants; and the apartment, though crammed with laborsaving devices, was little bigger than a peasant's hovel, and considerably more claustrophobic.

We had been there for only moments when she thrust herself at me. Her blood was racing, and scented with erotic secretions. She kissed me. I tasted blood on her chapped lips. I pulled away. "Be careful," I said. "I don't have the same desires as you. I don't feel lust. Not like that."

"Then teach me the other kind of lust."

"I'm afraid you would not like it."

"Yes, yes, I know the desolation, the loneliness of eternity. I don't care! Don't you understand? I've always wanted to be a vampire. I've never been able to get this close to one before. Not for certain. I'm a historian. I want to get the long view. I want to see man's destiny unfold, bit by bit. I hate being a human being."

"It's not what you think it is." How could I tell her about those flashes from my childhood, those faded images that still haunted me with their unattainable vividness? My world is a gray world; only the infusion of blood brings to it a fleeting color, and that only a simulacrum of color, awakened by long-lost memories; now, 500 years beyond the end of the world, I had become even more of a tragicomic figure. How could this woman ever know, unless I made her know? And then, poor thing, there would be no turning back.

I did not want to make her like me. I had tried that once. It had not eased my loneliness. And my creation had betrayed me. But the woman could be useful.

For now I would pretend to hold out the possibility that she might one day become immortal.

"Make love to me," she said.

She smiled a half-smile and beckoned me into an inner room. There were mirrors everywhere. With great deliberation, she began to remove her clothing. There was a pleasing firmness to her, though she was not young. An Aztec woman of her years would have been worn out, her fists hardened from pounding laundry or tortillas. It would be necessary for me to go through the motions of lovemaking. In the end I did not mind. She had been menstruating.

Afterwards, I lay on the bed and watched her sitting at the mirror, painting her face. She opened a drawer and took out a gold pendant in the shape of a crucified man. Suddenly I understood why I had not perished along with the rest of the world. I had unfinished business.

"Where did you get that amulet from?"

"You recognize it, don't you?" She stood up, clad only in the pendant and her long dark hair. "I'm afraid you're not the first vampire I've dated. Actually I wasn't entirely sure he was one, until now. They don't make a habit of telling. But you've just confirmed it."

"I have to find the person who gave it to you."

"I'll take you to him," she said.

• • •

Once more we crossed the bay in the steel chariot; once more my memories came flooding back.

They had seemed insane to me, those man-beasts; there were only a handful of them, yet they scoured the land as though they were an army of thousands. In only a short while they had conquered a city but a day's journey from Tenochtitlan. But in the palace of Moctezuma there was a strange calm. I did not know why. Each day, I sacrificed the requisite numbers of victims at the appropriate hours; I did nothing that dishonored the gods.

Except, of course, for the little lie I had told my king; it had not been Huitzilopochtli who had commanded that the man Hortator be consecrated as the Unblemished Youth. I had said so to ensure that the man would survive and remain useful to me. It was not the first time I had invoked the voice of the Hummingbird to bring about some personal decision. When one has been the mouthpiece of the god for centuries at a time, there are times when one's identity becomes blurred. Besides, what harm could it do? Hortator was the perfect choice, even if the god had not made it himself.

I visited him each evening in the compound sacred to Xipe Totec, where the four sacred handmaidens dressed him, bathed him, and tended to his sexual needs, for he was no longer free to walk about the city at will. He was, indeed, unblemished, a prime specimen of Aztec manhood, lean, tall, well proportioned, and fine featured. The god would be pleased when the day came for him to be flayed alive so that his skin could be worn by the priest of Xipe Totec in the annual ceremony that heals and renews the wounded earth and brings forth the rains of spring. There was only one thing wrong with it all; the Unblemished Youth did not seem particularly honored by the attention. It was all most unusual, a sign of the decadence of those times.

"I don't want to do it," he told me, "because I don't believe in it." For a nonbeliever he was certainly reaping its benefits — being massaged by one handmaiden, being fed by another, and the gods alone knew what was going on under the gold-edged table behind which he sat. "I mean that it's no use; the blood of human sacrifices isn't what makes the sun rise each morning; the god of the man-beasts is clearly more powerful than Huitzilopochtli even as Hummingbird was mightier than the gods who came before. I don't mind the pain so much as the fact that I'd be dying for no reason."

"You've been poisoning the king's mind, too, haven't you?" I said. For Moctezuma seemed to have lost all interest in the future of his empire.

"I am the Unblemished Youth," he pointed out. "It was your idea. And as you know, that means that my advice comes from the gods.."

"You hear no voices from the sky!" I said. "It's all pretense with you."

"And what voice from the gods told you that I was to be kept alive to teach you the ways of the white men?"

He knew I had lied. Only one whose mind had already been tainted by the man-beasts' ideas would even have imagined such a thing. "But I do hear voices," I said.

"Then let me hear one too."

"All right."

I told him to follow me. We took a subterranean passageway — for he could not be seen to wander the streets of the city — that angled downward, deep under the great pyramid of Huitzilopochtli. The walls were damp and had a natural coolness from the waters that seeped underground from the great lake of Tenochtitlan. Hortator stopped to admire the bas-reliefs which depicted the history of the Mexica people in their long migration toward the promised land; there were sculptures in niches in the stone, some decorated with fresh human skulls or decaying flowers, some so weathered that they could no longer be identified, being the gods of unremembered peoples who had long since been conquered and assimilated by the Mexica; many parts of the tunnel were ill-kept; our torches burned but dimly here, far from the outside air.

At length we reached a chamber so sacred that even King Moctezuma had never set foot within it. It was guarded by the god of a civilization far older than ours — Um-Tzec, the Mayan god of death, whose skull-face was etched into the stone that blocked the entrance.

I whispered a word in the long-forgotten Olmec language, and the stone slid aside to reveal the chamber. Hortator gasped as he read in the flickering torchlight the calendar symbols and the glyphs that lined the walls.

"But —" he said, "this is the lost tomb of Nezahualcoyotl, your namesake, the first great king of the Aztecs!"

I smiled. I held up my torch so he could see all that the room contained — treasures of gold from ancient cities — magical objects and amulets — and a great sarcophagus, carved from solid obsidian.

"The tomb is empty!" he gasped.

"Yes," I said, "it is, and always will be, by the sacred grace and will of Huitzilopochtli, Hummingbird of the Left."

"The black robes told me of creatures like you. I've never seen you eat; you seem to subsist on blood. You're one of the undead, a creature of the devil. You sleep by day in your own coffin, and by night you prey on human blood."

I laughed. "What strange notions these man-beasts have! Though I admit that I have sometimes taken a nap inside the sarcophagus. It's roomy, and very conducive to meditation."

I showed him the treasures. Every one of them had an ancient tale attached to it, or some mystic power. The ring of concealment and the jewel for scrying the past. The great drum fashioned from Xipe Totec's skin, which, when beaten, confers the power of celerity. "Feel it, touch its tautness. That is your skin too, for you are Xipe Totec."

"There is only one Xipe Totec, who gave his life for the redemption of the world, who was killed and rose again on the third day."

"I'm glad the Spaniards haven't robbed you of that truth!"

"On the contrary," he said, "they taught it to me. And they say that theirs is the real Xipe Totec, and yours is an illusion, the work of the powers of darkness." He pulled out an amulet from a fold of his feather robe, and showed me the image of Hesuskristos; a suffering god indeed, nailed to a tree, his torso cruelly pierced, his scalp ripped by thorns. "It is an admirable god," I said, "but I see no reason why, accepting one, you must heap scorn on the other."

"Oh, they are not so different, the new gods and the old. The black robes have sacrifices too; they burn the victims alive in a public ceremony called auto-da-fe, after first subjecting them to fiendish tortures —"

"Wonderful," I said, "at least they have some of the rudiments of civilization."

"I did not say their god was better, Nezahualcoyotl; only that he is stronger. Now show me how your god speaks."

"I will need blood."

"Take mine," he said.

I took my favorite blood-cup, carved from a single, flawless piece of jade, and murmured a prayer over it. I did not want to scar the Unblemished Youth; I knelt before him and pricked him lightly in the groin with the fingernail of my left pinky, which I keep sharpened for that purpose; I drained an ounce or so into the blood-cup, then seared the wound shut with a dab of my saliva.

The drawing of blood caused the man to close his eyes. He whimpered; I knew not if it was from pain or ecstasy. I called on Huitzilopochtli, drained the blood-cup, tossed it aside. The warmth shot through my ancient veins, pierced my unbeating heart; it was a bitter blood, a blood of destiny. I emptied out my soul. I waited for the god to speak.

And presently it came, a faint whisper in my left ear, like the fluttering of tiny wings. I could not see Huitzilopochtli — no one has ever seen him — but his still small voice lanced my very bones like the thunderous erupting of Popocatapetl itself. *The world has turned in on itself,* said the god, *and the fire of the sun has turned to ashes.*

"But — what have we done wrong? Didn't we slaughter hecatombs of warriors to your glory? Didn't we mortify our own flesh, build pyramids whose points grazed the very dwelling places of your Kindred?"

The god laughed. *The cosmos dances,* he said. *We are at peace.*

In my trance state I saw Hortator standing before me, no longer in the consecrated raiment of Xipe Totec, but naked, nailed to a tree, the skin scourged from his back, the blood streaming from his side and down his face, and I cried out, "You abomination! You travesty of the true faith!" and I rushed toward him. When I was with the god I was more powerful than any human. I could rip him in pieces with my bare hands. I had him by the throat, was throttling the life from him —

You will not kill him, said the god. All at once, the strength left my hands. *Instead, you will make him immortal.*

"He doesn't deserve —"

Obey me! He too is a prophet, of a sort. Do you not understand that he who rises to godhead, who cre-

ates a world, a people, a destiny, plants inevitably within his creation the seeds of his own destruction? All life is so — and the gods, who are the pinnacle of life, are as subject to its laws as any other creatures.

It seemed to me that I no longer understood the god as clearly as I had once, when I came down from the high mountain to bring his message to a tribe of wanderers. His words were confused now, tainted. But he was the god, and I obeyed him without thought. I knelt once more before Hortator, and I began to feed, mindless now of damaging his flesh, for I knew that he would never have to suffer the rites of Xipe Totec. I fed and fed until there was no more blood at all, and then, slashing my lip with my razor fingernail, I moistened his lips with a few drops of my own millennial blood, blood that ran cold as the waters under the earth.

I cried out: "Do you see now the power of Huitzilopochtli? I have killed you and brought you back from the dead; I have awakened you to the world of eternal cold. . ."

But Hortator only laughed, and he said to me, "I heard nothing. No hummingbird whispered in my left ear. The black robes were right; your gods do not exist."

"My gods have made you immortal!"

"I am already immortal; for the black robes have sprinkled me with their water of life."

I could not understand what had happened. Why had the god commanded me to make him my Kindred, then allowed him to mock me? Why could Hortator not hear the voice of the deity when it reverberated in my very bones? The very fabric of the world was unraveling. For the first time in a thousand years, I was afraid. At first I could not even recognize the emotion, it was so alien; it was almost thrilling. I reached back farther and farther through the cobwebs of memory. I saw myself as a child, scurrying beneath my mother's blanket, fleeing the music of the night. With fear came a kind of melancholy, for I knew that I would never again truly feel what it was like to be alive.

Once, it seemed, I walked with my god; daily, hourly I heard his voice echo and reecho in my heart. Then came a time when he spoke to me but rarely, and usually only in the context of the blood-ritual. And now and then, I began to speak for him, inventing his words, for the people did not hear him unless I first heard him; it was I who was his prophet. Was it those little lies that had made my god abandon me now?

I cried out, "Oh, Huitzilopochtli, Huitzilopochtli, why hast thou forsaken me?" But the god did not see fit to respond.

• • •

We stopped at a bazaar to buy clothes more suitable to my surroundings. Julia picked out some black leggings which could be pulled over my loincloth, shoes made from animal skins, and an overshirt of some soft white material; she paid for the items with a rectangular plaque, which the vendor slid through a metal device, after which she made some mysterious marks on a square of parchment.

Then we drove on to another part of the city, one where the buildings were more ornate, not the monolithic towers of stone and glass I had seen before. We stopped in front of a low, unpretentious-looking building; Julia bade me follow her.

Inside, the surroundings were considerably more ostentatious. There were paintings, a floor covered with some kind of red-tinted fur, the pieces joined together so invisibly that one could not tell what animal it had come from. The place was full of all manner of people, jabbering away in many accents, though I did not hear anyone speak Nahuatl; perhaps my native tongue had gone the way of the language of the Olmecs.

We stood, a little uncomfortably — for though no one questioned our being there no one made us welcome — and I began to notice a pervasive sickliness in the air — the sweetness of putrefying flesh that has been doused in cloying perfume — I knew that it was the odor of the dead—I knew that I was in the presence of others of my kind — not one or two but dozens of them. What had happened in the past 500 years? Had I been reborn into a world of vampires? Again fear flecked my feelings, the same fear I had felt when I doubted my gods for the first time.

"Your friend is sometimes to be found there," Julia said. She pointed to a door, half-hidden by shadows. "Go along. I'll stay here and have a glass of wine."

"You're not coming with me?"

"I can't," she said. "No human being has ever come out of that room alive. But if you're really what I say you are, you won't have any trouble. That room," she went on, her voice dropping to a whisper, "is the Vampire Club."

"Why are you whispering?"

"I'm not supposed to know." Her eyes sparkled. I could see that she loved to flirt with danger; that was why she was so obsessed with my kind.

I put aside my fear. I had to confront Hortator. Already I knew that he was close by. From the dozens of clamoring voices in the building, my attenuated senses were able to isolate him. I could even hear his blood as it oozed through his veins; for every creature's lifeforce pulsates to a personal rhythm, unique as a fingerprint, if one has only the skill to pick it out.

I was becoming angry. I stalked to the door and flung it open. There came a blast of foul and icy wind. I stepped inside and slammed the door shut. There was no mistaking the odor now. I descended steep steps into a tomblike chamber where several outlandishly attired men and women sat deep in conversation, sipping delicately from snifters of blood.

"Rh negative," said one of them disgustedly, "not exactly my favorite."

"Let me have a sniff — *pe-ugh*! Touch of the AIDS virus in that one; oh, do send it back, my dear Travis."

"Whatever for? I think it lends it a certain *je ne sais quoi*," said Travis, "that ever-tantalizing bouquet *de la mort. . .*"

Two other creatures looked up from a game of cards; their faces had the pallid phosphorescence of the dead; their eyes glittered like cut glass, scintillant and emotionless.

A slightly corpulent man, sumptuously clothed in velvet and satin, waved languidly at me. "Heavens," he said, "what a surprise! We don't get many Red Indians here."

"Get him out of here," one of the cardsharps hissed. He was attired like one of the Spanish black robes.

"Yeah, dude," said a young man, of the type Julia had described to me as punk. "Or card him at least." He cackled at some incomprehensible joke.

"Whatever for? He's obviously one of us. Either that, or he's in desperate need of the services of an orthodontist," said the man in the velvet.

"We don't know him," said the other cardplayer, a woman, whose hair stood on end and fanned out like the tail of a peacock, and who wore a full-length cloak of some thick, black material.

"Perhaps we should ask him who he is. See here, old thing — very, very old, I'm afraid — I'm Sebastian Melmoth, your humble host. And you are?"

"I am Nezahualcoyotl," I said, "the Voice of the Hummingbird. I'm looking for a certain person. He calls himself Hortator."

"Oh, I see. Well, you really mustn't get to the point quite so fast; it's not very dignified, you know. Let a century or two go by first."

"I have let five centuries go by."

"Perhaps you'd care for one of our sanguinary cocktails?"

"I've already supped tonight, thank you."

"And might I ask you what Clan you belong to?"

"I know nothing of Clans. If you won't tell me the whereabouts of Hortator, please direct me to someone who can."

"Are you an anarch?" asked the woman with the peacock hair. I could only look at her in confusion.

The other cardplayer rose and sniffed at me. "Unusual bloodline," he said. "Not a pedigree I'm familiar with."

"Now look here," said Sebastian Melmoth, "he's obviously a vampire. But he doesn't seem to have the foggiest notion about how to behave like one. Tell me, Nezzy old chap, if you were in fact to find Hortator, what would you do?"

"I shall kill him."

The others began to laugh at me. I felt like some peasant on his first trip to Tenochtitlan. "Why do you mock me?" I said.

"Well!" said Sebastian Melmoth. "That's simply not done anymore. Not without the consent of the Prince.

Who doesn't even know who you are, so I don't see why he would grant your request."

It was then that I heard his voice. "Kill me?" The voice had deepened with the centuries, but I still recognized it. There he stood, towering over Melmoth, in the full regalia of a Mexica warrior, the jaguar-skin cloak, the helmet fashioned from a jaguar's head, the quetzal plumes, the earrings of gold and jade. Behind him there hung a life-sized painting of the white men's Xipe Totec, the god nailed to a tree; a soldier was hammering a stake through his heart; a beautiful woman watched with tears in her eyes.

"Kill me?" he repeated. "Why, Nezahualcoyotl?"

"Because you tried to kill me!"

"That was a foolish thing. I admit it. I placed too much credence in the Spaniard's superstitions. I know now that you're not that simple to kill. In fact, you look very well for someone who hasn't had a drop of blood in half a millennium."

"You are part of the old things, the things that should have died when the world ended. I understand now why I have been preserved by the gods. It is so that I can take you with me, you impious creature who twice refused the honor of a sacrificial death. I have been sent to put an end to your anomalous existence so that no part of the Old World will taint the New."

"Did your god tell you this, old man?"

Suddenly I realized that I had heard no voices from the gods since awakening inside the glass box in the San Francisco Museum. There was no more certainty in me, there was only ambiguity and confusion. My grand revelations no longer had divine authority. Perhaps it was true that they were the hallucinations of a madman. Perhaps if I had my votive objects I could summon back the voice of the hummingbird — the sacred blood-cup, the drum, the gold-tipped thorns for piercing my own flesh.

"Huitzilopochtli!" I cried out, despairing.

"You fool," said Hortator. "No god brought you to this place. There is no divine plan. It was I who told Julia Epstein where to dig. It was I who chose the moment to bring you back out of the earth. It was I, not Huitzilopochtli, who summoned you hither!"

"Why?" I said.

"Oh, don't imagine that I want to renew some monstrous cosmic struggle between you and me. It's much simpler than that. Buried with you, in the chamber at the heart of the pyramid, there were certain artifacts, were they not? Magical artifacts that will enhance my power. Your coming back to life along with the items I need is something of an inconvenience, but I'm sure you won't last long, because you simply don't understand how things work in this new world, this age of vampires."

● ● ●

Then it was that the memory of the apocalypse returned to me, bursting all at once through the wall I had erected to shield myself from its pain. I could not bear these creatures of their future, with their petty rules and their ignorance of the great cycles of the cosmos. I turned and strode away, taking the steps two at a time until I reached the Alexandrian Club, where Julia was sitting nervously at a corner table.

"Where did I come from?" I screamed at her. "How did you come to possess my body? And where are the artifacts I was buried with?" I had to have them. I had to try to summon Huitzilopochtli. Surely I would hear his voice again if I went through the ritual of the sacred blood-cup.

"Quiet now," she said, "you're making a scene."

"I have to know!"

"Yes. Yes. But not here. It's dangerous for me."

We drove into the darkness. San Francisco sparkled with man-made stars. A thousand strange new odors lanced the air: frenzied copulations; murderers and thieves skulking through the back streets; and the blood music, singing to me from every mortal inhabitant of the city, from within the topless towers of stone came the pounding of a million hearts, the roar of a million bloodstreams. Oh, one could be a glutton in this city, if one were a creature such as I. No wonder they had congregated here.

"I told you," said Julia. "Things are different now."

"What did Hortator mean when he said that he had summoned me back from the dead — by telling you where to dig?"

"Oh, he was being melodramatic. But he did drop a few hints."

"Before or after he made love to you?"

"You're not jealous, are you?"

"Of course not." I was silent for a while. The woman had a way of baldly confronting me with the truth. I didn't like it. I loathed the very idea of a city crammed with vampires, living by complex rules, observing silly hierarchies. But what could I do? The car raced over the bridge once more; Tenochtitlan too was a city of many bridges, a floating city. San Francisco was like a bloated, savage parody of my vanished kingdom.

Julia said, "I'll tell you, if you like. We have a series of weekly lectures at the museum. Hispanic studies, you know. Hortator came to a few of them. He would ask penetrating questions. Then he started telling me things. There was a big earthquake in Mexico City, you know. The Velasquez Building was leveled to the ground. He told me — convinced me — that there was a major find hidden beneath it, a secret room, he told me, next to a secret passageway. He told me he'd seen it in a dream. I laughed when he drew me a map. Well, that was the thing, you see. We had been using sonar to excavate those tunnels, and the computer scan matched his drawing to the centimeter."

"And you found me there."

"You were lying in a massive obsidian sarcophagus. You had a stake through your heart. I assumed — foolish me — that because of that, you were quite, quite dead — too many Dracula films, I suppose — so that it would be safe to put you on exhibit."

• • •

Memories of the apocalypse. . .

The king in all his splendor. This time not on the crest of a grassy hill, watching a pretended battle, but atop a pyramid of stone, looking down on the conquistadores as they swept through the city in a river of blood and fire. Man and beast conjoined now, the man-things glittering in their silvery skins, the beasts whinnying and pawing the pathways paved with the dead, arms and legs flying in the air as the cannonballs smashed through stone and adobe and human flesh.

And I beside him, I the mouthpiece of the god of the Mexica, aghast and powerless, raging. "You didn't have to play dead for them. They're just mortals. You've treated them like gods."

"They are gods," said Moctezuma. "There was nothing I could do."

Hortator had poisoned his mind. He had fed Moctezuma a diet of his own bad dreams, told him that the Spaniard was indeed Quetzalcoatl.

I looked into the eyes of my king; and I saw such sadness, such desolation that I could not bear it. It must be a terrible destiny to be the one chosen to preside over the end of the universe. Was there no way to turn back the sun? No. Beside us as we sat, each one wrapped in his private melancholia, my deputy priests were grimly carrying on the day's duties, plucking out the hearts of victims who waited in an endless queue that stretched all the way down the thousand steps and into the conflagration in the market square.

"Don't tell me that you accepted the word of this man-beast as the word of a god!" I cried.

"Wasn't it?" the king said. "In truth, I felt a certain wrongness about it all."

"Then let me call on Hummingbird to turn back the tide of time!"

"What difference does it make now?"

"Majesty," I said, "when the king himself no longer believes in the old truths, how can the earth sustain itself?"

"Perhaps I've been a little distracted," said the king. He was wavering.

I knew that I could not stand idle. I left the king's side, I entered the sacred chamber behind the altar, whose walls were caked with the blood of 10,000 human sacrifices. I paused only to suck the juices from a fresh, still-palpitating heart that one of the priests handed me. The soldiers were hacking off the limbs of the still convulsing victims, casting down the arms and legs, as has always been the custom, for the poor to dine on. The sight of the city's daily routine being carried out even now, on the brink of utter annihilation, would have moved me to tears, except that I had shed none in a thousand years. The priests worked quickly and efficiently, up to their elbows in coagulating gore. I hardly looked at them; I chucked the drained heart onto a golden platter before an image of Hummingbird, then entered the secret passageway behind the altar that led downward, downward to the hidden chamber where lay my sarcophagus and the tools of my art.

In the tunnel, the sounds of death were muffled. Cannon like the distant whisper of thunder in the rain forest. The screams of the dying faint, like the cries of jungle birds. The clash of metal on stone like the patter of rain on foliage. I took the steep steps two at a time. Soon I was in the heart of the pyramid.

When I reached the chamber, I found that the seal was broken. Not with the magic words, but shattered with gunpowder. Several of the man-beasts were already there, ransacking the place, gathering up the treasures into sacks. "How dare you?" I screamed. The man-beasts rushed at me. I summoned up my inner strength. I struck out blindly with both fists, and two of the Spaniards slammed against the stone walls. One of them died on the spot; the second more slowly, a little string of brain oozing down from his helmet. The third man-beast gaped, turned tail, started to run. Then his greed got the better of him and he returned to gather up one of the sacks of gold. He glanced at me; I was draining his dead friend's blood into the sacred blood-cup so that I could call on Hummingbird.

I closed my eyes. I called on the name of my god.

Huitzilopotchtli. . .

I felt myself sinking into the well of unconsciousness that was the presence of my god. I heard the familiar buzzing in my left ear that presaged the coming of Huitzilopotchtli. I smiled.

My child. . .

Came the whisper of the Hummingbird's wings, the tiny voice from the heart of the flames. I thrilled to its dark music. I allowed it to wash over me like the currents of the sea. I relinquished my being. The presence of the divine was more fulfilling even than the taste of blood, than the memory of women.

My *child*. . .

Abruptly, the trance was broken. I was jolted into consciousness. Even now, telling the story to Julia 500 years later, the memory will not come back as a woven fabric; it is in tatters.

Hortator stands before me, no longer in the attire of the Unblemished Youth, but wrapped in a metal skin from head to toe, like one of the conquistadores. With him are a dozen of the white-skinned creatures. He has delivered to his masters an entire world, an entire civilization.

"I know what you are now," he cries, "creature of Satan. They've told me everything." Several more of the Spaniards come in behind him, brandishing their swords and their flaming torches and their muskets. Seeing their dead comrades they cry out, back away; but Hortator laughs. "I know what you are now, and the Jesuits have told me what I must do to kill you."

Confused, uncomprehending, I lash out —

He dodges my blow, leaps across the sarcophagus, seizes the drum of Xipe Totec and begins to pound on it, a slow relentless rhythm. I scream. He pounds. I lunge. He leaps, each leap drawing more celerity from the power of the drum. He flies along the walls, he twists, he turns, he is a whirlwind, a tempest —

Huitzilopotchtli! I cry out.

No answer. I reached into the profoundest darkness of the well within. Where was my god? I see Hortator bearing down on me, brandishing a sharpened wooden stake.

As though from infinitely far away I seem to see the stake rive my stony flesh, rip apart my ribcage, pierce my heart. . .

Huitzilopotchtli!

Huitzilopotchtli!

Then, and only then, the god responds. The pyramids above us start to tremble. Cracks appear in the ceiling. Rocks start to rain down.

"Flee!" cries Hortator. I hear, through the fog of pain, their footsteps, metal clanking on stone. I hear some of them cry out as the cave-in crushes them.

I clutch at the wooden stake. But it is too late. I feel its leaden weight within me, feel it still the sluggish pump that is my heart, I feel the blood slow from a spurt to an ooze. I feel my heart muscle tighten around the unyielding wood like a vagina. I feel violated. I feel powerless for the first time since my changing. Then, all at once, I am spiraling downward toward the long sleep of ultimate forgetting.

• • •

And now, another underground passageway, another secret chamber. Five hundred years in the future, in a world I did not belong in, I stood with Julia Epstein among the shelves and shelves of artifacts of my people, all labeled, boxed, marked in white paint in the strange curlicuish script of the man-beasts.

Crate after crate I ripped open. "What is it you're looking for?" said Julia. "This is valuable stuff — you can't just throw it around like it belonged to you."

"It does belong to me."

"Half a millennium ago. But they're priceless antiquities now. And they haven't been appraised by the insurance company yet, so —"

I saw a tattered quetzal-feather robe that had once belonged to King Moctezuma's grandfather. I saw my sacred blood-cup, chipped now. I lifted it from its box. . .

"Careful with that thing! It dates back to Olmec times."

"I know. I made it."

She was silent for a moment. "The drum!" I said. "There was a drum fashioned from human skin."

"I've seen that," she said, "in Hortator's apartment."

So that was how he had made it out of the collapsing tunnels — with the power of celerity conferred by the drum of Xipe Totec! I was furious now. He had no right to my ritual objects. I was more determined than ever to exact revenge. Perhaps he thought I would be a useless anachronism, but I would teach him not to usurp my magical tools. They had told me at the Vampire Club about new laws that forbade the killing of vampires without permission from some prince, but what did I know of princes? What did I care? I was more ancient than any prince.

But even as I spoke, we heard the sound of shattering glass, and the high-pitched wail that I now knew to be an alarm that would eventually summon the museum's security. Then came a distant thumping sound, uneven, like a fibrillating heart. I knew that sound well. The hollow pounding contained in it the scream of a dying man.

"Hortator!"

"Why do you have to go on fighting him?" Julia said. "Don't you realize that the war between you two has no meaning any more?"

"Julia, I must have a little of your blood."

She closed her eyes, craned her neck, bared it to me as a warrior bares his heart for the sacrifice. "I need the blood," I said, "so I can summon forth the voice of the Hummingbird."

"There's no voice," she whispered. "It's in your mind, the right brain speaking to the left, a hallucination of godhead. Don't you understand that people don't see visions and hear voices anymore? You come from the age of gods; we live in the age of consciousness; it's not the god who commands us anymore, it's we ourselves, our ego, our individual being. People like you, people who still hear the voices of gods, they put them in insane asylums now."

What was she telling me? It made no sense. How could humans exist without prophets to transmit the commands of the gods? How lonely it must be for them in this future; to be like little islands of consciousness, not to be linked to the great cycle of the cosmos; to be not part of one great self but merely little selves, with little, meaningless lives. I could not, would not live that way. I took her in my arms; I made a tiny incision in her neck with my little fingernail; I drew a thimbleful of blood into the sacred cup; deeply I drank, and as I drank I prayed: Huitzilopotchtli, Huitzilopotchtli, do not forsake me now.

Hortator burst into the chamber. The alarms were screeching. "The rest of the treasures of the room have now been brought to San Francisco," he said. "That's why I told Julia where you could be found. I need the other ritual objects. I need the powers they can bestow on me. As for you, you're just a historical oddity."

But I could feel the strength of Huitzilopotchti course through my flesh.

As Julia, faint from her bleeding, sat, dazed, on my old sarcophagus, still in its wooden crate, Hortator and I battled. He threw me against the wall; I lacerated his face with my fingernails; he whirled about me, pounding his drum, my drum. Each of us drew on his dark powers. A mortal would not have seen us battling at all. He would have felt now a tremor, now a flash of light, now a ripple of darkness. I leaped onto the ceiling, I sped along the walls, defying the earth's pull with my speed; but Hortator was equally swift. His fangs glistened in the manmade light. We fought hand to hand on the lid of the sarcophagus where Julia still lay. We tussled on the concrete floor of the storeroom, and still the siren wailed.

"I'll really kill you this time," Hortator shouted. "The black robes told me a stake through the heart would kill you. I know better now."

And still I had not heard the voice of the Hummingbird. It was beginning to dawn on me that there was something to what Julia said; that perhaps this was no longer an age of gods. The last time the god had spoken, had he not said, Do you not understand that he who rises to godhead, who creates a world, a people, a destiny, plants inevitably within his creation the seeds of his own destruction? I did not understand then, but I understood it now. My existence showed to ordinary men that there was something beyond mortality; but beyond my own immortality there was also a kind of entropy. In being granted the ability to see the grand scheme of the universe, to live for centuries and know the higher purposes of mankind, I had also learned that all, even the most sublime, is vanity. I was full of despair. How could I belong to this future? How could I live amongst dozens of creatures like myself, arcane hierarchies all selfishly struggling for domination over one another? I knew that Hortator would hound me to my death. I could not live in a world where I could not hear the voice of my god.

We had battled for what seemed like days, but I knew that only seconds had passed; so quick were our movements that time itself had seemed to stand still. He had me pinned to the ground. I felt not only his weight but the weight of this whole bizarre new universe. And with a free hand he continued to drum, frenzied now, his eyes maddened, his lips frothing. I waited for him to drain me of all my blood, to desiccate me, to consign me to the well of oblivion forever.

Then, at that moment, the siren ceased. Hortator relaxed his hold on me. A shadow had fallen over us. I smelled the presence of another Kindred. I could feel the concentrated power, a puissance that nearly matched my own.

"Prince," Hortator whispered. He stepped back from me, then fell to the floor in supplication. I could not see this Prince, so thoroughly had he cloaked himself in magical darkness. But I knew him in the shadow that suffused the air.

"Oh, Nezahualcoyotl," said the prince, whose voice was as reverberant as a god's, "what am I to do with you? You have arrived in this city, yet you do not even come to pay homage to me as is our custom; and already you've created all sorts of controversy. The Vampire Club talks of nothing else but you. You're an anomaly; you challenge our most basic assumptions about our people's history."

I said, "I did not mean to offend you. My quarrel with Hortator is an ancient one, and not your affair; and I see now that the things we quarrel about have become irrelevant. I have no real desire to live. Let Hortator take my ritual objects and grow in power; and let me return to the earth."

"It is true," said the prince, "that I have the authority to grant you death. But how can I? You are older than I; you are so old that even the concept of the Masquerade is foreign to you; it is I who should bow to you, but I cannot. There can only be one prince.

Nezahualcoyotl, you must find your own destiny in some other place. Or else there will always be some who will look to you for leadership, anarchs who will revere your disregard of our rules of civilization and who will claim that your greater age gives you greater authority. Nezahualcoyotl, you must leave. I cannot command you. I, a prince, must ask it of you as a favor."

And now the security guards were entering the room. It was just as it was in Tenochtitlan, the enemy storming the secret chamber just as my world was disintegrating all around me. The prince did something — used his powers of hypnosis perhaps — for the guards did not seem to see me, Hortator, or the rippling darkness that was the prince of San Francisco.

"Are you all right, Ms. Epstein?" said one of them.

Julia was struggling to get up. "I — must have passed out," she said. "Something — someone — perhaps a prowler —"

"No one here now, ma'am. But they've made quite a mess."

"Are you sure you don't want me to get a doctor?" said another guard.

"I'm fine, thanks."

"Let's see if we can find him lurking around somewhere," said the first guard, and they trooped away. Astonished, I looked up. I thought I glimpsed something — a swirl of shadow — vortices within vortices — the eyes of an ancient creature, world-weary, ruthless, yet somehow also tinged with compassion. I knew that I he was right. I could not stay in San Francisco. I knew nothing of the feuding factions of the vampire world, the warring Clans, the Masquerade; I belonged to a simpler time.

"I will go," I said softly.

Then Julia said, "And I will go with you."

I said, "You don't know what you're saying. You think it's some romantic thing, that there's glamour in being undead. Look at us; look at how we have relived, again and again, ancient quarrels that the world has forgotten; the vampires that rule the world are but shadows, and I am less than a shadow of their shadow."

Julia said, "Only because you have not loved."

She came toward me. In her eyes there shone the crystalline coldness of eternity. I had not wanted to transform her into one of my kind. I had sought only to use enough blood to sustain me, to let me see my visions. She had not yet become a vampire; what I saw in her eyes was the yearning. "It's a historian's dream," she said, "to pass through the ages of man like the pages of a book, to perceive the great big arc of history. It's not just that I love you. Even if I didn't, I could learn, in eternity, to love."

Hortator hissed, "Only the prince can grant the right to sire new Kindred!"

But the prince said only, "Peace, peace, Hortator; will your anger never be slaked?" And then — and I could feel him fading from our presence as he spoke — he said, "Do what you wish, Nezahualcoyotl. Be glad. We will not meet again."

• • •

I have returned to Tenochtitlan. It is a gargantuan madhouse of 20,000,000 souls, but it is still called by the name of my vanished tribe, the Mexica. My official title is Meso-American Studies Advisor to the San Francisco Museum Field Research Unit, Mexico City. Julia and I have a charming apartment; one side overlooks one of the few areas of greenery in the city, the other one of the worst slums.

Julia tells me that a philosopher named Jaynes has written a book called *The Origin of Consciousness in the Breakdown of the Bicameral Mind*. It is a book that explains how, in the ancient world, men did not possess consciousness of self at all, but acted blindly, in response to voices and images projected by the right side of the brain, which they perceived to be the direct commands of gods, kings, and priests.

It is a strange world indeed, where people see no visions, and where a book has to be written explaining away the gods in terms of ganglia and synapses. I do not like it. I do not like the fact that I have been cut off forever from the divine; that I am no longer a prophet, but merely one vampire among many.

Yet the city does have its charms. Its nightlife is thriving and decadent; its music colorful; its alleyways quaint and full of titillating danger. And then there are the people, the descendants of my own people and the Spaniards who overcame them. Julia and I often make time to enjoy the inhabitants of our new home.

There are many poor people here. They pour in from the country, seeking out a better life; often they end up working as virtual slaves in huge factories that pump out cheap goods for their richer neighbors to the north. Sometimes they become gangsters or beggars. Sometimes they find a charitable person to take them in, as domestics, perhaps, or live-in prostitutes.

But sometimes, ah, sometimes, they vanish without a trace. ♀

POWER

by Don Bassingthwaite

The telephone's shrill scream startled Emily enough that the scalpel she wielded with delicate precision skipped wildly. The cold blood of the dead man on the table trickled out over her fingers. She pursed her lips with frustration and reached for something with a broader mouth than the simple, institutional water glass that stood ready on the edge of the table.

Her fingers closed on a stainless steel basin. The falling blood struck the metal with a sharp, almost musical patter as she stripped off her latex gloves and strode across the room. She got the phone on the third ring.

"Morgue."

"Miss Grange. . ."

"Doctor."

"Sorry, Dr. Grange. This is John, upstairs. There's someone here to see you."

"What does he want?" She glared at the dead man on the autopsy table. The flow of blood was slowing already — he had been dead almost too long. She picked up the phone and walked back towards the body, the extension cable slithering over other sheet-draped tables. "I'm not expecting anybody."

"He says it's family business."

Emily cradled the telephone receiver between her head and shoulder and used her free hand to press down on the corpse's belly. Under the pressure, more blood spurted into the basin. "Tell him to use the usual door."

She heard John repeat the information. There was a new voice in the background, one with a French accent. John spoke into the phone again. "He doesn't know where it is. He's a distant cousin."

A grimace struck her face. "Is he tall, black hair, gold-rimmed sunglasses? Wearing a jacket with an orchid in the button-hole?"

"I don't know what kind of flower he's got. . ."

Of course not, Emily thought. She moved her hand to the body's chest and pressed again.

". . . but that sounds like him."

Damn. "Tell him where the usual entrance is. I'll be waiting for him." She hung up without waiting for a response. Leaving the telephone balanced on a nearby body, she picked up the basin and carefully poured its contents into her glass. Then she settled down to wait.

It had been 12 years since Emily's Embrace, and her abrupt reassignment to night-shift forensic pathologist in the San Francisco Medical Examiner's Office. Twelve years as a vampire, and in that time, she had gotten to know almost all of the Kindred in San Francisco. There weren't that many vampires in the city who had French accents. Only one would have the nerve to identify himself as a "distant cousin," a member of one of the Clans that lingered on the fringe of the Camarilla. And he had come himself — his "business" must be important. The visit was almost welcome. Very few Kindred regularly came to the Medical Examiner's Office in the Hall of Justice. Even fewer came to her domain in the basement of the north wing. Most vampires sent their retainers when they had business with Emily, and the business was always the same.

Cover up the mistakes. Hide the stray evidence that popped up from time to time when a vampire lost control and killed someone. Provide death certificates that listed a more mundane cause of death, and make sure the body was disposed of cleanly. She was an important link in the Masquerade. The Prince had praised her work.

Her fingers tensed on the glass and she had to set it down before she broke it. The Prince's words were empty. She deserved more than this! Her domain was the Medical Examiner's Office, her subjects the Medical Examiner, the other forensic pathologists, and a few of the regular police. No one respected what she did. She was a lackey, a convenient service to be used when it was necessary and ignored the rest of the time. The other Kindred shunned her. Some important link! This was not the future a bright, ambitious medical school graduate had seen for herself. It wasn't even the future a more mature forensic pathologist, 48 but still ambitious, had seen in the first weeks after her Embrace by Clan Ventrue.

The sudden sound of the door buzzer wasn't enough to surprise her this time. "Come in, Jean-Claude, the door's unlocked."

"Can't you come out?"

Emily ground her teeth in frustration. "My equipment is in here." She pushed herself to her feet and began preparing another autopsy table. There was a burst of obscene French from the corridor. She smiled coldly. "I'm waiting."

The door burst open. Two large men staggered into the room. Between them, they bore a bundle wrapped in a blood-stained sheet. She motioned them to put it on the table. "Jean-Claude?" she called.

The vampire rushed into the room as though passing through the doorway was some kind of torture. He had a handkerchief over his nose and mouth, as if he smelled something bad, and his eyes darted wildly around the room. He dismissed his servants with a curt gesture. They filed silently out of the room and closed the door behind them. Only when they were out of the room did he remove the handkerchief from his face. "How can you stand this place?"

"It's necessary. And you get used to it," she replied tightly. "If it bothers you so much, don't breathe."

"I'm not. But the smell is still. . . everywhere! It sticks to everything. I'm going to smell like a corpse when I leave!"

"You get used to it," she murmured. More loudly, she said, "You're the first Setite I've had come to me."

Jean-Claude frowned, the expression creating deep furrows in his handsome face. "The Followers of Set," he muttered with something that sounded like shame, "do not normally seek out the services of others."

"Not normally?"

"I would prefer you to keep my visit here to yourself." He pulled back the sheet to expose the corpse he had brought. "He was one of my followers."

It was the body of a young man, perhaps in his early 20s, the ragged remains of his clothing plastered to his body with blood. He had been handsome, she supposed. His skin was deeply tanned, his muscles tightly defined, his remaining features clean and classical. But his death had been ugly. His body was almost a tatter of slashes, scratches, and bites. One of the deeper puncture wounds had probably destroyed something vital before he could die from loss of blood. Blood still seeped from some of the cuts. The body was fresh. The blood would be fresh, barely cold, still with the tang of life. . .

Emily realized that she was licking her lips. The glass of blood she had drained earlier stood nearby. She grabbed it and drank deeply. The blood was stale, the death older, but it would serve to keep her mind on the task at hand. Jean-Claude was staring at her with a look of disgust on his face when she lowered the glass.

"That was revolting. How can you drink dead blood?"

He looked as if he might throw up. Emily considered taking another drink to see if he would but thought better of it. She set the glass down before turning back to the corpse. "You didn't come here to discuss my feeding habits. What happened to him?"

"A. . . ceremony got out of control at the temple." He shrugged. "My other followers attacked him."

"What with?"

"Knives. Pieces of broken glass. Their teeth and nails. It happens occasionally. With some drugs, a group can turn ugly like that." Jean-Claude snapped his fingers for emphasis.

Emily pulled the blood-soaked sheet away from the body completely. "If this happens 'occasionally,' I'm surprised I haven't seen you in here before."

"Most times it doesn't end in death. I try to make sure of that. A dead follower is of no use to me. This time it happened too quickly. He was dead in seconds." He shrugged again. "What can you do with him?"

She picked up a clipboard and pen. "Usually, I can list the death as a suicide, but I don't think that's going to work this time. I'll have to call in the next-of-kin, have them identify the body, then convince them it was a mugging or something. We'll cremate the body afterwards." She tapped the pen against her teeth in thought and nodded to herself. "That should work. What was his name?"

Jean-Claude glanced down at the bloody body. "Does it matter?"

"Yes, it does. I have to put a name on the death certificate and I have to find his next-of-kin. Who is he?"

"I don't know."

"I find that difficult to believe."

"He was a new recruit to the Temple." He picked up a flask of distilled water. Emily was surprised to see that his hand was shaking. "Someone brought him in for the first time last week. A lot of my followers try to maintain their anonymity. I usually let them for a while."

"Did he have any ID on him?"

"Someone stole his wallet."

Emily was tempted to throw the clipboard down in frustration. She held on to it. Jean-Claude was nervous, desperate for her help. She might be able to gain something useful out of this transaction. "Then who did he come with?"

"I don't know. All my followers ran. They're loyal to the temple, though. They won't tell anybody about it."

"I don't care about your followers! Isn't there anything you can tell me about him?"

"No!" Jean-Claude snapped back. "That's why I need your help! I don't know who he is, I don't know who brought him, but if anyone is looking for him and can connect him with the temple, I'm in trouble! I need you to cover for me, you blue blood. . ."

"That's enough." Emily straightened and glared at him coldly. Internally, she glowed warmly with victory. "Don't forget that you do need me. It's going to be a little more tricky, but we can still do it. You'll owe me, though. There's going to be a little bit of confusion tomorrow morning. We have an unidentified body next door ready to be cremated. One body under a sheet looks a lot like another body under a sheet, especially when the toe tags have been mixed up."

"And the death certificate? The next-of-kin?"

"The death certificate will be very ordinary. It will say that he died from a stabbing during a mugging." She shrugged exaggeratedly. "The body is found on the street and brought in late. I make some preliminary notes and then leave the autopsy for the day crew. Some idiot cremates the wrong body, we sack him, and I'm forced to fill out a death certificate based on my notes. The next-of-kin won't matter at all, although I'm sure they'll turn up eventually."

"Someone could still trace him to my temple."

"We say that the body was found somewhere dark and nasty but not too far from somewhere with lots of people. Somewhere he could have wandered or been lured away from. A night club strip. I have some influence with the officers who patrol a suitable area. They'll remember finding the body and they'll have the reports to prove it." She smiled reassuringly.

"But what if he wasn't the type to go to a night club?"

The smile wavered but didn't disappear. "Jean-Claude, if he was the type to go to your temple, he was probably the type to go to a night club occasionally. Even if he wasn't, I suspect that he would have lied about where he was going anyway. If he told anybody at all. Relax. It will work."

Jean-Claude looked relieved. "This stays quiet?"

"It's foolproof. No one will ever find out. Just remember — you owe me a favor."

"Absolutely! Emily, I could kiss you!"

"A favor is fine."

"Anything! My temple is at your disposal!" He virtually danced out the door.

Emily watched him go. When he was out of sight, she permitted her smile to grow wider and more predatory. Jean-Claude was not the most powerful or widely respected vampire in San Francisco. Most of the Kindred loathed him, in fact, but he did have connections. And a favor owed was a favor owed. This was her chance to reach for a bit more respect from the other Kindred. This was what she deserved!

Her eye fell on the corpse Jean-Claude had brought, and she smiled again. If she was only going to incinerate it, she would be a fool to let the blood go to waste. She dipped her finger in the blood and touched it gingerly to her tongue, testing for the taint of vampire vitae. Not long after her Embrace, another vampire had tried to trick her into a Blood Bond by putting his own blood into a corpse. She certainly wouldn't have placed Jean-Claude above suspicion of doing the same thing.

The corpse, however, was clean. Emily whistled with happy expectation as she picked up her scalpel. She had fresh blood and, more importantly, she had Jean-Claude.

• • •

"What happened, Barr?" Emily reached back into the car and pulled out the black bag she carried to crime scenes. The flashing lights of a multitude of police cars and ambulances tinted the entire scene red. She hated field calls, but at least she got to the bodies quickly.

"Drug gang mostly, Dr. Grange." The lieutenant squirmed under the weight of the bullet-proof vest he carried, then set it down altogether. "Might have been some cult activity — I heard chanting or something. Some gangs are like that. You felt that big quake a while ago? That happened while we were going in." He opened the door into the gang's warehouse hideout for her. "After you."

Emily stepped past him. It was surprisingly quiet inside. Barr fell into step beside her, his face grim. An ambulance crew was taking a wounded officer out on a stretcher. He murmured weakly and reached out for Barr as they passed. Barr held on to his hand for a moment, then let him go. One of the ambulance attendants caught Emily's eye and shook her head with resignation. The man on the stretcher had lost a lot of blood. It was obvious that he would be dead before morning. The smell of the dying man's blood, the smell of a great deal of blood, was heavy in the air. She was glad she had fed before coming.

The center of the warehouse was clear of crates. This had been the scene of a gun battle, dirty and brutal, in the close quarters. Barr dismissed the two constables who stood guard. Emily knelt to examine one of the several bodies lying scattered around the area. "How many of them were there?" she asked.

"These ones and about 10 more that got away down into the sewers." Barr indicated an open trap door nearby. "We're looking for them now. They were tough bastards — just stood right up to it."

"How many wounded?"

"On their side? Not a one. They only left the dead behind."

She looked up at him. "And on ours?"

"Just Long." He struggled to maintain a stolid face. "Everyone else got off lucky, but Long took one in the chest. Cop-killer bullet, must have been. Cut through his vest like butter."

"Wasn't he under some sort of cover?" Emily opened her bag and pulled out a syringe.

"He was being a damned hero. Said he was going to take out the big man. I was near him. He pumped four good shots into that son of a bitch but they took him down anyways." He regarded the bodies of the gang members sourly, then cursed loudly and slammed his fist into the side of crate.

Emily turned to look at him evenly. "Barr, why don't you go back outside. I only have to get some blood samples. You don't have to stay."

"I have to. . ."

"Go." She locked eyes with him. His will was strong, but hardly strong enough to resist her. His mouth moved on its own for a moment, then he smiled and laughed.

"Sure, why not!" He turned to leave. "I'll just send the Forensics crew on in when they get here."

"Oh, I'll probably be finished before that." She almost smiled herself. It was so much simpler to do what she had to without the idiots from Forensics fumbling around in her way. It was fairly standard to take blood samples at the scene, but not her usual two or three from each body. One of the first things she had done after her Embrace was condition the Forensics crew to arrive on the crime scene a good 30 minutes late. Forensics had since become legendary on the police force for their tardiness. And no one else really wanted to be around when a forensic pathologist was working.

Emily took a syringe of blood from the first body, transferred it into a capped plastic vial, labeled it, and placed it carefully in her bag. She filled another and then moved on to the next body. Each gang member could provide her easily with two vials of blood. Three was greedy, and Forensics, for all their stupidity, might notice. Once the bodies were in the Medical Examiner's Office, she could take as much blood from them as she wanted.

At least the cause of their deaths was obvious. All of the gang members had come down in a hail of police bullets. Most lay in a cluster near the trap door to the sewers. She ran her hands through their clothing quickly, then stared in surprise at the ring she pulled from the pocket of one gang member.

The head of a cobra with exaggerated fangs stared back at her. The symbol of a Follower of Set. She double-checked the other bodies. Two others wore similar rings on their fingers, the third wore one beside a St. Christopher medal on a chain around his neck. All Followers of Set, but mortals.

"Emily. . ."

She whirled. The voice came from nearby, from a narrow gap between two large crates. There didn't seem to be anyone there, but even as her eyes wandered away there was a flicker of movement. Jean-Claude appeared from out of the shadows, propping himself upright against the cases. He was bleeding from a number of gunshot wounds. Four, she realized. The blood that fell from the wounds turned to dust before it hit the floor.

"Help me," he begged her, "Take me out of here." He stepped out away from the crates and managed a few steps before he fell. Even so, he continued to drag himself towards her.

Emily kept her distance from him. He desperately needed blood, and a desperate vampire wasn't picky about where he got it. She tried to think as she moved away. He was virtually at her mercy. If she wanted to, she could probably capture him easily. The Prince had been unsuccessfully hunting for the Setite temple since the first rumors of Jean-Claude's arrival in San Francisco had begun to circulate. If she presented Jean-Claude to Vannevar Thomas at his court, she could become the toast of Kindred society.

However. . . she bit her lip in thought. Vannevar Thomas knew about Jean-Claude himself. He hated him in fact. Even the most accidental encounter between the two of them inevitably resulted in harsh and icy words, though nothing more. The Prince had never moved against Jean-Claude personally. Rumor in the Kindred community had it that he regarded it as simply too dangerous. Was presenting the Setite to him likely to change that? And what if Jean-Claude escaped or was set free? Emily had no illusions about the treatment she would receive from him. She had already invested in him by covering up for him. If she saved him now, he would be very firmly in her debt.

She pulled two vials of blood from her bag. "Drink these." She rolled the vials carefully across the floor to him. Jean-Claude pounced on them like a cat, although the coordination necessary to open the vials seemed to have eluded him. He simply put the ends of the vials in his mouth and bit down until the plastic shattered. The fact that this caused more damage to his abused body didn't appear to matter to him. He swallowed the blood and the bits of plastic together. The worst of his wounds began to close.

"More!" he gasped, "Please, Emily! Give me more!"

Reluctantly, she pulled out two more vials and rolled them to him. This time he got the caps off and drank more neatly. When he finished, he was still gaunt from lack of blood, but his wounds had healed. Emily risked coming closer. She almost panicked when he jumped at her and wrapped his arms around her, but then she realized he was hugging her.

"I never thought I would be so happy to see a Ventrue. We were conducting a ceremony and the cops came. . ."

"Quiet!" She pushed him away. "Tell me later — I don't have you out of here yet."

"I'll go through the sewers!"

"No! They're searching them already, and they're armed. You aren't strong enough to fight them. I have a better idea. Don't go away!" She pushed another vial of blood into his hands. "Try to leave the bodies alone."

She walked quickly back out of the warehouse. Most of the ambulances were gone now. A few waited behind to carry the bodies back to the morgue. Forensics had finally arrived as well and was chatting with the remaining police officers as they unpacked their equipment. She picked one of the ambulance attendants at random. "You. Get a stretcher and a body bag and come with me."

"My partner. . ."

"Can warm up the ambulance. You don't need him. Come with me." Emily let a trace of ire creep into her voice. "Now." The attendant didn't question her again. Once they were back inside the warehouse, she stopped and made sure that he wouldn't remember anything about what was going to happen.

Jean-Claude was pacing nervously when they returned. When he first saw the attendant, he stiffened. She realized that the hungry vampire probably only saw the man as a source of warm blood and hastily stepped between them. "He's your escape, not your supper." She pulled the body bag off the stretcher and unfolded it. "Get in."

"You must be joking." Jean-Claude regarded the heavy black plastic with undisguised loathing and poorly hidden fear.

Emily crossed her arms and shook her head sternly. "It's the only way you're going to get out of here without arousing suspicion about where you came from. I can control one or two mortals, but not the 10 or 12 that you would have to walk past outside. You barely have the strength to walk anyway."

The Setite crouched down beside the bag. "It stinks like a corpse," he muttered resignedly.

"It should."

"Isn't there any other way to do this?"

"No. Besides, you'll only be in it for a few blocks. I'll follow in my car. The ambulance will stop once we're away from here and I'll take you the rest of the way with me.

He slid his foot inside as if stepping into a sleeping bag. "Where are we going?"

"Back to the morgue. I have blood there."

"Marvelous." He wriggled down into the bag and stared up at Emily as she tugged the zipper closed. "More corpses."

"Be thankful — you could have been one yourself." She gestured for the attendant to help her. Together they lifted the bag onto the stretcher. "Be quiet and hold still once we get outside. We'll go out the side door to avoid everyone."

"You're a wonder, Emily." Jean-Claude's voice was muffled. "You are wasted working alone with the dead."

She grimaced, though she knew he couldn't see it. "Tell me about it!"

"No vampire has helped me this way before."

"It's not coming free." She nodded for the attendant to start forward. She didn't want to run into the Forensics crew on the way out.

"I know, but. . . I mean, I'm almost sorry for dragging you into this thing with Doc Michaels."

Emily stopped, stunned. A cold chill ran through her body. The attendant kept going, and she had to take several quick steps to catch up to him. "What thing?"

"You don't know?" He sounded surprised. "Doc was blackmailing me. Turns out the young man I brought you last week was a favorite vessel of his. He wanted revenge and a cut into my drug deals. He said he knew where the temple was and that you helped me. I didn't believe him. He must have tipped off the police. He said he was blackmailing you, too." He paused, then added, "Until Doc said that, I was wondering if you had betrayed me." There was the hint of an edge to his voice.

If Emily hadn't already been dead, her heart would have stopped. She reached out and touched Jean-Claude through the bag. "No. I didn't. You're going to be coming out now, so be quiet. I'll be right back — I'm going to take the ambulance with you."

She felt numb inside as she ran around the building to the ambulances. "Doc" Michaels was a vampire of her Sire's generation. One of her Sire's blood siblings, in fact. One of the Prince's brood. He had his fingers in virtually every hospital and large clinic in the city, and she was the only other vampire in San Francisco with the medical training to understand how potentially powerful that made him. Her little domain in the Medical Examiner's Office brushed up against the bulk of his empire. Every time Doc stirred, Emily got shaken by it. If he knew about her dealings with Jean-Claude. . . she swallowed, abruptly aware that she might be playing right into his hands. Jean-Claude might not know it, but Doc

Michaels' long fingers even extended into some of the ambulance companies. It was the only way out of the warehouse, though. She crossed her fingers and prayed that this ambulance crew was nothing more than what they seemed.

It wasn't hard to spot the ambulance attendant's partner. As she had suggested, he had the ambulance running, ready to leave. He sat in the driver's seat, hands tapping the wheel in time to music on the radio. Emily walked purposefully up to the passenger door and opened it. When he glanced up, she caught his gaze and held it. "Go to the side door," she instructed him, climbing into the passenger seat, "then help load the body there into the back."

She leaned her head against the cool glass of the window, letting the ambulance driver carry out her commands. How could Doc have found out about her? One of Jean-Claude's followers? No, he had sworn they wouldn't talk about the murder. Except that Doc could be very persuasive, especially when he had a scalpel in his hand. Jean-Claude? The Setites were devious. But why? He was in the same trouble as her. Could Doc have discovered his dead vessel and somehow Embraced him? Not likely. The body had been cremated right on schedule the morning after Jean-Claude had brought it to her.

At least she knew why Doc hadn't actually contacted her with a blackmail threat like the one he had delivered to Jean-Claude, Emily realized bitterly. It was Jean-Claude he was after. He would have little to gain from blackmailing her. There was no prestige in running the Medical Examiner's Office, even though it was the only large medical-related institution in the city that he didn't control. There was no power either, really. It was without status and without power, just like her. She was beneath his notice. She choked back tears of blood. No

Kindred, except Jean-Claude, took any notice of her at all. Yet if Doc Michaels were suddenly to disappear, she would be the only one in the city who would really be able to replace him effectively. And he didn't even think she was worth blackmailing. . .

The plan seemed to spring fully formed into her head, jerking her upright with the force of its entry. Emily pursed her lips tightly as she thought. Doc had played himself into a losing position. She turned to look at the ambulance attendants as they loaded Jean-Claude into the rear of the ambulance. "Take me to a phone booth."

A dog skittered out of the way as the ambulance accelerated.

● ● ●

"Emily?" Doc Michaels called as he stepped into the morgue. "Are you here?"

Emily was pleased to note that his nose wrinkled in distaste at the odor in the room. She had turned the ventilation system off when she arrived several hours ago. "I'm here," she said quietly, in her smallest voice. She stood up from her desk and came around in front of it to greet him. Sitting behind a desk was a position of power — she wanted him to perceive her as weak. "Please. Come in."

He continued to stand in the doorway. "Perhaps it would be better if we went somewhere more comfortable?"

"I don't want any of the others to know about this. I can't go out." She stepped back as if she were nervous, and accidentally bumped into a corpse on a gurney. The room was packed with them. "Does anyone know now?"

"I haven't told anyone about your call." He started to step away from the door, then stopped. Emily wondered if he was suspicious. "My car is just outside though — and very private."

"No!" She forced a note of panic into her voice.

"Very well then." He walked completely into the room, twitching violently as the cramped conditions forced him to edge between two more corpses. "I must admit, your message last night mystified me. You sounded frightened. It's no secret your Sire and I are not on the best of terms, but the Followers of Set? Why would you think I. . ."

Emily saw Jean-Claude appear from the shadows by the door only a second before he leaped at Doc. The Ventrue's words ended in a sudden grunt of surprise as Jean-Claude tackled him. "Now Emily!" screamed the Setite, "Now!"

Her hand went almost automatically to the nearest sheet-draped corpse and felt for the sharp stake that was hidden there. There were several others like it around the room, since she had had no idea exactly where she would be when the time came to act. She almost had the stake in her grasp when Jean-Claude and Doc Michaels crashed into the gurney and spun it aside. Emily was left with only a sheet in her hand. She dived for another stake.

Doc Michaels had been an old man when he was Embraced. He still looked like a kindly, grandfatherly family doctor. Unfortunately, physical appearances meant little among the Kindred. Jean-Claude seemed young and strong, but the old man was matching him blow for blow. Emily had suspected that would happen. The two vampires rolled over and over on the ground as they fought. She couldn't get a clear chance at Doc. At the same time, she didn't want to try to separate them physically for fear of being drawn into the fight. She saw only one thing to do. When their struggle brought them close to a gurney, she tipped its dead burden off and on top of them. The two sprang apart instantly, repulsed by the corpse. Jean-Claude actually retched. Doc snarled and coiled, preparing to leap at his distracted attacker.

The stake went into his back and through his heart with a kind of dry hiss, as if she were stabbing a desiccated mummy. Doc Michaels shrieked and tried to lash out behind him. His fingers caught at her clothing, then fell away loosely as paralysis spread through his body. He tumbled to the floor. A horrible expression of rage and shock was frozen on his face.

Emily bent down and lifted him, careful not to dislodge the stake. He was surprisingly light. She held him with one hand as she opened one of the drawers that lined the wall of the morgue. It almost felt as if she were tucking a child into bed when she laid him out on the cold metal. Doc Michaels made a very natural-looking corpse, as if he had only recently died. Suddenly, she felt her Hunger rising. Ventrue were very particular about the source of their nourishment. Emily had discovered quite early that her Embrace had left her with a cruel and ironic need for cold blood taken from dead bodies. The body of a vampire was as cold and as dead as a body could be. She brushed Doc Michaels' collar aside to reveal his neck. The temptation was strong to drain the life out of him, to make the transfer of power complete. Very strong. She bent down, lips drawing back from eager fangs.

Jean-Claude grabbed her from behind and pulled her away. "No!"

"Let me go!" She struggled against him, but he held her firmly. "I want his blood, Jean-Claude. I need it!"

He twisted her around so that she could no longer see Doc Michaels' body. "You need him more! What if you need something someday? Information? Kill him now and all you will have done is commit Diablerie! Is it worth it?"

Emily pressed her Hunger back down. He was right. She relaxed. "Let me go." He did. She walked purposefully over to the drawer and slid it shut with a resounding slam, then looked up at the Setite. "Thank you."

"It would have been foolish to destroy such a resource."

"As foolish as attacking him prematurely? You were only supposed to close the door and lock it from outside."

"He knew something was wrong."

"I could have dealt with it — the bodies in the room unnerved him. I could have had him staked before he did anything." She sighed and wiped the back of her hand across her mouth. The blood was hers and not Doc Michaels'. Somehow she had split her lip in the struggle. "It doesn't matter now anyway. Did you get your followers and servants gathered back together?"

"Yes. I was fortunate."

"Take your people back to his haven. Make it look like it was broken into. Make it look like a Sabbat raid. That should keep everyone paranoid for a while. It will take the heat off us. Take care of anybody in his car, too. And remember, Jean-Claude, you owe me very big."

"What if someone comes looking for him?" Jean-Claude indicated the drawer that contained Doc Michaels.

Emily pulled a ring of keys from her pocket and locked it. Then, with a grunt, she broke the key off in the lock. The drawer was officially empty and they had no shortage of other drawers for real bodies. No one would worry about fixing that lock for a long, long time.

• • •

Emily picked up the telephone before the second ring. "Morgue."

"Congratulations! I understand the Prince has just confirmed you as guardian of Doc Michaels' affairs."

"That's the easy way of saying he doesn't understand which end of a hospital the patient goes in, Jean-Claude. But thank you. It's actually going to take several weeks before I have complete control."

"What are you doing now?"

"Paperwork. They just brought in the body of a suicide from earlier tonight on Montgomery. He jumped from halfway up the Russ Building. Very messy."

"Still hard at work. You don't have to do that any more."

She laughed. "I'll let the day crew handle this one, but I do enjoy my work sometimes. And so do you. What do you want?"

"You know me too well. There are five coffins on a boat coming into harbor the day after tomorrow. Can you arrange to have them taken past customs without being opened?"

"You're racking up favors-owed, Jean-Claude. And you're not the only one now."

"Just the first. It's good to have friends in high places."

"Consider it done."

"Thank you, Emily. I owe you."

"You owe me a lot."

"Good night, Emily." Jean-Claude hung up the phone and leaned back in his chair. A slow, evil smile spread across his face as he picked up a serpent-head ring from his desk. He had sent flowers to Constable Long's funeral. He always liked to reward his followers for their loyalty, and Long's fatal self-sacrifice in shooting him right on cue had been invaluable. It lent an air of truth to his story about the "surprise raid." He wondered if poor, innocent Doc Michaels felt the same oblivion as Long. The old Ventrue had almost given away his ignorance before Jean-Claude had been able to silence him in the morgue. He kissed the ring, then addressed it as if he were addressing the follower who had so recently worn it.

"We have her, Long. We have her." ⚲

DARKENING OF THE LIGHT

by Bill Bridges

The sun had sunk below the earth, darkening the light in the world of men. Heaven was obscured by the night and the forces of the dark came forth. This was as it always was and always would be. The continual cycle of yin and yang, light and dark, day and night. Ever changing, ever staying the same. Don Benedict knew this from long experience. But tonight, for the first time in many years, he was unsure of the future.

Before him was the parchment paper where he had written the hexagram. The yarrow sticks lay bunched to the side, having done their part in the divination. Don Benedict stared down at the result of the oracle and was worried. It was the Ming I, the Darkening of the Light, or the "wounding of the bright." Earth above, fire below. There were no moving lines, no clues towards further elaboration. The Judgment advised perseverance in the face of adversity. It spoke of a man of dark nature in a position of power threatening the "wise man."

He stood up and began to pace. Only half an hour ago, he had risen after the setting of the sun. As usual, he dressed himself and then brought out the I Ching, the Book of Changes. Not a night passed in which he did not consult its wisdom. This was not so much out of a need for guidance as it was a desire for greater understanding of the book's mysteries. He felt that if he could unlock its secrets, all the answers to all the questions about the Orient could be had. He was not Oriental himself; he had been born in Mexico. Years spent among the residents of Chinatown, however, had wakened in him an interest in the Chinese and their ways. This was not out of a desire for power, unlike the pursuits of many in his Clan, but a quest for solace.

As he walked about the room, encircling it like a impatient tiger, he thought about the hexagram and its possible interpretation. He had been unnerved when, while throwing the stalks, the earth had begun to shake. It was a series of tremors that passed soon, but Benedict was sure it had colored the reading. He thought about the hexagram and its possible interpretations. Normally, the oracles in the book were addressed to the reader, the "wise man," the one who had been smart enough to seek the wisdom of the I Ching. But Don Benedict was unsure if the oracle was written for him, or about him. Don Benedict could very well be the dark man referred to, a man with power who sought to do ill to the wise. And was this not so? Don Benedict had done much harm to others, and would continue to do so for his very survival.

He wondered how many more nights he could go without blood. He would certainly need some before the week was through, but he felt fine for now. Perhaps the oracle referred to something else.

He stopped his pacing. The Embrace — the Darkening of the Light. Would he be called upon soon to pull another into the night with him? He shook his head. If so, then he would refuse, no matter the reason. It was better that others die rather than suffer his fate.

He then noticed the envelope on the table. The sigil of his Clan was stamped upon it. He wondered when it had arrived. Messages such as these were sent only through magical ritual. They had no courier, for they simply appeared to their intended recipient. He opened it and quickly read the note, placed it onto the table and put on his coat.

He then went out into the dark night.

• • •

He arrived later at the fine mansion in Pacific Heights. The doorman took his coat and Don Benedict walked down the hallway. He did not look at the expensive statues or pictures on the walls; he had seen them before. He came to the large double doors with the odd carvings, and rapped lightly on the head of a miniature lion battling a dragon. In a few moments, the door opened and he walked through into the plush office.

He stood quietly and patiently waiting for the man behind the desk to acknowledge him. The man was reading a newspaper intently. Don Benedict could see that it was written in Chinese. He then had a good suspicion as to why he had been summoned.

The man finally looked up and said, "Be seated."

Don Benedict walked over to the chair before the desk and sat down. He made himself comfortable and then looked at the man and said, "My Lord Honerius, how may I further the Clan?"

Honerius pushed the newspaper towards him and leaned back in his chair. "I am somewhat distressed at what I have been hearing from your district, Don Benedict. Please see page three, the first article."

Benedict took the paper and read the article, reading it much faster than had Honerius; his Chinese was better. He put the paper back on the desk and said, "I see, but I don't believe there is any cause for worry. The shipment from Hong Kong was ordered by. . . an upstanding member of that community."

Honerius frowned. "No smoke here, Benedict. Do you refer to the Dowager?"

Benedict looked annoyed. He did not enjoy forthright speech. It was vulgar. "Yes, my Lord. She informed me long ago of her intent to order a sleeping berth from her homeland, one which would allow her to rest in style."

"If that were so, then the coffin would have been empty." Honerius said. Benedict raised his eyebrows. "Whatever was in that jade coffin destroyed Harris as he attempted to investigate."

"I do not understand. That was to be the Dowager's —"

"Is it possible this Dowager lied to you?" Honerius interrupted, staring at Benedict intently.

"The Dowager does not, of course, tell me everything. But she would not have risked such a grave error as this. I suspect this is as much of a surprise to her as it is to us."

Benedict was silent for a moment as he thought, while Honerius watched him. He finally asked, "What do we know of the vampire that exited the coffin?"

"Next to nothing. We know he — it — is skilled in ritual, for it cleverly covered up its actions from scrying. Once Harris had opened the coffin, it was instantly upon him. It made quick work of him and fled into the city, leaving the opened coffin behind. The coffin is now in our possession, and members are attempting to gain what information they can from it. No luck so far."

"The Dowager must know by now. I must go see her and explain."

"Explain, Benedict? It is not your job to explain!" Honerius slammed his hand loudly onto the table. "You must demand an explanation. This is directly in conflict with the accord we made with her. I have so far been able to keep this from the ears of other parties, but I do not know for how long. I want this situation wrapped up before then!" He pointed harshly at Benedict. "It must not be known that Clan Tremere cannot enforce its control over Chinatown! We cannot have foreign Kindred entering the city without our permission! If this happens, Vannevar will attempt to control the situation himself, and our Clan's power base will be set back drastically."

"I understand, Lord. I will handle the situation immediately," Benedict said.

"See that you do." Honerius sat down and leaned back in his chair. "I have not been very strict with you in the past, unlike other members of this Chantry. I saw that it would hinder your relationship with Chinatown and your contacts there." He began to idly fondle a heavy paperweight before him, a miniature globe modeled after a medieval map, except adapted to the modern earth's curvature. "I have allowed you extraordinary secrecy concerning these contacts of yours. If you wish to maintain the freedoms you have had, then act quickly and correctly in this. You have the strength to represent the Clan, both martial and occult; you know your place in the Pyramid. You cannot expect promotion without obedience to Clan laws. Do not forget that you are one of us, Benedict. Now go."

Benedict stood up and bowed slightly to Honerius. He then left the room. His mind worked furiously over the problem as the doorman put his coat on for him and he walked out into the chill San Francisco night. As the doors closed behind him, he knew they would not open easily for him again if he did not succeed with his mission.

He walked quickly down the street to find a cab to take him to Chinatown.

• • •

The taxicab pulled up across the street from the Chinatown Gate. Don Benedict paid the driver and got out. As the cab pulled away he stood staring at the gate. It was so new and gaudy; a silly ornament for silly tourists. The people beyond the gate did not need such a thing to remind them of their homeland and heritage.

Don Benedict crossed the street and stood looking up at the gate. The Dowager enjoyed this edifice. She was delighted when it was first proposed and had made sure that it was completed. The Dowager liked gay and happy things. She had also asked that Benedict enter by this gate whenever he came to see her. To do otherwise was rude. So, Benedict honored her little tradition and always came through the Chinatown Gate.

He walked under it and passed through into another world. He walked up Grant Avenue, through the crowd of late-night shoppers. Asians, both American and Chinese, mixed with tourists from all over. The smell of Chinese cooking wafted out of the many restaurants. Benedict stopped when he reached California Street. He stared across the lane at Saint Mary's church.

It was called Old Saint Mary's now by mortals, but it was still new to Benedict. He remembered it as it had been the day it was dedicated. He remembered the first Mass there and how proud he had felt: another church by which the heathen frontiersmen and native savages could be brought to God. But there were very few natives left by then. He and the other missionaries had seen to that.

Don Benedict moved on. He crossed the cable car tracks and traveled deeper into this pocket of American Asia. He turned left on Sacramento and walked up the hill, past Waverley with its temples and Hang Ah Al alley with its playground.

A dog ran from the alley over to him and sniffed at his feet. Benedict stopped and looked down at the dog. It was a mangy, hairy mutt, probably one of the many strays that wandered the alleys of Chinatown. Benedict was surprised, for it had been a long time since a dog had been so bold with him. They mainly stayed well away, or barked at him from afar. He put his hand out to pet the dog, but it jumped back and ran away, down the alley it had come from. Benedict shook his head; he wondered if he should get a dog himself. He would have to give it some blood to keep it from running away like this dog, but it would perhaps add life to his home. He recalled that dogs were symbols of loyalty to the Chinese.

He continued up the street and turned right onto Stockton and crossed over to the Chinese Consolidated Benevolent Association, the Chinese Six Companies. He stopped and looked at the lion guardians, carved in stone. They warded the building from evil, yet they had never prevented him from entering. He stepped past the ornamented gateway, beneath the dragons, birds and fishes which frolicked there. He knocked on the red doors and waited for a reply. The doors soon opened and a Chinese man looked out at him.

"Yes?"

"I have come to see the Dowager," Don Benedict said.

The man's eyes narrowed but he nodded slightly. He opened the door wider and Benedict stepped in. The main hall was large and impressive. Three long tables with chairs were in the center of the room. Flags, both American and Chinese, hung on the walls. A very formal and serious place. Here, disputes between rival tongs were once arbitrated, all under the watchful yet invisible auspices of the Dowager.

The man motioned for Benedict to follow him. Benedict knew the way. He had been here many times before. He knew the man he now followed; he had been coming here before this man was even born. Yet it was the same response every time. The Dowager was strict on the importance of appearance. It made up for the lack of her own.

The man led Benedict to the wall, where he placed his hand and exerted a delicate amount of pressure with only his middle and final fingers and lower palm. A door swung open and Benedict walked through to the stairs leading down. The door closed behind him, but the paper lanterns lit the passage well-enough to see. He came to the bottom and walked up to the doors, identical to the red doors above. Two golden dog statues were to either side, similar in duty to the lions above, but they also had never halted his passage.

He stopped before the door to compose himself. He centered his body and began a quick breathing exercise. He then performed the Thaumaturgy he had learned from his Eastern studies. Channeling his *chi*, he controlled the flow of his blood, sending it to his skin, flushing the skin with a rosy red. His hair grew brighter and his eyes sparkled. He was no longer a pale man who spent too much time in the dark, but a ruddy, tanned son of the *conquistadores*. Don Benedict appeared as he had in life.

He straightened his suit and knocked on the doors. They were immediately opened by a servant. A small palace lay beyond, a relic of a bygone age in a far-off land. Benedict stepped into the Dowager's home.

"Ah, you're here! Oh, Father Benedict, I had so hoped you would visit me."

The Dowager sat on a dais, surrounded by pillows and Chinese servants. She wore the most beautiful silk dress in the world and fanned herself with a golden fan that was once the Emperor's. All about her was jade. But all these things could never bring back her beauty. The Dowager was hideously ugly, as repulsive as any of her Clan: Nosferatu.

Benedict bowed to her. "Empress, I am glad to see you well. The sun hides at night, ashamed before your radiant beauty."

"Oh!" The Dowager smiled and sighed, fanning herself. "Oh, Father, only you can say such things to me. And I believe them when you say it, for you can see the beauty of a soul. You see inside of me. You are so good, Father Benedict."

Benedict sat down on a pillow across from her. "Please, Empress. I am no longer Father. Call me Don or Benedict."

"Ah, Father. It is a most wonderful night, is it not?" She said as she continued to fan herself.

"Yes, it is." Benedict replied. She had always ignored his request and continued to call him by his old title. There were a few moments of silence, as both of them waited for a polite amount of time before business could be discussed. Even then, Benedict knew they could not speak too plainly; it was not the way.

Finally, the Dowager said. "It is so uncomfortable lately. I get almost no sleep at all. All these pillows, they are for the servants to sleep on. I so want to sleep as

I once did, in a coffin of jade. I even had one sent from China, all the way from Hong Kong. But, alas, it has not arrived."

Benedict waited a few moments before responding. "I have heard of a shipment from China, just in yesterday, at the Embarcadero. But an incident arose concerning it. Many men are confused about the events."

"The Embarcadero? Perhaps this is the same incident I have heard of. The servants say so many things all day long, I cannot help but listen sometimes. You know how it is." The Dowager was silent for a moment, as she continued to fan herself. "I do hope my wonderful jade bed is all right."

"I am sure it is fine, Empress. Those who have intervened in this incident are responsible gentlemen. I am sure I can put in a good word with them. But they will ask me so many questions. I wonder where I am to find the answers."

The Dowager looked worried, as if she was unsure how to say something. They sat in silence for a while until Benedict intervened. "Sometimes it is wise to speak one's mind, lest further confusion is the result."

The Dowager looked at him and stopped fanning herself. "Oh, Father. There is danger all about. The times are not as they once were. The laws of heaven are unheeded by men, and the evil trample upon the righteous." She sat back and stared at the ceiling. Benedict frowned. She had been about to say what was on her mind, but now she was lost in memory.

"Do you remember when we first met, Father? We were both so young then. Our deaths had been but a mere decade behind us. We are almost the same age, you and I. You were at Saint Mary's, in the park, staring at your church. How long had it been since you entered? I watched you for a long while, and I knew you had a strong soul, the soul of a righteous man. That is why I finally approached you. I was so lonely, for few would speak to me here in this strange land. Yet you did. You spoke so wonderfully too. I knew then that there was hope for us, you and I, unlike those around us, who were engulfed into the night. We did not need the sun, for we knew it was in our hearts.

"It was you who made me forget my vengeance, Father. It was your good soul. So much evil had been done to me. I was so pretty! I was the most beautiful girl in China. All knew that I was to be the Empress, for none deserved to touch my beauty but the Emperor. But there was one who saw my beauty and wanted it for his own — the demon foreigner! From the shadows he watched me, and knew he could not have me. Oh, such a jealous evil one! Could he not be content to watch? No! He took my beauty from me! He could not stand to see my beauty when he could have none of it!

"I wanted so to kill him, but I was too scared. Had I not died and become his demon child? Would not the Celestial powers punish me further if I destroyed my new father? I knew there were rules even in Hell against such things. I fled. There was nothing else I could do. I came here, with but a few loyal servants. And here I found my friend, Father Benedict." She looked at Benedict and smiled, but did not lift the fan again.

"You have brightened my night, Empress," Benedict said. "I was alone with my thoughts until you confided in me. I needed so to have someone confess to me, as so many had before my second death. I thank you."

The Empress sighed and began to fan herself again. "We must be content with our place in the universe, Father. We once served the light, and now we serve the dark. This is how things are; it is the cycle. Why struggle?"

They both sat in silence for a while. Benedict was annoyed at the things the Dowager had said, for they were similar to his own thoughts of late. He had always accepted things as they were; the wheel of fate could rarely be turned to one's own advantage. He had once served his Church with pious and unquestioning duty, as he now did his Clan. It was no good arguing or struggling against it, for who would hear? The Dowager spoke again.

"We are not in a good position, you and I," she said. "A rival has come to Chinatown. He wants to take my place and power. He does not like Westerners."

So that was it. An Asian vampire was attempting to take Chinatown as his territory. This was not only bad for the Dowager, but for Clan Tremere also. He had spent years buildings his contacts here. They would disappear overnight if this strange vampire succeeded.

"What can you tell me of this stranger?" Benedict asked.

"He is a very dangerous one. He is not as old as you or I, but he is strong with the anger of youth. He has many powers granted him by the demons of the night. Much magic is at his command. He hides in fog and strikes from fog."

Benedict hid his consternation well. The Dowager spoke like a commoner, one afraid of the mysteries of the night. Could it be she knew very little of the vampire, and was trying to hide the fact from him? No, it was more likely that all she knew of this thing was what she had heard as a child, and so spoke of it as a child would.

"There must be many legends concerning this one," Benedict said. "I am sure they are most illuminating."

"He is said to be a great sorcerer," the Dowager said, "skilled in the arts of the elements. "He can weave the substance of smoke to his desire, and make solid the insubstantial. In his hands, the very mists of the night are weapons."

Benedict was not sure what to make of this. If this vampire had power over smoke and fog, then San Francisco would be a powerful place for him, with all the mists coming in from the bay. "Can this legendary one himself take the form of smoke?"

"I have never heard so in the legends. He commands these things, but is not of them. He also knows well the art of calligraphy and talismans." The Dowager reached behind her for a wooden box, carved with beautiful birds. She placed it before Benedict and opened it. Inside, laying on a satin lining, were three strips of colored paper, each with a different symbol written in colored ink upon them.

Benedict recognized them: Taoist talismans, each holding a powerful magic spell, designed to release the spell as the paper was ignited. He looked carefully at them. The Dowager had taught him something of their manufacture, and he had made a few of his own in the past. He recognized one as a warding from evil, and another as a fire symbol. But the third was unknown to him.

"These will protect you from the evil one," the Dowager said. "The one there will defend the owner from spells, causing them to perish. The one here will cause an enemy to ignite into flame, thus destroying him. And the one here is special, for it represents the element of wood. It will provide a weapon whereby mastery over his body can be obtained." Benedict understood; it was an interesting spell. The Dowager continued, "Take them, Father. For you will need them against this demon."

Benedict frowned. "I thank you, Empress. But what of his martial prowess?"

"Formidable," the Dowager replied. "But your own kung fu should protect you. Are you not a master of Pa Kwa, Eight Trigram Boxing?"

"I have had many years to develop my skills," Benedict said. "Are there any servants you can lend me in my task?"

The Dowager began to fan herself. "Oh, but I need all of them here. I have too few left. If this demon were to see them, he might blame me for letting them stray. I would not like a visit from him, even if his intentions were good."

Benedict understood. The Dowager did not wish to be involved in this undertaking, in case Benedict lost. She would then still be able to ally with the vampire if necessary.

"I must go forth then," Benedict said. "But I do not know where to look for my adversary."

"These gossiping servants of mine! What tales they tell. I have heard that there is a small store, one which sells imports from China, in which many interesting things can be found. It is called the Hsi Lu Trading Company. If one were to go to this store, he would find a set of stairs in the back which leads below the street, to the underground world. I have heard that many go there after arriving here from abroad. But the store owners are very rude, and they do not allow any of our Western hosts in. I am sure that a wise gentleman would have little trouble convincing them, however."

Benedict knew of the place. He had seen it before, during his wanderings in Chinatown. It was down one of the many alleys that hid behind the main streets. He smiled. He bowed to the Dowager, took the wooden box, and stood up. "I thank you for your gracious hospitality, Empress."

"Please visit me again, Father. I look so forward to hearing of your adventures." The Dowager fanned herself as she said this. Benedict knew this was her defense for showing emotion. He saw worry on her face, something she rarely displayed.

He knew she had a difficult position, an exiled Empress-to-be of a Western vampire Clan trying to maintain a hold over an invisible population of Asian Kindred. He knew there were some Asian Clans in Chinatown, some who had never been heard of by the Camarilla. But even with his relationship to the Dowager, she was very careful to keep them secret from him. This new one must be of a Clan even she could not control.

He knew he could wrest such information from her, and she would still forgive him. She was unaware of the Blood Bond he had subjected her to long ago, when she was new to the city and the West. It was this Bond which fueled her deep affection for him. But he had never pressed the Bond, had never used his hold over her overtly. He was afraid that the Bond was all that kept her love for him.

Benedict turned and walked out of the room, back into the dim passageway. As he climbed the stairs, he thought about his next actions. He had been underneath Chinatown before, but he had been escorted by the Dowager's servants. He had sensed that much was hidden from him down there, a world where many supernatural refugees from China hid from western eyes. He would have to pierce the veil between them. This foreign vampire had made the first move by killing Harris. Now Benedict had to find him and bring him under Clan Prestation. He doubted this would happen. From the way the Dowager spoke, he knew he would have to fight this vampire. To the final death.

• • •

The small, tight alley stretched for half a block before it dead-ended in a brick wall. To the right of this wall was a small shop, with a tarp hanging above and colored banners with Chinese characters. The narrow door was open, and light spread out into the alleyway, along with the thick incense smoke which burned within.

Benedict walked quietly down the alley to the shop and stopped at the window, looking in. Behind a counter sat an old man with a long pipe. He blended in with the exotic commodities scattered around him and all about the room: fu dog statues, authentic woks, bamboo chairs, banners and wall-hangings, many small statues, and other Chinese knickknacks. Benedict stepped into the room from the alleyway and the old man frowned.

"We closed. Go away," the old man said.

"I am simply looking for the stairs," said Benedict.

"No stairs! You go!" the old man yelled. Benedict met his eyes, and the old man could not look away.

"Show me the way," Benedict said.

"Yes. . . yes, this way," the old man said, as he stood up and moved to the back of the store. Don Benedict followed. The old man parted a curtain and pointed to a trap door with a large ring. He could not tear his gaze from Benedict.

"Open the door," Benedict commanded, and the old man bent down and tugged at the ring with both hands. The door pulled open with a creak, kicking dust into the air. The cloud settled slowly around the room. Benedict looked into the hole and saw a set of stairs leading down. There was no light. "Bring me a lantern," he told the old man, who then walked into the front room and soon returned with a lit candle.

"This all I have," the old man said, holding out the burning candle, set in an ornate bronze holder. Benedict took it from him.

"Go back to watching the store. I never came through here," he said.

"Yes. You no come. I not know you." The old man walked back into the front room and sat down behind the counter. He picked up his pipe and began to smoke again, as if nothing had disturbed him.

Benedict walked down the stairs, holding the candle before him. The stairs went down for some ways before he came to a landing where another set of stairs led down. He kept going, deeper into the earth. He was sure that the distance was illusory, though. At the most he was below the sewer level. He doubted the underworld extended any deeper than that.

He came to the end of the stairs and before him was a large tunnel with a "T" intersection. It was an old sewage tunnel, dry and crumbling. He stepped forward and looked to the left and right. The tunnel extended into darkness either way. He listened, but the silence was complete. Far off, he faintly heard rushing water, somewhere down the left fork.

Benedict thought about the situation. The vampire he sought was using the tunnels to hide in. He would want to maximize the security in case other vampires like Benedict came after him. In this case, would he choose to hide near the rushing water, to hide his own voice, or away from it, so that he could hear the sounds of others approaching? Benedict considered the character of this vampire: he had to be audacious to do what he had done so far, yet he could not be too powerful or he would not hide in the tunnels. What would be his weapons of defense? He used fog to his best advantage, according to the Dowager.

Benedict knew which way the vampire waited. He would be to the left, where he could use the spray from the rushing sewage water to substitute for fog. Benedict went left.

After ten minutes of walking Benedict saw a faint light ahead, coming from a side tunnel. The sound of the rushing water was louder, but its source was still farther ahead. He extinguished his candle and crept forward. He heard voices coming from the tunnel and stopped to listen. They were too far away to make out, but he recognized the Mandarin Chinese dialect. He quietly moved closer until he was next to the side tunnel. He smelled incense and could now clearly hear the conversation. It was two men, arguing with each other.

". . . leaving it there was idiotic! Who knows what method they have of tracking us? I tell you, you are arrogant and risk everything!"

"Shut up! I know what I am doing! I covered my tracks with spells. Do you not see? This way, they will think that the ugly bitch is to blame, that she is hiding something! They will turn against each other and we will reap the benefit. I will rule Chinatown!"

Benedict looked around the corner and saw the two men. The tunnel led to a large chamber, festooned with tables, chairs, and a bed. Silk wall hangings covered the grimy sewer walls. The two men stood in the center of the room facing each other. One of them was a Chinese man, dressed like a businessman. The other was a large, athletic-looking Chinese, dressed in gray. A fog of incense lay heavy over all.

"Fool! She knows them too well!" said the businessman. "They will see that you are to blame. She will lead them to us."

"Ha! Let them come! I am not afraid of them," said the large man. "These Western vampires have not seen the might of my magic! I will teach them!"

"Then you may begin your lesson with me," Don Benedict said, stepping from the tunnel and into the room.

Both men gasped and stared at Benedict in shock. The large man recovered quickly and smiled. He stepped forward. "So! It is one of the crawlers in darkness, come to pay respect to the new ruler of Chinatown!" The business man moved to the back of the room, trying to hide.

"I am here to have many questions answered," Benedict said. "You are an unwanted guest into these domains, and you must explain yourself."

"Ho! Do not speak to me like that! I have killed men for speaking to me like that. I do not have to answer to you! "

"You do not belong here. These are not your territories. There are age-old rules for these things. Ignorance of them is no excuse."

"I need no knowledge of laws! These are my laws!" and he held out his fists and snapped into a kung fu fighting stance. Benedict recognized the form as Chang Chuan, Long Fist. Benedict took a defensive Pa Kwa stance. The man nodded. "So, you are not entirely Western, yes?" he asked Benedict.

"I have many skills." Benedict replied. "Will you give me your name?"

"I am Feng Sha, the Wind Killer, of Clan Yin Shan! You would do good to fear me," the man said.

Benedict only smiled. "The Dark Mountain Clan? I have never heard of it. I am Don Benedict, of Clan Tremere."

"Ha! Clan Tremere! A joke! I have heard of your Clan. Did not your ancient master have to steal his powers from another? You are but a dog to them, a dog fetching sticks, with no will of your own!"

"Untrue. Do not confuse structure with weakness. Our Clan's very powers rely on strength of will. You would do good to remember this."

"Will? How can will come from a mere pawn? Are you not what they call, 'a brick in the Pyramid?'"

Benedict's eyes narrowed; this one knew some Clan secrets.

"Yes, I have heard of your Clan," Feng Sha continued. "Men of greed snatching knowledge from dusty ruins. Are you like this? I think you seem different — civilized; you know many things Chinese. Why do you not join me, and we shall rule this city together, a union of East and West?"

"I am the agent of my Clan in this matter," Benedict replied. "It has been declared so by the powers that guide heaven and hell. My fate is the Clan's fate."

Feng Sha began his move before Benedict had even finished speaking, but Benedict deftly side-stepped the leaping kick. Feng Sha landed and ran at Benedict with a furious series of punches. Benedict blocked all of them and then stepped to the side and punched Feng Sha, slipping under his arms and landing the blow hard into his ribs. Feng Sha was knocked back with the force of the blow, expelling air with a grunt as he fell.

"Do you submit?" Benedict asked.

Feng Sha gave him an evil look and said, "Never!" He then began to twirl his arms in a circular pattern. The incense fog in the room began to swirl and move towards him, as if he were the center of a swirling vortex. He yelled out and the fog suddenly formed the shape of a sword in his hand, solidifying out of wispy air. "Ah ha!" he yelled and ran at Benedict, swinging his sword in massive, circular strokes.

Benedict began furiously dodging, moving about the room, retreating after Feng Sha's advance. He moved past a chair and flung it at Feng Sha. The smoky sword splintered it in half with one blow. Feng Sha kept coming. Benedict was unnaturally fast, moving with a speed most mortals could not perceive, but Feng Sha had kept up with him, and even seemed to move faster.

Benedict leapt over Feng Sha, landed on a table, and hopped over it just as the sword came down upon it, splitting it asunder. Benedict reached into his shirt pocket and pulled out one of the Dowager's talismans. He barely dodged another blow as he fumbled into his pants pocket for his cigarette lighter. He ran behind another chair, kicking it at Feng Sha, who almost tripped on it before he kicked it out of the way. This gave Benedict enough time to light the paper.

The paper burnt to cinders in an instant and a great gust of wind leapt from the ashes towards Feng Sha's sword, blowing it into mere mist and out of the room. Feng Sha looked at his empty hand and yelled in anger. Don Benedict ran into the tunnel, seeking enough time to light another talisman.

Feng Sha began to whip his hands about in a swirling pattern, and again the incense coalesced, increasing in mass, growing into a carpet of fog. Feng Sha leapt onto it and it rocketed from the room into the tunnel. Feng Sha yelled in triumph as his flying cloud shot towards Benedict, standing a ways down the tunnel.

Benedict leapt to the ground just in time as the cloud shot over him. Feng Sha's hands flew into a frenzy of gestures, and the cloud halted and spun around. Benedict, on his knees, pulled the second talisman from his pocket and flicked the lighter to ignite it. The lighter sparked but no flame came forth. Feng Sha was now gaining speed and approaching quickly. Benedict flicked the light again and still it failed to light. He tried again, as Feng Sha reared back his fist, mere yards away from Benedict and closing fast. This time the lighter flared and Benedict held the talisman over it. In less than a second, the talisman was mere ash, and a roaring gout of flame leapt forth from it, engulfing the onrushing Feng Sha.

Feng Sha yelled as the flames licked at him, igniting his clothing. The cloud disappeared and he fell to the ground, rolling about to extinguish the flame. Benedict ran forward and prepared to kick him, but his enemy was too quick. Feng Sha rolled aside as Benedict's foot landed hard where he had been. The flames were now out, but he was blackened and smoking.

Feng Sha stood up quickly and uttered a cry as he snapped his hands into a martial gesture. Instantly, the smoke wafting from his charred clothes collected into a ball and shot towards Benedict's face. Benedict was temporarily blinded as the cloud hit him. He waved his hands, trying to scatter the cloud and fell as his right leg snapped under Feng Sha's kick. Even with his bad burns, Feng Sha still fought with formidable skill.

Benedict retreated, blocking Feng Sha's punches, ignoring the pain from his broken leg. Feng Sha halted his attack. "Do you admit defeat, Tremere? All your magic has not defeated me. I have held back up to now! Do you submit?"

Benedict concentrated as Feng Sha spoke, sending blood to his wound. It began to heal up. The bone was not set right, but Benedict could fix that later. The pain died, but Benedict could now feel the weakness from blood loss. He needed more blood. "Why must we fight, Feng Sha? Can we not work this out like men?"

"We are not men!" Feng Sha yelled. "I can tell you are old, but have you learned nothing in your years of death? You act like a man. You even kow-tow to your lords like a man!" Benedict had stood ready, concentrating, focusing his will while Feng Sha spoke. "You are of the night, and thus belong to no one! I will — *yaargh*!!!" Feng Sha yelled in shock as the ceiling collapsed upon him. Benedict concentrated harder, forcing more stones to loosen and fall. Feng Sha was soon buried under an avalanche of stone.

Benedict did not pause; he ran forward to finish off the buried Feng Sha. Before he could reach him, the stones exploded outward, flying into and past Benedict, but not strong enough to injure him. Feng Sha stood, flushed red and sweating blood.

Feng Sha ran forward with unholy speed and swept his foot out, knocking both of Benedict's feet from under him. As he fell, Benedict prepared to roll back up, but Feng Sha was too quick. He kicked Benedict's back with incredible force. There was a horrible snapping sound and Benedict fell, unable to move, his back broken.

"Well, Tremere?" Feng Sha said, his skin almost glowing with the blood he had expended to escape the stone mountain. "You must admit defeat now! You have not broken your chains, and I stand victorious! I do not want to kill you — I want you to tell your masters that I am unbeatable!"

Benedict internally sent blood to his back, and it began to heal. The bones were set wrong, but this was a minor problem compared with paralysis. He could move again now, but he felt the Hunger awakened in him. He would have to end this soon.

Benedict slipped the last talisman from his pocket. Feng Sha saw what he was doing and moved to kick the lighter from his hands. Benedict moved so the blow landed on his back instead. More bones broke, but Benedict could still move. The talisman caught fire and Benedict threw it at Feng Sha. There was a creaking sound, as of wood breaking, and Feng Sha yelled out. He fell back, staring at Benedict in surprise and anger. A wooden shaft poked out of his chest, right out of his heart. Feng Sha fell over, unmoving.

Feng Sha's eyes stared at Benedict, seething with anger. Benedict stood up. He would now take this vampire back to the Chantry where his secrets would be snatched from him. He walked over to Feng Sha and stood over him.

He looked into Feng Sha's bloodshot eyes and was suddenly aware of the blood pulsing there, throbbing in the veins, a river of red life. He saw the trickle of blood around Feng Sha's chest, where the wooden shaft had appeared. He saw the red stain all over Feng Sha's skin, where blood had oozed forth from his exertion. He closed his eyes, trying to gain control. He could not succumb now; the Clan needed this vampire's secrets too much. Benedict opened his eyes again and looked into Feng Sha's eyes, which were now staring at him in horror, fully aware of what Benedict was fighting against. With incredible effort of will, Feng Sha opened his mouth to say something. All that came out was a trickle of blood.

Benedict lost the battle. He fell onto Feng Sha and tore his throat out, gulping up the torrent of blood that gushed forth. He drank and drank, aware of nothing but the ecstasy of a hunger finally satiated. Then, he was engulfed in a tingling wave of current, traveling from his mouth to everywhere in his body at once. It was an ecstasy of power unparalleled. Nothing mattered anymore: not knowledge, not Clan, not self.

When it was over and Benedict opened his eyes, Feng Sha was dead, a pale corpse, quickly decaying as time finally caught up with him.

Benedict sat by the corpse for a while and then stood up. He searched the chamber, but there was nothing of interest there. The businessman was gone, but Benedict could find him later. There were enough things in the room to act as an occult channel to him.

Benedict lit his candle again and walked back to the stairs.

• • •

It was a cool evening as Benedict sat on a bench in St. Mary's Square. He thought about the events of the last week. He had caught up with the Chinese businessman, Feng Sha's aide, the next evening. The man had been packing, preparing to leave town. He had shrieked in fear as Benedict came in through the door, after breaking the lock. All Benedict could force out of him was an odd statement, before he collapsed, dead by a strange Thaumaturgical spell. The man had said, "I am but a servant! More will come. . ."

The Dowager had been quite satisfied with the outcome of the affair, although she ignored Benedict's question about the businessman's last utterance. Honerius was angry that Feng Sha had been killed before his secrets could be had, and was concerned about the businessman's statement. He spoke of the need for better intelligence on the affair and mentioned sending Benedict to Hong Kong, but as yet, Benedict had heard no more on the issue.

Benedict thought about his frenzy and its results. He had the blood of Feng Sha in him now. It was powerful, yes, but he did not care. That was not as important to him as what had happened when he lost control. Something had snapped. A cycle had been broken.

He looked down the street at the church. He had not been through its doors since his death, over a century ago. He thought about the light spreading out of the doors from inside, the light of a thousand candles. He thought about the oracle, the Ming I. He had feared that he was the evil influence it spoke of. But there had never been cause for worry; he was indeed the dark man, he knew that now. What had been broken were the bonds of the human condition, the chains that had held him to his place, a slave to what was expected of him. He was free.

After a while, Benedict stood up and walked over to the open doors of the church. He took his candle out of his pocket and walked through the doors to light it. ♀

DANCING WITH THE DEVIL

by Keith "Doc" Herber

Delfonso awoke late. He had overslept again; he could feel it.

He stretched in his coffin, felt his joints creak, then sat up. He was awake.

Gaining his feet, he groped the old adobe wall for the light switch. Overhead, a bare bulb sprung to life, splashing the ancient corridor with yellow light.

Delfonso stretched again, rolled his head around, working the stiffness out of his neck. He was an old vampire, among the oldest in San Francisco. And if not the oldest, certainly the longest resident undead.

He felt as though he'd been asleep a long time and wondered if he had not slept through a whole night, failing to wake altogether. It had happened before — only a few times — but enough to raise Delfonso's concerns. As vampires grew older, he had learned, they often slept longer, more deeply, and through almost anything.

Delfonso had been undead nearly 500 years. Perhaps it was catching up with him.

With a pale-white hand he brushed the dust from his black trousers, his fingers finding the small rip where he had snagged them the night before on the seat of his limousine. He had ordered Juan to fix the broken spring first thing the next day.

Looking into the small mirror hanging on the wall across from the alcove containing his coffin, Delfonso smoothed his black dress coat, straightened his collar and white tie, and, with delicate fingertips, brushed smooth his narrow, closely trimmed mustache and tiny, pointed beard.

He must appear respectable.

He felt the urge to go out tonight. Hunger gnawed. How long since he had last fed? A week? Ten days? He couldn't remember. All he knew was that as he grew older the Hunger seemed to wane. Oh, it was still as demanding, but it came less often, forcing Delfonso to kill less often.

He would have to call Juan from the upstairs phone, he thought to himself, get him over right away. What time *was* it?

To his right, the corridor led to a narrow wooden stairway that reached the house above; at the other end stood a heavy, rough-timber door, mounted with black iron hinges and lock. It was to this door he now walked. Pulling an antique key from his pocket, he unlocked it and pushed it open, revealing a midnight-black chamber beyond. He snapped a wall switch and light sprang up. The room was filled with ancient instruments of torture: the rack, strappadoes, and other examples of the Spanish Inquisition's trade shipped here centuries ago from Mexico City, Delfonso had them installed in this underground chamber — a chamber once connected to the adobe mission built here in 1776 by the Franciscan father, Junipero Serra. Serra had disapproved of the chamber, but Delfonso had then been posing as an agent of the Inquisition sent from Mexico City. Fear kept the father from protesting too much.

Delfonso had made good use of the chamber, encouraging recalcitrant Indians to accept the word of God, and occasionally chastising a Spanish soldier from the Presidio who had strayed from the righteous path. Originally a scheme hatched by the vampire to afford him a steady source of food, it was while torturing one of his victims that he had at last, finally realized the role he was meant to play in this world. He was an to be an avenger sent from heaven to save the most desperate of lost souls. Many had found God while writhing on his rack. Delfonso, watching their agonized throes, eventually found God too. After hundreds of years "lost in the wilderness," he had come to discover *why* he was. He returned to the warm embrace of his Catholic religion, once more assured of his salvation in the hereafter.

Gently, with a loving hand, Delfonso stroked the dark-stained timbers of the rack. So many had died on this machine — in immense pain and suffering — but how many souls had Delfonso saved? How many had he, at the last minute, saved from Eternal Damnation and sent winging to heaven?

Delfonso had lost count.

Turning to a small niche in the wall, he struck a match and lit a small votive candle within. Light filled the opening, revealing a statue of the Virgin Mary. Delfonso genuflected, quickly muttered a Hail Mary, then made the sign of the cross. Before extinguishing the candle, he drew out a small silver crucifix from inside his shirt, kissed it, then touched it to the even colder lips of the statue.

Tonight, he had promised the Virgin, he would save another soul.

• • •

Once upstairs, Delfonso telephoned his Filipino chauffeur and told him to bring the car around. They would be going out tonight. Putting a CD on his large stereo system, he listened to the opening strains of *La Boheme* while waiting for Juan to appear. The chauffeur lived a few blocks away and it would be a few minutes before he arrived.

While he listened to the music, Delfonso's eyes roamed over the souvenirs, trophies, and other memorabilia crowding the house's small living room: a large, antique globe; a bookshelf crowded with old volumes and binders full of maps and charts; a pair of antique Spanish lances and shield mounted over the fireplace. Delfonso noticed the dust thickly coating everything and made a mental note to have Juan come in and clean sometime soon.

His eyes came to rest on the old Spanish helmet sitting on a walnut end table. Looking at it, he was taken back to his early days in the New World whence he had come, the poor third son of a Spanish nobleman, desperate to make his own fortune. Carrying banners, Delfonso and 400 other Spaniards had marched inland in search of gold and Indian souls to save. They discovered the Aztec civilization, its gold, and worse, its infernal rites. Delfonso could still remember the endless lines of captives marched up the broad temple steps to where the priest Nezahualcoyotl would carve their living hearts from their bodies and offer them to the sun god. The Spaniards had been horrified by the spectacle and soon after overthrew Moctezuma II, ending the savage worship.

But before that would happen Delfonso himself was to die in this horrible manner. Captured by the savages one evening while separated from his troops, Delfonso was carried to a secret temple outside the Aztec city. Here, the Indians threw him on his back across the sacrificial altar, holding him fast while a priest raised a jagged obsidian blade high in the air, then plunged it down through Delfonso's chest, hacking away the Spaniard's still-beating heart.

Delfonso winced at the pain of the memory.

He had awakened some time later, near midnight, choking on a vile fluid being poured down his throat. Surprised to find himself alive, Delfonso listened as the Aztec priest explained what had been done: how Delfonso had been killed then resurrected with the living blood of a secret and eternal race. The priest was aware that the coming of the conquistadors meant the doom of his people — as had been prophesied for so long — and, knowing that he would die, the priest intended the lineage of Nezahualcoyotl to continue. Delfonso recalled having the distinct impression that Nezahualcoyotl himself was not aware of the "favor" the priest was doing him.

After the Aztecs had fallen to the Spaniards, Delfonso found himself alone in the wilderness, an untrained vampire Childe whose mentor had been slain, and who knew little of himself other than he was no longer of his own kind. Years he had spent in the jungle, dwelling on the outskirts of the slowly expanding Spanish settlements, preying on pagan Indians and the occasional Spaniard. He thought of those years spent alone, his very soul in mortal jeopardy. . .

A soft knock at the front door brought him out of his reverie. Juan had arrived.

Rising from his chair, Delfonso grabbed his cape and hat hanging on the wall and, opening the door, stepped out into the damp, heavy air of the city's Mission District.

● ● ●

Expertly, the young Filipino driver maneuvered the black stretch Continental through the Friday late evening traffic.

"I think Domingo is probably down around 24th Street," Juan said, glancing over his shoulder to where Delfonso lounged in the back seat.

"Head down that way, then," ordered Delfonso. "He should accompany us on our foray this evening."

The Filipino smiled and nodded. A ghoul now working for Delfonso nearly six years, Juan hoped that someday Delfonso would adopt him as Childe. Delfonso found Juan properly subservient and respectful, but not the sort he would consider raising to vampire — although he never indicated this to Juan.

The limo made its way steadily south down teeming Mission Street alive with excitement and action on a weekend night. Lower middle-class at best, the Mission district is a sprawling flatland nearly surrounded by hills and mountains, its streets a never-ending series of wall-to-wall cheap stucco or frame houses now inhabited mainly by Hispanics. Located south of the city proper, the district was built up during the late 19th century, a blue-collar neighborhood successively inhabited by Scandinavians and Germans, then Irish, then Italians, and now Mexicans and other Latino groups. Even the small enclave of Chinese hail mostly from Peru and speak fluent Spanish.

Louder, noisier than ever, its streets plied by low-riders booming salsa and with Mexican restaurants on every corner, the Mission District seemed to Delfonso fated to be home to a never-ending string of ill-educated, uncultured immigrants. He had lived here since 1906, after losing his suite and nearly all his belongings in the Palace Hotel fire following the great quake. Uninsured, and finances dwindling, he'd moved to his present home in a part of the Mission untouched by the holocaust. He had lived here ever since. Hardly a day went by that he had not had occasion to regret it.

He scanned the streets, filled with pedestrians, lingerers, girls in low-cut dresses too tight and too short. Sinners, he thought to himself.

Sinners — every one of them. Would they someday be redeemed?

"I think I see Domingo," Juan said over the back of the seat. "Over there, in that crowd."

Delfonso sat forward, looking through the windshield at the corner where Juan pointed. He easily spotted Domingo.

A squat, hefty Mexican, Domingo had been Delfonso's Childe for almost 40 years now. Born in Los Angeles, the man had come to San Francisco in 1943, one step ahead of the draft board, and soon after met fatefully with a hungry Delfonso. A dope-peddling zoot-suiter back in L.A., Domingo had proven useful to Delfonso. Domingo had a street presence Delfonso lacked, and did a much better job of controlling the local area than the elder Spaniard could ever hope to. True, he could terrorize in a way that Domingo couldn't, but Delfonso felt he could not — perhaps would not — meet and mingle with this half-breed crowd of Indians and Spanish.

"Pull over and blow the horn," Delfonso told Juan.

At the sound of the horn, Domingo looked up and saw the limo waiting at the curb. A quick knocking together of fists with the gang members he was talking to, then he was walking toward the limo. Delfonso watched Domingo's strut. Just slow enough to impress his friends, but not so slow as to anger his master. Domingo could play the line.

"Good evening, Mr. Delfonso," said Domingo, sticking his head through the opened window, grinning, showing his gold tooth.

"Hop inside," Delfonso told him. "We go hunting tonight."

Domingo waved his friends off then clambered into the front seat, next to Juan.

"Heyyy," he drawled. "It is a good night for hunting, eh amigo." He smiled at Juan.

Juan grinned back, and winked.

"Head downtown," Delfonso ordered the driver, then settled back into the deep-red velvet seat while Domingo filled him in on street happenings.

While the limo crept steadily north, Domingo described current conditions in the Mission, moneys collected, and suspected infringements by "poachers" — vampires from other parts of town hunting and feeding in the Mission District. Vannevar Thomas, reigning Prince of the city, kept a sharp eye on the boundaries between provinces and violations were dealt with harshly.

But Delfonso soon found the talk growing stale. The two had really very little in common aside from a similarity of native language. The older Spaniard found himself growing bored.

"I require privacy," Delfonso finally said. "Notify me if you spot a likely prospect."

Pushing a button in the armrest he watched Domingo's scowling, thick-headed face disappear behind the opaque screen rising up out of the back of the front seat. The passenger compartment was now sealed and although he could still hear the muffled conversation of Domingo and Juan, Delfonso chose to ignore it.

Delfonso relaxed back into his seat, letting his mind wander. His idle fingers again found the tear in his trouser leg and he thought of the broken wire in the limo seat. He bent forward to see if Juan had repaired it as he had asked him to and was appalled to find that, although the wire was now safely clipped, the chauffeur had patched the fabric with nothing more than a piece of red cloth tape that *almost* matched the red of the velvet upholstery.

"Damn," Delfonso told himself. Was there no one he could trust to do a proper job anymore? Then, taking a good look at the limo's interior, realized how worn and threadbare the whole vehicle was getting to be. Even the exterior — as polished as Juan might keep it — on closer inspection showed numerous chips and dents inexpertly filled and repainted. Delfonso realized the car was getting old and a little care-worn.

Much like himself, he thought.

They reached broad, busy Market street, and Juan turned right, heading northwest; the Moorish-styled clock tower of the old Ferry building stood proudly at the end of the street. Built in 1898, it was one of the few major structures in this part of town to survive the great earthquake. Ahead, on the right, a few blocks this side of the Ferry building, was the spot where once stood the grand and resplendent Palace Hotel, Delfonso's home from 1876 until his forced move to the Mission in 1906. Dwelling on the top, seventh floor, he was one of many permanent residents that lived in the luxurious place. From the gallery outside his apartments he could gaze down upon the Grand Court far below, watching the coming and going of guests riding in carriages that entered and exited via the circle drive in the hotel's interior.

Posing as the Spanish Count Delafonsa, the ex-conquistador had spent the best evenings of his existence there. Famous and distinguished guests from all over the world stayed at the Palace which, with 800 rooms, was the largest hotel on the West Coast and one of the largest in the world. Surpassed by none for service, food, and elegance, its furniture was special ordered, as was the solid gold place setting for 100. The hotel's restaurants were unsurpassed, the owner going so far as to lure away the chef from New York's famed Delmonico restaurant. Delfonso, over the years, had spent many a wonderful evening with the likes of such people as Oscar Wilde, Edwin Booth, and even — on the night before the great earthquake — the incomparable Caruso.

Delfonso had attended the grand balls staged there, the lavish parties, and even the funerals of a few distinguished guests. In those days Delfonso had moved with the best society San Francisco could offer, mingling with Floods, McKays, Hopkinses, Stanfords, and Crockers. He had, with Englishmen Ned Greenway, helped establish the city's first social register, and because of his noble descent, was often consulted on matters of etiquette and protocol. Inside tips from his Nob Hill acquaintances helped him to amass a fortune in the silver market, and this money he poured back into theaters and operas, raising the social status of the city. San Francisco had been truly great then, he told himself.

A knock on the opaque glass panel startled him. He jabbed at the button in the armrest, dropping the screen 10 or 12 inches.

"The usual route?" asked Domingo.

"Yes, yes," Delfonso answered impatiently. "Up through North Beach." Then he closed the screen again.

Juan turned north on Kearney, moving up through the dark and nearly deserted Financial district.

Unlike most of the vampires in the city, Delfonso, by dint of his long-time residence here, had been granted extended hunting privileges, allowing him to seek prey outside his usual Mission District boundaries. Others complained, but because he was so discreet, and because of his dwindling need for food, Vannevar had so far refused to revoke the privilege. Only Chinatown was off limits to him, and even that not officially. But Delfonso stayed clear of the area, regardless. The mysterious and grotesque thing that dwelled in an underground warren somewhere beneath that crowded and evil-smelling quarter of town was jealous of its territory. Although Delfonso feared little in San Francisco, he had learned to honor the wishes of that thing known only as "Grandfather."

They crept north along Kearney, skirting the southern border of Chinatown, heading toward Broadway and the old Italian section beyond. This was the first inhabited part of the city, back when it was known as Yerba Buena, and not San Francisco. The street they were on, now blocks from the waterfront, was once nearly the edge of the cove that once stood here. Since filled in with rubbish, abandoned ships, and goods whose prices on the market had fallen below reasonable level, it now supported some of the largest skyscrapers on the West Coast, including the strangely pyramidal TransAmerica building.

A few blocks further brought them to Pacific Avenue: the old Barbary Coast, once roamed by the worst sorts of thieves, murderers, and prostitutes. It had provided Delfonso with some of the most degraded sinners he'd ever attempted to save, but was now given over to antique shops, graphic design firms, and light industries.

Crossing Broadway and Columbus the air was suddenly filled with light and sound. Traffic was heavy and the sidewalks crowded with people: singles, career-types, yuppies dressed in expensive leather coats haunting cafes and bistros, drinking cappuccinos, chattering brightly, desperately trying to score.

They swung back toward Grant, then north again, past the crowds in front of the Saloon, Grant-Green, and other music clubs along this strip. Although prospects seemed numerous, Delfonso saw nothing to catch his eye. He ordered Juan to keep driving.

They swung west, moving slowly along Fishermen's Wharf, even at this hour still flush with tourists. He saw a few possibilities, but nothing that urged him to stop the car and "invite" one in. Some of them, on some other night, might have tempted him — but not tonight. Tonight, he had decided, he would need a *real* sinner, someone truly deserving of the fate he had in store for them. A fallen and disgraced soul that Delfonso might raise to momentary glory before doing them in.

He dropped the screen a few inches. "Juan!" he ordered sharply. "Take us to the Tenderloin."

● ● ●

A few minutes later found the black limousine prowling that part of San Francisco long known as the Tenderloin. Searching carefully, they worked their back and forth across the face of Lower Nob Hill, tracing the one-way streets back and forth. First Post, then Geary, Eddy, and Ellis, working their way downhill, deeper and deeper into the seediest part of the city. The type of woman Delfonso looked for — a prostitute — was plentiful, as were drug pushers, addicts, thieves, and others. But to take a working prostitute right off the streets might lead to trouble. He would have to make a deal with the local pimp, the vampire in charge of running the Tenderloin, an Irishman named Sullivan.

They finally located Sullivan down on O'Farrell Street, near the gaudy and tasteless Mitchell Bros. Adult Theater. The vampire leaned against the wall of the building, partially lit by the glow of the neon sign. His pale skin stood out in the darkness, exaggerated by his Levi's, dark shirt and pea-jacket, and the knit watch cap he habitually wore.

Sullivan spotted the limo as it pulled near, and stood up straight, watching its approach.

Juan parked the Continental at the curb and Sullivan, unbidden, approached, glancing up and down the street as he drew near. Delfonso powered down the rear window, and the screen separating him from Juan and Domingo, as well.

"What do you want?" said Sullivan, charmlessly, leaning through the rear window. Once a sailor out of Massachusetts, his 30-year old face was rough and lined. Badly trimmed red hair stuck out from under his cap, and his beard, also red, was short and stubbly.

Domingo turned sharply around in his seat. "Hey, gringo! Have some respect, you know? My man here is no street punk, eh?"

Sullivan shot Domingo a glance that might have killed, but Domingo didn't bat an eye.

There was no love lost between these two; Delfonso moved to interrupt.

"Now, now, there's no need of all this. After all, Domingo, we are in Mr. Sullivan's territory and we should behave as proper guests."

Domingo never took his eyes off Sullivan, but he said no more.

"Mr. Sullivan?" Delfonso said.

Sullivan looked back toward Delfonso, ignoring Domingo still boring holes into him with mean, slitted eyes.

"We would like to make a purchase tonight."

This had happened before. Sullivan knew what the old vampire wanted.

"How much you lookin' to spend?"

"About a thousand dollars, I would think."

"That's not very much. I don't even know if I got anything that cheap," said Sullivan.

"I don't require quality," Delfonso explained, smiling. "In fact, the lower the quality, the better."

Sullivan hesitated — looked up and down the street again.

"No. Not for a grand," he finally said. "You're asking me to take a perfectly good whore off the street — permanently. Even the worst of the junkies can turn in that much in three or four days."

"How about twelve-fifty?" offered Delfonso.

"Make it fifteen," countered Sullivan.

"Fourteen hundred?" asked the Spaniard.

"Deal." Sullivan stuck out his hand.

"Pay the man, Domingo," said Delfonso.

"Now," he asked, "who is it we are looking for?"

Domingo fished out a handful a wrinkled bills, counted out the proper amount, and stuffed it in Sullivan's hands. The Irishman, fanning the bills, made a quick count then shoved them in the front pocket of his jeans.

"Her name is Christy," Sullivan said. "Or Christine. I forget. Anyway, bleached blonde hair, kinda frizzed. Real skinny. You can spot her for a junkie a block away. She should be working down around Turk or Golden Gate somewhere. Just prowl around down there. You won't miss her."

"Thank you, my good man," smiled Delfonso. "A pleasure doing business with you, I'm sure."

Sullivan grunted something affirmative and stood back up. Juan waited for a break in traffic then pulled smoothly away, leaving the tall, lean Irishman standing on the sidewalk.

* * *

Down on Turk they were in the darkest and lowest part of the Tenderloin. Sandwiched between housing projects and the ornate, expansive Civic Center Plaza, the area was roamed by the worst elements of the city — veritable predators and prey. Pondering this, Delfonso found he did not like the comparison with himself and his business here. But his was a different mission than that of some others. Tonight he would save a soul, perhaps.

They spotted Christine on the corner of Turk and Polk — as Sullivan had said, from nearly a block away. Thin to the point of emaciation, she watched warily as the lone, black limousine rolled toward her down the street. When it stopped in front of her and the rear door opened, she sauntered over, doing the best she could to wiggle what little hips she had left.

"What can I do for you, mister," she piped, trying to sound casual, seductive.

"Step in," said Delfonso, his eyes glowing a bright red from the darkness within.

Without a word the hapless woman stepped into the limo. Now under the power of the vampire, her will was no longer her own.

At the last moment Delfonso decided they would go for a drive rather than go straight back home to the fate awaiting Christine in the secret underground chamber.

"Take us through the park, Juan," he asked. "I feel like a moonlight drive."

Indeed, the moon had risen throughout the evening, up over the Bay to stand at almost zenith in the sky above. Nearly full, its cold, pale light shone down on the city, glowing off the fog rolling in from the Pacific.

Juan's route through Golden Gate Park carried them past the glass-paneled Conservatory and the California Academy of Sciences building built in 1916. Nearby stood the old Music Pavilion, one of the few remnants of San Francisco's Mid-Winter Exposition of 1894. Delfonso had spent many a lovely evening at that fair, more often than not in the company of a lovely young lady or two. In those day he had made the perfect escort: sophisticated, charming, elegant, European, and completely honorable. Never once in all those years, Delfonso thought with a smile, did anyone ever accuse him of attempting liberties with a lady. No, the sort of liberties that Delfonso took were with ladies of an entirely different caste; and they were the sort of liberties that few of his Nob Hill friends would ever guess.

"Do you see, dear," Delfonso asked, pointing out the window as they passed. "I once listened to nighttime concerts at that Pavilion, enraptured by the music, with the beautiful Emma Flood on my arm. Yes those were wonderful evenings. And here. . . here stood the Tower of Electricity with its thousand lights and bright beacon on the top. Electricity was a new and marvelous invention in those days, you know."

Christine did not respond. She sat silent, stupefied, in her seat.

"I'm sorry, my dear," he apologized. "I chatter on when you're not really in the mood for talk. I apologize."

He studied the woman's face, silhouetted by moonlight. Although her skin was coarse and pocked from drug abuse, her features were finely made, and delicate. She had blue eyes much like Emma Flood's, although a bit cloudy. Her forearms were covered with needle scars.

"Perhaps some fresh ocean air will restore your spirits," he said, cheerfully. "Juan?" He dropped the screen a couple inches. "To Ocean Beach please. The lady wishes a drive along the water."

Christine, sitting motionless, said nothing.

The limo wound its way through the park, past ornamental lakes, cultivated gardens, and stands of exotic flora: Australian tree ferns, rhododendron, eucalyptus. At the end of the park they swung out onto the Great Highway and began coasting south, along the broad, gray expanse of Ocean Beach. The wind, as usual, blew in from the sea, the fog bank rising from the waters to drift over the western portions of the city, shrouding it in damp, gray cloud. The breakers rolled up to shore, the surf pounding the beach. Behind them, the Cliff House stood brightly lit atop the bluff overlooking Seal Rock.

"I have a fondness for the salt air," Delfonso told Christine. "It reminds me of times long ago."

Christine again said nothing.

For a time they road in silence, Delfonso gazing out the window wistfully, Christine silent. Delfonso ordered Juan up Twin Peaks Boulevard, running along the city's three central mountains. From this vantage point the city's distant spires and towers sparkled as though dressed in thousands of jewels: a veritable Oz on the water.

"A city of light and life," Delfonso observed. "So much life."

"You know," he said, turning toward the still-silent Christine. "Years ago they dug up all the cemeteries in the city. They moved all the dead out of town in order to make more room for the living. All my old friends, kicked out like so many vagrants. What do you think of that?"

Christine didn't respond.

"They live in Colma, now — south of the city."

The small town of Colma, in the center of the peninsula, is home to San Francisco's dead. Thousands of acres are covered by numerous cemeteries — Russian, Chinese, Catholic, Jewish, and others. The few living residents of Colma community are employed caring for these cemeteries. It was to Colma the limousine now headed. Delfonso had decided to pay his old friends a visit.

Parked at the entrance to Wood Glen cemetery, Delfonso told Domingo and Juan to wait with the car while he and Christine wandered out into the well-groomed graveyard on foot. The moon was now past overhead, sinking slowly toward the ocean hidden beyond the ridge of the Santa Cruz Mountains running along the coast. Over these mountains the ocean fog crept slowly inland — ghostly ragged fingers pouring slowly down the slopes.

"Look he said," gesturing with his arm at the acres of tombstones glistening white under the bright moonlight. "Here lie the fairest of the city's fair, the greatest of its great!"

Pulling the unresisting Christine along by the arm they walked along the rows of endless graves, Delfonso reading names aloud, telling her their stories, their triumphs and defeats.

"Here's a Crocker grave," he said. "You remember Charles Crocker, don't you? One of the Big Four railroad tycoons? He built the huge mansion on Nob Hill near the Hopkinses and Stanfords."

Christine showed no sign of recognition.

"Certainly you can't forget the famous Crocker spite fence?" he asked.

Crocker had tried to buy the entire block but one stubborn homeowner refused to sell the modest home he'd built on the corner of the lot. Crocker went ahead and built his mansion anyway, then, in an attempt to force the poor man to move, constructed a 30'-high fence of concrete surrounding the shabby little home, virtually shutting out all the man's windows save those facing the street.

"Crocker never was one to take 'No' for an answer," Delfonso chuckled.

"And here's Barnard's tomb," Delfonso cried, half-dragging the girl toward a white marble mausoleum set atop a slight rise. "One of the city's shining examples of civic responsibility — at least until he got caught in bed with a wife other than his own," Delfonso chuckled. "Shot dead by a jealous husband, but nothing that would keep San Francisco from throwing him one of the best funeral parades ever."

And so it went on, Delfonso half-escorting, half-pulling the bewildered woman through the moonlit cemetery, pointing out names familiar to him, some he'd even forgotten until now.

A tombstone made him pause. He read the name aloud: "Flood. The Bonanza King."

James Flood and his three partners — McKay, Fair, and O'Brien — had early on cornered the Nevada silver mines and cashed in big on the Comstock Lode. His mansion, of Italianate design and built of brownstone, still stands on the corner of California and Mason Streets, the only millionaire's edifice to survive the fire of 1906.

Gazing on the name carved in marble, Delfonso was again reminded of those grand and wonderful days living in the Palace Hotel: the potted palms, the uniformed help, the grand restaurant in the court.

He looked at the girl next to him staring without comprehension at the tombstone. No longer did he see the emaciated prostitute he had picked up on the streets. He saw instead Emma Flood, the silver baron's beautiful, young niece from Sacramento. Young, vivacious, Emma had been a favorite of Delfonso's, and he one of hers.

A sudden thought struck him.

"Mademoiselle?" he asked coyly. "Would you honor me with the next dance?" He made a slight bow in Christine's direction.

Not bothering to wait for an answer, the vampire lifted Christine's arms and, humming Strauss, began waltzing the woman across the cemetery, their forms spinning lightly under the cold and silky moonlight.

Faster and faster they whirled, Delfonso's voice lifted in song, ringing across the deserted cemetery. As they danced, the tombs and grave stones melted away, becoming the white linen-draped tables of the Palace Ballroom during the Friday night Cotillion. Crowds watched from the sidelines as Delfonso and the lovely Emma Flood tripped lightly across the floor. Other dancers gave way, retiring to the sidelines to watch, relinquishing the entire dance floor to the lovely couple. Emma laughed gaily, giddy from the dance, and Delfonso caught the envious looks cast at him by the younger men attending the ball. Let them envy us, he thought. Smiling widely he spun the light-footed Emma through a series of fast spins that left the gaping crowd speechless. They then applauded while Delfonso and Emma beamed back at them, radiant in the moment.

At the end of the song, to the sounds of more applause, Delfonso politely bowed to the young woman.

"Perhaps you should return to your beau," he said. "I think we have made him a bit jealous. Perhaps you should put his fears to rest. . ."

Emma said nothing — only smiled then turned and walked away, back to the young men waiting impatiently on the sidelines.

Delfonso sat down on the nearest chair, resting, looking over the faces of the crowd. He could see them all clearly: the friends, the rivals, even a few that had eventually fallen to Delfonso's Hunger. They were all here.

The sound of a woman's scream shook him awake. The crowds of people melted away into nothing, the tables and chairs became tombstones once again. A second scream — suddenly choked off — brought him to his feet. Alert, he realized he'd been lost in a daydream.

Up the rise, a short distance off, stood the limousine. Two dark figures — Juan and Domingo — huddled nearby. Shocked, Delfonso could see them sharing the corpse of Christine in feast.

"Stop!" he shouted, sprinting back to the limo. "God! Don't do that!"

But it was too late. Christine was dead, already a good portion of her blood drained away. Juan had jumped up at the sound of Delfonso's voice, but Domingo remained where he was, crouched over the corpse.

"We thought you gave her to us," the Mexican said. "You sent her over to us."

Regaining his composure, Delfonso realized Domingo was right.

"Yes, yes, of course," he corrected himself. "By all means. . ."

The two immediately fell back upon the corpse.

Delfonso chose not to watch, instead waiting patiently in the back seat of the car for the two to finish their meal. A few minutes later Juan and Domingo got back in.

"Where to, sir?" Juan asked.

"Take us home," Delfonso said quietly.

"We are finished tonight?"

"Yes," Delfonso answered. "I'm afraid I no longer have an appetite." ⚲

THE ART OF DYING

by Lawrence Watt-Evans

The lights came up in a sudden blaze, driving the darkness away from the easel, back to the studio loft's furthest corners, confining the night's gloom to the shadowy spaces behind the sparse furnishings — and of course, to the world outside.

Bethany suppressed her displeasure and discomfort at this abrupt, unexpected brightness; she would have thought that Anton would have chosen softer, more romantic light, but apparently he was sincere in wanting her to *see* his work.

She glanced at the canvas, not expecting much — not expecting anything, in truth, but to not even look would have been rude, and she liked to think that she was never unintentionally rude. Anton seemed so very intense about his artistic efforts; she really had to at least pretend to take them seriously.

The casual glance lengthened, and turned into a stare. She took a step toward the painting, her gaze fixed on the bright image.

A moment ago Bethany had been concerned only with the dark burning of the Hunger and the delicious anticipation of feeding, with the almost painful teasing she had been subjecting herself to as she let Anton babble. She had been caught up in the perverse enjoyment of delaying the moment when she would taste Anton's blood, in increasing the tension between need and satisfaction so as to heighten the eventual pleasure.

Now, though, that tension had vanished; the Hunger itself was nothing but a minor distraction as she studied the intense colors, the textured surfaces of the painting.

It was a cityscape, San Francisco at dawn, knives of sunlight cutting between the gleaming towers and shattering to jeweled shards on the waters of the Pacific.

It was utterly beautiful.

She stared at it, drinking it in with her eyes, wanting to absorb every detail.

"Glare," she said, her eyes still fixed on the painting. "Too bright."

Instantly, Anton twisted a knob and the light dimmed. "I had the lights way up so I could work on it," he said. "It was bright, but I didn't see any glare. I guess your eyes are more sensitive than mine."

Bethany smiled to herself. "Yes," she said.

"You like it?" Anton asked.

Bethany struggled for a long moment, and at last managed to tear her gaze from the picture and look at the artist's intense bearded face, at his black hair and guileless eyes.

That man had created this beauty.

She shouldn't have been so surprised, she told herself. After all, she had met Anton when that earthquake, earlier this evening, had startled them into bumping against one another at an artists' reception at the Palace of the Legion of Honors. Why should it come as a shock to learn that he, too, was an artist? Who else would she expect to meet at an artists' reception? She had gone mostly because it was a pleasant diversion on a quiet Friday evening, and what made it pleasant was the art, and the artists.

Of course, the surprise wasn't that he was one of the hundreds of kine in the Bay Area who put brush to canvas; the surprise was that he was a true artist — in Bethany's opinion, an artist of real genius.

That opinion might not carry the weight of some, after a mere 40 years of undeath, but Bethany was confident of her conclusion. If this painting was not a work of genius, Bethany told herself, then she was no true Toreador, she was as bad as those Poseurs of Serata's.

No, even those fools with their fads and flash, even the youngest Childe in the Clan, would see Anton's brilliance in an instant.

"It's wonderful," she said, smiling at Anton.

He smiled back, a smile of pleased relief. "Would you like to see some others?" He gestured at a dozen other canvases, leaning face-in against the east wall of the studio.

"Very much," she replied, thrusting away, for a moment more, the pulsing Hunger that drove her.

One by one, he lifted the canvases and displayed them, while Bethany stared in wonder at street scenes, sunsets, still life, each with that distinctive hard-edged, brittle light, like nothing she had seen before. While none of the other paintings were quite as magnificent as his most recent work, it was clear that that new creation was merely a continuation of ongoing artistic development, not a wild, one-time fluke.

Anton was a genius, the most brilliant painter Bethany had ever met in the flesh.

"Why haven't I *heard* of you?" she asked.

He shrugged. "I haven't exhibited anywhere yet. Haven't tried. I have an inheritance I live on, and I wanted to build up a body of work, my family always said my work wasn't good enough. . . do you *really* like them?"

"I *love* them — and I love *you*! Come here!" She meant it — she loved him, as he would love a fine wine. She threw out her arms to him.

She would have to be careful. She was very hungry, but she must not drink too deeply.

Not yet.

This one must be saved, must be made one of the Kindred, not given to useless, ungrateful death — but she could not do that without permission of the Prince. She was no anarch.

She would have to speak to Vannevar Thomas as soon as she could; she could not allow Anton to face the everyday risks of mortal existence a moment longer than absolutely necessary. Such talent must be saved for the ages.

As his arms went around her, as her lips neared his throat, she took one more glance at the painting.

Very careful.

• • •

"Bethany!" The voice was deep and penetrating.

Bethany paused, startled; she lowered her bulky parcel, then turned and peered through the dimness and smoke of the Alexandrian Club's main lounge.

She saw a figure approaching, and recognized it. "Stefan," she said in flat acknowledgment.

"I almost didn't see you," Stefan said as he squeezed his way through the crowd; the black leather of his tight pants brushed audibly against someone's clothing, and the silver pendants on his chest jingled.

Bethany had not particularly wanted to be seen, but she saw no reason to state the obvious; she simply waited.

"I didn't expect to see you tonight," Stefan said. "Weren't you going to some sort of event? Our host said you were."

"Over hours ago," Bethany replied.

"Oh, but. . . surely you didn't leave alone!"

"Is there something you want, Stefan?" she asked, already tired of the pretense of friendship. Stefan was one of the trend-following fools in Serata's circle, and there was no love lost between that group and Bethany's own, more traditional faction of the vampiric Clan.

"No, no — not at all! I was just surprised to see you." He smiled. "Pleasantly surprised," he hastened to add.

"I don't know why," Bethany said. "I come here often. If either of us should be surprised, Stefan, I would think it would be I. You are scarcely a regular here."

"Ah, Bethany, you misjudge me. While I can scarcely tolerate the self-proclaimed Artistes who run the place, I must admit that this is a fine place to meet with others of our kind, and when I return to the City to pay my respects to my Sire I often stop in here afterward."

Bethany bristled at the slighting description of the club's management — both Cainen, who ran the Alexandrian Club upstairs, and Melmoth, who ran the secret club beneath, were *her* own kind, and kindred spirits, as it were.

"You come here, even though you don't like the management, and yet you ask what *I'm* doing here?"

"No, no, sweet Bethany," Stefan protested. "I merely express my pleased surprise at my good fortune, that our visits should thus coincide! I had resigned myself to missing the pleasure of your countenance."

She turned away from this flattery, picked up her parcel, and took another step toward the alcove beneath the stairs.

"Oh, don't hurry off!" Stefan protested, stepping quickly beside her.

"Stefan, I have business elsewhere." She pushed past him and ducked into the alcove.

He followed her as she opened the heavy oaken door and hurried down the 13 steps into the stagnant gloom of the Vampire Club.

At the bottom she paused in the tiny foyer, and Stefan joined her. The foyer was small enough that the two of them, and Bethany's package, made an uncomfortable crowd.

"Aren't you going to knock?" Stefan asked, reaching for the massive brass ring.

Bethany brushed his hand aside.

"Stefan," she said, "I am here on business, to see the Prince, who I'm told is visiting my Grandsire. *You have no business here!*"

Stefan smiled, his long white teeth a flicker of light in the darkness. "All the Kindred are welcome here, Bethany. I would not *dream* of interfering with your business, whatever it is — but I'm as welcome here as you are."

She glared at him; untroubled, he reached past and lifted the heavy knocker. Three times he let it fall against the carved oak while Bethany simply stood, her gaze hostile.

As the door swung open, Stefan remarked, "Besides, I hardly see what the great secret is — it's obvious that that thing you're carrying is a painting, and I presume it's a gift for the Prince. Why should the presentation be private? Afraid he'll see just how poor your work is?"

"It's not my work!"

"Ah, then your artistic judgment."

"At least I have some artistic judgment, you bloody *Poseur*!" Bethany snapped, pushing past Stefan into the main lounge of the Vampire Club.

His laughter trailed after her as she descended through gloom and stale air to the lower deck.

In this place nothing lived, nothing breathed — but the undead moved in their semblance of life, past paintings that mocked the living, glorying in their own darkness. Here, Bethany met with her Prince.

Twenty minutes later, the preliminary formalities out of the way and the situation explained, Bethany carried the painting into the library, where the light was best, and carefully unwrapped it. A nude's oil-paint eyes looked on from one wall, while Vannevar Thomas, vampire prince of San Francisco, and Sebastian Melmoth, master of the Vampire Club, watched with interest.

"The mission of the Toreador Clan is to preserve great art," Bethany said, talking to cover her nervousness, "and great artists, through the Embrace." She saw Melmoth's lips quirk with amusement at her presumption, and realized that she was telling her elders things they had known for longer than she had existed. "While of course I am still young by the standards of our kind, I have faith in my own opinions — I would never have been taken into the Clan myself, were I no judge of art. And in my opinion, Anton Prihar is truly a great artist." She pulled the last of the wrappings away, and held up the painting she had borrowed.

For a moment there was utter silence as Bethany's audience took in the painting — the towers cut by golden glory, the water spattered with diamonds of light. Then Stefan, standing in the doorway, began applauding. Bethany almost dropped the painting; she had been so intent on the two elders that she had not seen Stefan's arrival. "Superb!" Stefan called.

Thomas turned. "And by what right, whelp, do you dare intrude on this discussion?" the Prince snapped.

Stefan's hands dropped, and he bowed respectfully. "Your pardon, sir; I am here as the representative of Allanyan Serata, Primogen of the Toreador Clan in your city. It seems plain to me that this matter concerns her."

"Ah," Thomas said. "And how is it that Mistress Serata was aware of this meeting?"

Stefan looked suddenly uncomfortable.

"She isn't!" Bethany shouted. "Stefan just followed me! He's just trying to make trouble; he's hated me for decades!"

"Oh, Bethany, I don't hate you," Stefan protested. "I am simply drawn irresistibly to save you from your own fo —"

"Silence!" Thomas said.

Stefan stopped in mid-word.

"I asked you a question, Stefan," Thomas said quietly. "And I did not ask you, Bethany."

Bethany cast her eyes downward as Stefan admitted, "Bethany spoke the truth, O Prince: I met her upstairs by chance, and followed her here. I did so, however, because my Sire has charged all of us who curry her favor to keep an eye on the actions of those who would deny her authority as the eldest Toreador in the city — this Melmoth, the one who calls himself Tex R. Cainen, and all their descendants, all their followers in the. . . shall we say, the aesthetic disagreement that divides our

Clan? You know they call us mere Poseurs, that they're so caught up in past glories that they can't see. . ."

"*We* can't see! You're so dazzled by flash and glitter that you throw away all aesthetic judgment. . ." Bethany began.

"I need no speeches," Thomas interrupted. "You may dispute art theory elsewhere, not in my presence."

"My apologies," Stefan said, smiling ingratiatingly. "But I truly am here as Serata's representative."

Thomas smiled back. "I see," he said. "And as Serata's representative, would you agree that this Anton Prihar should become one of the Kindred, that his skill might be preserved?"

"Oh, absolutely!" Stefan said. "Bethany's stumbled on a real gem this time, no question about it!"

"You are, of course, an irrefutable authority," Melmoth murmured quietly. Stefan ignored the sarcasm.

"And if I say that San Francisco is overpopulated, that there are to be no more Kindred created at this time?" Thomas asked.

"Then we would have no choice but to obey," Stefan said with a cruel smile.

"Yes, sir," Bethany said, ignoring Stefan's obvious pleasure in her discomfiture. "But please, don't say that."

"The work is quite remarkable," Melmoth said, to no one in particular.

Thomas threw a quick glance at Melmoth, then at Bethany. "You all agree, then, that this painter should be Embraced?" The three Toreadors all indicated silent assent.

"Very well," Thomas said. "I will permit it."

"Oh, *thank* you!" Bethany said.

Stefan bowed. "I will inform Serata at once," he said. "I have no doubt that she will wish to Embrace this artist herself."

Bethany turned, shocked.

"But I found him!" she said. "His blood is *mine*!"

"And if Serata says he is hers?" Stefan asked, smiling. Bethany, wordless with fury, turned to the Prince.

Stefan quickly said, "Surely, the Prince will not deny the rights and privileges of the Primogen, to favor this foolish young creature? Allanyan Serata is an elder of the Fifth Generation; Bethany is what, Ninth?"

"Eighth," she said coldly. "*I found him!*"

"And would you refuse him a chance at greater power than your own?" Stefan asked her. "Is it, perhaps, your own power, your own ambition, that interests you, rather than this human's art?"

Bethany's hands came up, curved into claws.

"And pray, sir," Melmoth interjected, "What is *your* interest in denying this young lady her treasure?"

"Spite," Bethany snarled. "It's just spite."

Melmoth cast an expressive glance at the ceiling, then at the Prince.

Thomas gazed contemplatively back.

"Sebastian," he said, "you see my predicament. These two have pitted the authority of the Primogen and the natural respect for one's elders against proprietary rights. I feel like Solomon confronted by the two mothers disputing over a child; how to resolve this, save by refusing this man the Embrace, and thereby letting his talent die in a few short years?" He started to turn back to the others, not expecting a reply.

Melmoth surprised him by murmuring, "I always wondered why Solomon didn't ask the child which was its true mother. Surely even an infant knows that much

— and this Anton Prihar is no infant, as his painting makes plain."

Startled, Thomas paused. A slow, thoughtful smile spread across his face.

"Indeed," he said. "Indeed!"

• • •

The two vampires stood side by side before Anton Prihar, their dark clothing and black hair islands of night's darkness in the brightly lit studio, their pale faces colorless blanks against the vivid hues Anton had chosen for the walls. To the artist they appeared an intrusion from some hostile, washed-out other world.

As, of course, they were — they belonged to the world of eternal night, the world of the Kindred, a world he had never known existed until meeting Bethany the night before, a world whose intrusion he had tried to stave off.

"Choose!" Stefan demanded. "We bring you eternal life, centuries in which to create beauty; you need merely tell us which you would prefer to escort you into immortality, little Bethany, or the great Serata."

"What does it matter?" Anton asked despairingly, the useless silver cross dangling from his hand. "Why should I care?"

"Your power would be greater as Serata's Childe," Bethany explained. "I can't deny that; it's a fact of our existence. But she and her followers have no true understanding of art, Anton; they're mere Poseurs, dabblers, prone to trends and fashions, with no appreciation of lasting greatness."

"Ha!" Stefan said. "We aren't afraid of change, if that's what you mean — we appreciate innovation and originality, we aren't caught in the outmoded patterns of the past."

Anton paid no attention to Stefan; he looked at Bethany, then down at the cross, then back at the vampire.

"When we met at the museum," he said, "I thought it was fate. I thought the earthquake was destiny at work, throwing us together that way. But I thought you were a woman, not a bloodsucking monster."

"I am a woman," Bethany protested. "But I'm *more* than that. And you can be, too."

"You drank my blood last night," he accused her.

"Yes," Bethany said.

"You're a vampire."

"Yes."

"But the cross doesn't affect you." He jingled the silver chain.

When Bethany and Stefan had arrived at the studio door, returning the borrowed painting, Anton had confronted them with the talisman, thrusting it in their faces; they had ignored it as Bethany asked, "May we come in?"

Anton had admitted them, and listened as they explained the choice the Prince had set before him. Now the artist was asking questions, and Bethany did her best to answer — she did not want to deceive him. She wanted him to know what lay before him, to understand that he need never die.

"No," she said, "crosses and silver don't affect us. Nor garlic, nor the rest of it. All myths."

"And you don't sleep in coffins all day, and come out at night?"

Stefan smiled sardonically as Bethany admitted, "We don't necessarily use coffins, but that part is basically true. Sunlight burns us, can destroy us."

Anton glanced at the painting, at the knives of sunlight cutting through the city streets.

"You give up something, yes," Bethany said, "but you'll be free of age and death forever."

"And you drink blood. You prey on other people." Anton put a hand to the bandage on his throat.

"But you don't need to hurt them," Bethany insisted. "It can be pleasurable. You saw that."

Anton nodded. "In the stories, vampires can hypnotize their victims," he said.

"Yes," Bethany said.

"So I couldn't resist if you just came in here and attacked me again."

"No, you couldn't, not for long," Bethany agreed. "But the Prince has ordered us to offer you a choice between Serata and myself."

Stefan, bored by this, growled, "Choose, mortal. Bethany or Serata?"

"I need time," Anton said. "I need time to think about it."

"What is there to think about?" Stefan demanded. "We offer you eternity, and you have a choice between more power or less — choose now!"

"I need time," Anton said, "to put my affairs in order."

"No one needs to know you've crossed over," Bethany pointed out.

"Still, I need time," Anton insisted. "You're asking me to choose between a total stranger and a woman who is nearly so, between power and something that might be love — or might not. You two claim to be eternal — what does one day matter?"

Bethany smiled wryly. "It doesn't," she agreed. "Tomorrow night, then?"

"Serata will not be pleased," Stefan warned.

"Come on," Bethany told him. She took Stefan's arm and pulled him toward the door; he shook her off and marched out, Bethany close on his heels.

• • •

The fog was thick the following night, spilling through the streets in opaque billows, cutting off all vision and blurring all light; perhaps, Bethany thought, that was why Stefan was late, why she had arrived alone and found the door of the studio standing open.

When she saw the door open, for a moment she feared that someone had broken in, that Anton had fallen prey to human avarice — or Serata's.

There had been no robbery, and Serata had not disobeyed the Prince; a dozen paintings were set out on display, untouched. The one that Bethany had borrowed had a place of honor in the center. The note was pinned to that last finished canvas, and addressed to her — not to Stefan, only to her.

"Dear Bethany," she read, "I have made my choice."

She looked up for a moment, then continued reading.

"I had thought that you understood and appreciated my work," the note said. "You certainly praised it highly, and in your own way, I suppose you did appreciate it — but it's plain that you didn't understand it, nor did that other person, Stefan, who you brought here."

Bethany glanced at the painting, momentarily puzzled. "Perhaps I could have explained it to you," Anton's words continued, "but I don't think that Stefan or the creature he serves could ever have accepted it. All my life, other people have made my decisions for me — sent me to the best schools, found me the right jobs, always acting for my own good — until I inherited my grandmother's money and could finally do what I pleased.

"And now, I've succeeded too well, and Stefan's mistress would act for my own good, and destroy what she seeks to control. I can never be what you are, what you want me to be, any more than I could be what my parents wanted me to be.

"Goodbye, Bethany. I know you meant well."

Bethany dropped the note and looked up again, at Anton's body dangling from the noose, turning slowly, limbs stiff — he had obviously died hours before, perhaps just minutes after she had last seen him alive, and there was no hope of revival to either life or a vampiric approximation of life.

Even had revival been possible, Bethany thought, she would have respected this final artistic decision — or at least, she hoped she would have. Her gaze fell back from Anton's remains to his works.

His body hung below the broad studio window, below the row of too-bright lights, and the corpse's black shadow twisted across a dozen paintings, paintings that, one and all, showed bright sunlight slanting across the sky, illuminating fields, forests, streets, and spires, sunlight gleaming from whitewashed walls, sunlight scattered by dancing water, sunrises, sunsets — everywhere, on all sides, in every painting, the sun that Bethany had not seen with her own eyes for more than 40 years, the sun she had asked Anton to give up forever, the sun he could not live without. ◊

DESCENT

by Sam Chupp

"Really, Anastasia, I didn't think you'd show, especially after that earthquake." Selena smiled. It was a shark's smile, sure and predatory. She was dressed to kill, as well: a velvet dress, green, with a beautiful stone circle Sumerian pendant depicting Inanna, Queen of Heaven. Anastasia smiled back the same way, her eyes hard. It had been a long time since she had been forced to play dominance games with another vampire.

"Oh, Selena, you know, I so dearly love Luigi's. That's why I'm here, really. Ah, isn't that Inanna! Wasn't she the one who lost her life in the Underworld?" Anastasia said, smiling.

"She found great power with the Queen of the Damned, actually. And returned to rule." Selena's eyes glittered.

"Who's your blonde friend?" Anastasia smiled. She brushed her thick, auburn hair back from her face and her dark eyes glittered. The maitre d' hadn't even noticed her leather jacket and jeans: perhaps he'd been expecting her.

Selena prodded the teenaged, blonde surfer boy with a single, gloved hand. The boy was obviously uncomfortable in his white tuxedo, and he stumbled forward. Selena smiled wickedly back at Ana through the veil of her midnight hair. She smoothed the silk sheath dress she was wearing as she watched Anastasia's reaction. "Go on, boy. Tell Mistress Ana your name." Selena's leer, her red lips and tongue, disgusted Ana.

The surfer smiled, dully, slowly. "I'm. . . my name's Dinner, ma'am." His voice was thick and sleepy.

Anastasia flinched, almost imperceptibly. But Selena caught it. "What is it, Ana? Do you not like your wine white? I imported him from Marin County. Would you prefer a less fruity, more robust vintage?" Selena had a habit of referring to blood as wine.

Anastasia smiled slowly. "Although your hospitality is without question, Selena, I'm not thirsty at the moment. Thank you for the offer, however."

"Not thirsty? How strange. I myself am never one to turn down fresh young things like this one. But I understand: you prefer a more feminine blush these days. What's her name? Susie?" Selena motioned for the surfer to step back to her.

"Sofie. Her name's Sofie. I thought you wanted to talk about old times?"

Selena brushed her hair aside, her green eyes narrowing. She smiled impishly, her whole demeanor changing in a second. "Oh? A sore spot for you? Don't tell me you've gone and fallen in love with her?"

Anastasia returned Selena's look with stony silence. A waiter took this opportunity to change the plates on the table: the soup went away, replaced by the salad.

Selena was first to break the silence. "Well, so. I see that's not a topic you're interested in discussing. Is there something beside the weather that we can discuss?" Selena's voice was icy.

"I would imagine you'd be full of gossip from the east. How is Jeremiah, Tabitha? I've not heard from them in some time." Anastasia said, picking at her salad. She was amazed at how old habits returned to her. She used to be a master at maintaining the Masquerade, especially in public and especially in restaurants. She noticed the Selena made no such pretense — perhaps Luigi's was Kindred-owned.

"Jeremiah is doing boring Toreador things, and Tabitha is doing boring Tremere things. They're both boring. And you would know that if you weren't hiding in your ivory tower here in San Francisco." She motioned to the surfer, who kneeled next to her and presented his wrist.

"Oh look, Ana. Poor boy's got slash scars. Probably has a rough life. Poor thing. Well, you're about to feel better, honey." Then, there, in the balcony of Luigi's, Selena sunk her fangs into the surfer's wrist and began to suck deep draughts of blood. He smiled in dull pleasure, closing his eyes and savoring the feeling.

"Don't you think you should leave him some to get home on?" Anastasia said, trying to keep her composure. Even though she was not hungry, and had not needed to feed as much lately, the smell of the rich surfer vitae was tempting.

"Oh really, Ana. You're so very droll. The last bits are the sweetest, you know." Selena said, smiling, licking her lips. The totally drained surfer was lifted onto a cart and taken out. A waiter stepped forward with a napkin, and Ana looked up at him in surprise.

Selena smiled, dabbing some vitae from her chin. "I wanted us to be completely comfortable this evening, Anastasia. So I took the liberty of arranging things. Don't worry about your precious Masquerade tonight. None will be the wiser for our celebration." Selena's skin had grown pink, her hair shinier, her whole body more shapely.

"Oh? And what are we celebrating?" Anastasia felt a wave of nausea well up inside her, and forced herself to maintain a mask of propriety.

"Our friendship, of course. And independence. You are independent of the Camarilla, the Circle of Seven's iron grip. And so am I," Selena said, smiling victoriously.

"What? How did you swing that? Your Sire get you a research grant?" Anastasia narrowed her eyes.

"Hardly. I've decided to go freelance. Totally. Tremere for hire. And I tell you, Ana, I've met the most interesting people in Mexico."

"Mexico? Why would you want to go there? The place is crawling with the Sabbat," Anastasia said.

"Exactly," Selena said, smiling, her eyes gleaming.

Anastasia put down her fork. She looked at Selena, looked at the inhuman coldness in her eyes, for the first time seeing it. Then she looked away. "Oh, Ana. Ana. You are so naive. You and your hermitage, your cloister. You're right to turn away from the Camarilla — what have they ever offered you that was of value? They ask you to deny what is truly you. The Beast Within."

Anastasia looked up at her, eyes afire. "I. . . I may not be involved with the Camarilla. But I am still loyal to my Sire."

"Your Sire? And when was the last time you spoke with Etrius?" Selena said, smiling.

Anastasia's eyes narrowed to slits. "I speak with him at the Esbats, as you well know. Or have you forgotten the lore that the Tremere taught you?"

Selena licked her lips and brushed her raven hair aside again. "Ana, that's just it. I've learned so much more among the Sabbat. They have powers, and paths, and rituals that are much more potent than any of those taught to us in the Camarilla."

"Yes, I imagine so. It's quite easy to gain power when you sell your soul for it. So tell me, Selena: who is your infernal master?" Anastasia said, finally finding her anger. She felt it building within her, welling up.

"Those old wives' tales about the Sabbat and the Infernal are just that. And I never took you for an old wife, really Anastasia. How dramatic. The way you talk, you'd expect me to burst into flame at any moment."

Anastasia rose and smiled as sweetly as she could manage. "Don't give me any ideas, Selena. Now, if you excuse me, I've suddenly lost my appetite for this conversation." She whirled and stalked down the stairs.

From the balcony, Anastasia could hear her laughing. "You'll be back, my sweet. You'll be back," Selena called.

•••

Ana took a cab across town, and made her way to the market, where she purchased a handmade wicker picnic basket from a street vendor. She began to fill the basket with wonderful things, things that she knew Sofie loved.

Ana loved tasting the sweet flavor of the warm Valpolicella wine in her blood, loved the sweet tang that garlic and basil and oregano brought to her lovers' vitae.

She threw herself into shopping, trying to forget the disturbing things Selena had said.

Ana decided she would take Sofie and drive up to the beachhouse, where they'd spend the rest of the night. It would be nice to get away, away from Selena, away from San Francisco, away from other vampires.

She smiled thinking of the light Sofie's eyes would have when she saw the caviar, the *foie de gras*, and the anchovies, all wrapped in green foil. She even smiled at the vendors who wished to haggle with her, and who were surprised that, be it Italian, Greek, or even Chinese, she answered each in their native tongue. Soon her basket was filled with jewel-like parcels, wrapped neatly in their individual packages, giving off a redolent scent of luxury.

All this preparation was for the midnight picnic on the beach that had become their tradition at the house. Ana shook out her hair and smiled absently as she thought of the daring race they would play with the sun as it burned over the cliffs and pierced to the ocean: about how sweet those last kisses were, before retiring for the day. Sofie would be able to sleep next to her while the jealous sun burned in the sky. It would be heaven.

Ana began to feel filled up with the combination of anticipation and longing that she felt. It consumed her. Sofie was the moon and sun in her life. Sofie was what made each step worthwhile. Sophia, bringer of wisdom, Sophia, bringer of peace. That gentle spirit, a magical woman who did not even know the simple magic that she carried in her fingers, the grace and beauty that she held in her eyes. This was why Ana loved her, why Ana had forsaken her own kind for a simple life with her, away from the intrigues of the Kindred.

Anastasia had met Sofie by pure chance, had stumbled into her life as the result of an accident, and had stayed with her because of something totally coincidental and unexplainable. Sofie painted Ana's dreams, painted the landscapes of her daytime slumbers. She did so with a clarity and accuracy that was unnerving and disturbing to Ana, who held herself quite an authority on the occult and magick. Sofie fell in love with Ana's dreams, and with the vision of Ana, and finally with the reality of Ana. When it came time to reveal her nature, Anastasia had steeled herself for the possibility that she would have to blot out her existence by commanding Sofie to forget her forever.

She needn't have worried. Sofie had smiled her sweetest smile and said, "Then, my love, let us seize the night, as we can never be together during the day."

Ana could almost feel the love that she shared with Sofie as a palpable thing: it surrounded her, kept her warm, kept her calm. Just now, relaxing, she realized how much Selena had goaded her, how close she had been to losing control. She walked the rest of the way up Russian Hill, and through a secret garden to get to the wellnigh hidden brownstone they rented.

The door to the attic apartment in the brownstone was properly locked, so Anastasia was spared that initial shock of dread and panic when one finds one's door ajar, hanging open there like a murderer on a noose. No, she was lulled into a sense of security as she opened the door and made her way through the silent attic, intent on the meal she would soon be creating. It was not until the pungent smell of her lover's blood wafted up to her nostrils that she was hit with the wave of terror.

Ana screamed. She ran down the spiral staircase that joined the lightproof attic with Sofie's studio. She ran through the studio, following the blood-trail that had been left, sickened by the panic and the fear and the intangible desire she felt spring from the warm blood. The blood trail led up to a beautiful antique dressing mirror, one that Anastasia herself had procured for Sofie, who so loved mirrors. The bloody footprints around the body led up to the mirror, and vanished.

Anastasia threw back her head, unwillingly, totally consumed in her frenzy. Skirling, whipping winds rocketed through the suite, breaking ancient porcelain and toppling an expensive antique laboratory set of glassware, shattering it. She lifted her arms up in total submission to the rage, allowing it to consume her and fill her up completely.

The winds stopped, but as if in answer to this chorus of destruction, another sound replaced blowing winds: the crashing of shattered glass. One by one, every pane, cup, plate, mirror, picture frame, and blown-glass art piece exploded in a shower of tiny glass fragments.

And, like the eye of a hurricane, there was sudden calm. Anastasia sank to her knees and then to the floor in supplication to ever dark power and every God she had ever known. She even cried out to Caine in her agony, to come and take her from this pain.

She sank into a timeless state, where her senses dulled and she was unaware of the shards of glass that peppered her skin. She held her eyes, weeping bloody tears, unable to move otherwise. She crouched there for a long time, until the first light of dawn crept over the tops of the expensive houses on the hill.

That light, as faint as it was, caused her to look up. Ana saw through blood-sheened eyes the dawn approaching, and began to feel drawn to it, as she always did. Only now she felt that she would not have the self-control to swing close the heavy shutters that would protect her from the sun.

Anastasia looked at the dawn, helpless to stop it. She knew that she would soon be struck by a sunbeam, but she could not bring herself to care. She looked about the room for something of Sofie's, something she could gaze upon in the bright sunshine before it took her unlife forever.

She saw Sofie's first painting, a beautiful seascape, with a little girl and a dog, hanging slantways in its now-glassless frame. She looked up at it, and sighed, smiling through her tears. She would soon join Sofie. She felt a warmth on the back of her neck, and felt her skin start to bubble under the heat.

And then, as if in answer, she felt a twinge, a definite pang of some kind, some sense which begged to be listened to. She focused her awareness on that twinge, on that merest sliver of a feeling, and felt it brighten. She felt her certainty grow that Sofie was indeed still alive. Her powers, latent and bound though they were, did not fail her. Sofie was still alive, no matter how ridiculous that seemed.

Pain. Pain was needed. Pain, after so much shock, after so much delirium. Pain, to awaken her senses and focus her priorities. She grabbed a shard of glass and jabbed it into her palm, watching it sink in, watching her black blood well up around it. The pain was enough.

She got to her feet and slammed closed first one, then the other heavy shutter, collapsing against it. Anastasia slumped down until she was resting on the floor, her back against the warm shutter.

Then, from exhaustion and wounds, Anastasia fell into unconsciousness.

She dreamed. She dreamed of a happier time, a night almost four years ago. She saw herself and Sofie, on the beach. The moon was bright. Sofie was naked, as she always was on beach, and wet from the water. "No, Ana, no. I want you to promise me. I want you to put away your super powers. I don't want you to use them anymore."

Anastasia shook her head, trying to focus on Sofie. "Why my love? Why? They are a part of me."

Sofie put her fingertip to Ana's lips. "No. No, Ana. They are a part of your old life. Your old ways. And now you're with me. Remember what you told me about that Goal-condra thing?"

"Golconda. Yes. I remember." Anastasia was smiling at Sofie. When she wanted to be charming, she was charming. It didn't hurt that she was teasing Ana the entire time, turning slightly in the firelight.

"Well, that proves it. No more ESP. No more spoon bending or door opening. Nothin'. Okay? You got it?" Sofie was smiling, but her voice was firm.

Anastasia looked very serious. "You're serious, aren't you? You really want me to throw everything away?"

"Not everything, Anastasia. You'll still have me. What do you want? Maybe that's what you have to ask yourself."

Anastasia watched the surf come in, watched it wash out. "I want. . . I want to be with you. . ."

"So promise me. Promise me, and I won't bitch about it any more." Sofie dug in the sand with her toes.

"But. . . what if I need my powers to protect you?" Ana said, looking far out to sea.

"I'm not saying you should throw them away. . . just don't use them. Unless you have to. And I mean, there better be a damn good reason. Now, will you pinky swear?"

"Pinky swear? What's that?"

Sofie laughed. It sounded like the surf in her dream. "You know, a solemn promise. How would you put it? An oath. You gotta swear."

Anastasia smiled at Sofie. She shook out her hair and drew her close. "No, Sofie. I have a better idea. A much better idea."

Then she was suddenly in the beach house, bent over a leaf of parchment. The parchment contained the carefully worded terms of her promise, and she signed it in her own blood. Sofie looked solemnly at Ana, and realized that it was one of those issues that she would not bend on. Ana held her hand while she made the pin prick. Sofie signed her part of the contract in her own blood. She remembered celebrating that pact as one might celebrate a marriage; it was a honeymoon of sorts. The dream turned to the silvery nights they spent by the sea.

The telephone rang. It rang again, incessantly. Ana's eyes were nearly sealed shut from the bloody tears she'd cried, but she managed to open them and find the telephone. The digital clock on the VCR told her it was evening again.

It was Selena's voice. "I imagine by now you've discovered my little plot."

Frenzy boiled up inside her, and she choked it back down. "Where is she, you bitch!"

"Please, please Anastasia. Such language. Let's be civilized shall we? You can certainly sense that she is still alive, no? Or are your powers weak from disuse?"

Anastasia struggled to hold on to her rage. Although she couldn't sense Sofie with her Pact-bound powers, she felt strongly that she would know if Sofie was dead — the sense she had felt earlier had not diminished.

"What do you want with me? What do you want to secure Sofie's release?"

"Ah. 'Secure.' 'Release.' You're talking like a general, Ana. Why not come down from that high horse and talk to me? Remember me, your Selena, your Moon? I have not changed. Perhaps it is you who has changed.

Tell me, are you happy under the yoke of your Sire? Are you pleased that he can control what you do? Are you happy in the Camarilla?"

Anastasia nearly dropped the phone. Looking around, she noticed where she was for the first time. She had managed to crawl, bloody from the piercing glass in her skin, to Sofie's futon, which was ruined now with her black blood. She was weak, hungry, and the Beast within her was rattling its cage.

"Selena. I'll do anything. Just don't harm her. I swear, if you hurt her, I'll make sure you burn in the sun."

"Anything, Anastasia? My, my. The Ana I once knew would've never been so desperate-sounding. She would've steeled herself, and even sacrificed a petty mortal if it suited her purpose. Where is the Ana who faced the Primogen of New York?" She laughed. "Oh, and Ana — I don't have to remind you that you're in no position to make threats."

"Don't toy with me, Selena. Name your price."

"My price? My price? Why, that implies that it is something that can be paid, as a debt is paid. As a Boon is paid. No, no, Anastasia, what I want is something much more than a price. I want your oath. I want your loyalty. I want your soul. I want your blood. I want you, Ana, sweet Ana. And you can have your pretty girlfriend as a pet, if you wish. But you'll serve me. Me, and the sacred Order of the Black Hand, the Sabbat."

Hearing this began to free the Beast, the collar around its neck loosening, weakening. Anastasia's fangs slid into her mouth, and she felt their sharpness next to her tongue.

"And if I refuse?" she whispered, trying to sound cowed when she wanted to loose her hate on the Sabbat bitch.

"Your Sofie will be made glad to join us, and be our cute plaything for a time until we stake her for the sun. You remember what I do with playthings, don't you Ana? Or perhaps you have been neglecting that side of you, as well?" Selena's voice was like frozen diamonds.

Anastasia shuddered. The Beast began to howl against its collar, the leash slipping out of her hands. She watched her fingernails change into talons. "Yes. I remember."

"Very well then. I hope you won't be offended, but I have taken the liberty of preparing an initiation rite for you. Tomorrow evening, when the moon is new, we will perform it. We will welcome either you, or a newly Embraced Sofie, into our brood. If you wish to join us, you'll be there. The church on Beacon street. But I'm sure you already know that, you being such the clever girl. And so well behaved!"

Her voice was rasping, irritating, provoking. She knew what she was doing, and Anastasia was powerless to prevent the Frenzy she was provoking.

"I will be there, Selena," Anastasia said. Her hand shook as she put the phone down on the cradle. She moved to the vase on the fireplace, picked it up, looked at it, considering. Her palsy got worse, her taloned nails scraped against the fine porcelain, and then the vase slipped from her hands. It shattered on the hearth.

Looking down, her eyes clouded with red, she saw the parchment with her blood pact written on it. Her monstrous claws caressed the paper, and she felt a twinge of pain as she saw Sofie's signature in blood there on the page. Her powers, her old life, her old self was waiting, contained in the words of the pact, waiting to be released. And it could only be released one way: through fire, pure cleansing fire. That would make the pact null and void. She thought a moment of Sofie — how she would be alone, terrified, weak, helpless to resist the powers of the vampiress who held her. Her head felt numb, dull, cloudy. She couldn't think straight. She knew that if she took this step she would be breaking a solemn oath, one that she had made in all serious dedication. But Sofie was in danger, a heartbeat away from living life as one of the Damned.

Her claws parted the stiff parchment of the pact with ease. It shredded into long narrow strips with one pass. They fluttered to the floor. Ana felt her power returning, slowly, being freed as it was bit by bit. Without a word, she summoned fire from her blood magic, fire from her own hand to destroy the pact that she had signed.

It burst into flame, another tie gone, another step taken.

Then the Beast struggled again, and this time caught Anastasia unaware. It slipped loose its chain and ran free, blood hunger driving it onward, on to the Hunt.

Time blurred. Ana ran through the streets, her powers cloaking her, her bloodthirst driving her every step. Turning down an alley, she fell upon another kind of hunter and his prey. She fell upon the unlucky rapist, tearing the man apart and feasting on his blood as it welled out of the wounds, rending his flesh as she fed. It wasn't long before the man's heart beat its last, and the world was free of one last foulness. But it had been so long since she had fed, and she was so thirsty, and the Beast demanded more. Her will was like a feeble reed in a torrent of floodwater, and the Beast set her upon the hapless victim as well.

The woman started to flee, but in her frenzy she caught her as well, and could not stop herself from draining the victim, the fear and pain in the victim's blood changing to ecstasy as she drained the last drop, desperately, unthinkingly. Then the cloud of blood-fire lifted, and she realized what she had done, and she held the empty corpse of the woman and cried blood tears over it, having taken one more step closer to her old life.

It was as if the stench and foulness of the city rose up around her to coat her in corruption, to make her its own, to Embrace her again. Standing up to leave, she looked at her blood-soaked hands and realized that she had taken another step down the path away from the light she had shared with Sofie.

"Aren't y'all gonna take care of that little messiness before you go?" A coarse female voice whispered in the dark. Anastasia whirled, her Beast still near the surface, and her night vision revealed a harlot stepping from the shadows.

The harlot looked at her, up and down. "You must be a new lick in town. I'm Princess Victoria. Pleased to meet you." The harlot smiled for a brief moment, and Anastasia's senses flared around the woman, telling her that she was Kindred — as well as a man in whore's costume.

Anastasia waved her hand and the two corpses burst into flames. "Does that satisfy my lady?" She said, her eyes narrowing. She was used to more respect from other Kindred. But that had been long ago.

The Princess immediately reacted to her power, stepping back. "Ah, ah'm terribly sorry ma'am. . . I had no idea that one of the Tray-mare would be stalkin' about my part o' town. I didn't mean no disrespect, you understand. . ."

"I see. Well, then, you can go about your business then. And say nothing to anyone about this."

"That's what I was gonna say, ma'am. That I wasn't gonna say anythin'. But, you see, the Prince, his name's Vannevar, he's a wonderful man. He asked us to tell him if any new licks come into town. And, well, ma'am, I feel kinda obliged to tell him. Unless you were just on your way to see him. You know, to present your-self. . ."

Anastasia's eyes narrowed to slits, and she reached out with her long-unused powers of domination. "Listen to me, you false strumpet, I'll do as I please, and you'll forget that you saw any of this! Do you understand me?"

The Princess's eyes blurred, her body went lax, and she nodded. "Yes ma'am. I do. Thank you, ma'am."

"Very well. Walk north until you reach the street, and awaken to yourself there. Begone!"

Anastasia watched the Princess walk out of sight, and turned and stepped out of the alleyway. The fires had already died down, leaving nothing but gray ash to swirl about in the eddies of wind that blew through the city.

She shuddered, realizing how far she had fallen in so short a time. She contemplated things: if she continued along this path, she would have to present herself before the Prince before too much longer, or else her Sire would have to defend her before the Camarilla.

As she walked home, healing the thousands of tiny cuts on her body as she walked, she failed to notice a pair of gleaming red eyes watching her from a darkened alley.

● ● ●

Anastasia invoked the powers of the Path of Finding, the path she had herself created, and followed the threads of possibility through the city to the church that Selena had described over the phone.

A white-haired vampire met her at the door to the ancient church, black, woolen cowl draped across his mocking grin. She had garbed herself in her ritual Tremere robes. The Eye, the Wand, and the Athame of her office hung from the sash. The vampire turned and called out to the gaping hole of a stairwell leading down: "One comes before the Gate, demanding to be allowed in to Hell! What should I tell her?"

"Tell her that all are equal in Hell, and that she seeks her own doom," came a voice, the ritual response. Ana thought it was Selena's, echoing up the stairwell.

The white-haired vampire smiled and blood oozed from the sides of his mouth. "Blood. Blood. Blood. We are all equal in the Blood." He grinned and reached out his hand; in it he held a burlap bag, open. "Your things of office, you will leave them behind. All are the same in Hell."

She heard a girlish scream, a human scream, echoing up from someplace, someplace far away. "Ana! Don't listen to them! Ana! Get away! Get away from here!" It was Sofie. She was silenced, Ana knew not how, but the quiet was brutal.

Anastasia hesitatingly placed her Wand in the bag, followed by her Athame, and finally, her hands shaking and knuckles white, her Eye, the dark, round onyx jewel glittering in the candlelight. Glad she was that he did not ask to remove her ruby earrings. The white-haired devil vampire then began to laugh, threw back his head and let his fangs grow. She saw his forked tongue dancing about his lips and she shuddered.

"The toll is paid! Lay open the gates for the Damned!" he said, his voice a shrill mockery of humanity.

Two heavy cast iron gates, which had obviously been a decoration in the days when this place was a working sanctuary, flung open. They were covered with entrails from some unrecognizable sacrifice, and the charnel smell coming up from the steps was enough to cause nausea in even Anastasia, whose tastes had been dulled by centuries of unlife.

She carefully stepped down the stairs, bracing herself: they were slippery with blood. She would've certainly been driven close to frenzy if she hadn't been so full with blood, she realized. Everything seemed to appeal to the Beast within her, and she knew it would soon wake from its uneasy slumber.

She suddenly felt a revolting caress, felt sinuous fingers touching her body from all around, and she stood stock-still, knowing that anything that happened here would be a test of sorts. She felt softness on her arm and around her neck and smelled a mixture of woman scent, fresh blood, and earth. She felt a kiss on her shoulders, on her cheek, and on her forehead, and she endured them. She saw the blood-and-earth-streaked face of the one who blocked her way further: a Sabbat woman with streaked red hair, and a wicked smile.

The woman turned and called down the steps as the man had, before. "Hey-yah! Hey! There's one here at the stairs of Hell, coming down the stairs! She wants to pass! What shall I tell her?"

"Tell her that she is doomed, and follows her own folly! Tell her that all truths are bared in Hell, and in Hell, all are naked, so that fires may burn them." Selena's voice again, Ana thought for sure.

The Sabbat bitch smiled a greedy smile as she put her claws up to Anastasia's fine Tremere robes, and ripped it off, exposing her naked body underneath. The woman leered at her. She threw the fine velvet aside and growled at Anastasia. "Go forth with you, Damned soul! Get ye hence!"

She felt a strong hand push her down the stairs, and nearly fell the intervening distance, but caught herself as she came in sight of the floor. The room was bathed in red, the heat was thick and heavy here. Black smoke choked the ceiling, blackened the place, from the many small fires that had been lit here. A hole rose up in the center of the place, and that was the only way smoke could get out.

Selena stood, naked, the headdress of Hell on her head. Two large oiled and tattooed men stood to either side of her, and she had a black, glass dagger in her hand.

"So, there comes one to the fires of Hell, to see what she can see! Why do you come, little girl?" Selena said, mockingly, laughing.

"I come to join the Black Hand," Anastasia said, hoping that the reply was sufficient, not knowing the proper response.

"You? You? Foul creature, do you think you're worthy for the strength of the mighty Black Hand? Do you think the Strength of Caine would take you into their order? How arrogant and stupid a child you are. Take her! Punish her for her insolence!"

The two guards grabbed Ana from either side, and she did not resist them. They bound her feet together, and clasped iron around her wrists. She felt totally powerless, and it was only the comforting presence of the twin ruby earrings that kept her from losing control.

She recoiled in horror, however, when the wooden stake struck her heart, and then she was mostly paralyzed — her heart was not fully penetrated, so she could still move a little. Then she felt twin spikes, twin hooks pierce her back in throbbing pain, and felt her entire weight placed on them. She was hanging on twin meathooks, her feet dangling in the air. Her feet left the ground. She felt her supply of blood leaking down the side of the wounds, felt the terrible cold of the steel that passed through her whole body. She was totally immobile.

Ana felt the Hunger begin to well up in her as the blood flowed out of her faster and faster. Staked though she was, she began to struggle in her grisly bond, and for the first time a sound issued from her mouth, a low growl, animalistic, and full of hunger.

"Yes!! Yes, Anastasia! Now you see! Now you know! Let it come, Anastasia. Do not fight it. You will be reborn! You will be reborn as one of the rightful daughters of Caine! Let it come! Let your hate reforge you!" Selena whispered in her ear, and she retched blood in response. Selena petted her as if she were a sick child.

Anastasia knew that they were trying to make her one of their own, breaking down her humanity and forcing the Beast in her to come out. She shook with impotent rage.

Then she saw Sofie. The white smock she'd been wearing when they took her was torn and bloody, but she was still breathing, still alive. The two brutes brought her in and chained her to the wall, her hands over her head, facing it. Selena then took a scalpel and began to cut the smock from her, and Anastasia had to watch in horror.

Sofie's back was a network of lines that were bleeding once the smock was cut away, and the fresh smell of the blood wafted over to Anastasia and filled her with self-loathing, desire, and disgust.

"Do you desire her, still, Anastasia? Well, I'm afraid that there's another who does as well. The right of feeding has already been claimed." Selena waved to the white-haired devil, who laughed maniacally and leaped forward. He grabbed Sofie's arm and sunk his fangs into her, feeding on her rich vitae.

Anastasia howled. She struggled on her hooks, so much so that Selena was afraid she'd be ripped in two by the meat hooks. Frenzy was past her as she watched what that white devil did to Sofie while he fed, and she felt every ounce of her humanity straining as she was forced to endure the torture along with her love.

When it was over, they opened the manacles and Sofie slid down the wall, the blood from her wounds causing a sickly wet slap on the flagstones.

Anastasia was an angry Beast then, and it was only Selena's powers of domination that kept her in control. Fixing a look in Ana's eyes, Selena told her "Silence!" With that, Anastasia calmed, but the fire behind her eyes was still there.

Selena stepped before Anastasia, who mustered all the control she had. In her hand was a bloody piece of cotton, one of the shredded strips of Sofie's frock. "Do you find this delicious? Did you like what we did?" She asked Anastasia, holding the strip under her nose.

Anastasia swallowed back the black bile rising in her throat and nodded, trying to let the feral fire in her eyes reflect madness, trying to convince Selena that her attempts at destroying her humanity had been successful. Selena smiled as Ana licked at the blood on the cloth.

Selena stepped quietly over to Anastasia and removed the meat hooks from her back. She unlocked the chains that bound her arms and legs, and the stake which pierced her heart. "You must now stand, newest member of the Sabbat. You must now partake in our Rite of Initiation. Share blood with us, Anastasia. Prepare to become known by the One-Who-Walks."

Anastasia smiled dully, but said nothing more, trying to show feral light in her eyes. She barely retained her sense, her humanity, but as long as she had will left, she would survive.

While they prepared the cup of blood for their hated ritual, she quietly undid the earrings on her ears, and popped the ruby stones from their fastenings. Anastasia watched in horror as Selena raised her hands in silent supplication to an unseen force. "Oh, One-Who-Walks, Dread Zarastus, I implore thee, come forth and mark one of your own!" Selena lit, one by one, big black candles that were arranged on the altar where the blood cup rested.

Anastasia slipped the rubies into her mouth and closed her eyes, willing them free of their enchantments. She had to swallow quickly as potent vitae washed into her, flooded through her. Just two quarts of blood from her Sire, but it was potent blood at that, the blood of Etrius, the archmage! When next she spoke, it was not only in her own voice. Her Sire's voice mingled with her own, and she spoke with unearthly tones.

"Selena! Long have I sought another chance to battle you, now it seems my Childe will carry the fight for me!"

Selena whirled, hearing the voice of her ancient enemy, Etrius who had betrayed her and all her kind and branded them all with the Curse of Tremere.

"Etrius?" She called aloud, her voice quavering with barely controlled fear. Her hands dropped to her sides, and the flames on the black candles were snuffed immediately.

"Etrius?"

"Let us say my power is in the blood, Selena! Taste its strength!" And with that, Anastasia sent twin curling bolts of lightning shooting at the Sabbat priestess.

She had no time to delay, and took the full brunt of the powerful blast, her hair singeing off in the process. Again, twin blasts flew forth from Anastasia, and she could feel the waning power of her Sire's blood being spent in their very essence. She screamed aloud in pain, but that did not stop her from reacting to the attack. With two grand gestures, she raised her arms and made a flinging motion at Anastasia.

Almost immediately, Anastasia felt invisible shackles to replace the iron ones that had held her before. With her Sire's blood gone from within her, and with the near-shattering of her own mind, she could not think of a counter-charm to break the bonds. They were proof against her magic, as well. She struggled against them, in vain.

Selena smiled as she watched Anastasia struggle, the Sabbat priestess's face scarred with black gashes from the lightning. With a simple gesture, Selena sent the nearby stake back into Ana's heart, paralyzing her again. The white-haired Sabbat brought Selena the twin earring settings.

Selena smiled. "I see. 'Principle Focus of Vitae Infusion,' isn't it called. . . your Master's vitae? Tsk, tsk. Your sincerity was ever at suspicion, of course, but I had begun to believe that you were ready to embrace the Beast within you. I can see that I was foolish to think one of Etrius' whelps would ever see the true source of Kindred magic. I have risked much in initiating you to this, our sacred order, Anastasia! You have cost me much, and caused a sacred ritual to be ruined. And now you will pay the price for your lack of vision!"

With a gesture, Selena made the invisible chains pull her down to the floor, where she was forced into a kneeling position near the center of the room.

"Sofie doesn't seem to be feeling well. Poor dear. I'm afraid she's going to bleed to death. You're going to be forced to watch her slowly die, unable to do a thing to help her." Anastasia struggled again, but to no avail.

"I imagine that we will see your attitude change during the night, and I think that tomorrow night you may be ready to join our ranks. That is, if you are still alive. You see, the sun comes in to this place. There's a tiny hole in the ceiling, and a little beam of light filters down here on sunny days. Of course, tomorrow could be dreary. I do hope so for your benefit."

Behind her, Selena's warlocks were gathering together the items they had used in the ritual.

"Oh, and, Anastasia, in case you were wondering: this room is warded against all Disciplines and magicks, except mine. It was only the potency of your Sire's blood that broke the ward, and then only briefly. You'll not find an easy escape from this place!"

Selena left after donning her robes, sweeping her cloak behind her, her pack of Sabbat warlocks following. She heard Selena say, "No! Leave those here. They can only be used by her Sire to follow us." There was the soft clink of a bag dropped to the ground, and the group departed. Upstairs, she heard the scrape of iron against stone as the gates were slammed shut.

• • •

Anastasia passed into a numbness, locked as she was by the magical chains. Her mind raced, going back through all her magical training, trying to find something, anything that would save her. There was a gray time, and Sofie moaned and passed in and out of consciousness.

Soon, the light of the sun began to show down from the hole in the ceiling. Sofie stirred. Anastasia turned her head slightly towards her, having discovered that the magical chains allowed her a little freedom of movement.

"Sofie! Sofie! Are you awake?" Anastasia called. A wave of sleepiness washed over her as the sun was rising in the sky.

"Sofie!" Sofie's eyes were half-open, and she looked up at Anastasia. "Ana?"

"Sofie! You have to get me that bag. Get me the bag, sugar. I can save us both."

Sofie crawled her way towards the white cotton bag, wordlessly. Ana wasn't sure if she realized what she was doing. She carried it back in her teeth, and Ana saw in horror that one of her legs had twisted around, broken and utterly useless.

Sofie upended the bag and Anastasia watched as her Eye, her Wand, and her Athame spilled out onto the floor. "The Wand, Sofie. Give me the wand. That stick there. Tuck it in my hand."

The sunbeam was burning its way across the floor. Anastasia's heavy-lidded eyes were barely able to stay open. Sofie uttered a muffled shriek of pain as she moved her body to put the Wand in Anastasia's hand.

Closing her eyes, Anastasia invoked her will, the Blood within her, and the power that streams through both. She felt the Wand react to the power, felt it growing warmer and warmer. She felt the power within her begin to form. When she had shaped it to completion, she let the power go. She felt a surge go through her chains and then. . . nothing. Nothing had happened.

"Damn it! The power wasn't enough, and now I have only a scarcity of vitae! I've failed you Sofie!"

Sofie looked at Anastasia. "Ana? Is that you? I'm gonna die, aren't I? You're really here?"

Anastasia nodded. "Yes, I'm here"

Sofie looked wide-eyed at the sunbeam, burning its way across the floor. "You need blood? I could give you mine."

Anastasia turned away from her. "No, hon, that's fine. You need all of yours. I'm just trying to figure out. . ."

Then she smelled the fresh scent of her lover's vitae. Sofie had cut her wrist with the Athame. "Don't waste it," she said, as she moved forward, forcing her wrist to Ana's mouth. Ana looked at her, and saw the commitment in Sofie's eyes.

"I love you Ana," Sofie said. "I can't live life without you."

Ana took Sofie's wrist into her mouth. Ana steeled herself but could not resist the tremendous ecstasy that flowed through her. Giving in to that feeling, Ana brushed Sofie's mind in a familiar way, and the mental bond they always shared during lovemaking was established. For a second it was as if time stood still, and their souls mingled in that connection. Sofie had made her decision, and gave of herself. Ana felt her lover's last drops of blood leaving her body, felt her essence slip across the connection.

With but single gesture of the Wand, Anastasia was free.

• • •

Anastasia put the white rose on the gravestone, and finished her ritual. A drop of blood was called for, and she took it from her tears. She drew a pentacle on the marker, calling for all spirits in the area to watch this place and keep it safe. She took some of the earth from the fresh grave and put it in a pouch.

She had called Etrius to arrange for the burial, he was happy to hear from her and even managed to show sadness at her having lost Sofie. He was more than willing to help her with the financial arrangements: provided that she present herself to the Prince of San Francisco immediately.

She walked back down the hill, closed the cemetery gate behind her, and stepped to the waiting limousine. Her driver was a ghoul of the Tremere elder, who had already telephoned her at her brownstone to pay his respects. As the limo passed through town, up Russian Hill, on the way to Sebastian's Club, she caught a glimpse of her former home, her Ivory Tower, the brownstone she and Sofie shared. She realized that it would never do as a Haven in this city, that she would have to move uptown, perhaps closer to the Chantry.

Whether Selena had known she had escaped or not, the Sabbat bitch had not come seeking her. Perhaps she wasn't as powerful as she had thought. Anastasia was still deeply concerned about the name Zarastus, One-Who-Walks... could that be her Sire? Or perhaps a darker creature, for the Sabbat were said to truck with forces from Hell?

She would meet the Prince garbed in her robes of office, having reclaimed and mended them from the vestibule of the church. Checking them before she changed in the limo, she found something, something which told her that Selena wasn't finished with her.

It was a pendant, a stone circle. On one side was Sumerian art, the visage of the Goddess Inanna, Queen of Heaven, and on the other, the Crescent Moon, Selena's sigil. ☥

EXPENDABLE

by Lois Tilton

Kyle woke to the certain, gut-deep knowledge that something was wrong.

He rolled into a crouch, the lethargy of sleep replaced by sudden dread. All senses alert, scanning the fetid darkness. "Fang," he whispered out loud, but there was no answer from the silence.

"Fang!" This time his call was a cry of desperation, and the dull echoes rang back at him, mocking: Now you're alone. . . alone. . . alone.

He had learned, in all these years since his escape from the vampire, what it really meant to be alone, to hide in the dark, to run from the sight of a human face, speaking to no one — no one except a mongrel dog. If it hadn't been for Fang, he was afraid he might even have forgotten how to speak, so far away from the world he had hidden himself. The dog had kept him human all this time. At least. . . he could let himself believe he had some faint vestige of humanity left to him. For he knew what he had become, and the knowledge was the root of all his despair.

More than just a companion, Fang was his guard, standing watch during the daytime hours when he was helpless and vulnerable. But now it was sunset, Kyle was awake, and there was no sign of the familiar presence. Fear churned deep in his belly. What had happened to the dog? A car, some lunatic with a gun? Or some other, more sinister element? The earthquake last night had really bothered Fang. Maybe it had disturbed his senses somehow.

"Fang!"

This time, as the echoes of his cry faded down the length of the empty tunnel, he thought he heard a response, a faint howl, almost like a wolf's.

The sound finally brought him to his feet, running quickly down to the abandoned access shaft. San Francisco was like a molehill, riddled with tunnels. Someone had begun, then abandoned this project maybe as much as a hundred years ago. Kyle didn't know or care why. But now he hesitated, as he always did, emerging into the world aboveground. Tonight, without Fang at his side, the last fading streaks of sunlit cloud beyond the city's hills seemed colored with menace.

The recent recession had accelerated the decline of this part of the waterfront into decay. But despite the air of desolation, Kyle didn't dare call Fang aloud, not out here in the open. Instead, he searched with all his senses cast as wide as possible, for a sound of him, for the faint, inexplicable touch of the animal's mind. And felt it, from somewhere in the direction of the docks.

After a few minutes, he caught sight of the familiar form coming toward him, but his relief was cold, because Fang was limping. Recognizing him, the dog whined, a sound of pain and distress, and Kyle suddenly caught the unmistakable scent of blood.

Something raked in his gut, a burning, acidic Hunger. In his mind, the vampire's voice laughed mockingly: Feed it, boy! Feed the Beast! Let it howl!

He clenched his teeth against it, so hard that his fangs bit down on his lower lip. He felt the sharp heat of his own blood burning his tongue. Somehow, the taste of it helped him regain control. As Fang came limping up to him, Kyle fell to his knees, put his arms around the rough, matted gray coat, sticky and clotted with gore. The dog had been hurt. One ear was ripped half-off, and there were bite wounds on his face, neck, shoulders.

The animal whimpered again and pushed eagerly against him, licking at his face. Kyle knew what he wanted and allowed him to lick the blood from his lower lip, where it had run down to his chin. He closed his eyes and held him tightly, feeling the animal warmth of the living creature, the heart that beat so strongly. He was worried sometimes that he might have passed on the terrible curse of his blood to the dog, but Fang was unquestionably still alive.

"What the hell did you run into out there, boy?"

Fang had no collar to protect his throat, but for his own reasons Kyle would never put a collar on any animal, especially not Fang, who had come to him freely.

It had been near the foot of the bridge, in a night shrouded by fog. He was constantly drawn back to the bridge, where it had all begun, meaning to put an end to the curse of his unnatural existence. A million times before, chained in the vampire's cellar, he had told himself that it had all been a mistake, that he had never meant to jump, not really.

But that night, when it was too late and he was finally free from the vampire who had transformed him into another, then, he did jump, only to find himself being dragged down by the water to the bottom of the bay. Not needing to breathe, of course he couldn't drown. He couldn't die. He couldn't even die.

He had crawled out at last, weak with exhaustion after fighting the current and the weight of the water. Some rusting wreckage offshore had sliced his hands and arms. He was lying there at the foot of the bridge with the blood dripping slowly onto the ground, when a shadow had fallen over his face. At first he thought it might be a wolf, with the lolling red tongue and sharp white teeth, but the head was too massive, the gray coat shaggy and tangled.

The dog licked at his face. He felt the breath, the hot, soft tongue wiping away his tears. Then the animal yelped sharply, shook his head from side to side. Kyle had struggled up to his elbow, tried to wave him away, but the dog approached again, slowly, stiff-legged, whining. His muzzle pushed against his hands and licked at them, lapping up the slowly seeping blood.

From that time, Fang had never left him — not until tonight. Now Kyle let him lick his face clean of blood again, while he carefully stroked the shaggy wounded head and neck.

"There it is! That's the damned mutt!"

Kyle sprang to his feet, and Fang at his side spun around to face the enemy, teeth bared, snarling.

There were two of them, approaching with a light, confident swagger. As he caught sight of their faces, though, revulsion struck Kyle. They were monsters, visibly monsters. Tusks protruded from elongated muzzles, nostrils gaped. One was entirely hairless, which exposed his misshapen skull; on the other, shaggy brows accentuated the bestial ridge over his eyes. There was no living warmth to them, no heartbeat. With horror, Kyle realized: they were what he was.

Do I look like that? Involuntarily, his hands went to his face, and the strangers laughed mockingly. "What'sa matter, cat? Can't find your mirror tonight?"

"He can't stand it he's not pretty like we are!"

As they laughed, Kyle said nothing, remembering the vampire's warning: They'd find you out there, boy. The Kindred. Eat your heart out right on the spot. They don't tolerate strangers in their territory.

In hiding all these years, afraid to let anyone know of his existence — his own kind most of all. Now Kyle wanted to run, but he knew how fast they'd be on him if he did. He had to stand and fight. And there was Fang.

One of them took a step toward the dog, saying, "Like I said, when I get my hands on that damn mutt —"

Fang's matted fur had risen to a ridge along his spine. His growl had a menacing pitch.

"Leave him alone."

The monster turned to Kyle. "What you say?"

He clenched his fists, taking his cue from Fang. Tightly, "I said, 'Get out of here, leave the dog alone.'"

They circled to surround him, their hideous faces distorted by fanged grins. "Well, listen to the neo! Telling us to get out!"

"Hey, this is Sewer Rat turf. We don't like no strange licks on our ground."

"And we don't like no damn dog following us around, spying. Gonna take care of you and your mutt."

The bald one swung on Kyle. There was some kind of blade in his hand. Kyle barely glimpsed the gleam of metal, the monster struck so fast, but Kyle twisted away in time. Then Fang, snarling, leaped to meet the attack.

As the dog's teeth closed around the monster's arm, Kyle was staggered by a blow from behind. He turned, weaponless, and saw the shaggy-browed one swinging a motorcycle chain. On the end was a spiked metal ball, and the tearing pain in his back knew it was what had hit him.

"C'mon," whispered the monster, still grinning hideously. "C'mon, alley cat, let's play!" The chain swung in a circle. Around. Around.

And because he was desperate, because he knew he was cornered and trapped, Kyle did the only thing he could. He grabbed for the chain, hoping to pull it to him or jerk it out of the monster's hand.

But instead he took the blow across his wrist, cracking the bone. The chain swung back again, and down, and the spikes raked him from his shoulder across his chest. He stumbled back. The chain hit his left elbow. At the sound of his cry, his enemy laughed, swung his weapon again, this time at the side of Kyle's head. He only barely managed to dodge away from the vicious spikes.

He could hear Fang yelping in pain, but he couldn't do anything to save his dog, he was almost helpless himself now.

"Hey, hold it!"

Someone's voice. Someone. . . a woman's voice.

He turned toward it, but this time he couldn't dodge the chain fast enough. The force of the blow knocked him to the ground.

"I said, 'Hold it!'"

Kyle was on the ground, curled up to try to protect himself, waiting for the chain to hit him again. But the ground, suddenly, shifted under him, the earth itself trying to shake him off.

Through a painful haze, he realized: it was a quake!

For an eternal moment, it was all there was, the uneasy earth shuddering. It was impossible to think, to react. Then it was over, and in the sudden, awed silence, he heard the woman's voice again, exactly as if nothing had happened.

"Don't you two jerks listen? I told you to hold it. This isn't the right dog!"

"Huh?"

She was getting up from her knees, brushing off the rags she was wearing. "This isn't the same dog, clotbrain!"

"Oh. Yeah, well, what about him?"

"You two just get out of here. I'll take care of him."

"He was on our turf."

"Yeah, and the damn dog almost ripped my arm off!"

"Did you hear what I said?"

"All right! OK!"

The two picked themselves up and retreated, looking back with sullen resentment. Kyle stared at his rescuer. What he saw looking down on him was a bag lady, authentic from the shapeless hat down to the men's basketball shoes. But in another moment something seemed to shift in his blurred vision, and he could see beyond the wrinkled face to another, even more grotesque, sister to the monsters who'd attacked him.

Then he heard a whimper, and he looked up to see Fang lying a few feet away, panting shallowly.

Gritting his teeth against the pain of movement, he crawled to his dog. If Fang had been hurt before, it was nothing to this. The injured animal whined again, and licked his face where the spikes had torn it.

"That your dog, huh?"

He glared defiance at the bag lady/monster. "Yeah, he's mine."

"So, well, sorry about the mess here. The boys made a mistake. They were looking for someone else, some lupe who's been shadowing us for a couple days now. In fact, I think your dog here had a run-in with it. That's how the mix-up happened."

Grief and anger made him reckless. "Hell of a lot of good it does, being sorry."

"Hey, dog's not gonna die or anything, you know. Not if he's yours."

Kyle stared dubiously at Fang, then touched the place on the side of his face where the dog had licked. Fang did seem better now. The dog's wounds had stopped bleeding.

He looked away quickly, not to see the blood, not to want it. The Hunger pang knew better. It had been too long since he'd fed. But no matter how strong the bloodlust, he would not use Fang that way.

"And just whose whelp are you?"

He didn't mean to answer her, but she took hold of his hair and dragged his face up to meet hers — her true face, shown to him now it all its hideous nakedness, the illusion gone. "What is it with these new generations? They don't seem to hear a thing I say! Who are you, neo? Who gave you the Kiss?"

He understood her then and shook his head. "He. . . never told me his name."

She snorted in amused contempt. "He never released you, either, did he? What'd you do? Run away? You did, didn't you? I oughta turn you in, y'know."

Turn him in? To whom, or what? Kyle didn't know what she was talking about, exactly, but the vampire had warned him: "As far as the Kindred are concerned, boy, you're not supposed to exist. They'd kill you on sight."

Now he said nothing, not knowing what might be dangerous to say.

She only shrugged. "Not that the Rats give a damn." She was staring at him now, even closer. "Tell me, what is that? Around your neck?"

He realized then for the first time that his shirt must have been torn in the fight, and he tried to conceal the shameful metal collar around his neck, but she pulled his hand away, stronger than he was. "Well, well! This is interesting! You may be worth my trouble, after all! Do you know what these symbols are on this thing?"

He didn't answer.

"Your Sire put this on you, did he?"

He tried to pull away, but again she made him look at her, and he felt his will crumple. "Yes! He put it on me! He kept me chained to a wall. For years. Every couple of days, he'd come and. . ."

Kyle couldn't make himself say it.

"He fed from you?" She was clearly fascinated.

He turned his face away. Against his will, he was reliving those years chained in that black cellar, like an animal, the collar around his neck. The constant, terrible, devouring Hunger in his gut, relieved only when the vampire would come into the room and throw him some beast — a dog or cat or laboratory rabbit. The self-disgust he would always feel as he ripped at their flesh with his fangs, sucking out the blood. And the vampire watching, laughing: "That's right! Feed, boy! You need to build up your blood!"

Sometimes, instead, it was plastic bags of blood, cold and black and tasting faintly of decay. From some hospital dumpster, maybe. Spoiled blood, diseased blood. Always, driven half-mad by the Hunger, he would drain the bags, down to the very last foul drop.

"I said, 'How'd you get away?'"

"Huh?" Kyle hadn't been listening.

"With that thing around your neck — how did you get away?"

"It was the quake. The big one."

"Hey, you're not that old!"

"No, I mean the one a few years ago." He shook his head, couldn't remember the years. "The quake hit, and the wall collapsed where he had me chained. I pulled the staple out."

"And your Sire? What about him? Don't tell me he didn't come looking for you."

"I don't know. He wasn't there when it happened. He wasn't ever there during the day."

Which was a lie. She looked hard at him a moment, as if she knew it was a lie, and he struggled to pull his eyes away from hers.

Then he was released. "So, what are we going to do with you now?"

"Just get the hell out of here, all right? Leave me alone!"

"Oh, no!" she laughed. "We can't do that. The boys may have made a mistake about your dog, but they're right, this is too close to our territory. I'm surprised you got away with staying here this long. Besides, what would you do? How many years do you think you can spend down in the sewers without going crazy? What do you exist on, you and that mutt — the garbage and rats out of the dumpsters?"

The humiliation, the truth of it, rankled. "I survive," he snarled.

"You don't know anything, do you? About the Kindred. What we are. The Traditions."

"I know all I want to know."

"Don't be stupid. You're one of us, whether you like it or not. But what you don't know can get you killed. That's right: killed. In case you think it can't happen to you."

He glared at her.

"Look, with no Sire, no Clan, you've got no standing, don't you see? No one responsible for you. We don't all of us think the same way about the Rules, but nobody wants trouble coming down on all our heads. And that's just what you are — trouble."

She stared down at him, then seemed to make up her mind. "All right. You wait here. I'll be back. I know where I can take you, for now. Oh, in case anyone asks, I'm Vika."

With a flutter of rags, she disappeared into the night.

Kyle waited, only because it was too much effort to do otherwise. From time to time, he let Fang lick his face or one of the other places the spikes had torn him, though the bleeding had mostly stopped. He hurt all over. The cracked bone in his wrist grated every time he tried to move. There was no way he could pick up Fang and carry the dog back to the tunnel, and no way Fang could walk with his injuries. So he sat there with him, and he waited, and he felt the Hunger growing in his belly, gnawing on him, raking him with its claws.

All the things she'd said just served to confirm the warnings the vampire had given him years ago. That others of his kind would destroy him on sight if they ever found out he existed. A stake through his heart —

The way he'd driven a stake into the vampire. When the wall collapsed, setting him free and pinning his tormentor at the same time. A long, sharp spike of wood, right through the heart.

Only, he didn't think it would be a good idea to let Vika or any of the rest of them know about that.

• • •

After maybe an hour, a black panel truck came bouncing over the ground and pulled up next to them. Vika opened the door, not a bag lady anymore but something like an over-the-hill hooker on her night off, wearing a scarlet cheongsam style dress, very tight, with the slit all the way up to the top of her hipbone. There was a face to match, but Kyle could see the illusion wavering if he stared hard. He looked away, avoiding the sight of yellowed tusks and gaping nostrils.

"OK, climb in."

"I'm not leaving the dog," he said stubbornly.

"Not leaving the dog." She got out of the van, opened the back door, then came and looked down at Fang. "Come on, boy, into the back." Fang whined.

"Tell him to get into the van," she told Kyle.

Kyle stood up painfully and went to the back of the truck. "Into the van, boy." To his surprise, Fang got to his feet and limped toward him. Vika grabbed hold of the dog and lifted him up until he could climb inside. "See, I told you he'd be fine. A day or so, and he'll be good as new. All right, now you."

Kyle shrugged off her help and got into the passenger side by himself.

It was unsettling to be riding in a vehicle after so long. He found himself clutching at the door with his cracked wrist while Vika drove heavy-footed through the nighttime streets. As they came careening down Powell, all he could think of was whether her brakes had been serviced lately. Where does a vampire monster go to get her brakes relined, anyway?

Something rolled out from under the seat, and he picked it up, saw it was an airline bottle of vodka. Unwillingly, he thought of Bloody Marys. He was half-tempted to turn around and see if there was a body or something in the back of the van with Fang, but it was partitioned off. The fact did nothing to ease his nerves.

As if she could sense his thoughts, she slowed down at a corner, causing a half-dozen streetwalkers to look up and display their wares. "Care to stop for dinner, first?" she grinned at him.

He shook his head, fighting down the Hunger inside him, the part of him that wanted blood, pumping hot and rich as he fed.

"No!"

She sneered. "Too bad. But I didn't think you were the type."

Soon they were coming into the Marina District, and Kyle started to get even more uneasy, wondering just where they were going. But when Vika turned into a drive leading up to the gate in a high wall, his misgivings turned to actual panic.

"Hey, wait! We can't go in here! I mean. . ."

She grinned again. "Yeah. Look at you."

He hadn't seen himself, hadn't really looked at himself in years of hiding away in the dark. But now he did, and the shame almost made him sink down to the floor of the van. His clothes had been stripped off winos passed out in the alleys. They were torn, stained with layers of filth and grime. His hands — he stared at them

— were dark with ground-in dirt. His nails were black. He realized that he smelled repulsive.

"No! I can't go into a place like this!"

But Vika ignored his protests, drove past a guard house, through the gate past the large brass plaque that said:

THE ALEXANDRIAN CLUB
FOUNDED 1917
PRIVATE
MEMBERS ONLY

"Don't worry! There's no dress code." She pulled up in front of the clubhouse. "Come on, let's go."

He was going to refuse, but she tossed her keys to the uniformed valet coming up to the van, and he had no choice. To his surprise, she went around to the back and helped the dog down. Seeing Fang, Kyle was even more ashamed. The dog was a mess, even more so than ever, with his fur all matted and clotted with blood.

"Look," she said, seeing that he was going to refuse to go into the place, "This is neutral ground, all right? No matter what your Clan, if you're Kindred, you're OK here. Just remember: you're under my protection." She looked down at the dog. "And he belongs to you."

Kyle noticed that she had totally dropped the illusion now, was headed toward the door naked-faced, all her grotesque features exposed for whoever to see, and he finally figured, hell, if she could go in there looking like that, maybe he could, too.

But one look at the inside of the club, opulent with all the wood paneling, the rugs, and he stopped cold. Vika ignored him. She went over to a man leaning against the desk at the side of the room.

"Hey, Tex, you on the front desk tonight?"

"Well, Vika, honey! You know how hard it is to get good help around here." He grinned, even while he was glancing back over her shoulder at Kyle, who wanted to evaporate into nothing. "We don't see you around the club much these days, do we?"

She shrugged. "When I've got business. I got business now. But, listen, maybe you could get someone to take care of my protégé, here, OK?"

He raised a slightly dubious eyebrow. "Your get?"

She laughed. "Not likely! Not with that face! Let's just say he's under my protection for tonight, OK? Oh, and the dog's his. Maybe you could, like, get them cleaned up some? They had a little misunderstanding with the boys."

"It's on your tab, Vika."

"Ain't it always! Thanks, Tex."

She disappeared, and the man named Tex watched her leave the foyer. He turned in Kyle's direction. "So. It's been a tough night, huh?"

Tex's voice had a soft twang, and he was wearing a fancy cowboy shirt with slash pockets. But he was a vampire. He had no human warmth, no heartbeat. The utter incongruity was about all that kept Kyle from fleeing back out the door. That, and Fang.

Tex leaned down to carefully rub the animal's wounded head.

"Looks like your dog here could use himself a big old raw steak. And maybe you're a little bit hungry, yourself?"

Kyle nodded, all the response he could manage. As Tex led him into the opulence of the lounge, a young living woman in a low-cut evening gown crossed the room. Kyle stopped, drew back, even as the Hunger lusted to dig its fangs in her bare throat, drink up her spurting blood. He repressed the urge desperately, imagining the horrible, obscene rites that must go on in a place like this — no matter how classy it looked like on the outside.

Tex turned and gave him a searching stare. "Around here, Kindred keep their hands off what doesn't belongs to them."

"No, I didn't. . . I wouldn't. . ."

Tex nodded. "Just so you know. It's not my business. Vika says she's responsible for you, she stands for your sins. Just — remember."

Kyle nodded again, completely lost and intimidated in this place.

"Good." Tex gave him another look, then said, "Come on." He led him through a dining room where a couple sat at a table drinking coffee, and through into a gleaming kitchen. The cook working at one counter gave him a familiar nod as he crossed to a refrigerator, pulled it open and took out a familiar-looking plastic bag filled with dark red fluid. "I think maybe you'd rather have this. Am I right?"

"Please," Kyle said hoarsely, and watched with hungry intensity as the vampire in the cowboy shirt decanted the bag into a large glass and put it into a microwave.

"We keep quite a bit of this on hand," Tex said conversationally. "I admit, I don't care for the stuff myself, and most of our guests bring their own retainers, but we get some like you, too. Trick is. . ." he popped open the microwave, "to warm it up just enough to take the chill off. Here."

Kyle reeled at the warm scent of the blood. With shaking hands, he took the glass from Tex and inhaled a deep swallow. The Hunger protested momentarily that the blood wasn't pumping hot from some dying victim's arteries, but it soon subsided. This blood was fresh and clean, and the warmth made it seem almost alive.

"Thanks," he finally gasped, setting down the empty glass.

"No problem, that's what we're here for. Now maybe you might like to clean up a little?"

"Please."

Tex showed him to the well-appointed men's room with a shower stall in the back, and Kyle gratefully stripped off his filthy clothes and started to scrub the grime out of his skin, one layer at a time. For the first time in years, he felt almost human again, and there in the shower he paused for a moment, wondering if he could ever go back to his unlife of hiding underground, and what other existence there could be for the kind of thing he was. This place, this club, was so far outside the possibilities he'd ever been able to imagine. Could it possibly be that he belonged here? Tex's look of warning made him doubt it. Not all alone, at any rate.

When he finally came out of the shower, there was a folded pile of clothes left discreetly on a counter. His old ones, thankfully, had disappeared. There were cord slacks and an olive-brown turtleneck sweater that fit him almost perfectly. He pulled the turtleneck up to hide the metal collar around his neck, grateful for whoever had chosen it, and without thinking he looked up at the mirror to see if the collar was visible.

And he saw his face.

For a moment, the shock left him unable to think. Then he wiped the steam away from the mirror and just stared. It was his face, unchanged from the last moment he'd seen it, almost 10 years ago. He touched it — the eyelids, the nose, the mouth. Then the half-healed marks of the beating he'd taken just a couple hours ago, still sore to the touch. But it was still him. He could see himself, and he hadn't visibly changed at all.

His finger probed his mouth, felt the fangs there, retracted. Almost not at all. Vampire, he said to the image in the mirror. Admit it, finally. What you are.

Or, as they seemed to call it around this place, Kindred. But, he recalled, he was kin with no ties, no rights, not even the right to exist.

He left the room, wandered back out into the lounge, no longer feeling like they were going to throw him out with the trash. Another couple was in the dining room now, one human and one not. A waiter came up to him. "Sir? May I help you?"

"I wanted. . . have you seen a dog? A big, gray dog? He was hurt."

"Your retainer? Yes, Sir. He'll be brought to you when the vet is finished with him."

The vet?

"Will there be anything else?"

He hesitated. The Hunger was subdued in him, but still alive. "If I could. . ." How do you ask for a glass of blood, slightly warmed to take the chill off?

But the waiter seemed to know before he could ask. "Another drink, Sir?"

Gratefully, he replied, "Yes, please."

"Perhaps you'd like it in the bar."

The bar was all polished brass and dark red velvet, the color of blood. In the back of the room, the girl in the evening gown was leaning over a billiards table. The waiter brought his drink to a table, and Kyle sat down, sipped the tepid blood, and tried to understand how a place like this could exist. How it could seem so normal.

After a while, the waiter came in leading Fang, and Kyle knelt down to see the dog, who panted and wagged his tail furiously. He'd been washed, clipped, and a couple of the worst wounds sewn up.

"Is that your dog?"

The girl was looking at them. "Yes, he's mine."

"Poor thing. What happened to him?"

"He got into a fight. With some other dog, I think." The scent of her living warmth was starting to effect him. He turned away and took a large sip from his glass.

Then he saw Vika coming into the bar with a man dressed in a black suit, another vampire. At a single gesture from the vampire, the girl put her cue down on the billiards table and left.

"Around his neck?" he asked, and pulled down Kyle's turtleneck without asking permission. Something in his manner made Kyle simply hold still for it.

For a moment the vampire examined the metal collar, tracing the symbols on it with a fingertip. "Yes, I see. Yes, you're quite right, of course. It is certainly Hervi's. This is very much of interest to the Chantry. We are in your debt."

"I can deal with that," Vika retorted smugly.

Then the vampire grasped the collar in both hands, subvocalized a phrase, and twisted. The ring separated into two parts.

Kyle gasped, clutched his neck. "How did you —" But the look the vampire gave him made the question die in his throat.

"The Chantry would of course be even more interested in finding Hervi himself."

Vika nodded briskly. "If I find out anything, I'll let you know." She glanced at Kyle. "How can you drink that puke? Never mind, let's go."

But the vampire placed a cold hand on Kyle's shoulder. "One might say that this was a matter for the Chantry, too."

"One might, if the Chantry acknowledged him. Are you gonna sponsor him, Sion? No, I didn't think so. Then again, one might say this whole mess oughta go to for judgment to the Prince. Or maybe even a Conclave. You wanna call a Conclave?"

"We don't lay our affairs open to outsiders."

"From what I've heard," Vika said carefully, and Kyle noticed she kept her eyes turned away from Sion's, "maybe you don't lay all your affairs in front of the Chantry. Maybe I should go to Honerius with this matter, instead?"

The vampire scowled. "We'll be in contact. This issue isn't settled."

"I'll be in touch," Vika said, bodily half-lifting Kyle out of his chair.

"What's this all about?" he whispered furiously when they were outside, heading to her van. "Who was that guy?"

"Business," she said shortly, opening up the back to let Fang in. "My business."

"Well, what about me? You let him just take that thing!"

She snorted. "You wanted to keep it around your neck? Anyway, Sion's Tremere. Your Clan. Or at least, they'd be your Clan if you had one, which you don't, 'cause you're not bound to them and they don't like that kind of thing one bit."

She gunned the van into life and headed down the driveway at an unsafe speed. "I was almost sure when I saw that thing around your neck — those symbols. Information's my business, in case you couldn't tell. So, your Sire's name is Hervi. He was deep into Thaumaturgy — Blood Magic — a while back, but he carried things too far. Way too far. Tremere's been looking for him for a long time now. There was talk of a Blood Hunt, even. No one knew he was here in the Domain. Makes things real interesting, y'know."

"I don't know a damn thing that's going on around here!"

She laughed, a sound that was starting to get on his nerves. "I know you don't. That's why you're not going anywhere right now, isn't it?"

She pulled the van over abruptly. Kyle looked around, anxious. He wasn't quite sure where they were.

"I could tell you some things about yourself, things you really ought to know if you're gonna survive. Like, for example, why some people are gonna want to get their hands on you, real bad. Only, in the information business, things have to go both ways. You know what I mean?"

Kyle looked away uncomfortably. "I don't know anything about this Hervi, whoever he is. Only what he did to me."

"Or where he is now?"

Kyle felt the dead, cold weight of his lie. He kept his eyes turned away from hers, not daring to meet them and be trapped. "I told you, I don't know! There was the earthquake, the wall collapsed, and I got away!"

"And Hervi never found you again?"

"That's right!"

She shook her head. "No, that's not right. With that thing around your neck, he wouldn't have had any trouble at all."

Involuntarily, his hand went to his throat, where the weight of the metal collar had choked him for so long. "I don't know why, then. Maybe he's dead?" Getting dangerously too close to the truth.

She shook her head again. "Hervi? Dead? Not bloody likely. Not that one!"

But the image came into his mind: the vampire lying there on the cellar floor, half-buried under the collapsed stone wall. How he had picked up the sharp piece of splintered wood, raised it over his head, brought it down with all the force he could, to drive it through the vampire's heart.

He decided to dare it. "Why not? Why couldn't he be dead? Maybe he. . . got caught outside in the sun somehow, when the quake hit."

She looked thoughtful. "Maybe. Accidents can happen to anyone, I guess. But Hervi was a lot more than he was supposed to be. If he is dead, well, I know of more than one lick who was real hungry for his blood."

Kyle was still remembering those years chained naked in the cellar, the vampire bending over him, fangs digging into his arms, his thighs, the dark blood smearing the vampire's face afterward, and the sensuous way he'd lick it from his lips. Hervi. Giving him a name didn't change anything. "I hated him so much. I never knew. . . vampires would. . . do that kind of thing. To each other."

Vika shrugged, put the van into gear again. "Like I said, there's a lot you don't know. That's just one reason the Elders want to get their hands on your Sire Hervi."

"A lot you won't tell me."

"That's right. Not for free."

She was pulling into a parking space now, somewhere just off Broadway. "Now what?" he asked.

"Now what is I'm hungry, that's what. You can drink swill out of a plastic bag if you want, but I'll take the real stuff, thanks." She twisted around under the seat, exposing more than a little of her legs and rear end, and came up with a pair of spike heeled shoes. "Damn things," she muttered viciously, getting out of the van. The red-lipped illusion of a cheap hooker was clamped on tightly over the ugliness of her real face. "Oh, and get that dog out of the back."

He did, and sat up front with Fang's head in his lap, wondering at the animal's remarkable recovery. It had to be the blood, he thought — his blood. But what was the dog now?

His own injuries were healing just as quickly. In a pensive mood, he made a small cut on the outside of his good wrist and held it out to Fang, who licked the welling blood eagerly. It certainly didn't seem to be doing the dog any harm.

He had too much time to think, waiting. If anyone had told him, back almost 10 years ago when he walked onto that bridge, that this was what it was going to be like. . .

I wasn't going to do it, he protested again. I wasn't going to jump. Not really.

But now what? He'd freed himself from the vampire's cellar, but then shut himself up again in the tunnels, another version of the same prison. Now here he was in this van —

Then he heard a familiar laugh, answering a man's voice. "Oh, yeah, Baby, we're gonna have a great party, right here in back of my van! You'll see! Got a bed back here, and booze, and everything!"

The back door opened, the van's shocks sagged and protested. "See! Now ain't this better than some seedy, flea-bitten cheap hotel!"

In the front, Kyle was forced to listen as Vika entangled her victim with sex and alcohol. Soon he could almost taste the sharp, tantalizing scent of human blood, warm and alive. His fangs ached to extend themselves, the Hunger in his belly twisted. Fang lifted his head and whimpered softly.

Kyle held the dog tight. He wanted it. Wanted it so much. Shortly later there was a tap on the partition behind the front seats. "Hey, you wanna come back here to give me a hand?" His own, one-time experience had led him to expect a corpse with a torn-open throat. Instead, Vika handed him out a man who looked like he was passed out, but unmistakably still alive, and without even a visible wound on him. "You didn't —"

"Kill him? What, you think we all kill every time we feed? Just dump him over there, next to the curb. He'll wake up in the morning and think he had a damn good time, that's all. Unless he gets rolled, of course, but that's not my business."

There was a smear of blood on the man's cuff. Kyle stared at it avidly, aching with need, despite the blood he'd consumed in the club. It was never enough, not really. Not like the real thing.

Vika laughed unpleasantly. "So! You want some?"

He dropped her victim. "No!"

She stood looking at him. "Tell me. You ever done it? I mean, really done it?"

"Once," he admitted, full of shame. "I killed her. And. . . I liked it too much."

"Sure you did. And now you let it claw you up on the inside, trying to deny what you are. Oh, I've met your kind before. They don't last long, let me tell you."

She got back into the van, waited for him. "OK, you did it once. And you couldn't stop till it was too late? Right?" She didn't wait for him to acknowledge it. "Then what?"

"I ran."

"Ran away and left the body, right? Now that's why the Kindred can't afford to have someone like you running around loose, leaving a big mess behind. No self-control, no common sense!"

He said nothing to defend himself, only looked up sullenly when he saw they were pulling into a parking garage. "Now what?"

She rolled her eyes. "In case you haven't noticed, it's getting late? Or do I need to tell you what happens when the sun comes up, too?"

In an instant of panic, he twisted around to look out at the fading night, as if the sunlight were going to burn through the back of the van at that moment. In fact, with everything that had happened, the impending sunrise had been the last thing on his mind. "So what do we do?"

"Well, I can't take you back with me. The boys wouldn't like it. You're not our kind. And I still want to hang on to you for a little while. So, like I told the john, it's real comfortable in the back. Nice and snug. And dark.

"But you better go let the dog out for a while before you bring him inside."

• • •

Vika seemed to have the dog on her mind a lot. "Take the dog out," was just about the first thing she said when they woke up at sunset the next day.

"Why don't you get that dog something to eat?"

"Doesn't that dog need some exercise?"

Kyle wasn't exactly stupid. He figured she was talking on the van's cellular phone whenever he was gone with Fang, that she didn't want him to hear whatever she was saying. It was business.

And it didn't seem to be going very well, either. Vika was visibly nervous as she drove through San Francisco's hilly streets, looking back behind her in the side mirror. Business. Buying and selling. And he was the commodity. He was — or what he knew about the vampire named Hervi.

Dangerous business. "So what's in it for me?" he wanted to ask. "After you're paid off and they've got what they want, what happens to me?"

Kyle's lie was a strangling lump in his throat. None of them believed him. Or wanted to believe him. Or maybe they had some way to sense he knew more than he was saying.

I killed him. I drove a stake through his heart and killed him.

Vika parked the van again. Kyle looked out. They were in the old military cemetery on the grounds of the Presidio.

She turned to him. "Stay here. I've gotta meet with some people."

He stared through the film of dead moths that smeared the windshield. He could see her approaching the Two Bits monument. She'd changed into dark jeans and a leather vest laced at the front, dug out of the piles of garments that littered the back of the van. Toward her, a figure was coming from out of a grove of trees, a man wearing black, a vampire. Kyle eased the door open, glad the interior lights didn't work, and slipped out.

Both of them in black, Vika and the one named Sion, standing by the grave. Arguing, bargaining, haggling over the terms of their deal.

Kyle took a few steps closer, hoping to catch their words. He had to know what was going on.

Fragments floated toward him from the dark:

"So, you're sure about that?"

". . . the Chantry. . . our affair. . ."

". . . life is forfeit already. . . Diablerie. . ."

". . . a matter for the. . ."

". . . worth my while. . ."

What the hell? Just as Kyle was about to step closer, further out of the van's shadow, Sion suddenly raised his eyes in his direction, and Kyle felt a sharp shock run through his nerves. The vampire turned back to Vika, but at that moment there was a movement from a grove on the other side of the monument, and a small group emerged, swaggering, openly displaying their weapons. Kyle recognized the Sewer Rats from his previous encounter and wasn't quite sure whether to be relieved or not, but prudence quickly sent him back to his seat in the van while the two vampire factions confronted each other.

It appeared to be a stand-off. Finally, while her allies covered her retreat, Vika got back into the van. Kicking the engine to life, "Thought I told you to stay put!"

"I've got a right to know what's going on!"

She glanced behind her in the side mirror, keeping her speed down to avoid the unwanted notice of the police. "You wanna know what's going on? All right, it seems like your Sire Hervi isn't dead, after all!"

"But —" Kyle tried to swallow his dread, but it clung to his throat. "How do you know?"

"They have ways of finding out that kind of thing."

"The. . . Tremere, you mean."

"Right. Or, at least, that's what Sion says."

"And they think I know where he is?"

"They think they can find him, maybe. Through you. I don't ask how. Not my business."

He shook his head, denying everything, wishing, now, that he could acknowledge his lie. "So, then why didn't you sell me to them? I mean, that's what this is all about, isn't it?"

"It's complicated," she muttered. "I don't know if I trust Sion. I think he's operating on his own, outside the Chantry. That's not good." She looked at him directly. "You know what Hervi was doing, right?"

"Um, Blood Magic, didn't you say?"

"Yeah. He was into that. Maybe more. Maybe worse than even what you know. They say — that Hervi's a lot older than he's supposed to be. There are people who'd be willing to pay a whole lot to get their hands on him. They aren't necessarily the kind of people you want to deal with, though."

Kyle thought he knew what she meant — vampires, killing other vampires for their blood. It made his own blood feel cold, if Vika was afraid to deal with them.

"I think I maybe made a mistake, going to Sion instead —" Her voice broke off as she took another look back in the mirror. "Oh, hell!"

Suddenly Kyle was pressed back against the seat as the van shot forward. He tried to look back, but he couldn't see what or who was chasing them. Vika drove like a possessed being, teeth clenched, manhandling the steering wheel, taking corners at reckless speed, and Kyle could feel the van go airborne as they crested the hills and landed with a clash of overstrained shock absorbers. From the back, Fang moaned in fear.

"Is it him? Sion?" Kyle demanded, but Vika didn't answer him, only gunned the van forward through a red light. "I thought. . . you didn't want the cops on your tail!"

At least there were no sirens.

Finally she pulled into an alley, cutting her lights and letting the van coast to a stop, all the while staring back into the mirror.

"You lose them?" he asked.

In answer, she slumped back against the seat. "I don't know. I think — yeah."

"So who was it?"

"Don't know." She laughed weakly, a different sound than Kyle was used to hearing from her. "Not Sion, I'm almost sure! I don't even know it was us they were after! But sometimes you can't afford to hang around to find out. Things are stirred up these days. A lot of things. You're not the only one with problems, I can tell you that!"

Fang howled from the back. "I've got to see the dog."

The animal flung himself into his arms, a hundred pounds of dog almost knocking him over. "It's OK," Kyle told him. "It's OK now."

"Get back in," Vika called from the front. "You can bring him up here with you." Although she looked as if she regretted that decision when the dog squeezed into the seat between them, tail beating hard.

"What if it had been them?" Kyle asked her. "Whoever you were afraid it was?"

She laughed again. "They would have drained you dry, boy. Like a husk. And me, too, probably, just for the hell of it. Not the kind of people you want to show up at your party. I don't even know if your friend Hervi could handle them."

Cold dread choked his throat again. "And they know about me?"

"If they don't already, they will, sooner instead of later." The hard look was back in her eyes. "Look, right about now you're starting to look more like a liability than an asset. I know you know more about Hervi than you're letting on. Hervi's the one they're all after. Now, if I had information that could lead them to him, maybe people'd be willing to forget about you."

He hesitated. She wanted to sell out Hervi herself. And what did he have to lose? Not a good question to ask, not in the company he was mixed up with now.

"Suppose. . . I could show you where it was? The place he kept me?"

She grinned hideously. "That'd be a start! I was hoping you'd be reasonable. Where do we go?"

"Like I said, I ran away from that place, and I wasn't planning to go back. Somewhere in the park. I don't know exactly. Maybe I can recognize some landmarks if I see them again."

Vika wasn't quite happy about that, but she backed the van out of the alley and started down Presidio toward the park. Kyle didn't say much at first, except to give directions. He still wasn't sure. Finally, "What if Hervi does turn out to be dead, after all?"

"Don't know. Depends if there's any proof, I suppose. Damn, this looks like a dead end. Are you sure you know where you're going?"

"I told you I wasn't sure! Maybe that should have been a left turn, not a right." After another minute, "If he's dead, would they still want me?"

She shrugged. "You sure seemed convinced he's gotta be dead, don't you? Any particular reason?"

He said nothing. His nerves were crawling with anxiety. The dog sensed it, and kept whining restlessly.

Vika kept having to shove his tail out of the way so she could drive. Finally, when they had passed the same corner the third time, she said irritably, "This is taking too long! I'm about out of gas, and all we do is keep driving around and around in circles. And this damn dog is driving me crazy! I'm gonna stop so you can get him out of my face and into the back again."

She pulled over, and Kyle and Fang jumped out. There was a scent of eucalyptus in the air, and something about the look of the hill off to the right, something familiar. It had been just about this same time of year. . ."

Fang sniffed at a tree, doglike. "Maybe I'd better walk him a little before I put him in the back," Kyle called to Vika.

"OK," she replied from the driver's seat.

Kyle casually followed Fang into the trees, then looked back quickly to see if she was following him. Come, he called to Fang with his mind, and set off at a run.

He was taking a big risk, and he knew it. He had enemies out here in the night, maybe Vika's enemies as well as his own. There were too many things about the situation he didn't know. Most of all, how far Vika could be trusted. It could well be that this was a big mistake, that leaving her protection was the worst thing he could do. But the more he learned about the other vampires, the more he didn't think he could trust any of them. They sure didn't seem to trust each other very much.

Things were looking more familiar, now that he was outside and on foot, the way he'd been that night he made his escape. Running, desperate, half-crazed after his years of captivity, thinking only to put as much distance as he could between himself and the cellar where the vampire lay with the stake through his heart. Dead. Or was he? Was he somehow still alive, after all this time?

Now he could remember. The hill behind him when he'd turned around to see if the vampire was pursuing him through the night. Remembering now how much the night had changed for him, how clear and bright it was with his new vision, how sharply visible it all was.

Now, with his dog running next to him, he retraced his flight as closely as he could, deeper and deeper into the woods.

The ravine was almost impossible to see until you came on it, with trees growing precariously on the steep sides. The cellar was down there. It was what remained, he supposed, of some centuries-old cabin that had once occupied the site before the land had tumbled into the gorge.

It was almost impossible, even now, to recognize the place. The quake had been years ago. Rocks and earth had slipped down into the ravine, trees had toppled and new ones grown up. On the slopes, brush and undergrowth had crept up to disguise the effects of the earthquake and erosion, hiding the entrance to the cellar, concealing it from sight. It wasn't hard for Kyle to believe that no one had happened onto the place in all the time since his escape.

"Stay," he told Fang, then climbed down the eroded slope to the cellar's entrance. It was dark inside, and the faint odor it exhaled filled him with a gut-deep unreasoning terror.

I can't go in there.

The vampire was in there. The vampire was in there, and he wasn't dead, he had never been dead, all this time.

I should go back, he told himself. I should go back and tell Vika I've found the place, let her go inside, let her deal with it.

But he couldn't trust Vika. With her, it was and would always be a matter of business. He was expendable, and he knew it. Expendable and more than a slight inconvenience.

He had to face the vampire himself.

His mouth felt dry as he took the first step through the open door into the fetid interior. The earth floor still held the odor of old, spilled blood. This had been his prison, where he'd been chained in the dark like a starving animal. And on the other side of the fallen wall, the vampire's secret retreat, where he engaged in his foul experiments, where he slept in the daytime. But now the walls were collapsed, and half-buried under the fallen stones —

He was still there. The vampire was still there, the stake still protruding from his chest, hands still vainly clutching the wood where it impaled him.

For a long time, Kyle just stood in the entrance, staring. It was only when the sky started to take on a noticeably lighter shade that he realized his time was running out, that he was going to have to find shelter or else be forced to spend another night in this place, alongside —

"Well! So you got your memory back, after all!"

At the sound of that laugh, he spun around, galvanized by shock. Vika stood above him, grinning with that grotesque expression she deliberately used to unsettle people. "Was wondering when you'd finally break for it. So, this is what you were looking for?"

His fists tightened, but Kyle knew when he'd been outmanipulated. "He's in here. And he's dead, like I told you."

"Really?" He watched her climb down to the entrance. "So, this is the place," she said again. "Nice. Cheery. Let's have a look, then."

Kyle turned away. "Go right ahead. This is what you wanted. I'm getting out of here."

"No. I don't think so. Unless you think you can get past me. Now, why don't you go in first?"

Reluctantly, he stepped inside ahead of her. "There," he pointed to the staked figure beneath the collapsed wall.

And he heard her laugh. "You idiot! You. . . ignorant Childe! You thought he was dead? Like that? You thought you'd killed him? It was you, wasn't it, who staked him?"

"The wall fell, like I said," Kyle muttered tightly. "He was pinned down. It was my only chance to get away."

Vika went closer, climbing over stones, and looked down on the staked vampire. "So, this is Hervi. Whoever woulda thought it?"

Irritably, Kyle said, "All right, there he is. All yours." He glanced at Hervi, hardly able to believe that even the vampire could still be alive like that, after all this time. But it was true. He hadn't decayed, hadn't changed, like he was in some kind of suspended animation. Not dead. Not dead, after all. It made Kyle shudder in irrational terror to think that he might still come back to life, might sit up and bare his fangs.

Vika glanced back toward the entrance, where the sky was now

discernibly lighter. "Looks like we might as well stay here today, then I can get the boys together tomorrow night."

"Oh no. No way! Not me!" Kyle backed away from her. He never wanted to spend another day in this place. And the more so now, with the vampire — with Hervi lying there. Not dead. "You've got what you want, you don't need me any more. So you can call off the hunt, all right? I just want out of here!"

"That is unfortunate, then."

At the sound of the voice, both Kyle and Vika froze.

"Sion!" Vika hissed his name like a curse.

Kyle recognized the vampire in black as he stepped inside the cellar. He felt his nails dig into his palms.

Sion grinned. "It appears that we'll all have to spend the day in here — one way or the other. Oh, and Vika, I wouldn't be expecting your brood to show up this time. I believe they've been unavoidably detained."

Sion laughed with malicious enjoyment at her expression. Then he stepped closer and took one intent, avid look at the staked figure on the floor and smiled in satisfaction. "It has been a long time, Hervi! And under such circumstances!" He glanced from the helpless vampire back to the entrance. "Yes, there is just time enough! But first, my inconvenient friends. . ."

"Sion, no!" Vika protested, backing away from him. "I don't want to have anything to do with all this!"

"But it's too late for that. You see, Vika, you're already involved. It's a drawback to the information business, you know — sometimes you end up knowing too much for your own good. And now, of course, you've witnessed a terrible crime. It's only too bad you couldn't get away in time to report it to the authorities.

"Look at me!"

While Kyle watched in horror, Vika turned slowly, unwillingly, to meet Sion's compelling gaze. She stood as if paralyzed in front of him while he pulled a sharpened hardwood stake from inside his coat and plunged it deep between her ribs.

For a moment, she still stood upright, blood welling from her mouth and nostrils, before she slowly crumpled to the ground. Bloodscent filled the cellar.

"And now. . ."

Kyle made a single, desperate move to escape, but Sion stopped him with a word. Then his piercing eyes seized hold of Kyle's will.

"Kneel down."

No! Kyle's mind protested, but he was powerless. He knelt, unable to do anything but obey.

"Look at him. Look at your Sire, your progenitor, your maker."

Kyle's vision fixed on Hervi, on the vampire's sightless, staring eyes, on the ancient, bloodstained shirt with the wooden spike projecting from it. Sion bent, ripped the shirt away, revealing where the wood had penetrated the flesh, the blackened, congealed blood that had oozed out so long ago. Hervi's blood.

The vampire's blood. The scent of it! Kyle felt the sharpness of his own fangs in his mouth. Hunger clawed at his gut.

"Yes!" Sion hissed avidly. "You want it, don't you? Of course you do. I can see how much you still hate him. No one will doubt what must have happened here. How you came back, looking for vengeance. . ."

Sion's hand closed around the jagged piece of wood.

"How you drained the blood of your own Sire!" Slowly, he pulled it free, letting a few drops of the thick, sluggish, black liquid seep slowly from the dark pit of the wound.

And deep within the dullness of the vampire's eyes, a gleam seemed to flicker. Clawed nails flexed.

"Take it! Now!"

Kyle fell on Hervi, biting down with his fangs, tasting the vampire's blood, reeling with the sensation of it, sucking it from the wound, wanting more, wanting it all —

"Enough!"

Kyle heard the order, but the bloodlust in him struggled against it.

"Stop!" And in a softer, more malicious voice, "Don't be greedy, Childe! Don't take it all!"

This time, reluctantly, Kyle obeyed. Hervi's blood was rushing through him, exhilarating. So much richer than the one time he'd taken human blood, the one time he'd killed.

The avid gleam in Sion's eyes was brighter now. "Of course, there can be only one penalty for what you've done." He was still holding the bloodstained spear of wood that had impaled Hervi. But just as he was about to stab it through Kyle's chest, a rush of gray fur came through the cellar entrance, and over a hundred pounds of furious dog struck him from the back and knocked him to the ground, snarling, biting.

Sion twisted to stab at the dog, but as he tried to defend himself, a pair of black-nailed hands reached out to seize his throat. Hervi, reviving quickly, sank his fangs into the other vampire.

Alive again. Kyle's eyes went wide with horror at the sight of Hervi alive again: the vampire, the vision that had haunted him for so long. While the two vampires struggled, rolling on the ground, locked together in a bloodthirsty, deadly embrace, he backed away in fear, calling Fang to follow him, thinking only of escape.

But then he felt a new rage welling up hot from some place inside him, more than just Hunger, more than bloodlust. There was the being who had tormented him for so long, free again to roam the night, to perpetrate more evils. To hunt him down. . .

No. This time he had to end it. End it for good. As Sion flailed at Hervi with the broken spike of wood, Kyle seized hold of his arm and wrenched it from his grasp.

With a strength he'd never known he possessed, he drove the makeshift stake into Hervi's back.

The ancient vampire screamed once, a thin, knife-edged howl of excruciating pain. Kyle stabbed him again, again, blood spattering his face.

Hervi's grip loosened, but as Sion broke free, Fang attacked him again, tearing at his throat. Kyle looked desperately around the cellar, where the light from the entrance was growing stronger. "Fang! Back!" He picked up a stone, as heavy a one as he could find, and brought it down on Sion's head. Bone cracked. The vampire jerked in a spasm. Kyle brought down the stone again. Again.

The air in the cellar reeked with blood now, but for once he felt sated. Or maybe it was the quickly approaching dawn. But was Sion really dead? Even with his skull crushed to a pulp, could the vampire somehow still come back to life?

He couldn't let himself take the chance. Against the wall Vika still lay with Sion's stake through her ribs. He jerked it out and saw her eyes flutter open, but Kyle went back to Sion, drove the stake into his chest. The vampire twitched slightly, and Kyle leaned on the stake mercilessly, pushing it deep, deep into his heart, pinning him to the ground.

As he stood, shaking in reaction to what he'd done, Fang whined. He grabbed the dog in a hug. There was a rope around Fang's neck, gnawed off at the trailing end. Kyle loosened it, threw it away. "Good boy," he whispered.

He knew it was too late to leave this place now. He could already feel the pangs of weakness as dawn filled the sky outside.

He fell back to his knees, consciousness fading. Daybreak had caught him. As he faded, Fang licked at his face, telling him it would be all right. His guardian would be watching over him until sunset came again. ♀

HOMECOMING: AFFAIRS OF THE HEART

by James A. Moore

Jeremy Wix sat slumped back in the passenger's seat of the Jeep. His eyes were half-closed and his Stetson was pulled low over his head, making him appear as if he were asleep, when in truth he was very much awake. Beside him, Dawson drove on through the night, heading towards a city that had never seen him before.

"Where's the turn off, Jerry? And please, try hard to remember that I've never been here. Don't pull a Seattle on me, okay?"

Jeremy sat up a little taller, looked around the area with a blank face and casually pointed. "Next exit. And will you knock it of about Seattle already? Christ, next you'll be blaming me for the goddamn traffic."

Dawson shrugged his shoulders and grinned amiably. "Hey, you're more than welcome to walk if the company bothers you. I've got better things to do with my time than play chauffeur, y'know."

Jeremy grabbed the door of the moving car, reaching through the open window, and sank his fingers into the aluminum. His voice when he spoke again was very soft, almost a whisper, not at all like his normal gravely tones. "By all means, let me off here. I imagine I'll make it through to San Francisco." His eyes were now wide open, staring out at the distant lights of the city.

Dawson ignored the request, and turned towards the exit lane, neglecting his turn signal. "Your problem," he mused as he accelerated into the sharp right turn, "is that you have no sense of humor. Used to be I could hassle you and just get a little hassle back, not a load of crap about making it on your own."

They drove on in silence for the next 20 minutes, the tension between them unbroken. "I'm sorry, Dawson. It's just. . . It's not easy coming back here." Jeremy was silent for a few more minutes, then he shrugged his shoulders and continued. "I spent my whole life here, my mortal life, and then I was forced to leave. How the hell am I supposed to come back here and act like nothing happened?"

Dawson shook his head, a half-smile smeared across his face. In the sodium lights of the freeway, he looked downright sinister, the way the shadows pooled at his eyes and his cheeks, he looked worlds meaner than he was in reality. "I know what you need. Drop the face."

Jeremy turned and looked at his friend as if he had lost his mind completely. "Are you crazy?" Dropping your face was one of those little terms that Dawson had come up with, a term that meant letting the mortals see just how nasty you looked without the illusions that hid your damnation. Both Jeremy and Dawson were unfortunate enough to have Faces that they needed to wear, though each had his own reason.

"Naw, we ain't in the city yet, why not?" He grinned, a wide, slightly vicious expression, and winked. "No one to see us do it, Jerr. We could just watch the faces on the other drivers. Heck, you could pull out the camera if you wanted, take shots of these schmucks."

Jeremy smiled in spite of himself, and reached for the Polaroid Instamatic that he was carrying in his over night bag. "What the hell, no one here to see it."

They pulled up next to a Ford station wagon that had seen its best days well over a decade ago. sitting in the driver's seat was a portly Latino somewhere in his mid-fifties. The man was bobbing his balding head side to side, following the beat of a Top-40s classic song. The song was old enough that Jeremy couldn't recognize it immediately; such songs grew rarer all the time. Dawson spoke softly, whispering almost, and started the count-down. "One. . . two. . . three!" Dawson's hand struck the horn on their Jeep, and the man's bobbing head turned to face in their direction as the shrill honk cut through the night air. At the same time, both Dawson and Jeremy let the man see their true faces.

It was only for a second, just long enough to watch the man's eyes bug halfway out of his head and to see the color drain out of his face. Just exactly and precisely long enough for the man to realize that neither of the people he was looking at were human. And just long enough for Jeremy Wix to snap a picture of his stupid expression.

Then it was over. Then they were just two guys in a Jeep having a good laugh.

By the time Jeremy and Dawson had reached the edge of San Francisco proper, Jeremy was in better spirits. He kept looking at the photo from his Instamatic, amused by the expression on the man's face, and bitter about what had put the silly look there in the first place.

Five years ago the bitterness would have been the only thing that really mattered, it would have brought a rage upon his soul that was capable driving him to violence. A lot had changed in the last five years, and now he could focus on the humor of the situation. Dawson claimed that he had no sense of humor, Jeremy knew better, it was just that there was so little in his life worth laughing about.

Dawson cleared his throat noisily, and Jeremy looked towards him. "Look, I gotta get out of here, Jerry, I need to take care of some business over in Oakland." He stared a Jeremy Wix for a few seconds, wondering what was going on deep behind the mask that Jeremy always wore, the mask that said all was right with the world, or at least it wasn't any worse than it was yesterday. "You gonna be OK?"

Jeremy smiled back, it was a weak smile one made small by fear, but it was real at least. "Yeah. Yeah I'll be fine. Get out of here. I'll call you when it's all taken care of." Dawson looked ready to stay right beside him through the whole visit, and Jeremy knew he would if he was asked. Jeremy did not ask. "Hit the road, Dawson, I'll let you know what happens, assuming I still can, but you don't want any part of this, believe it."

Dawson nodded slightly, seemed almost ready to volunteer for combat, and then nodded again. "We'll see ya, Jeremy." The Jeep started roughly from the side of the road and took off like a bullet. Jeremy Wix watched the spot where it had last been for several minutes before heading on his way. The city had changed in 15 years, and he supposed that was to be expected, but the changes hurt in a soft way. Still, it was the only place he would ever be able to call home. Jeremy shifted the Army surplus duffel bag on his shoulder, leaned to the side a little for balance, and started on his way. From this moment on, until he met with Vannevar Thomas and, hopefully, gained the right to live in San Francisco again, he was a wanted man.

Dawson had let him off on Fifth Street, not too far from his first destination. Only 12 blocks. Jeremy could have asked for a lift all the way to where his mother was mourning the death of her life long husband, but Jeremy had learned a long time back never to trust anyone that far, never to tell anyone where you planned to spend your time, not even your good friends. That was not the way the game was played when you were undead.

The walk was painful, dredging up more and more memories of how his life had been before the Embrace, when he was handsome, when he was still human. By the time he had arrived at Union Square, the light mist that had been threatening to become fog had carried out its threat. Rather than making him lonelier, sadder, the fog revitalized him. The fog was a part of Jeremy's home as much as anything else in the city.

Jeremy Wix was just starting to reflect on the smells that made San Francisco — the occasional waft of sea water spray, the smell of damp litter hidden in the gutters, the faintest hint of sourdough bread from one of the numerous over-priced bread shops — when he was struck hard enough on the shoulder to actually stagger him.

Jeremy stared at the bastard that had just collided with him, a lean, well muscled man, scarcely any older than 18 to 20. He was dressed in evening finery, ready for a night out on the town, and by the looks of him, ready to go pick up his date for the night. Jeremy almost let the man's rudeness go, almost ignored the man entirely, then the man opened his mouth and sealed his fate. "Why don't you look where the hell you're going, asshole."

Jeremy's hands pulled into fists without his even having to think about it. "Hey, pretty boy, come here."

The man turned to look at him with what almost equated to shock on his face, as if the idea that Jeremy might actually be talking to him was simply beyond his comprehension. He started walking away, an almost laugh, almost sigh of disgust going past his model perfect lips.

Jeremy was beyond the point of caring. There was too much going on in his life, there was too much to worry about, and he simply couldn't bring himself to let the man go on his way. Besides, he was hungry. "I said come here, pretty boy, I want an apology."

The man was a good four or five inches taller than Jeremy's 5' 10". At a guess he had about 40 extra pounds on him as well, and it looked to all be muscle. Jeremy waited to see when the man would make his move. The man simply waved him away with one hand, turned, and made to leave again. Jeremy Wix made a casual assessment of his surroundings, made certain that absolutely no one was around to see what was occurring, and made special note of the alley that was off to his left. When he was positive that there would be no witnesses, he tossed the man towards the alley's opening, not much of a toss, just enough to get him moving in the right direction.

"Shit, you don't know how to listen very well, do you?" the startled man yelped, more surprised than anything else. Jeremy took another quick look around, made absolutely certain that there was no one in the vicinity to see the two of them, and then grinned amiably. He shoved the man back into the alley with a smooth push on the his expensive looking leisure suit. "Boy, I can't tell you how nice it is to see a friendly face my first night back."

The man slammed into the dirty brick wall with enough force to knock the wind out of him, and Jeremy heard the sound of loose change clattering musically off of an overturned trash can not far away. A much warier man was gaining his feet when Jeremy reached him. Jeremy kept his voice even and friendly as he pulled the man close. "I was just thinking to myself. I was thinking: Jeremy, what you need is a little something to eat before you get home," he mused as he slapped the shocked man's face hard enough to actually hear the hinge of his jaw dislocate. He talked over the man's muffled scream, smiling into the pain widened eyes as he lifted his victim completely off of the ground and pressed him into the wall again, making certain not to let the man's head hit first. It was no fun if they were unconscious.

The man tried to talk,"Whyrnooingthhith? I'm thorry. Pleath, chust leaf me alone!" Jeremy was more adept than most at hearing words mangled by speech impediments. Hell, speech impediments were very common among his kind. "Why are you doing this? I'm sorry! Please, just leave me alone!" About every other word was even mildly coherent. Jeremy guessed at the rest of what the man said. "Why? Because I can, and because you really pissed me off. But mostly, because I'm a bad liar. See, my dietary habits forbid me the pleasure of Mom's cooking." He frowned slightly, looking at the squirming fool in his hands, ignoring his prey's attempts to break his grip. "I'd hate to lie to my mother. I'd hate to tell her that I'd just eaten, if in fact I had not."

Desperation allowed the handsome man to move, he kicked Jeremy in the balls. Jeremy acted as if nothing had happened, and his assailant started to get really nervous. Jeremy didn't know exactly what the thoughts going through his victim's mind were, but he could guess: Maybe he was thinking that there were things more important than whether or not he was going to be late for picking up his date; things like living to explain to his fiancee why he hadn't been able to meet with her and her parents for dinner. Jeremy forced the thoughts from his mind; it was far too late for feelings of guilt. Besides, the nastier parts of his mind were enjoying the show, and his personal favorite part was about to begin. It was time to make the man understand what he was up against. Jeremy surveyed the alleyway one last time. After he was reassured, he dropped the Face that hid what he had become from everyone who might see him.

Todd Kingsley, until recently from L.A., looked at the dark blue, warty skinned demon in front of him and started thrashing anew. The devil in blue jeans reached for his face and tweaked his nose hard enough to rupture the cartilage that gave his sinuses access to air. Todd whimpered, felt his eyes start to sting with the burning water of tears, and continued to kick ineffectually at the monster's crotch and stomach.

Jeremy Wix waited patiently for his opponent's eyes to clear and then, for maximum effect, smiled broadly, revealing a set of teeth that would have made a Doberman pinscher jealous. They were long and sharp, and spread all over his mouth as if vying for space in an overcrowded bus.

Jeremy lowered the rude man until they were eye to eye, and winked slowly. "You did me a real favor, guy. I never could lie to my mom worth a piss. Thanks." Jeremy savored the sensation of his teeth ripping into the throat of his prey, relished the taste of hot blood flowing into his mouth and past his own gums, caressing his tongue with the sultry, rusty taste.

When he was done feeding, Jeremy carefully licked the wounds, curing them with his saliva. Normally, he would have let his foolish victim live, let him have nightmares about what could only be a serious nightmare. But he was nervous, and he really couldn't afford to leave any trace of evidence that he had done anything wrong.

He tried to make the breaking of his victim's neck as pain-less as possible. Sometimes, he really hated himself.

Only 20 minutes later, Jeremy stood at the entrance to his family's home, and politely knocked on the door. In less than a minute, Alicia White was looking at him from the across the threshold, a look of pleasant shock on her face. Jeremy, face now back where it belonged, hidden in a sheath of illusion, placed his finger against his lips and gestured for silence. The woman was almost as dear to his heart as his own mother, and he hugged the maid fiercely, aching at how much he had missed her despite how few times he had thought of her consciously.

Alicia led him to where his mother sat, reading a book about financial security and looking a hundred years older than her 58 years. From where he stood, he could see the gray roots that she had carefully dyed, he could see the marks that even the best plastic surgeon could not quite erase. Mostly he could see her pain, her grief at the loss of her husband. It tore a gaping wound in his soul to see her suffering. "Mom, I'm home." The words were even more of a croak than they normally were.

Anita Wyzchovsky looked at her son face to face for the first time in 15 years, and the tears she had held at bay for the last week poured past her carefully applied make-up in a deluge. Mostly blinded by tears, she stumbled across the room to where her only child stood, and threw her arms around his chest, burying her face in his neck and sobbing her grief onto him. Jeremy Wyzchovsky held his mother closely, using only a small portion of his strength to support her, holding back his own blood-red tears with only the greatest of efforts. They stood that way for several minutes, until the crying jag was over.

Jeremy did his best to comfort his mother's soul, trying to relocate the parts of himself that he had deliberately lost some time back. He smiled at the right places, keeping his answers as close to the truth as he could, giving what comfort was possible for him.

"Oh God, Jeremy, let me look at you." Anita stared into her son's eyes, amazed at how healthy he looked. "You've hardly changed at all."

"I wish that were true, Mom. I've changed a lot, just not so's you'd notice it with ease." She stared at his perfect teeth, his stylishly long hair, with just the slightest touch of silver starting at the temples, she lost herself in his cool, blue eyes. For 15 years the only communication had been on the phone, maybe an occasional card or package at the holidays. He looked away from her, sorrow written across his handsome features, and sighed softly. "I was so sorry, Mom. I know me and Dad never got along the best, but I was so sorry to hear abou. . . about the accident."

Anita Wyzchovsky felt the water works start up again, wrapped her arms around her son one more time, and started crying. He held her, he crooned meaningless phrases and promised that everything would be all right, but somehow, the words and gestures seemed almost practiced. She took the comfort, she allowed herself to be fooled, but a small part of her refused to be fooled. Her son had changed in some fundamental way, he had been hurt as few people could be without scarring, and she had no idea what might have caused his pain. She wanted to ask him what had happened, wanted desperately to know what had made him so cold, she never said a word.

When he was ready, he would talk. They spent the next hour consoling each other, making conversation and promising to see each other again, soon. It was after he had left that she started really thinking about the hesitation in his voice, the odd catch when he first mentioned his father's death. She found herself wondering if maybe her son knew something that she did not. She started wondering what her son had really come back to town for, and if maybe, just maybe, he knew something about the death of her husband that she did not.

When he had finally managed to break free, he stumbled from the house on Nob Hill, the section of town where his family had lived for the last few generations, and threw himself into the first dark area he could find. Safely away from prying eyes, Jeremy Wix allowed himself to cry for what he had lost. He cried for his mother's grief, he cried for his lost chances to be with his father, chances that would never have mattered if they had not been taken from him by force. He cried for the pain he had let back into his soul and he cried in fear, knowing with little doubt that he would never be allowed to return to San Francisco, and damn the information that he hoped to barter with Vannevar Thomas.

When the tears had finally stopped, Jeremy Wix set his shoulders, readied himself for his upcoming confrontation, and headed towards the last location he knew of for the Prince of San Francisco. "You'll let me stay, Thomas. You'll let me stay, or so help me God, you'll live to regret the decision."

● ● ●

Joseph Cambridge sat in his "office," one of the many row homes that made up so much of the good sections of San Francisco, and stared at the television screen in front of him without acknowledging the pleas of the latest commercials to try the exciting new products being released on the market.

Instead, he listened to the cultured tones of Vannevar Thomas explaining that Jeremy Wix was back in town. A thin smile spread across his toadlike countenance, and he fingered the rusty leg brace that supported him.

"I trust that this will be taken care of, Vannevar. I have kept my word to you, I have accepted your punishment — harsh though it was — and I hope that I can expect this problem to be taken care of before I have to get involved myself." Joseph Cambridge pressed the button marked "Off" on his remote control, and let the light of the television fade, drowning his room in darkness.

"No, I understand completely, sir. No, of course I shall allow your people their chance to find him. I'll make it even easier on you. I'll meet you at your offices, that way you can keep your eyes on me." He listened patiently to the Prince's response, nodding as if the Prince could possibly see him in the darkened room. "Nonsense. It's no inconvenience at all. This is as good an excuse as any to come see my sister. Yes, please do tell Donna that I'm on my way." A long pause then, as the prince conveyed the message and gave Donna Cambridge's response. "Yes, I'm looking forward to seeing her as well. Perhaps we could finish that game of chess we started? Your turn, if I'm not mistaken. Has it already been six months? Well then, I'd say we were over due to finish this particular game. I shall see you shortly, Vannevar. Say 20 minutes? Wonderful."

Joseph Cambridge sat for a few moments in the darkness of his plush apartment, trying to force the eager smile to stay off of his face, trying to prepare himself for the right level of indignation, knowing for certain that Jeremy Wix would be arriving at the Prince's offices only a short while after himself. "Yesss, Vannevar. It is most definitely time to finish this particular game."

• • •

Jeremy Wix saw the two men tailing him almost as soon as they started to follow. It was a necessary adaptation to his mortal life style, he had to know when he was being followed, he had to know how many followed him at any given time. Vampires did not believe in playing the same games as the humans they fed on, their games were a great deal more subtle, and normally involved the use of loyal human retainers. Jeremy could tell by the way that they followed him, letting him gain a great deal of distance before they closed back in on him, that the fools following him where mortal, like as not a part of the prince's veritable army of retainers, and that they were there primarily to watch him at this point. He risked capture long enough to place a phone call.

He placed the quarter in the phone's slot for change and dialed his mother's number from memory. A large and slightly mangy mongrel started sniffing at his leg, and for the moment, he ignored the beast.

His mother answered on the second ring, sleep blurring her voice slightly. "Mom? No, listen to me. I left a small package in the side of the sofa where I sat, between the cushions. I want you to read the papers that you find there. They'll explain a great deal, and when I come back tomorrow night, we can talk about what they say. Listen to me, listen carefully."

Jeremy spent several moments he could ill afford to waste listening to his mother's questions, and then cut her off abruptly. "Mom, be quiet for a minute, please. Just listen. Thanks. Now then, the pages are written on flash paper. They're gonna read like a bad piece of horror fiction, but believe me, you do not want to get caught by anyone in this town with those pages on you, or anywhere near you. Yes, I'm very serious. If someone should knock on the door, if Alicia should happen to ask you about the pages, lie through your teeth and deny any knowledge of them. If someone should ask any funny questions... what? No, not funny hah hah, funny strange. Like the stuff you expect in a spy movie. Right, like on *Mission Impossible*. If any one asks questions, yes, even Alicia, you burn those pages. All it will take is a single match. They'll go up in one hell of a flash, there'll be nothing but a little bit of ash, scatter the ash if you end up burning them. It's very important, Mom. More important than you could possibly know. And Mom? Never, ever, ever tell anyone about what those pages say. We'll talk tomorrow night. I love you too. Good night, Mom. Sweet dreams."

Jeremy reached out to pet the mutt at his heels, but it shied quickly, a small growl coming from it's muzzle. "Yeah, you ain't anything special to look at either, Fido." The dog snapped once and skittered away, half expecting to be kicked. Jeremy didn't bother; he liked dogs, it was humans that always pissed him off.

He was heading for the two men following him, when someone called out his name. "Jeremy Wix!" He turned to look at the source of the voice, and suddenly felt deceptively strong and incredibly shapely arms wrap around his neck. The body that hugged him closely was one that he knew well enough to have dreamt about on more than one occasion.

Jeremy stared into dark eyes that fairly sparkled with amusement and allowed himself to grin. "Carlotta! How the hell are you?" He looked at the complete package of Mediterranean beauty in front of him, and smiled ear to ear. "Damn you're looking good." He hugged her again, honestly glad to see a friendly face.

Carlotta smiled mischievously, wiggled against him suggestively, and replied, "I'd say the same back..."

They finished the line together. "But it would be a lie." She hugged him closely, placing her lips to his ear, and gave him the warning. "I don't know why you left Seattle, but you shouldn't have come here. Those two delicious looking lumps over there are Vannevar Thomas' men."

He pulled back from her and smiled again. "Thanks for the warning, Carlotta, but I had already figured that part. I was just about to have a little talk with them when you showed up."

"Why are you back? From what you told me you're not exactly a welcome sight around here." He could stare at her little pout for months and never get tired of seeing Carlotta.

"Hey, it's where I'm from, sweety, I had to come home." The obligatory leering wink at Carlotta, and a suggestive grind of his own, "If I'd known you were here, I'd have come back a long time ago."

He risked a look at the two goons, they were looking everywhere but at him. The wary mutt was going past them, paused long enough to salute a telephone pole, and headed towards Nob Hill. "You missed all the fun, Jeremy, We had a little quake earlier on, should have seen the looks going down at the Vampire Club."

Jeremy smiled, ruffled Carlotta's hair, knowing that she hated it, knowing that she would tolerate such nonsense from him, they were, after all, friends. She swatted his hand away affectionately. "I imagine there'll be plenty more, this is San Francisco after all." He thought about it for a second, asked her one last question. "Is that were you hang out in this town, the Vampire Club?"

"Sweety, there is no other place for our kind to hang in San Francisco, any one tells you otherwise is lying."

Jeremy Wix held her delicate fingers in his hand for the briefest of times, smiled once more. "If I survive tonight, I'll meet you there soon." The smile faded from both of their faces, they knew full and well the implications of what he had just said, he was banned from the city, his most likely punishment for being here was death. "Give me a Kiss goodbye?"

Carlotta's smile came back. "Not a chance in hell, Jeremy." She kissed him lightly on the lips. "Just a kiss for luck. See ya around." Jeremy watched her go, hoping he'd be able to keep his promise to see her soon, and doubting it.

Jeremy left the phone booth, walking back the way he had come. The two men were doing their best to look as if they were interested in reading the menu from a Chinese restaurant.

"I'm guessing that you gentlemen work for Vannevar Thomas?" The first of the gentlemen in question looked over at the second. The second of the gentlemen nodded almost imperceptibly. "Good." Jeremy smiled, held his hands above his head in a mocking gesture of surrender. "Take me to your leader, I'm ready to throw myself on his tender mercies."

Both men looked understandably wary, but also managed to look truly relieved at the same time. Jeremy Wix gave them no trouble.

Within 30 minutes, he stood before the double doors that led to the offices of Vannevar Thomas, a tight, dry lump trying to nest in his throat. He wondered almost idly if he had made a colossal mistake when he murdered his dinner earlier. Either way it was too late to change the past. That lesson at least, he had learned just over 15 years ago.

The two men escorting him knocked softly on the right hand door, and a few moments later, opened both of the doors in unison. Jeremy smiled at the clockwork precision of the gesture, and stepped forward.

Before him stood the prince of San Francisco, looking as regal in his three piece business suit as anyone ever had. Beside him was Donna Cambridge, and the frosty look she showed him stated clearly that nothing had been forgiven. Lastly, standing next to Donna and ready to pounce should anything at all attempt to harm his sister, stood Joseph Cambridge. Joe was expressing his raw hatred of Jeremy Wix with bared fangs and burning eyes. If he'd been permitted, Jeremy was certain that he would have killed his nemesis on the spot.

With an easy stride — casual and assured, but not too pushy — Jeremy Wix walked into the offices proper, preparing to gamble his life away.

• • •

Anita Wyzchovsky looked at the yellowed pages in her hand and trembled, almost certain that her son had gone completely insane. Almost, but not quite. The letter explained an awful lot in a very small amount of space. She could tell that most of the letter had been written a few months back, only the first and last pages had been written recently, the rest of the pile of papers was wrinkled, water marked, the beginning and end were still perfectly clean.

She sat in her bed room, at the vanity where she always put on her face, and started to read the letter again. From the living room, she heard Alicia cry out, heard the sound of a dog barking, and then the sound of something breaking. Anita shot out of her seat, wrapped her terry cloth robe tighter, and rushed to the living room to see what the problem was. The shaggy mongrel that was causing so much racket was wagging his tail furiously, bouncing playfully as poor Alicia tried to grab his fur. Anita smiled despite the broken vase on the ground and joined into the chase.

The mutt had no intention of being caught, and the two women, far past their primes, never had a chance.

Before all was said and done, Anita and her live-in maid had surrendered, breathing hard and chuckling about the mongrel that had escaped into the depths of the house. "Sooner or later, he'll grow sleepy, and then we can get him out of here," Alicia remarked. "I don't know," mused the recent widow. "He's kind of cute in a way. Maybe we can let him stay."

Alicia looked at her employer with one raised eyebrow. "Do you expect me to wash a monster that size?" Alicia placed a look of long suffering on her face, and the two women had a short laugh. Almost on cue, the mutt was at the door, whining loudly and scratching at the base of the front entrance, desperate to get outside. Alicia rose and let him out the door, her employer sighed from the couch. "Story of my life, Alicia: chase a man around, invite him to stay, and watch him leave me." Alicia forced a laugh, but knew that Anita was mostly serious. Anita said she was going to turn in, and Alicia bid her a good night.

Anita Wyzchovsky climbed back up the stairs, moved slowly back to where she had placed the letter from Jeremy, and reached for her matches. She stared long and hard at the place where the letter had been. It was gone. The only possible answers, made easier to swallow by the dog hairs in her room, was that the mongrel had chewed them up, or that she had lit the pages before she went downstairs. Either way, Jeremy had nothing to fear, the pages were destroyed and no one had seen them save for her.

Sleep was a long time coming, made longer still by the worries that her only son might already be dead. At least now, she understood a little better.

* * *

The three figures stared calmly at Jeremy Wix, and he felt — or at least imagined he felt — his heart skip a few beats. For a long moment no one spoke, and Jeremy felt all of the bravado he had stored in his body fade, blown away from him like smoke in a hurricane. Jeremy could not decide which face to study, he decided to study them all.

Vannevar Thomas was immaculate, the very personification of every image seen in a fashion magazine. No hair was out of place, no seam on his pure silk suit misaligned. There had been a time when Jeremy himself looked almost as good; that time was longer in the past than he cared to think about. Jeremy fondled the gold necklace and the crucifix the necklace held in place, absently noting the warty flesh that had grown over one of the sections of chain when he became. . . when he changed.

Only the most casual of glances was spared the progenitor of his damnation. Joseph Cambridge bore a face that he would never forget in all of his years, a face that still haunted the occasional dream he allowed himself to remember. Why should he want to study something he already knew all too well? A look in the mirror was all that was required to let him see a creature equally disgusting in visage.

Donna Cambridge was another story altogether. The look of barely contained contempt on her smooth, china-pale face was enough to make Jeremy want to crawl back into the sewers. As much as he hated her brother, Jeremy still loved Donna. The feelings may have only been sentimental reminiscences of a time when he could walk along side the most attractive of people without fear of reprisal, but the pain those bitter memories caused was just as real as it ever had been. Perhaps I was wrong, he thought to himself. Perhaps we could have been happy together. He crushed the thought as quickly as it forced its way to the surface of his mind.

As he studied the faces of his peers, so, too, did they study him. For all he could tell, they had all found him bitterly wanting. The thought that he may be unworthy of their approval was enough to force himself back into a proper position of defiance. Fond memories may well have driven Jeremy Wix home after 15 years, but it had been — and continued to be — his anger that permitted him to face his creator, his judge, and his heart's desire again.

Jeremy was preparing to break the silence, when Vannevar Thomas saved him the trouble. Like the rest of the Prince, his voice was cultured and beautiful. . . . Everything that Jeremy no longer was without his Face. "Well, this is an unexpected surprise. I seldom have an outlaw in my domain come to me willingly." The Prince stepped forward, serenely, with unconscious dignity, and extended his hand in formal greeting. The hand was as solid as iron, and no doubt strong enough to rip the bones out of his own hand. Jeremy tried not to flinch as they shook.

"How are you, Jeremy? I trust that there is a legitimate reason for your return to San Francisco and for keeping me from my evening engagement?" The tones were almost casual, it was the implied strength of the friendly handshake that caused Jeremy to step back slightly.

"Yes sir. I wish to petition you for the right to return to San Francisco. I–I want to come home, sir."

Before the Prince could respond, Joseph Cambridge had stepped forward, blurring with the speed of his motion, and grabbed a very large handful of Jeremy's tattered jacket in his massive hand. The fire in his eyes was bright enough to make Jeremy flinch as he was heaved into the air. There was a horrible sensation of deja vu, and Jeremy found himself pinned against the wall of the Prince's offices. The voice that erupted from Joe's mouth was thunderous, loud enough to shake the earrings that had long ago fused themselves to Jeremy's flesh. "*You what?!*" Had such a thing still been possible, Jeremy Wix would have wet his pants. Despite his own anger, he could never fully forget the tortures and the fears that his Sire had inflicted upon him.

Joseph Cambridge made as if to reach through Jeremy's chest and rip his heart from his breast. Jeremy did not doubt for one second that he could do it. There was the briefest satisfaction in Jeremy, seeing in his peripheral vision that Donna's stony visage had cracked, seeing that at least a part of her still seemed to care. Her eyes had grown wide, her head was shaking softly from side to side, and her hands were reaching out, reaching to stop her monstrous brother from killing him.

She needn't have bothered, the voice of Vannevar Thomas was enough to end the murderous act. "Stop it, Joseph. This is my decision to make, not yours." The Prince may as well have been telling the gardener to be more careful when trimming the roses for all the force thrown into the comment, but the command had the desired effect. Joseph Cambridge slowly lowered Jeremy Wix to the floor, a barely audible growl rising from his throat throughout the process.

"You're luckier than you know, pretty boy. Luckier than you have a right to be." The words were whispered softly as Jeremy's feet gently touched the plush carpet in the room. Joseph Cambridge stepped back to his sister's side.

"If you're going to misbehave, Joseph, I'll have you escorted back to your home. Am I making myself clear?"

"Yes."

"Hmm. Good. Now then, Jeremy, why on earth would I want to let you back into the city?"

Jeremy Wix straightened his jacket, glared at Joe Cambridge with a bravado he most certainly did not feel, and turned to the Prince. "I have information that you might find useful. Information that I would be willing to exchange for immunity from punishment for all past crimes, and the right to stay in San Francisco."

"Vannevar, This is preposterous! You know what he did to Donna, you know what he is like! You can't possibly be considering a pardon for whatever pathetic information this. . . this bastard may have!" It was almost a plea, those words that rumbled from deep inside Joseph Cambridge's chest. It was almost a demand as well.

Vannevar Thomas turned gracefully to look at Joseph Cambridge and lifted one eyebrow, smiled slightly. "I believe I should like to hear what the information is, before I decide, Joseph. If you don't mind, that is, I'm only the Prince, and I realize that what I may or may not think means nothing to one of your own prestigious station, but it is after all, my job to hear all sides of an argument."

Joseph Cambridge bristled at the obvious sarcasm in the Prince's voice, decided instead to plead his case again. "Vannevar, he'll do you no good. His kind hasn't the heart to care one way or the other."

Before the Prince could respond, it was Jeremy's turn. "My kind? I guess you'd know all about that wouldn't you, you made me what I am." His voice was once more barely a whisper. Joe seemed nonplused by the change, Donna and the Prince both seemed more perceptive.

"You deserved worse! I should have torn your heart out and fed on it you bastard!"

Jeremy was halfway across the room, charging towards Joseph before he had given any thought at all to the matter. "It would have been better than this, you fucking freak!"

Joseph Cambridge stepped forward to meet him, ready for combat and ready to destroy what he had created. Perhaps it was anger, perhaps it was the desire to acknowledge all of the truth, to see at last all that fate had done to both of them. The two revealed their true natures, revealed for all in the room to see, just what it meant to be Nosferatu.

Joseph stood on his leg braces and towered fully a foot over Jeremy. His skin was a pale toothpaste blue as opposed to Jeremy's darker skin, but his face was just as hideous; it was covered in cysts, cross-hatched with folds of warty flesh. His teeth were bared, strong teeth in rows as numerous as those of a shark, sheathed partially in gums the color pitch. He was just as hideous as Jeremy remembered, just as horrible to see as Jeremy himself.

Joseph Cambridge backhanded Jeremy Wix hard enough to blast him into the desk of Vannevar Thomas. Jeremy and the heavy oak desk both went over with a crash.

"No, Joe, don't hit him again!" Donna's cry made her brother hesitate for the briefest of seconds, just long enough for Jeremy to regain his footing. With a cry that was mostly animal, Joseph Cambridge charged forward again. Jeremy dropped into a better stance ready to kill the demon that had stolen everything that mattered from him.

Vannevar Thomas intervened. "*Stop!*" the word was not loud, but the power that backed the word was thunderous. Both Joseph and Jeremy felt the force of his command, muscles seized and refused to obey them. They were as still as statues.

The Prince stepped between the two, ignoring the hatred that fairly poured from them. His words were cold, cold enough to make them both listen. "This is my domain. There will be no combat here. For the last time, Joseph, the decision is mine to make, not yours. Furthermore, that desk is older than the two of you combined, and has a great sentimental value. If you've damaged it, I'll stake you to meet the sun. If you continue to act in this way, I shall be forced to punish you. Severely. Do I make myself clear?"

Joseph Cambridge calmed himself with a visible effort. Nodded his assent.

"Good. Jeremy, this is hardly the proper way to convince me that I should let you stay in San Francisco." There was almost no change in the Prince's demeanor, no shifting of his features, just a mild look of disappointment. "Perhaps you should pick up my desk and share with me what your information is and why I should find it useful. Does that sound good to you, Jeremy?"

Jeremy looked at Joseph Cambridge. Cambridge sneered back.

He looked at Donna Cambridge, whose face had again become as stone. He looked at Vannevar Thomas. "I would rather tell you alone, sir. One on one as it were." He turned away and hefted the massive desk back into its proper position.

Vannevar Thomas stared back with a slight smile on his face. "Very well, Donna my dear, why don't you take Joseph over to the pond in back? I should like him to see my new Koi. They really are amazing specimens, Joseph. Perhaps I can have a few of them delivered to your house."

Donna lead her gargantuan brother by the hand, smiling sweetly up at his glowering visage. Joe looked ready to finish the argument, but was apparently smart enough not to push his luck. Vannevar Thomas waited patiently, head cocked at an odd angle until they had been gone for some few minutes. "Now then, let's talk Jeremy."

• • •

Jeremy Wix walked slowly away from the Prince, turned and faced him, even as the Prince was seating himself behind the huge oak desk that covered one corner of the room. "You haven't given your word to me yet, sir."

Once again the Prince looked rather surprised, as if the thought that his promise was necessary hadn't crossed his mind. "My, you are the pushy one, aren't you Jeremy? Of course, if you weren't, you wouldn't be in quite the mess you're in now, would you?"

"No sir, I wouldn't be."

"What ever possessed you to do that to Donna, in the first place Jeremy?"

"Which part sir, breaking up or sending out the photographs?"

"Well, why not cover both? The breaking up and then the photos."

Jeremy shrugged, he had expected questions, he had even predicted this one. "I didn't promote the break up, Prince Thomas. I was caught in bed with another woman." Vannevar Thomas asked questions with his eyes, Jeremy added the details necessary. "She'd always knocked before, I guess the shock of seeing her brother after eight years of thinking him dead made her forget her usual manners." He shrugged again. "My own fault really, I should have locked the door."

"And the pictures?"

"Is this really necessary sir?"

Vannevar Thomas smiled thinly. "Quite necessary, Jeremy. Tell me about the pictures."

Jeremy sighed, wanting to be anyone but who he was, anywhere but where he was. "We argued a lot, I was a little vindictive, even though I shouldn't have been. I had some Polaroids of Donna in the nude, I wrote her name, phone number, and hourly rate on the back. I passed them out to some of the sleazes I met at a few bars." Jeremy looked at the Prince, the Prince looked back, expressionlessly. "It was juvenile and reprehensible, sir. I admit that."

"You understand the sort of trouble that you'll be causing yourself by coming back here? Joseph may not be among the Primogen, but he has substantial clout. He is second only to his Sire among the Nosferatu in San Francisco. He will most likely do everything in his power to destroy you."

"I understand that, sir."

Vannevar Thomas steepled his fingers for a moment, staring as much through Jeremy as at him. "Very well, you have my word. If the information is of importance, and is useful to me, I shall grant you immunity for past crimes and safe haven within the city of San Francisco and the surrounding areas over which I have control. Fair enough?"

"Yes, sir. Thank you, sir."

"I shouldn't thank me quite yet, Jeremy. I haven't agreed that the information is of great enough significance as yet."

"Point taken, sir." Jeremy fidgeted, not knowing quite how to proceed, and finally decided that the straight forward approach would be best. "I can give you the locations, within this very city, of two Setite hearts." He paused to savor the honest surprise on Vannevar Thomas' face, and the way the Prince suddenly sat a trifle straighter in his chair, ready to listen. "One of the hearts belong to Darrius Stone. Not the most powerful of Setites, granted, but certainly a fine way to keep your eyes on the rest of the Setites that want to make this area home."

Jeremy let the knowledge sink in, savored the moment while he could, and then placed his trump card on the table before him. "The other heart belongs to Jean-Claude."

Vannevar Thomas stared through Jeremy Wix for several moments, weighing the usefulness of the information proffered. Setites were the only known Kindred that could actually remove their hearts, making it much harder to truly hurt them. The catch was that if you had possession of the Setite's heart, you could kill the Setite whenever you felt like it. A solid bargaining chip, considering the number of Setites that seemed intent on making San Francisco their home. And Jean-Claude was certainly one of their leaders, if not the leader.

"You understand that I will have to test the validity of this information before the final decree is made?" The Prince's voice was as measured as ever, giving no hint as to just how important the knowledge was to him. Jeremy would have been surprised if there had been any other reaction from Vannevar Thomas. Jeremy Wix allowed himself a small smile of victory. "Oh, yes sir. I certainly do."

• • •

Less than an hour later, Jeremy Wix was once again a citizen of the city of San Francisco. Joseph Cambridge, despite his furious ragings, could not change the Prince's mind, and it was certainly not for lack of trying. Throughout the entire tirade, Jeremy Wix smiled serenely, normally staring directly at the creature that had Sired him. When the decree was formally announced, upon the retrieval of the two simple earthenware jars, Jeremy formally bowed to the Prince of San Francisco. He thanked the Prince for his time, and offered his services should the Prince need them. The last was not necessary, both he and the Prince acknowledged that the offer was not a part of their agreement, but it could not hurt to ingratiate himself to the man.

No one stared at the ceramic containers with more awe than Jeremy. It was almost comical to think of the efforts that had gone into learning the hearts' locations. Jeremy had broken his own personal code of ethics on at least four counts, just to gather the information.

He also took a moment of Donna's time to apologize for the way he had treated her so many years ago, saddened to see the wounds were still fresh enough to hurt her almost as much as they now hurt him. Seeing her up close, holding her hand briefly in his own, he remembered the good times that they had shared together even better. He almost let himself Kiss her, but only almost.

Donna was gracious, more gracious than she had ever been when she was merely human. Vannevar Thomas himself had Embraced her some 15 years ago as a way of maintaining a solid hold over Joseph. She had belonged to Vannevar body and soul ever since.

He also passed a smug, self satisfied wink in the general direction of the seething Joseph Cambridge, but only after the Prince explained that no direct action on Joe's part, against Jeremy Wix would be tolerated. Joseph Cambridge was not at all pleased about the change of events, but for just a moment, directly before the prince had ordered that no harm be done to Jeremy, he had been on the verge of a smile. Jeremy could well understand that Donna might hold a grudge against him, but Joseph? Did the man never forgive?

Bravado aside, Jeremy still had to admit to himself that he was truly terrified of Joseph Cambridge. Despite his heart begging him to come home, despite his love of San Francisco, Jeremy was forced to wonder if returning to the city would be more trouble than it was worth. Certainly, he had gone through quite enough effort to gather the locations of the two hearts, but that had been almost easy in comparison to the risks he had taken in coming home. The Prince's rule came back, no direct harm from Joe Cambridge. He could handle anything else that came along, he was certain of that. After a final nod to all three of his counterparts, Jeremy Wix left the Prince's offices and headed into the night.

Jeremy had to see his mother. And see her he did. He told her of the Kindred, and what his life had been like for the last 15 years. He spent the majority of the night talking with her, there was so very much to talk about.

Jeremy Wyzchovsky, called Jeremy Wix or even Pretty Boy — due to the features he affected, the features he had once truly had in all their effeminate glory — by most everyone that knew him, smiled more that night than he had in the last five years. He had much to smile about, he was home again.

Tomorrow was soon enough to ponder all of the implications about coming home, for this night at least, he was once again his mother's son. Right then she had more need of a son than she did of anything else. Seeing his mother helped him remember what he had once been, and if only for one night, he needed to be reminded. ⚳

MASQUERADE

by Kevin Andrew Murphy

James couldn't remember where he'd crashed the day before or when he'd last tanked up, but the bike was full and so was he. "Cool." Time to ride.

He dodged a cable car, flashing the tourists a smile, and slipped on his shades as he came to the crest of the hill. Minute and a half past sundown, clouds still gold to the west and silvered moon to the east, twin shadows washing up past the facade of the Fairmont and the old brownstone of the Pacific Union Club. Snob Hill, aka Nob Hill. But it was San Francisco and he loved it.

Except the traffic lights.

James remembered there was something he was supposed to do and took the delay to reach into his jacket's inside pocket. There was a memorandum book, open to today's date, and someone had scrawled on it in that spidery faggot handwriting he kept finding on all his things: "Fri. Oct. 29. Sundown. Sutro Bath's w/Dirk."

James put away the book and flipped off the asshole behind him, taking off down California Street. Dirk was cool, and it was a lot more fun running with him than that bitch queen, Belladonna, and her leather dykes. She had something stuck up her ass, and it probably came with batteries. Dead ones, in her case.

He cut down Hyde to Geary, taking it out across the city. Traffic was better, but San Francisco was never without its surprises. And a vampire didn't survive long without instincts.

James heard the fore-echo of a crash and swerved aside just as the car in front of him slammed on its brakes. "Fuck!" He realized then that the ground was shaking. Brakes squealed and people on the sidewalks gawked, and from somewhere in the distance came the sound of metal and glass.

And the scene before him melted like a bad director's interpretation of a flashback.

Masonry crumbled and the sky burned, dark smoke roiling in a phantasmagoria of time and pain, shrieks of men and horses in the background, and he tasted fear. Old fear.

"Momma!" came the child's cry from his throat and he saw a woman, blond hair coming free from its lace cap and antique nightgown billowing in the morning light as she rushed toward him, catching him up in her arms and hugging him close. Safe. Warm. Secure.

"Momma!" sobbed the child, and the memory was shattered by the very present and audible horn of the car behind. The reality of night and 1993 replaced the vision of the morning of 1906, and acrid smoke and burning air transmuted to the ordinary fumes of car exhaust.

James shook his head. Goddamn auspex. The power only gave glimpses of the future, usually too little too late, but hindsight came in full Sensurround whether you wanted it or not. As if he gave a damn what some turn-of-the-century brat thought of the earthquake or his mother. It had all happened before James had died — and before he'd been born for that matter — and nobody gave a fuck about the '89 Quake, let alone the 1906.

Not that you wouldn't think so from the way this one had stopped traffic.

"Goddamn tourists," James swore, slipping between a van with a Santa Cruz sticker and a Mercedes whose license plate proclaimed "Famous Potatoes." "You'd think they'd never seen a fuckin' earthquake."

James was glad he rode a hog instead of being locked in one of those stinking metal coffins. Geary was a mess, but he still made good time and got to the Cliff House just after the last glow had faded from the sky.

He cruised in beside a tourist mom and two daughters and killed the engine, turning on the charm. "Evening, ladies."

Omigod, he looks like Luke Perry. He caught the thought from the elder daughter. *Tres 90210.*

The mother's eyes went wide. James Dean? But he's dead.

"'Fraid so, ma'am," James said. "Dean's dead. But you can't kill a memory."

James snapped out and got a brief chuckle letting the three stare at the place he'd been. The youngest was of course the first to break the obfuscation. "Momma?" she asked. "Didn't we just see Jason Priestly?"

James slipped on down the steps, invisible to the tourists. Always give 'em what they want. It was the actor's job, and even in death he enjoyed it. He had half a mind to stage an Elvis sighting, but Dirk was waiting and the rest of the gang wouldn't appreciate the attention.

James sidestepped a mangy dog at the base of the stairs, letting it snuffle some yuppie type. Animals were tough to fool, and harder to frighten away than kids. And something in his sixth sense told him that this one was trouble.

The Gutters were hanging out in the ruins. James slipped out of the veil halfway down the beach and waved to get their attention. Dirk gave him the "Hi" sign, and everyone else played it cool.

Dirk, Joe, Little Mick, and Veronica. The core of the gang, all vampires. No humans, no ghouls. "Hiya Jim."

"Evening Dirk." He nodded to the others. He rode with them sometimes, but wasn't a Gutter. Too much of a lone wolf. "So wha'sup?"

Dirk waved for the others to go play with the tourists, then got out a cigarette and lit up, slowly. The flame flared bright, but James forced himself to stay cool. No flinch, Dirk thought. Good.

"You finished testing me, asshole?"

Dirk flicked the ash towards him. "Guess so. Wanted to see if you had the guts to run with the Sabbat."

James' guard was up and he looked, though didn't see any immediate threat. Dirk's aura was the same pale cobalt it always was, without the black veins of a Diabolist. Same with the rest of the vamps on the beach, and the humans too, though no surprise there.

The dog, however, was one fucking *angry* dog, red like a pool of blood, but edged with the bright green of curiosity, and bursting with lifeforce. Not a Diabolist, but dangerous all the same, and nothing he'd ever seen on a dog before. Maybe rabies.

But there wasn't anything on the beach like a Diabolist, even a wannabe.

James snapped back. "What the fuck you talking about, man?"

Dirk took a long drag, but James could feel the agitation behind the careful mask. "Sabbat's in town."

James shrugged. "So? Nothing new. Anyone who knows what's up knows they got spies. Only trouble's figurin' out which licks are Sabbat and which are just regular assholes."

"L.A.'s crawlin' with them."

"Sabbat or assholes?"

"Both." Dirk grinned. "Ain't you a vamp by way of the Queen of Angels yourself?"

James played it cool. "So's Tex, and he's like this with the Prince," he said, crossing his fingers.

Dirk laughed. "Can't prove nothing. Sabbat's everywhere. But rumor says a whole pack of 'em has gone on tour, hunting elders or anything else that looks tasty. Diabolists. Heard they offed half the primogen up in Portland, sucked on 'em 'til they were nothing but dust. But who knows. Maybe the old bastards just wasted each other."

"What's it to you? You don't hang with the Camarilla."

"Sabbat thinks I do." Dirk flicked the cigarette into one of the old baths. It hissed and died as it hit the water. "Doesn't matter what I think. And just because I don't hang with the old windbags and their bullshit doesn't mean I want to join the Sabbat and go to their little vampire revival meetings. Even if I don't end up on the communion plate."

James hadn't heard much about the Sabbat, but none of it was good, and Dirk's picture of Southern Baptist bloodsuckers was not something he wanted to think about. "What makes you think I'd want to join them? They're supposed to be nuttier than the Malkavians."

Dirk gave him a pointed look. "Weirder than Tupperware ladies on acid, Jim. But you go places I don't, so I thought it fair to warn you. 'Sides, I heard you got the 'spex, and a good pair at that."

That was true, though not something he generally let others know. James could read a room at a glance, or even the mind of a vampire elder. But it was an actor's talent. You had to know your audience before you could play to them.

He watched the ocean crash against the beach, taking the moment to breathe in and smell the salt air. Been a while since he'd done that, and it felt good. "So, you want me to keep an eye out and see if I notice any new Diabolists? No problem. The Kooks and Degenerates keep tabs on all the local snackers anyway, and the Prince snuffs most of them. Unless they're anarchs."

He glanced over at Dirk, but the other vampire's mind was unreadable, and his aura only showed a token flash of annoyance.

Dirk looked to his waterlogged cigarette. "The Sabbat aren't morons like most Diabolists. They're like you, James. They play dress-up. . . and they do it with their auras too." Like you, the thought slipped out.

James wondered what he meant by that crack, but waited to see what else Dirk had to say.

The head Gutter took a deep breath for effect, or maybe just to delay an unpleasant thought, since he hadn't needed to breathe for a long while. He let it out. "I've heard the Sabbat can blank their auras, or cover them up with a fake."

"Warlock shit?"

"Maybe. Maybe they're buff enough to do it on their own. Who knows? It's the Sabbat.

"But if there's any vamp who could spot 'em and trick 'em, it'd be you, Jim. You've got all the right skills, and you're smart enough to do it. And just crazy enough to try."

Dirk sounded like the producer who'd signed him on years ago. "So what do I get if I take the part?"

The Gutter smiled, letting his fangs show. "Take it as a dare. If you see a bunch of new vamps you can't read, or whose emotions don't change, or don't match what you think they should be feeling, that'll be them. Sidle on up to them. Smile. Make friends. Then do whatever takes your fancy."

Dirk took out another cigarette and lit up, match flaring. "After all, Jim, that's what you do best.

• • •

The wind whipped past the bike, and James fell away, red leather fading to black and brown hair to blond. Philip sighed in relief. It had been a while since he'd taken the Brujah out for a spin, and he hadn't thought he'd lose himself so completely in the role, let alone that he'd mistake his own memories of the quake for a psychometric flashback. But James dealt best with the rebels, and as he'd said, you gave the audience what they wanted. And you had to give yourself to the role if you wanted to play the part.

And the stage was now the Café Prague in the Haight, and that meant Toreadors. Virgil had asked him by, but hadn't said what he wanted to talk about. Which meant the *persona d' nuit* was Philemon, the model of Virgil's Clan — literally.

Philip composed himself for the role by cutting through the park. Philemon loved beauty, and even in the dying days of Indian Summer, Golden Gate Park was gorgeous, the meadows half-shrouded in fog and night.

Not that night was any problem for a vampire, especially with the moon on the rise, one day to full.

He lingered a moment at a stop sign to gaze into the mirror and let his vanity coalesce. Perfect skin, flawless as *bianca* marble. Lapis eyes. Golden curls. Such classically sculpted features as Michelangelo had only seen in dreams, and a body to make anyone die of envy, be they man or woman.

The Mask enhanced his beauty, and Philemon sighed. He was truly stunning.

As was the horn of the car behind him. "Philistine!" Philemon shouted back. "Don't you know Art when you see it?"

Philemon, however, chose to move, as there was beauty in motion, and none in the strident discord from the vandal's automobile. The noise was even more clamorous than the horns of the temple of Cybelle. But that was Rome, almost 2,000 years ago, and few would understand such a delicate allusion. Pity.

There was a slight delay en route to the cafe, when a police officer took exception to Philemon's perfect coiffure being displayed without a motorcycle helmet. Philemon was kind, explaining to the officer the error of his ways, and even favored the poor ignorant with a Kiss.

Philip licked his fangs. Tasty, but a danger to the Masquerade. He told the cop to forget about it.

Philemon was scandalized. What could ever have possessed him to have done such a thing? But *la!* An answer readily presented itself: The Prince's Masquerade was a work-in-progress, and one always had to make sacrifices for the greater sake of Art.

Such a waste, however. Philemon let a good dozen of the kine see his perfect form to best advantage by parking a distance from the café and walking up

Ashbury. Music filtered down the block, delightful '70s retro by Jellyfish, and Philemon bounced in time to the beat.

". . . congratulations . . . to him adulation . . . a blessed life begun . . . for the ghost at number one . . ."

Philemon nodded to his host of admirers, then paused when he saw the sign and giggled. Some mischievous sprite had shorted the neon, and now the second scroll of the "R" flashed on and off, transforming the Café Prague into the Café Plague and back again.

"A plague upon their houses," Philemon quipped. "A commemorative plague."

Laughing at his own wit, Philemon entered the café, wondering who he should first favor with his beauty.

". . . know you've been buried alive . . ."

His face fell, and the Mask almost did too. The vampire crowd was primarily Ventrue out slumming it. Not his sort of people at all. This was Philip's crowd.

Philip Van Vermeer IV, formerly Philip Van Vermeer II, was exceedingly put out. Here he was, made over into the ridiculously foppish guise of Philemon, tight leather butt pants and all, and there were mortals present so he couldn't drop the Mask, or even change the semblance of his clothing into something more presentable before his peers.

Nickoli, primogen of the Ventrue, raised a glass of red wine in toast. "Surprise, Philip!" he called over the music.

"Surprise," said the others, more sedately, and Philip took them in: Doc Michaels, the Ventrue Minister of Health; Donna, Childe of the Prince, showing herself to best advantage in an off-the-shoulder gown perhaps more appropriate to the opera — though nothing was ever inappropriate in the Haight; a brawny mortal or ghoul whom Philip did not recognize, though the face seemed familiar; and Vannevar Thomas, the Prince himself, having such force of presence as to maintain his dignity even while holding a balloon bouquet, of which the centerpiece was a large mylar orb ornamented with Care Bears and bearing the legend, "Today is your special day!"

Happy Deathnight, said a voice in his head.

Philip turned and looked into the sparkling blue eyes of Tobin Van Tuys, his great-uncle and Sire. And his mirror, despite two decades of apparent age and several centuries of true antiquity. The blond hair was thinning and handsome face lined, but otherwise Uncle Toby looked for all the world like the man Philip saw in the mirror each evening. Most evenings, anyway.

"Surprise, nephew," said the elder vampire. "We thought this a bit more to your taste than the Alexandrian Club. Celebrations at one's place of work always end up having the mien of an office party, no matter how splendid the setting."

Philip smiled. It was always so touching that a being of such great power took the trouble do something so simple and human. "Thank you, uncle," he said softly.

Vannevar and Donna came over, the Prince presenting Philip with the balloons with a courtly nod. "As the March Hare said to Alice, 'Happy Unbirthday.'"

"To you," added Donna, handing him two blood-red roses done up in florist's wrap. "From Vannevar and myself."

"Thank you," said Philip, knowing the precious significance of such presents — the roses, at least. "I had not expected to see you until Sunday."

The Prince inclined his head. "An engagement came free, so Donna and I were able to come. As for Sunday, All Hallow's Eve being what it is, I'm afraid we'll only be able to make our appearance and then vanish almost as quickly."

Philip smiled. "It is the night for apparitions."

"True," said Vannevar, "and summonses. No end to those, and even if Honerius is busy with his mystic nosepicking, somebody always has the rabbit by the ears."

"There are all sorts of engagements," said Donna enigmatically, looking to Thomas.

Though uncharacteristically nervous, Virgil gestured grandly, bowing to the company. "In fact, I have one myself later this evening, and so, I know, does Philip. So before we begin making like Vannevar's rabbits and make ourselves mad for time . . . ?"

Nickoli laughed and Virgil quickly ushered everyone into the back room of the cafe, the last words of a poem cutting off as the door shut behind them.

An old sound, Dixieland beat, with spoons and banjo and a mandolin. It reminded Philip of that fateful evening some 70 years before, when he had been in a similar back room, a speakeasy, with bathtub gin and black minstrels. There had been a firefight, and he had died. Only 23 and cut down by a stray bullet.

But his uncle's love had saved him. That, and the fact that his uncle was among the most powerful of the Ventrue and had been willing to risk the wrath of the Prince to embrace a dying mortal. It still amazed Philip to think how Tobin Van Tuys had felt that foolish child's dying breath and been able to rush across the city and save him.

Or damn him, depending on one's point of view.

Everyone was in the room and Philip took in his surroundings. The inner sanctum of the Café Prague was a small lounge appointed with '60s salvage art, cable-spool tables and suchlike, spaced at random amid bright posters from the Avalon Ballroom advertising various concerts from the Summer of Love. Such fun, thought Thomas, examining one whose day-glo letters proclaimed "The Congress of Wonders."

Philip agreed, remembering the comedians, and found a spot for the balloons and roses on an art nouveau hall tree set off to one side. He heard the *click* as Virgil turned the key in the lock and glanced into the mirror, allowing the Mask to drop and replacing Philemon's bondage ensemble and ludicrous prettiness with his own normal semblance and turtleneck and pants in basic black. He smiled to himself. Much better.

Either to sleight the Prince or from sheer bad taste, Nickoli had seated himself in the room's one obvious throne, a peacock chair with hideous paisley cushions. "Now that we are in private, Virgil, I would hope that we might have more satisfying libations." He gave a quick look to the mortal, then back to the cafe's owner, and raised his glass. "And I would like to know what it is you've been serving in place of your usual 'sangria.' Blood plasma mixed with red food coloring is bad enough, but this is particularly vile."

Doc Michaels answered. "Would you believe Ringer's solution mixed with black cherry Kool-Aid? Perfectly harmless injected into mortal veins, and therefore safe for Kindred digestion even, if not terribly satisfying." He bowed. "My own personal invention."

Nickoli set the glass down on a table decorated with pressed butterfly wings. "Thank you, Jenny Craig."

Donna chuckled and Philip let his attention be drawn to the mortal, who was the undoubted star attraction at the moment, and certainly not of the usual run if primogen felt safe discussing Kindred matters in his presence.

He was a young Italian man, neither ghoul nor vampire, but judging from his aura having at least the potential to be a mage. Just below average height — short, to Philip — and apparently no older than his mid-20s, he wore an impeccably tailored Armani suit with crimson silk accents and had the air of a banker or investment broker. Not surprising, since Philip knew that the moneyed professions were his uncle's particular preference. The man's face was darkly handsome, set atop a thick and powerful body, and if not for the lack of a neck, he could have done beefcake, the musculature obvious even under the charcoal silk.

Uncle Tobin smiled at Philip, then bowed and gestured to the mortal. "May I please introduce my personal guest at these proceedings — and also the evening's cake: Giancarlo Giovanni. Giancarlo, my nephew and Childe, Philip Van Vermeer."

"A pleasure," he said, heavily accented, and grabbed Philip's hand in a hearty squeeze.

Philip squeezed back and smiled, now recognizing the face. He had never met the man before, but Giancarlo was undoubtedly a member of the exclusive Giovanni Clan. The family look was unmistakable. Only the flush of life and a healthy tan had confused him. Though young now, Giancarlo was no doubt slated to become a member of his family's vampiric elite, explaining this small lapse in the Masquerade. "The pleasure is mine."

Giancarlo laughed. "Not yet, my friend, not yet. But you will find it well worth the wait. My family tells me my blood is quite potent, *abondanza* as we say, so there should be enough for everyone, yes? That should be magic enough for your palate, your uncle tells me, and while he has not told me the tastes of the good doctor, or the Prince and his lovely companion, I am assured that I am talented enough to suit the whole company. Fortunate, yes? This is a case of, how you say, 'having one's cake and eating it too.' But I am most interested to see how the Ventrue celebrate their deathnights, for I have only my own family gatherings for comparison, and those are rather formal affairs."

"Among the Ventrue, deathnights are an occasion for celebration." Philip looked over at the Care Bear balloons the Prince had given him. "Even whimsy. You are welcome to delight in my death."

"Then it is my pleasure to join you." The Italian gave his hand one last squeeze and looked him straight in the eye, and Philip, used to the shrouded minds of Kindred and the abstraction of unsuspecting mortals, was shocked by the stark clarity of the thoughts writ there. The mortal had been expecting the intrusion and Philip fell past the edge.

Is it true? asked the black pools of Giancarlo Giovanni's eyes. Are you truly mad, Philip Van Vermeer? Is that your true name, or form? Or is it a lie, in whole or in part, and is it your lie, or another's? Whose? What is it that motivates you and what do you want from this "life" of yours?

Giancarlo broke away, still smiling, and Philip's psyche shattered, unable to withstand the precisioned force of the inquiry.

Philip surfaced, watching as the guests arrayed themselves about the room, and tried to keep himself as tied to Philip's persona as possible while not losing himself to the Ventrue. He closed his eyes, feigning intense emotion while at the same time making his thoughts unreadable. Dear, sweet uncle Tobin, Sire in all but truth. It wasn't his fault. Philip had even believed the pleasant fiction of the speakeasy firefight the first few years of his unlife. Many still did, possibly even the Prince.

But Tobin Van Tuys knew it was a lie, and so did Phil. He'd been Embraced by a Malkavian anarch and left staked on his uncle's doorstep, an act of sheer spite. And perversity.

The joke of it was, only when he was among madmen was he in his right mind.

But this was Philip's party, and it was selfish for Philip to steal it for himself. Philip would make his uncle happy, and Tobin deserved at least that.

Philip Van Vermeer opened his eyes and glared at Giancarlo, planning to throttle the little Italian if he got a chance. How dare anyone put credence in that ridiculous rumor that he was a Malkavian cuckoo left on his uncle's doorstep as a prank on the Ventrue? Only a Malkavian would be mad enough to believe such a thing. Or a mortal puffed up on his own importance for knowing a few trifling secrets about the Kindred.

Of course, the lie had its uses. The Malkavians had designated him their representative on more than one occasion, and he'd been able to use the mad vampires' vote to further the interests of his true Clan. The Ventrue were more than pleased with his actions.

"Good friends," said Uncle Toby, and Philip quickly found a place beside Doc Michaels on the floor cushions. The Prince and Donna had taken the rattan loveseat for their own, making Nickoli look ridiculous in his isolation, and Giancarlo and Virgil had taken the laminated orange crates. "We are gathered here to celebrate the death of my Childe, Philip, without which he would not be with us on this night. It was 70 years and 70 minutes ago that I Embraced him as a member of our company, and I renew that bond now, a minute past the minute, so that the bond is that of love and not blood." Tobin checked his antique silver timepiece, then unsheathed the knife on the fob, cutting deep into his wrist.

Blood poured down, pooling into the cup formed by his hands, only stopping as it reached the brim. "Drink, my Childe, and be renewed."

Philip got down on one knee and bowed his head. "I am not worthy of this gift," he said the ritual phrase.

"None of us are worthy, my Childe. It is only by the Sin of Caine that we are Damned. Drink of the *Sangre Real*. Drink from the *San Greal*."

"*Sangre Real-San Greal*," chanted the other Ventrue. Blood Royal, Holy Grail.

"My thanks," said Philip, bending his head and drinking deep from the blood of the Ventrue, the purest line of Caine. The Royal Blood.

It washed down his throat, rich and warm, and Philip felt the wash of centuries.

Look here, said a voice, and Philip saw a man strike down his brother.

Look here, said another, and Philip saw his uncle, dressed in the clothes of a Dutch merchant Prince, a scene from the glory of Amsterdam.

See this, said a third, and Philip saw himself, slicked step haircut and collegiate suit, from the day of his death and Embrace, lying in the arms of his uncle. But staked. And his uncle wept tears of blood.

Know Her, said the voices in unison, and a tarot card fell down before his vision. Key II, The High Priestess, from Crowley's Thoth deck. "The Future is Uncertain." Then the Priestess laughed and her face melted and resolved into another woman's, blond and heartbreakingly beautiful.

Know Her, said the voices, then the woman laughed and he saw her soul, black with sin as if painted with a tarred brush.

Then the tar melted away and he saw her true soul, pale rose with longing and gray with loneliness. But dead.

End of the line! clamored the voices like a crowd of railway porters. End of the line!

The tar caught fire and bloody palms reached out and grabbed his face, pulling him past the burning woman, and Philip suddenly found himself on his feet. "Arise, you are one of the Chosen!" said his uncle.

"He is Chosen!" said the others present.

"Hallelujah," said Nickoli. "Now can we cut the cake?"

Philip fell back against the wall, reeling from the intensity of the vision, and his palms slid across the smooth paneling. His powers of auspex had grown over the decades, but had never had this intensity. Some of the power of his uncle's vitae had cause them to spike.

There was still the deathnight ceremony to attend to. Philip pushed himself away from the wall and licked the blood from his lips, wiping the rest from his face with a handkerchief.

Doc Michaels brought out a cooler chest and prepared the necessary equipment for a transfusion, while Giancarlo came over, smiling. "My apologies for not being an attractive young lady, but one cannot have everything, yes? Or as this is San Francisco, does it matter?"

Philip demurred. "A willing vessel is rare enough, and doubly so one who can serve as cake for a Ventrue deathnight. A lovely lady would be asking too much."

"Ahem," said the Prince, "I believe we have a lovely lady already present."

Donna blushed in a most lifelike manner and put her head against his shoulder. "Vannevar, please."

Philip bowed. "My apologies, my Prince, and to Donna as well. But were I to steal a Kiss, I'm sure I would never be satisfied with just one, and soon you would find me impossible to get rid of."

The corner of the Prince's mouth twitched. "Pleasantly, at least. But point taken. Donna is neither mortal nor free, and of the Ventrue present, I believe that we two are the only ones mutually to each other's taste."

Giancarlo laughed. "Well, then, Philip can always wish for a lady of his own, yes? But I think I will unwrap myself." He unbuttoned his jacket, folding it neatly and laying it over the back of an orange crate, and followed with his waistcoat and shirt, flexing slightly. Doc Michaels would have no trouble finding a vein for the transfusion, but might have to shave a bit first.

"Mmm," Donna purred and smiled, showing her teeth. "*Signori Giovanni,* I would love to invite you to my own deathnight." She paused then, looking to Vannevar. "If my Prince would not mind?"

Vannevar chose not to respond.

"We shall have to see," Giancarlo said diplomatically, then nodded to Philip. "Happy Deathnight, my friend. And *buon gusto.*"

Philip bent down to the Giovanni's neck. "*Gratzi, mi amico.*"

Giancarlo's blood was just as rich as he had said and Philip lost himself in the ecstasy of the Kiss.

• • •

Philip was nearly sweating blood. What a night. Sundown with Dirk, early evening at the Café Prague for his uncle, late evening at the Condor Club for the mortals, midnight at the Vampire Club for the dead, with a witching hour show for the half-dead at the Alexandrian Club upstairs somehow sandwiched in on both sides of the band. He'd done enough quick changes, in and out of character, that it was a wonder he still remembered who he was. Philip decided the old Malkavian hag who'd done him in had picked this night just to drive him crazy.

Of course, October 29 was the beginning of the three-day festival that culminated in *el Dia de Los Muertos*, the Day of the Dead, so lots of California Kindred had one of the next few nights for their deathnight. It made a certain amount of crazy sense, as befit a Malkavian. That it was also the Friday before Halloween, and full moon the next night, just added to the insanity.

At least the Alexandrian's curtain close was the last show of the night. "Bde-bde-bde — That's all folks!" Philip called out, sans the illusory Porky Pig head he would have used at the Vampire Club downstairs, and took his bow.

And saw Her.

It wasn't quite the same woman. Instead of the gauzy robes of Crowley's Priestess, she wore the black leathers of a mod, her hair dyed black and cropped short, ears set off by diamond studs. Her aura was neither the dusky rose he had last seen last, nor the blackened horror that the vision had shown him earlier, but totally absent, a blank in the wash of color in the room.

As were the four around her, chatting with the white and red column of egotism and anger that was Tomaine, the latest of the Brujah primogen.

Philip ducked behind the curtain, wondering what he should do.

"Philip!" cried a voice in delight.

He turned to see a jowly face descending on him: Sebastian Melmoth, owner of both clubs and vampire leatherboy extraordinaire. "Wonderful performances, all of them. Why, you mocked *me* even better than I mock myself — the mark of a true wit. And," he added in a conspiratorial undertone, "I must thank you again for taking the time on your deathnight."

Sebastian enjoyed dealing with Philip, so Philip let the Ventrue take the fore, hoping he could give Sebastian a quick brush off. "I am honored to perform here, especially on such an auspicious night as this. I know how eagerly those from your own Clan would wish to take my place."

"Poseurs all, I must confide." Sebastian lay a delicate hand on Philip's arm. "'Tis a shame they are part of my Clan, but even if they had some other name, they would still stink."

Philip smiled, and let Sebastian go on with his soliloquy.

"But a rose for a rose, as they say, and nothing smells sweeter than the rose of death." Sebastian held forth a pressed blossom, pale lavender despite its age, the stem studded with countless thorns. After a cursory glance around, he squeezed until his blood ran down the stem and the delicate petals stirred to life, brown leaves turning green.

Sebastian smiled. "I believe your preference is for the blood of magicians and psychics. May I present Mademoiselle Helen Blavatsky, a Russian hybrid tea, named for the redoubtable lady herself, who once gave me this as a present. I understand you had Italian cake earlier this evening, and Russian tea always goes so well with that, as I recall."

Philip took the rose and let it disappear up his sleeve. Tex had already given him a yellow one, and a half-dozen others had also presented him with the roses of death, in various symbolic shades. It was a true mark of favor.

But nothing he had time for now.

"My greatest thanks," he said and disappeared. With any luck, Sebastian would be befuddled enough that he wouldn't even remember talking to him. After the

Englishman bit enough drunks, he tended to forget a number of things.

A new song started up as he came onto the floor, Human League's "Mirror Man." Philip sighed. That was supposed to be his cue to go on stage, but what could you expect when Sebastian hired techs for their looks and not their talent?

Philip slipped invisibly through the crowd, looking for the pale candy-striped aura of Tomaine, and wondered what guise he should appear in. It was usually never such a decision; he could normally tell the sort of people folk liked.

But the Sabbat pack, if that was what they were, were here in disguise. Masked as it were.

"You know I'll change, if change is what you require, your every wish, your every dream, hope, desire. . ."

Philip knew a lot about masks and costuming. From the glance he'd had, and the company they were keeping, the new spies had taken on the role of Brujah anarchs.

Which meant that he should take the role of an old spy and an old Brujah. Perhaps someone missing in action from the Sabbat-Camarilla wars, forced to hide out in enemy territory. He smiled then and lip-synched the next line: "Here comes the Mirror Man. . ."

Philip trailed them through the rooms of the Alexandrian Club, watching as they tagged along with Tomaine, and wondering if the primo was to be the night's main course, or was just good camouflage. Maybe both.

He made a decision in the billiards room and took a cue from the rack, rounding a corner and taking on the guise of James.

"Hey! To'! My main man! What's shaking?"

Tomaine whirled, but the sight of a five-foot long stake was enough to give any vampire pause. "James," he said at last.

Philip was glad his Brujah ego had cruised through one of their rants when Tomaine had been around. Just enough for passing familiarity.

James, however, was getting into the role. "Who's the chick? Anybody care to shoot some pool?"

Tomaine took the bait like he'd hoped. "Unfortunately all they have here is billiards. Do you play?"

"Sure. Do you?"

The woman stepped forward then, cutting off the challenge and making her own play for authority. Classic Brujah. "The chick's name is Christine." She paused. "Are you really James Dean?"

James grinned. "Fuck me, lady. Dean's dead." He chalked the cue. "I'm really Jason Priestly got up in a red leather jacket, and I quit L.A. 'cause Shannon Doherty is such a bitch."

He looked into her eyes and tried to read her, but it was like looking into a steel mirror. James looked away. She was guarded all right.

She laughed, hard-edged and mean. Perfect Brujah. "Why don't you get your stick, Tomaine, then you boys can go at each other? I like to watch."

Tomaine signaled for a cue. "Watch your mouth, bitch, or I'll stick you too."

One of Tomaine's entourage racked up the balls while the others convinced the couple using the table that the bar would be more to their taste, whether or not they drank. None of them had an aura, and it was an even bet that their eyes were all the same steely gray once you looked deep enough.

The Sabbat was in town. James loved it.

He circled the table, running his fingers over the wood and checking the weight of his cue. He'd played here a number of times, though dressed up as that nutcase, Philip, or some other bastard who wouldn't draw too much attention. But it was Halloween weekend. No one would question a James Dean look-alike. And even if they did, this was the time for the dead to walk the earth anyway.

Fuck the Masquerade, though. If the licks hadn't wanted people to recognize him, they shoulda had one of the sewer rats make him and mess up his face. 'Course he would have wasted any rat who'd try to pull that shit on him, and that's why they hadn't given it a go.

He was glad the Brujah had taken him, and better yet that it was the Sabbat down in L.A., not these prissy Frisco bastards like Tomaine and their Camarilla and its stupid Masquerade. What was the fuckin' point of being a bloodsucker if you couldn't scare the shit out of some poor slob every once in a while?

James scored another point. Tomaine was an asshole. Good thing his pals from the Sabbat had showed up. They'd all waste the old toad and blow this fucking Masquerade bullshit sky high. This was what he'd been hiding out for all these years.

"Nice shot," said Christine, leaning on the edge of the table. "Now let's see you make the next one."

James grabbed her by the back of the head and pulled her close. "For luck," he said, kissing her hard on the mouth, and let his fangs spike his tongue mid-clench. The blood welled up and poured into her mouth, then James withdrew his tongue and sucked shut the edges of the cut, savoring the taste of his own vitae.

Anger and defiance flared in her eyes, but not her aura, and he jerked her head back so she swallowed from reflex, his blood coursing down her throat.

He let go of her and let her sag back into the arms of Tomaine, her eyes shining with the joy of the Kiss — though they were still the same steely gray to the 'spex. James had found a Sabbat all right.

He took the cue and wasted that ball and the next, finishing the game. "Two out of three, asswipe?" he asked the old Brujah.

It took four licks to hold him back.

"Enough of this!" said a voice. Sebastian Melmoth, the prissy leatherboy, stood there, trying to impress everyone with his stupid Toreador shit. "I will have none of this in my club!" He looked to James. "And I don't want to see your face in here again."

James grinned, pointing the cue at the older vampire. "What the fuck's wrong with my face, faggot?"

Sebastian appeared to calm. "My, my," he said. "Hiding behind a big stick, are we? Afraid to defend yourself with your own little splinter?"

James tossed the cue aside and put up his fists. "You want to go at it, then, faggot? *Mano a mano?*" A thought trickled into his brain from somewhere. and he took off his jacket, Black Sabbath T-shirt stretched tight across his chest: Marquis of Queensbury rules?

Sebastian stepped back and what little color his face had left drained away. James somehow knew the nerve he'd struck: Oscar Wilde had been locked up in prison for blowing the Marquis of Queensbury's son. What the fuck that had to do with Sebastian, he didn't know, but faggots were a bunch of clannish bastards, so the leatherboy probably knew, and it didn't take much to scare the fuck out of most of them anyway.

James put down his fists and sneered. "Blow me."

Sebastian purpled, blood rushing to his fangs, but he bit it back, refusing to frenzy. "Out!" he shrilled. "Out of my club! Out or I will call a Blood Hunt!"

"What the fuck's a Blood Hunt, you old fairy?" James laughed and watched as Tomaine actually restrained the mincing old Toreador. A couple of the bodyguards came towards him until James put up his hands. "Hey, back off or I'll say a few more things nobody wants to hear. And none of us wants that, right?"

The bouncers let him put his jacket back on. James turned to Christine and the rest of her crew. "Let's blow this place before the wildman there decides to blow us."

A path cleared to the door and James led the way out, singing, "Toreadoro, artiste poseur whore-o," and continued on into various other Kindred blasphemies and borderline violations of the Masquerade.

The valet stood outside the Alexandrian Club. "My keys," James said. "Hop to it."

The valet went to get the keys to James' chopper, hopping like a bunny all the way. Christine came up beside him. "It looks like the wildman already got that boy."

"Why do you think they call them car hops?"

One of Christine's crew giggled, a mousy little brunette got up like Stevie Nicks gone evil, black petticoats and all.

Christine put her hand on his arm, the fingers slim and delicate. "Tell me," she said, "are you really James Dean?"

"Dean's dead."

"True. But that doesn't answer my question. Are you James Dean?"

"What do you think, baby?"

She smiled. "I don't know what to think. *Tell me.*"

James felt the press on his mind and something snapped, a connection he'd thought he'd had. "Yeah," he found himself saying, "I'm James Dean. And if you fucking Dominate me again, I'll kill you, lady."

One of the other Sabbat members, a tall guy, spoke up. "James Dean died in the late '50s."

James turned on him. "Well look who believes everything he's told." He sneered. "I bet you think I got a condo with Elvis and Marilyn too, an' Jim Morrison comes over on Sundays for bridge.

"You guys are a bunch of assholes. I got stuck in torpor for 10 years after our pack got trashed, and I've been hiding out in this hellhole ever since. And the first Sabbat packers I run into since then give me a bunch of shit when they're just as dead as me."

"Why do you think we're Sabbat?" asked the tall guy.

"You guys ain't got no auras. Either you sold your souls, or you got something to hide." James shrugged. "So you ain't Camarilla, and you ain't anarchs. That leaves one thing."

A dark-haired guy wearing the Banana Republic catalog stared at him. "You don't have an aura either."

James grinned. "You show me yours, I'll show you mine."

The little mousy girl got in his face. "What's *La Palla Grande?*"

"It's Spanish for, 'The Grand Ball.' And *El Pollo Loco* means 'The Crazy Chicken' and it's a fast food joint. Who gives a fuck? The password's 'swordfish,' okay? I got wasted first battle after I got killed, so I didn't learn all the handshakes or get my Mouseketeer pin. Give me a break, OK?"

"*Tell me,*" said Christine, "are you Sabbat?"

"Yeah," said James. "Yeah, if you'll have me back."

• • •

James learned all their names by the time they'd broken into the Japanese Tea Garden. The tall guy was Brandt, and he was a La Bamba, or something like that, which meant he was hot shit and didn't show up in mirrors, not that it was something to brag about. The mousy gal in the wicked waif outfit was Katie and she was a Malkavian, though she wouldn't admit to it. James just sort of guessed after she said she was the reincarnation of Helen of Troy, but was going incognito so as to not cause another war.

The dark-haired guy was a Toreador who liked to be called Spike, though Katie called him Wilfred to annoy him, and the last of the crew was Morgan, who Katie said was a panda.

"That's *Panders*," Morgan snapped, though he really did resemble a panda in some ways: big, with black hair and very white skin and circles under his eyes.

Christine was the Priestess, and she was a Tzimisce. James had heard something about them, mostly that they were better warlocks than a lot of the Tremere, but she didn't say much beyond that.

James, of course, was a Brujah, and proud of it.

Brandt grabbed a drunk at the edge of the park and forced him to come along. James could see the man's terror in the flashes of his aura, but didn't give a damn. He was Sabbat, and this was the sort of thing Sabbat were supposed to do.

Katie and Spike tied the man to one of the benches. "Did you know my mother mated with a swan?" Katie asked conversationally while Spike took out an expensive camera and began taking pictures. "I've tried it myself, but I've never quite seen the appeal. Do you?"

"Ohgodohgodohgodohgod," babbled the man. "Ohpleaseohmygodohgod. . ."

"Actually it was a god," said Katie. "Zeus, to be exact, and I imagine my mother said the exact same thing when they got it on, though a bit more enthusiastically."

"What a loon," James said to Christine.

She smiled back. "We must excuse her. She's Malkavian. Madness runs in their blood."

"From what she says, it does a bunch of other stuff too."

"Hold that pose," said Spike. "Yes, yes, perfect." A bulb flashed, and Katie and the drunk both screamed.

"So whatcha gonna do?" James asked. "Never did Night of the Living Dead with the Sabbat. That's what this is, right? The first day of that Mexican thing?"

"*La Noche de los Muertos,* to be exact, but yes, you have the general idea. The extended festival begins tonight, and it's also the Friday before the full moon, so we have reasons aplenty to celebrate. But first," said Christine, taking a teapot from under counter of the tea house, "we must reestablish the vinculum bonds."

"Brandt," said Spike, "strangle him just a little bit. I'd like to do a study of the bruising process, and you're the only one whose hands won't show up." Flash. Flash. Flash. Flash. "Thank you, that was great."

Christine slashed her wrist with a small ritual knife and poured blood into the teapot. She offered blade and pot to James. "If you would, my dear?"

James chuckled. "Tea ceremony. Fun."

He cut his wrist the same way Christine had and let the blood flow into the pot. It reminded him of something he'd done earlier that evening, but he couldn't remember what.

Morgan was the next to add his blood to the teapot, then Brandt, Katie, and Spike. Katie giggled. "Oh boy, this is just like *The Mikado.*" She looked eye to eye with Spike, then, in unison, they began to sing, alternating verses: "My object all sublime/I shall achieve in time/To make the punishment fit the crime/The punishment fit the crime."

Katie began dancing, pouring the blood into six teacups, continuing to sing her mad little song: "For all of those dear little vampires/Who hold their humanity high/Those all are the people/I'd stake on a steeple/And let them all fry in the sky!"

They laughed and everyone downed their cups, including James. It tasted wonderful. Katie went and tapped another potful from the terrified drunk. "Saké anyone?" she asked and James raised his cup.

"Thank you for suggesting the tea garden," Christine said. "My troupe so enjoys coming up with innovative new rites, and we were afraid we were going to have to make do with a parking garage. But," she added significantly, "it's always good to follow tradition. And to keep up with the Craft. So I think the order of the night is a goat. After all, it is Friday."

She looked to the terrified drunk. "Strip him."

Brandt grabbed the man's clothes and tore, stripping him until there was nothing left but ragged shreds of cloth. "In life," Christine remarked, "I was a make-up artist. But I've found my art has become so much richer since then."

She took hold of the man's feet, molding and massaging them gently, then squeezed hard. James watched the bones twist and deform, flesh warping till all that was left were a pair of twisted hooves, forked like a goat's.

The man screamed and James watched as Christine ran her hands up, thick hair sprouting with the passage of her palms. The man's flesh writhed and grew monstrous, head elongating into the muzzle of a goat, hair sprouting everywhere, until at last Christine had her hands atop his head. She coaxed and molded two horns from the bone of his skull, which suddenly burst through the scalp dripping blood, growing to a foot in length. Katie and Brandt licked them like lollipops, and Spike's flashbulbs popped in a staccato strobe all the while.

Morgan stood back, appraising. "Wouldn't a Japanese demon have been more appropriate? This is a tea garden, after all."

Christine sniffed. "Critic."

Katie slashed the bonds that held the thing that had once been a man to the bench, and James felt his already cold blood turn to ice. It stumbled to its hooves, bleating in terror, then fell face first on the deck.

Morgan pulled it to its feet, clucking his tongue. The thing stumbled forward, stiltwalking carefully, and steadied itself against the railing.

"Get thee on top of me, Satan!" Katie cried, jumping in front of it, then laughed as it bleated and fell into the fish pond. Spike took pictures.

"Call it performance art," said Christine, but looked unhappy. James allowed her to serve him another cup of blood. "So, how is it you've survived so long among the Camarilla?"

James took a sip, glad the conversation was getting into familiar territory. "They're all stupid," he said. "Half of 'em had me as a matinee idol, and the other half believed me when they said I was taken by the anarchs. But that's mostly bullshit. What happened was that there was this nutty Malkavian with all sorts of personalities who'd been around since the '20s. He was damn good at doing the Mask of a Thousand Faces, so I just grabbed him and sucked him dry and took his place. Got his power and his money and all the bullshit favors his friends owed him, and nobody thought it weird that he had me as an extra personality. Piece of cake."

Christine sipped her blood. "Did you ever try to reestablish contact with the Sabbat?"

"Ever been in torpor for 10 years, lady? Phone numbers change. I decided to wait until you showed up." James poured himself the last of the pot, watching as Katie summoned ducks to attack the Devil, and Spike took pictures. "Took you long enough."

"What's the rush? We have eternity. But honestly, the Domain of San Francisco is well guarded, and you were reported destroyed. But we do have friends here. Tomaine seems promising and has offered us a safe house. You, however, were an unexpected surprise." She turned to him. "A very welcome surprise. I've always been a fan of your films, even when you were alive."

"Thanks," James said. "You do good work, too."

Brandt was holding the former drunk in the air, making Flying Devil pictures for Spike, while Katie soaked rice crackers in her blood and fed the ducks. "Perfect! Perfect!" shouted Spike. "Tea Garden with Satan and Ghoulish Ducks!"

Christine sighed. "Well," she said, "at least they're enjoying themselves. Tell me, the pack you were in: Did they ever do anything interesting or innovative?"

James shrugged. "Weirdest we ever got was inflating some guy's intestines and tying them into balloon animals."

"Seen it." The goatman bleated in terror and the ducks quacked happily. "There's got to be something more."

James took her hand in his own, letting his blood and some warmth flow into it, and hummed a snatch of a tune.

Christine looked to him, her eyes glittering like opals in the moonlight. "What is that?"

James squeezed her hand. "Tune I heard somewhere. Can't remember where." He hummed a bit more, then sang a line, "'She's been everybody else's girl. . . maybe one day she'll be her own. . .'"

"That's very pretty," Christine said at last.

"So are you." James smiled, realizing that beneath the eyeliner and bloody tears, her eyes were blue. "That's you, you know. What the song's about. Everybody else's girl."

Christine removed her hand from his and drew back. "What do you mean?"

James smiled. "I mean you. You don't exist, not by yourself. And I don't mean 'cause you're dead or 'cause you ain't got an aura. You aren't there for yourself. Tomaine needs a little Brujah bitch queen to hang on his arm, you do it. These jerks need a stage mother to keep them in line, you do that. You're being everybody but you."

Her face became a mask of stone. "How would you know?"

James laughed. "I'm an actor. I know an act when I see it." He put his hand out and took hers back. "And I know 'cause I've fallen into the same trap myself. Being everybody but me. That's me, the mirror man. But put a mirror next to a mirror, and what do you see?"

Christine paused, her face softening, then looked deep into his eyes. "Was it you, then, up on stage, as the comedian?"

James took on the semblance of Philip. "Enjoy the show?"

Christine did a double take, then laughed uproariously, the tension in her face melting and tears of blood running down her cheeks. "Wonderful! You did that whole scene with Tomaine and that swishy Toreador just for our benefit?"

James snapped back to himself. "Nah, I mostly did it to blow off steam. But I also had to see if you were worth it. Half the city thinks I'm a nutty Malkavian, and the other half think I'm a Ventrue spy impersonating a nutty Malkavian. Or a Toreador performance artist impersonating a Ventrue impersonating a Malkavian."

"And you are?"

"A Brujah doing whatever the fuck he pleases." James paused, seeing something in her eyes. "Ain't that what the Sabbat is about?"

Christine paused, smiling thin. "One last test, then, I promise you, I will believe you no matter what you say you are: What is the creed of the Sabbat, as it was told to you?"

James looked at her, then had the strange image of her face set in a tarot card. It was the Thoth deck, and Crowley had spoken his words best: "Do what thou wilt shall be the whole of the law."

Aleister Crowley adjusted his Egyptian robes and smiled. The woman was comely and nubile, and put him in mind of his Priestess. Or of Lust, once he got her to take her clothes off, and he did as well. "I am the Beast," he said.

The woman smiled. "Close enough."

Then they bit each other in a communion of blood and the joy of the Kiss.

• • •

It was an hour to sunrise, and Christine and her pack had taken off the little iron pins that protected them from perception by James' auspex so he could see their souls in all their blackened glory, streaked like tie-dye mixed with pitch.

Morgan looked at him, appraising. "It looks like you're no stranger to Diablerie yourself."

James shrugged. "A Camarilla here, an anarch there, who's gonna notice?"

"You've done quite well pulling yourself up by your bootstraps," Christine said. "From the look of you, you've had an even lower start on the totem pole than we did. But we can remedy that."

"You got some lick you want me to waste?"

Christine smiled. "Not just yet. But observe the sign." She pointed to a small plaque which read: "Please do not feed the ducks."

"Usually we'd leave our leftovers for the rats or dogs, but even ghoul ducks have trouble disposing of a body."

James laughed. "They're making pretty short work of the carp!"

Christine inclined her head. "True. But our guest here is a bit bigger than that. And while it would certainly be amusing to leave his corpse for the police and the Born Agains to find, it would alert the Camarilla and thereby compromise the Hunt."

James looked at the diabolic former drunk whose goat's eyes looked at him in terror.

"However, we can all have a snack, and then you may have dessert. Ladies and gentlemen?" she asked the rest of the pack.

As one, they descended on the goat man, sucking him dry.

Christine placed a hand across James chest, holding him back. "Save room for dessert, dear."

The weird corpse lay there, bloodless, then Christine motioned to Morgan. "You have the most interesting blood, Morgan, and Spike likes to capture these moments on film."

Spike readied his camera, then Morgan cut his finger and let a drop of blood trickle across the corpse's goatlike lips.

The nostrils flared, scenting, then the tongue came out and licked at the smear of blood. It went back in.

A second passed and the body convulsed, going through a transformation, and, if possible, becoming more monstrous. Muscles swelled and hair sprouted, horns twisting into impossible angles as the fangs grew longer than the lips.

"Yes! Yes!" cried Spike, going for all possible angles, and the creature screamed in agony as the flashbulbs popped in its giant eyes. James realized that Morgan had the blood of both Nosferatu and Gangrel running through his veins, transformed, perhaps, by Christine's magic.

"Kill it!" cried Katie. "Oh, kill it now, and bring me the golden fleece!"

"That isn't Helen's line, you twit," said Morgan.

Katie kissed James on the cheek. "For me, my hero, and the glory of Troy!"

James felt his passions boiling within him, and the Beast was let loose. He lunged forward, biting the creature on the neck. His fangs sank deep into the still-warm flesh.

"Now make a wish, dear," said the Sabbat priestess, "and blow out the candle."

The monster had only a drop of blood and its unlife was extinguished in a moment.

Christine placed her hands upon his shoulders, steadying him. "Keep drinking," she said. "Pluck the amaranth. *Sangre Real. San Greal.*"

The chant was taken up by the others and James wrestled against the monster, drinking, drinking deep, until he had sucked out its life and soul. The flesh turned to ashes beneath his fangs, and what had once been a homeless vagrant, then the likeness of evil, was now nothing more than a pile of dust.

And James felt its power explode through his veins and he laughed in exultation as he was Reborn.

• • •

Philip awoke the next evening with his first hangover in over 70 years. What had he been —

It all came back to him in a flash. No, it couldn't be. He pulled the covers back over his head, praying he would wake up and it would all be a bad dream.

Philip Van Vermeer IV took the covers off his head. He was acting silly, excitable, and highly irrational. Not that this wasn't the time for it, but there was no sense in crying over spilt milk. Or blood.

However, involuntary manslaughter was one thing; premeditated murder was another.

Diablerie was a third.

He usually did not resort to profanity, but sometimes the moment called for it: "Oh shit."

A sea of guilt washed over him and the Wandering Jew got out of bed. "Oh my God! My God! What have I done?"

He wept tears of blood and shame. God knew perfectly well what he'd done. He tried to find his penitential whips, but someone had hidden them, and the little bondage handcuffs in the bottom drawer didn't seem like the sort of thing God had in mind when it came to flagellation. Somehow, though instruments of pain, he knew them to be worldly things. "Forgive me, oh Lord!"

Who could he talk to? Who could ease his suffering and let him atone for his shame? He looked to his autographed picture of the Virgin Mary. He had her phone number, but portable telephones were worldly things as well, and he could not imagine having the audacity to call the Blessed Virgin using an instrument of the Devil. And he could not let himself be seen for the shame of it. "Oh woe! Oh woe!"

He began to beat his head against the wall, but Philemon stopped himself. What had possessed him to do such a thing? Guilt was all well and good, but no excuse to destroy the gods' most perfect creation.

He looked in the mirror, looking to see if he'd done his countenance any permanent damage, but then saw the stain upon his soul. Black! Black as leper's rot! Black as the waters of Tartarus!

Philemon screamed in horror and tore the mirror from the wall, dashing it to the floor. The glass shattered and he flung himself upon the bed, weeping. Oh woe! Oh woe! The stain would never come out!

After a long space of bawling and self pity, Philip sat up, wrung the blood out of his pillow and drank it. No sense in wasting blood, or crying over mistakes. What was done was done. And he was amazingly thirsty. And sore.

Philip took off his turtleneck and ran his hands across his chest. His muscles were hard as steel, and he felt stronger and healthier than ever before, fresh as a new-minted coin. Ninety-three years of death and abuse had been burnt away.

And deep within himself he felt a well of Hunger.

He smelled blood from his jacket. In the largest secret pocket were the death roses he'd been given, wrapped in silk, and he took them out, one by one. Lavender from Sebastian, yellow from Tex, white from Mary, red from the Prince and Donna, pink from Virgil, and pale gold from the doctor. And one great, crimson blossom from his uncle.

He brought them to his face, smelling their rich perfume. He was loved. Yes, he was loved. No matter who or what he was, he was loved.

But he was also hungry and the temptation was almost overwhelming. Philip dropped them in a bureau drawer and locked it tight, shutting away the sweet scent of power, the blood of Prince and primogen. To drink them would quench his thirst, yes, but it would also move him closer to bloodbond.

Philip went and got the phone, dialing the Club. There was no way he was going to work tonight.

"Hello," said the recording. "You have reached the private line of Sebastian Melmoth. Sebastian is off being witty so has no wit to spare for this message. When you hear the beep, he will have come to his wit's end. Please leave a message. *Beep*!"

"Sebastian, this is Philip. If you're there, pick up the phone. If —"

"Hello, Philip." The Englishman sounded tired. "What is it?"

Philip sighed. "I need to take the night off. Something's come up." He looked at the shattered mirror on the floor, knowing what it would show him in its countless reflections.

"Philip, I need you," Sebastian said. "It's Full Moon Saturday *and* the day before Halloween, and your act serves well to distract the guests and keep everything running smoothly, to say nothing of its artistic merits.

After you left last night, you wouldn't believe the nasty scene we had in the billiards room. We had almost three Kindred frenzy, myself included."

Philip gritted his teeth. "It was my deathnight last night."

Sebastian sighed floridly. "Ah well, you asked for nothing, and who am I to deny a dead man's wish? But don't remind me of my generosity if tonight is a dismal failure — or a smashing success! It will be an embarrassment for you either way."

"Thanks, Sebastian, and I'm sorry." Philip closed his eyes. "One other thing: The Sabbat's in town."

There was a pause on the other end of the line. "If that's a jest, Philip, it's not funny, and if it's news, it's nothing new. What are you trying to say?"

"Just watch out, Sebastian. Don't trust anyone." With that, he hung up the phone.

Philip looked at the shattered mirror. "Especially me."

Philip was hungry. He had to hunt.

And he could still smell the blood of the primogen in the air.

● ● ●

Don Juan had a wonderful time, and so did the ladies. He had never felt quite so refreshed or invigorated as he did now, though it had taken three of them to satisfy his passion. Luckily they all lived in the same dorm room, otherwise things might have gotten unpleasant. A gentleman should only leave a lady exhausted, not drained. Otherwise there would be no pleasure the next night.

Such was the way of the Ravnos. He whistled happily as he made his way out the door and onto the

USF campus, the buildings white as a flock of doves in the moonlight. How thoughtful of the Jesuits to have provided pretty maids by the score for a man of his tastes. Like a nunnery, but without all the inhibitions and silly vows.

And here was another pretty maid, dressed in black on black, with diamonds in her ears like twin stars. "James," she said, looking at him as if she sought recognition.

He bowed, doffing his cap and letting the ostrich plumes sweep the ground. "You have me mistaken, milady. I am Don Juan. But you may call me James if that will gain me the pleasure of your charming company."

She laughed gaily. "Oh, my, you're wonderful. Our troupe always needed an actor." She stepped closer. "You know, James. You almost make me feel like I'm alive again." She put her hand upon his. "It's only the bonds of the vinculum speaking, but I feel as if I've known you for a very long time."

Don Juan raised the lady's hand to his lips and kissed it gently. "And I, too, feel as if I met you somewhere before, in some pleasant garden with a pond, and I looked into your eyes as the children laughed and played in the distance."

He swept her into his arms. "Come with me. The moon is full and I will give you a night to remember. We shall make love by Selene's light as the oceans sing and the fairies dance upon the shore." Something bothered him, at the back of his mind, but he couldn't see why it mattered. "But how did you know to find me here?"

The woman reached into his pocket, beneath the velvet and the lace, and took out a silver ring set with a bloodstone. "I gave you my token, milord. I did not wish to lose you, and so sudden did you rush off that I am glad I gave you this token when I did."

He laughed, taking the ring and placing it upon his smallest finger. "I shall treasure it always."

The maiden's face took on a serious expression. "The others are off hunting, but we'll meet them at midnight. We can spend the next few hours together, James."

"Then that is as it should be, for tonight is the Hunter's Moon, and the others must hunt. But for us the chase is over, for we have found each other, and now the pleasure feast begins." The poor maid was obviously touched, mistaking him for some dead lover. But, of course, that's what he was, in a manner of speaking.

Don Juan chuckled. Who was he to deny a madwoman his company? "Come, milady. My horse awaits."

She laughed and joined him, taking the place behind him on his noble charger, Harley.

Harley made his way across the city, whinnying in that strange way peculiar to all enchanted steeds, until they came to the long lawns beneath the great Golden Bridge. "Look, milady," he said, finding a place for Harley beside the other magic steeds, "the fairies dance upon the waves and the lovers stroll upon the beach. But if you come beneath the mantle of my cloak of invisibility, we shall walk unseen as the spirits of the air."

She dimpled. "Your powers of obfuscation are indeed mighty, milord. Shall we procure refreshments as well?"

"We shall have the nectar of love, and that is all we shall need."

She made a little moue of dissatisfaction, but it looked charming upon her face. "But milord, I am thirsty."

"Then you shall drink from the wine of my love, milady, and I will seek sustenance elsewhere."

"You are too kind," she said, and let him lead her down the beach.

Don Juan laid his magic mantle upon the sand so that they were invisible to all who passed by, then began to undress the lady, one article at a time. She stopped him when he came to a jewel she wore in her hair. "Not that," she said. "It's my protection from auspex."

"You lie upon my magic mantle, sweet lady. You have no need to fear this fiend Auspex and his prying eyes, for he cannot see you here. And I wish to savor you in your full beauty." She allowed him to remove the pin and the rest of her garments, and he did the same with his as well, laying them upon the ground protected by his magic mantle, invisible to all but the fairies and the eyes of God.

He made love to her, slowly and passionately, but she lay there, stiff and unmoving as a corpse. "Oh Kiss me," she said. "Please give me the Kiss. It's only torture to draw it out like this." She began to cry, tears of blood flowing down her cheeks. "I can't fake it like you can. I never had the talent to be an actress."

"Milady, I fake nothing. My passion is true. If you cannot summon passion on your own, look into my eyes, and share in my passion, for I assure you, it is great enough for two."

Don Juan gazed into the eyes of the cold madwoman and opened the doorways of his soul as the enchantress had taught him, baring the secrets of his heart and letting his passion shine through. The woman began to quiver as she shared the ecstasy of the flesh.

And Philip looked into Christine's eyes as he lay atop her, minds locked open.

Her eyes widened in horror and she froze. You're mad, she thought. You're not Sabbat at all. You're a Malkavian!

I'm whatever you want me to be. Philip looked into her eyes. If you believe hard enough, you can be whatever you want to be. Even human. At least for a while.

Christine's mind tried to shutter itself off from him, but the bond was tight, and Philip saw, beyond the cruelties of the Sabbat, the sad and lonely woman she had once been.

And still was.

Philip felt himself conforming to her image, taking on another role, and let her see her soul reflected in his eyes, as it was and as it had been.

And Christine looked at the mirror in revulsion. How dare the Malkavian mock her so? She was Sabbat! She was the Priestess! And that sad and lonely girl had only been a chrysalis waiting for the dragonfly to emerge.

Christine grabbed the mocking madman's head and pulled him close, Kissing him full upon the lips and biting him hard. The madman bit back, and Christine felt the ecstasy of passion as they struggled in the bonds of the Kiss, his blood washing into hers and hers into his, warring for dominance as his eyes, his mocking eyes, reflected her own and her life and death.

Then the madman ceased to struggle and Christine watched as his life passed before his eyes and into hers, his blood and life draining into the black hollow of her soul. Images from his past and her past, melting into one another like a projected image in a hall of mirrors, his death, her death, his death, her death, on and on and on, flickering images merging them into a whole like a thousand stereoscopic cards, no one complete on its own.

Christine cried aloud in exultation as she was Reborn and the madman crumbled to ash. She had drunk his life and soul.

Then she sat down and wept tears of blood, for now she knew who he had been. And all he had ever wanted was to make her happy.

• • •

Christine rode the motorcycle down the paths and into the dome of the Palace of Fine Arts. She had reclaimed her ring and pin, and kept the jacket and bike as trophies, glad that her pack had not seen her moment of weakness at the end.

She put the regrets aside. Those who followed the Path of Power and the Inner Voice could not listen to such weak feelings. But she had to respect the Malkavian. He had fooled her for the moment, and his madness had almost caught her. Only her inner strength had seen her through the last struggle.

Her troupe stepped out of the shadows of the colonnade. "Where's James?" Katie asked.

"'James' is dead." Christine dismounted the bike and took off the Malkavian's helmet. "In point of fact, he never existed. He was simply a fictitious persona created by a Camarilla spy."

Brandt paused a beat. "The impersonator at the Alexandrian Club?"

"Yes," said Christine. "Hindsight is a wonderful thing."

"You made a mistake," said Morgan.

Christine gave him a look. "I corrected it. I never made claims to perfection. Only to being better than the rest of you.

"Besides," she said, reaching into Philip's jacket pocket, "the hunt would become dull if there were not an occasional danger from the prey. And this one was crazy. Like a fox.

"But the fox hunt was not without its rewards. Look what I have here." She showed them Philip's engagement calendar.

"So?" prompted Morgan. "Tell us what it is."

"A treasure chest," said Christine. "I have here the names and numbers of half the primogen in the city, including the Prince. Boons, prestation, all the nonsense of the Camarilla. And," she added significantly, "a perfect haven and a tasty snack at the same time. Philip Van Vermeer, our former James Dean, shared a haven with his great-uncle. And Tobin Van Tuys is one of the most powerful and respected primogen of the Ventrue."

"How did you find that out?" asked Morgan. "I'm sure this Malkavian, mad as he was, wasn't stupid enough to write down something like that in his notebook."

"Certainly not," said Christine. "But are you familiar with the legend that a dying man's life passes before his eyes? It's true. And I got to watch as I sucked out his. Diablerie isn't totally useless when used on those lesser than oneself."

She laughed, holding up the appointment calendar. "And between those memories and this, we have the makings of a grander scheme, for Tobin Van Tuys is scheduled to host the Ventrue Masque tomorrow evening at the Van Vermeer mansion. The guests arrive at seven, and the buffet is set out at eight. But we'll be there before that — Philip kept a few spare invitations for last minute oversights."

Spike grinned. "So one of us plays the uncle and one of us plays the nephew, and we just wait for the primogen to come calling?"

Christine smiled and nodded. "But not tonight. We've no way of knowing Tobin's schedule for this evening, and a sunrise scuffle is always messy and dangerous. But we know precisely where he'll be tomorrow: at home, awaiting the early guests. And worrying about his nephew who failed to call in the night before." She closed her eyes for a moment, savoring the thought. "And won't he be delighted to see his Childe return, along with a date and a trio of guests for the party."

"Trick or treat!" Spike and Brandt laughed as one.

Katie clapped her hands with glee. "Oh, this is even better than the trick with the wooden horse!"

"Just a variation on the same theme. The Trojan Horse meets the Grandma's House motif, only we're the wolves and we've already eaten Red Riding Hood." Morgan shrugged. "Oh well, we've worked with worse plots. At least what it lacks in innovation it may make up for in irony."

• • •

Christine finished molding Brandt into the likeness of Philip Van Vermeer, for he was the closest to the Malkavian in height and bearing. Something about the face, however, didn't quite suit her, and she wished she had the original there for a model, as well as the Hamlet costume the Malkavian had planned to wear.

"Just give him a half-mask and cloak and have him go as the Phantom," suggested Morgan, dressed as Vincent Price's version of the Witchfinder General — the ultimate critic. "You can fix the rest later, and I doubt if anyone's going to inspect him down to the last anatomical detail. We don't want to run late."

"True. But as this is the performance and not the dress rehearsal, I'd prefer to have everything right the first time. Besides, if the note of the evening is irony, I find the Malkavian's original idea of going as the Danish Prince to be particularly amusing."

Morgan chuckled. "There is the parallel with the uncle, yes."

"If you could oblige us with the costume then, dearest?"

Morgan nodded and Christine moved aside, letting the Pander go about his mumbo jumbo, slashing his wrists and having the blood fountain over Brandt's naked body. The vitæ turned black and clotted, coagulating into rich velvets and furs, silver buckles and gold chains, and for the last bit of the costume, Morgan reached up to his own face and tore through the skin, pulling forth his skull and presenting it to the Lasombra.

Brandt took it gingerly as the blood and gobbets of flesh putrefied into dark streaks of dirt and grave mold, and Morgan smiled, a new skull filling out the curves of his face, the Nosferatu blood adding a few extra bumps and twists and lengthening the fangs. "There you are," the Pander hissed through snaggled teeth.

"I'll fix you in the car, Morgan dearest." Christine shuddered, hating to see good work ruined, but went about giving Brandt his finishing touches, briefing him on what to do and say. "The uncle, however, is mine," she reminded him. "I will be the one to taste his power — and that goes double for everyone else," she said, turning to the rest of the troupe.

Katie appeared nonplussed, though the expression looked strange on her now wildly beautiful face, having had Christine remake her as Helen of Troy.

She flounced down onto the dirty couch of Tomaine's Tenderloin basement, arranging the purple skirts of her chiton. "It's Wilfred's turn. You got to drink James, so now Wilfred gets to drink the next vessel."

"Helen," Christine said simply, adjusting Brandt's chin to her liking, "James wasn't potent enough. You tasted his blood last night, and even after he Kissed the Devil, he was still a step below us. So it didn't give me anything but pleasure, and a bit of information." She looked to the mad girl. You could never tell when she would go over the edge, so it was best to placate her.

"Spike will have the next of the primogen thereafter, then you may pick from the rest of them."

"Like Paris got to do with the Goddesses?"

"Exactly. But there should be more than enough fine old vintages for us all to take one step closer to Caine this night."

Spike came down the stairs, dressed in motley as the perfect Harlequin — except for the camera. "Mission accomplished. The limo's running and the chauffeur's not."

"You dusted him," Brandt accused, looking at the ashes down the front of Spike's tights. "You pig."

Spike shrugged. "Hey, I was hungry. And I didn't think Tomaine would appreciate a body dumped outside his haven, living or dead. But if someone decides to dump some clothes and empty an ashtray. . ."

Morgan snorted. "Diablerie is one thing, Wilfred. But you give a whole new meaning to Saturnalia. Eating your own Childer. . . and so young too."

Katie bounced up. "At least he knows where his blood has been, unlike *some* people we could mention." She looked the other direction pointedly. "And I'm the only one who gets to call him Wilfred."

Christine turned away from Brandt. The Malkavian had been right — what they needed was a stage mother. "Now now, children. Play nicely. And let's all get upstairs before someone steals the limousine Spike left unattended in the middle of the Tenderloin."

There came the sound of a large vehicle pulling away from the curb, and Spike grinned, disappearing in a flash so sudden that if she didn't know better, she would have sworn he'd used obfuscation instead of celerity.

By the time they had gotten upstairs and locked the apartment, Spike was waiting behind the wheel of the limousine. A jogging suit and a number of gold chains lay in the gutter beside a dusty chauffeur's uniform. "Congratulations," said Morgan, opening the door of the limo, "you've set a new record for the 30-second Saturnalia."

"What can I say?" Spike grinned, domino mask skewed rakishly. "I've always loved Slurpees."

Christine lifted the skirt of her vestments and got into the back seat, careful of the headdress. For her part, she had chosen to go as Pope Joan, her robes blue as the waters of the Mediterranean, heavily embroidered and trimmed with cloth of gold, her hair carefully wimpled up under a papal crown, the whole offset by a large rosary with a beautiful jeweled cross as pendant. Just the right mixture of piety and heresy, and Christine was glad she'd taken the trouble to kill the priest and steal the relic. It made the costume.

A sudden blinding flash of light hit her in the eyes. "Hah! Got ya!" Spike laughed and Christine had half an urge to reach out and literally wipe off the smug look she knew must be on his face. But they hadn't time for 'Got your nose' at present, and she'd spent too much time on his make-up to ruin it now. "Just drive, Spike," she said through gritted teeth and throttled her scepter instead of him.

The Toreador laughed and pulled away from the curb, and Christine pressed her temples. Ever since draining the Malkavian, she'd been suffering from temporary blackouts. She hoped she would not share in his madness. To be one such as Katie would be a great shame, and a great impediment to her advancement within the sect.

But she couldn't show weakness before her troupe. She opened her eyes and over the course of the next few minutes fixed Morgan's face with the familiarity of old habit.

Chinese lanterns painted into jack-o'-lanterns hung all about the steps of the mansion, diffusing eerie orange light through the fog, and the strains of a Strauss waltz came through the door as Brandt lifted the knocker.

The door opened almost at once, and there, beside a doorman dressed as Death, stood the unmistakable form of Tobin Van Tuys, for all that he was got up as Hans Christian Andersen, with a book of fairy tales and a Little Mermaid doll tucked under his arm for those slow on the uptake.

"Philip!" he cried in delight, pulling Brandt into the house and hugging him mightily. "My dear boy, I was so worried about you! Why didn't you call?"

Brandt bowed, holding Morgan's old skull which now played the part of Yorick. "Alas, my uncle, I was the victim of motorcycle trouble and the villainous Pacific Bell. I found a nice safe place, however, but unfortunately not one with a working phone."

Tobin Van Tuys nodded. "Well, I am just so glad you're all right. But if you could introduce your friends?"

Brandt smiled. "Ah, uncle, how could you think of breaking with custom? We unmask at midnight and not before!"

Tobin laughed. "Of course, of course. Welcome to my house. Come freely. Go safely; and leave something of the happiness you bring!"

Christine laughed with the rest of her troupe and entered the mansion. She realized that they would have to stake Tobin Van Tuys first so that she could use him as model for Spike, since she couldn't be certain to get a perfect image if he'd already crumbled to ash from the Diablerie. But that would add to the pleasure and the artistic merit of the production. Katie would have to take pictures, of course, but while she didn't have Spike's eye, there was a certain originality to her use of camera angles.

The foyer of the Van Vermeer mansion was as she recalled it from her stolen memories: polished mahogany, drawing room to the right, library to the left, with a flight of stairs leading down to the main ballroom from whence the music emanated. But there were altogether too many guests.

Christine swept down the stairs, passing the enigmatic purple robes of a Venetian masker, and took in the crowd: Harlequins and Columbines, Spanish Devils, Cinderellas and Princes — Charming and less-so — a sequined Elvis, two Red Deaths, and no less than 10 interpretations of Count Dracula, some better than others.

A string quartet, masked in Mexican skulls, played from the corner, and couples swirled about the dancefloor. Too many. Too many guests by far for what they had planned, and more than half of them mortals from the smell of sweat and expensive perfume wafting across the floor.

"Oh Jesus," Christine swore, attempting to stay in character to some extent. Spike and Katie, oblivious to the complete shambles the script had fallen into, joined the waltz, dancing precariously close to the full open fire at the end of the ballroom. Brandt and Morgan went off individually to mingle.

"Champagne, your Grace?" asked the Steadfast Tin Soldier, or at least that's what Christine assumed the antique military uniform and the aluminum paint were meant to represent.

"Not just yet, thank you." She waved him away, later fending of paper ballerinas with hors d'oeuvres, witches with blue-checked aprons offering sweets, and a Little Match Girl who had apparently branched out into a full tobacconists line, including the Rastafarian varieties, as had the soldier from the Tinder Box. The Hans Christian Andersen theme was almost a recurring bad joke, though it did make the servants a bit easier to recognize. She didn't want to see what the Snow Queen had to offer.

The evening passed in a daze, guests coming and leaving, and then Christine found herself confronted by a short yet darkly handsome man, dressed in the full mail and tabard of a Knight Templar, broadsword slung across his back. "Your Grace," he said with a heavy Italian accent. "Might I have the pleasure of the next dance?"

Christine made herself blush. "And who might you be?"

"Merely your humble knight. But you may call me Giancarlo." He bowed low, then took her hand, kissing her ring.

The name seemed familiar, but Christine couldn't quite place it. Oh well, she might as well enjoy herself, and from the warmth in the mortal's hands, it seemed as if he might be a tasty snack if she could get him off somewhere alone.

He danced well and lightly, despite the armor, though she could see the sweat running down his face, and Christine felt quite giddy by the time they had finished two sets.

They ended beside the fireplace. Christine turned her back to it so she would not have to look at its light, but savored the warmth. "You dance well, my Servant."

"As do you, your Grace," said the Italian, panting heavily.

The clock began to sound midnight as Morgan came over, looking displeased.

Bong!

"Have you seen Spike and Katie?" asked the Witchfinder General. "I haven't seen them all hour."

Bong!

Come to think of it, she hadn't. "No. I suppose they're somewhere."

Bong!

Brandt arrived, still holding Morgan's old skull

Bong!

"Anyone seen Spike or Katie?"

Bong!

"No," she and Morgan said in unison.

A hush started to fall over the gathering as the last strikes of the clock sounded, and by the time the last of the bells had rung, the party was completely silent.

A space cleared in the center of the room, and Tobin Van Tuys stepped out. "'Ask not for whom the bell tolls,'" he intoned, "'it tolls for thee!' The gates of the Otherworld are open and the dead walk the earth! Samhain is upon us and we welcome the dead to our celebration at the closing of the old year! My friends, now we unmask!"

There was a sound of satin and tissue paper, the assembled company removing their dominoes or setting aside their lorgnettes, but Christine also heard the unmistakable sound of sliding steel. Giancarlo moved past her, broadsword unsheathed, and the sword's edge met the neck of Brandt.

With a snap and a spout of blood, the head of Philip Van Vermeer fell to the floor, rolling and bouncing alongside the skull.

Christine felt her muscles somehow moving beyond her control as she took her papal scepter, the handle polished ebony, and rammed it through the heart of Morgan — or at least where the heart should have been.

He placed his hand on the scepter and smiled, baring his fangs. "Some of us don't have our hearts in the right place, your Grace."

How dare he mock her so? She was the Pope! Pope Joan grabbed her blessed rosary and held it forth, showing the spawn of darkness the holy power of Christ. "Begone, foul fiend!"

The vampire hissed and recoiled, cursing most blasphemously at the power of the blessed rosary, allowing time for her faithful knight and servant to take up his sword and run the monster through, bearing it over into the firepit.

The beast exploded in flames, no longer remotely human as foul vanes and spurs burst through the flesh, like wicker beneath the paper mâché of some pagan effigy. It started to come forth from the fire, then paused as the sword caught on the logs behind and seemed to lose its will to fight. "Burning the Witchfinder General," it said, hissing like the flames. "There is a certain irony to that. A better ending than most."

It then collapsed in a cascade of black ashes and sparks of hellfire.

The sword clattered to the grate, then Pope Joan watched as the garments of the Danish Prince changed from black velvet to running red blood. "Betrayer," said the head of Philip Van Vermeer, eyes staring open, and the skull beside it laughed as the pooled blood reached it and began to dye it a vivid crimson, only to stop as a spark from the fire reached out and touched it. Flames sprang up and the blood burned as fiercely as would oil, incinerating the corpse and the skull.

Her head exploded with pain and her body did as well, limbs stretching and lengthening through the power of vicissitude. This could not be! She was the Pope! No, the Malkavian had driven her mad. She was Christine, the Priestess, the High Priestess of the Sabbat!

She fell to the floor, body spasming in agony, and her mind shattered as another will imposed itself upon her.

Philip sat up, sobbing tears of blood. So close. So close to losing himself completely to the madness. He heard the crackle of the flames behind him, then someone was helping him to his feet. "Ladies and gentleman," said the voice of Giancarlo Giovanni, "the masks are finally off! May I present Philip Van Vermeer, the master illusionist!"

Philip staggered, holding onto Giancarlo for support. "Bow," hissed the Italian.

Philip bowed and the guests applauded, the yellow and green of shock and revulsion changing to silvered emerald of uneasy amusement as he used the Mask to make the Priestess's robes resemble the Hamlet costume that Brandt had worn.

"All an illusion. . . yes, yes, all an illusion. . . some trick. . . I swear, he's better than David Copperfield," babbled different voices in the crowd, auras flashing the purple of denial.

"But it looked so real. . ." said some businessman's wife dressed as a fairy princess.

Philip waved to dismiss the thought and focused his will and presence. "*Think nothing* of it, my lady. Just a magician's tricks. Mirrors, flash paper, vampire blood — nothing real. Nothing to trouble yourself about."

Giancarlo bowed next to him. "It was the climax to one of those 'Host a Murder' things you Americans have devised. Most amusing. I was just doing my small part to help out."

There was uneasy laughter and the partygoers broke off into knots, making way for an imposing figure dressed as Louis XIV, the Sun King, still holding his golden mask before him.

The Prince took his mask aside. "A most interesting illusion. I would like to hear more of this — in private."

Uncle Tobin came forward, twisting The Little Mermaid in his hands. The book of fairy tales had been forgotten. "Of course, Vannevar. We may retire to my study. Music, everyone! This is a celebration!"

The band started up a hesitant waltz, but no one ventured onto the dance floor. Donna, dressed as Coya, the Aztec Moon Goddess, clung tightly to the Prince's arm, saying nothing, and both mortals and Kindred fell aside as the Sun King led the way upstairs.

Philip walked down the hall, Giancarlo on one side, the blood still on his sword, his uncle on the other. Tobin quickly opened the study and ushered everyone inside. There, on the sofa, lay the bodies of Katie and Spike, staked with what looked to be ironwood stilettos. Philip had no memory of having stabbed them, but he knew that didn't mean much.

The moment the door was closed, he fell into his uncle's arms and began sobbing, letting all the illusions drop.

"Hush, my child. It's all right. You've done well." His uncle looked into his eyes. Calm yourself, boy, he thought

Philip looked away. He didn't want to summon Philip just now, didn't want to lose himself in calm reflection. "I love you, Uncle Toby."

I love you too, my Childe.

"Ahem," said the Prince, waiting for everyone's attention. "I would like a few explanations. Philip's either hysterical here or has just died the final death out in the ballroom, a third child of Caine was incinerated, and we have two unknown Kindred besides. And Tobin mentioned something about the Sabbat, so I'd just like to know who and what everyone is before I dispense justice."

"I believe I may be of service." Philip looked, and Giancarlo Giovanni bowed his head to the Prince, bloody sword point first into the carpet before him. "My part in these matters has been small, yes, but I do know a few interesting facts."

The Giovanni strode over Spike's body, avoiding the eyes, and pulled a pin from the Harlequin's camera strap. A gasp came from the Prince.

"That," said the mortal, gesturing to the photographer, "is a Diabolist. And this," he said, holding up a small charm on an iron pin, "is the insignia of the Sabbat. By your leave, milord?"

The Prince gestured, looking away from the blackened horror that was Spike's soul, and Giancarlo raised his sword.

The cut came down, clean and neat, and the severed head rolled across the carpets of the study.

The Giovanni repeated the process with Katie, the Prince nodding as he showed him the insignia and once he saw the mad girl's soul. Her head joined Spike's upon the floor, the eyes still open and staring. "I love you, Paris," she said, bloody tears flowing down as she gazed into the dead eyes of the photographer. "I always will. See you next time."

Katie's eyes fell shut, and the head of Helen lay there, serene and beautiful.

"My thanks." The Prince looked to the Giovanni. "But I understood that your Clan was at truce with the Sabbat."

"My *family*," Giancarlo said, stressing the word, "has an accord with those who share their state, both Sabbat and Camarilla. But I am neither Kindred nor ghoul. I am a free agent." He reached out and pulled the papal crown from Philip's head, Christine's jeweled pin sparkling to one side.

The Prince stared, and Philip's uncle took one look at him and pushed him away, stepping back as if struck.

Slowly, Philip turned and looked into the mirror over the study's mantelpiece. Between the clock and the candlesticks, he saw the stains of Diablerie upon his soul, twice as black as before.

"My Prince. . ." began Tobin.

Vannevar Thomas stepped forward. "I cannot sanction Diablerie."

"No," Giancarlo agreed, "but you can pardon it."

The Prince looked to him. "Do you question me?"

The Giovanni smiled. "No, I remind you. This subject is directly responsible for ridding your domain of five of your most powerful enemies, assassins of the throne. Yes, he has done that which is forbidden by your kind. But if you reward him with stake and fire, or whatever you set aside for those who practice the Devil's Kiss, only think what message it is you send to your subjects."

Giancarlo turned to Philip, looking like the Prince of a different century or the Knight of Swords. "Pardon him, do not thank him, and let him have your protection as his only reward. There is ample precedent. That is what God did to Caine."

The Prince gritted his teeth, his face working, but his eyes unreadable. At last he spoke. "I thank you for your advice, counselor. This time it is good. I am surprised, however, that you didn't come dressed as Machiavelli."

Giancarlo bowed. "I had considered it, my Prince. However, I chose the Knight Templar as it was the only costume where I could both carry a sword and wear a mail coif."

The Prince nodded. "I understand." Vannevar looked to Philip and his uncle. "Privately, I thank you.

Publicly, I will pardon you and will swear to call a Blood Hunt on any but myself who takes action against you for this crime, or even speaks of it in my presence.

"But I will destroy you if you even think of doing such a thing again."

The Prince went to the door, pausing with his hand on the knob. "Tomorrow at the Vampire Club should prove sufficient for the announcement. You will have ample things to keep you distracted here this evening." The Sun King's mask came back up. "And I must thank you for your invitation, Tobin. Let it never be said that the Ventrue cannot throw an entertaining party."

The Prince left, Donna in his wake, still silent.

Giancarlo bowed. "I think it best if I leave you two for the moment," said the Italian. He left, humming some strange little tune as he cleaned the blade of his sword, and shut the door behind him.

There was silence in the room, only broken by the ticking of the clock on the mantel.

Uncle Tobin looked to him, emotions warring upon his face, then at last he opened his arms and hugged Philip to him.

Philip hugged his uncle back, never wanting to let go. "Oh uncle," he said, "it was so hard. To send my mind to you and to play the Sabbat at the same time. It was so hard to do it all. I was afraid I would go mad."

Uncle Toby held him tight. "Hush, my Childe. It's all right now. Everything is all right."

"I love you, uncle. I'm so glad you're all right." Philip cried tears of blood. "I was afraid I would go mad." ⚰

UNDERCOVER

by Matthew J. Costello

Morning and Maria Rodriguez hurried through the halls of Police Center, nearly running, thinking: Christ! If I'm late for this meeting I'm dead. But the drive up from Pacifica had been a bitch. Living alone was great, as long as you could get yourself out of bed.

Out too late last night? One Dos Equiis too many? Least I didn't screw him. Got to give me that.

She got to the desk outside the office of the Chief of Detectives, Homicide Division. The desk sergeant in a starched shirt with crisp collars looked up.

"I — I have an appointment with Captain —"

But the Captain's secretary already had the phone up to his mouth, had already hit a button, was speaking oh-so-quietly into the mouthpiece.

Then click, the handset was down on the base. "He's waiting for you." A smile — as if this cop knew secrets that I don't, Maria thought. "Go in"

Maria tool a breath, pulled down her skirt, straightened her jacket, and walked in.

Captain Max Cameron was a well-known figure. Especially these days, especially with the papers and the news keeping a running total of the body count. Eight people dead so far, and everyone waiting for the next mutilated body to surface. No pattern, no rhyme nor reason to the killings — a school teacher here, a bartender there. One tabloid ran a photo of a body recovered in the bay, near the bridge. The skin looked like tissue paper that a nasty cat went berserk tearing.

Maria stood at attention while Cameron dug in his drawer for something.

"Sorry I'm late, sir. The traffic —"

Cameron looked up and smiled, a disarming smile. The man was twice Maria's age, but her antennae told her to be alert. These days she got hit on from the most unlikely sources.

"Don't worry, Rodriguez. I've got some good reports on you. You're not afraid to get down and dirty, as they say."

So I'm going to Homicide, Rodriguez thought. That's good. Could make Detective there pretty fast. Course — I could also get killed.

"You busted those people at that club — what's it called?"

"The Night Wing, sir."

"Some kind of coke deal. Weird kind of club —"

Putting it mildly, Maria remembered. Everyone was in full S&M regalia, boots, leather, garter belts — and androgyny was in full flower. She helped get the dealers, but Maria felt that there was more going on in the Night Wing than simply a few deals for blow.

"Good stuff that. That's why we thought of you for —" Cameron was back looking in the drawers. "— ah. Here we are." He pulled out a detailed street map of San Francisco. Cameron looked up, smiled again.

He wants me to come to the desk, Maria thought. And she took a step while Cameron watched. Shit, she thought, don't let him make a pass. Not this morning. I want to try and be a professional cop this morning, that's all.

"Know what these are?" he asked, pointing to red dots on the map.

Maria shook her head.

"That's where we've found the bodies. One up near the old Presidio, another by the horseshoe courts — that must have been nasty for the old farts to find in the AM And another here, behind Japan Center. One red dot for every body."

Maria cleared her throat. "You want me to work homicides? I'd like that. That —"

Cameron shook his head. "Patience. You're getting ahead of me. And, yes, I want you to come on board. But it's how I want you to come on board."

Cameron took a breath. Maria waited while Cameron teased her. Then —

"What do you know about the Gutters?"

The Gutters. Well, not a hell of lot. It was a gang, but not like one of the bands marauding in East L.A. The Gutters were organized. There were rumors that they moved drugs, that they were contract killers, even rumors that there was no such group.

"It's a gang."

Cameron nodded. "We think — let's say, we have some evidence that some of the Gutters may be playing a little game." Cameron held the map up. "The body count game."

"Evidence?"

"We have a photo of a leader in the Gutters, a man who calls himself Mac. And we'd like to find out what this Mac is up to."

Maria nodded, the light bulb still not going off.

"We've heard that he likes women."

A slow glow started to appear. Maria shifted on her heels. There was a throbbing in her head. Maria looked for a chair, but the room was so dark, shades down, so hard to see.

"So the idea is for you to go undercover. Meet some Gutters, maybe hook up with this Mac. See what games the kiddies are playing."

Maria licked her lips. Say, "No," a voice suggested. Say, "No, thank you," turn around, and walk out. Life's too damned short.

"Interested?" Cameron said. "No pressure. Your decision."

And Maria cleared her throat and said, "Sure."

• • •

Maria checked herself in the window of the boutique. She was wearing tight shorts and her leather boots. Black stockings and a white blouse from a retro '60s store. Her third night out, and no luck so far.

OK, she thought, I look hot. Still no guarantee that I can meet a Gutter, let alone get into the gang. . . if there is a gang.

She was standing with a lot of other young people by Buena Vista Park. The summer night air was warm, with just a bit of dampness from the Pacific. There were glows in the darkness, the fireflies of crack bowls and joints passed.

She could have been wired. It was an option.

"Thing is," Cameron said, "if they find a wire on you, if they see a suspicious bulge, you're a dead woman. This way, you can get in, get out, and they won't know squat."

But now, standing with these kids, Maria wished she had some link to safety and sanity.

Testing, testing. Is anybody there?

But she was all on her lonesome.

She started moving through the crowd, looking for people who looked like they were the alpha males of this watering hole.

Across the street from the Dugout Bar, under a sputtering streetlamp, Maria saw some guys standing. Guys she hadn't seen before. Could just be three guys, or maybe, if I'm lucky, it could be something else.

She looked over at them, and then one guy started across the street before he was quickly stopped by another man dressed in jeans and black leather. Then that guy took the lead, walking over to Maria, coming close. He had dark eyes and jet black hair that caught the fading yellow light of the street lamp.

He walked over to Maria. "You look lost, babe."

Maria nodded. "Not lost at all," she said. Then right at him, studying the face, recognizing it as the same person in the photo, she added, "Just bored."

Then Mac's friends joined him. "If you're bored, we've got the cure."

Testing. One. . . two. . . three.

"Are you up to party?"

Maria looked away, then back to Mac whose smile seemed warm, radiant in the darkness. "Sure."

Funny, the name of this place was Twin Peaks Park. Twin Peaks, like that show. Maria had liked that show — the music, the strange characters. Everyone seemed weird, an outsider. Like me.

Mac stood by her and pulled her close.

"Wait — you're going to like this."

Maybe now is when I should try to leave, she thought. I can't just stand here and watch what they're going to do. I don't even have a gun. "A gun's too dangerous," Cameron said. "They might kill you if they found a gun."

"Hmmm," Mac said, pulling her tighter.

A couple turned a corner, heading up towards the Twin Peaks Park.

"You know what they're going to do, babe?" Mac said, His lips were close to her ear, whispering to her. Maria thought she should pull away. But no, that wouldn't be in character. She moved a bit, and Mac's lips moved down her neck, sliding, making goosebumps sprout on her.

"What do you think they're going to do?" There was a click, and then a blade flashed in the night. Mac's lips were still on Maria's neck. She felt him touching her, holding her.

Then Mac pulled away, and Maria felt loss, the warmth, the smell of him gone. Mac stood up and turned to the other guys with him.

I should look at them, Maria thought. Look at them, study their faces. But all she could see, all she could remember was Mac.

"Let's go," Mac said. And they followed the couple up the hill.

Maria saw the couple lying on the ground, twisting on the grass.

"We'll wait a minute," Mac said. "Give them a few more minutes."

Maria shook her head. "I — I don't think we should —"

"Should what, babe? You said you were bored, right? What's the problem?"

"We'd better go —"

I can't stand here and watch them kill these people, Maria thought. I can't let that happen.

Maria pulled away, but Mac's hand — cold, firm — was on her wrist.

"Can't leave now, babe. The party's just starting."

Maria tried to yank away, but his hand was like a metallic claw, tight and closed, and now dragging her to the couple.

"A pretty sight, don't you think? They don't even hear us, see us."

"Please," Maria said. And then Mac yanked her close, like snapping a doll on a string, and Maria was looking into his eyes. "This is what you came for, isn't it?" Mac pulled her closer, his lips brushing hers. "Isn't it?"

Then back to the couple. Mac took a step closer to them. The woman on the grass said something. Maria heard her say something, aware that there were people around. Maria could feel her fear, as if she was the person on the grass.

Maria saw the knife in Mac's hands. "No," Maria said, but she had stopped struggling, as if this was a show to be watched, letting it play out.

The man on the grass now stirred, aware that he and his girl were not alone. Mac stopped. "And now, it's time for the surprise," Mac said. He turned to Maria and put the knife into her hand.

• • •

Evening. The sun was down and the streets turned cooler.

Cameron said he'd wait for her. And Maria walked into the office, and the dark was soothing, peaceful.

"Go on," Cameron said. "You met Mac and others. And what did you learn about the Gutters?"

The shades were shut against the city lights. Maria pushed her hair off her face, looking around, smelling the air. She rubbed her lips.

"We went to the park."

"And they killed someone?" The Captain took a step towards her, smiling. "You watched them kill someone?"

Maria shook her head. "No. No one was killed."

Cameron smiled. "I don't believe you. I think you're scared."

Cameron moved past her to the door, turning the lock. The click was loud. "I think that something happened last night, that maybe you went to their lair, where they hide out. And I think that you're going to tell me what happened."

Cameron took a step.

"You see, you weren't really working for the SFPD. Not really. I had to have someone find out what the Gutters were up to. Why all the killing, why all the bloodlust when there's only one who should decide such things."

Maria stepped back.

"Oh, don't worry about calling out, Maria. The desk sergeant is gone. It's quite silent in here. No sounds can escape."

Another step backwards. Maria opened her mouth, so dry.

"Vannevar Thomas needed to know what these young ones were doing. They will be stopped, of course, but it will take time. They're so stupid, so rash, so greedy. But Thomas will stop them."

A breath. There seemed to be so little air in here.

Cameron works for man named Thomas. He's not like Thomas. But he does his work.

Yes. Of course. Like Mac said.

"Now, you will tell me everything."

Maria nodded. Yes, everything — the way it happened — in Twin Peaks Park.

The couple stood up, and now they drifted over to Mac, Maria, the others, laughing. And Maria saw that they all knew each other. She saw that now she was in the center of the circle, that they were all looking at her.

Their faces were hungry, full of desire. Only Mac's eyes had any warmth.

"You wanted to join us, and we'd like you —"

Mac brought Maria's hand that held the knife over to his wrist. And, with his eyes still on Maria, he began cutting.

"— we'd like you to join us."

The thin cut bloomed, as Mac's blood began to trickle out. He held his wrist up to her.

"Drink. Just a taste on your lips."

The wrist was there in front of her lips, then closer. Mac's voice whispered, soothing, hypnotically: "Drink."

Until Maria closed here eyes and pressed her mouth over the razor-thin wound, tasting the blood, feeling. . .

Wonderful.

Cameron froze. "Then, you are one of them?" Cameron's mouth opened wide, and he was genuinely surprised. This was something Cameron was unprepared for.

Maria backed closer to the door, feeling for the lock, turning the knob. It was deserted outside. Cameron had said so.

"Still, you will talk. They can't exist like this, killing, feasting, creating chaos, creating terror—"

The lock clicked, and Maria backed away, as the door kicked open —

And Mac was there.

She wanted to taste him again, touch him, to live as part of his soul.

Cameron's eyes widened. But he was too old, too slow to move, to avoid the knife that sliced him open, and then the savage bites. The human was too slow. And Maria laughed, giggled, watching Mac snap at Cameron's neck, making him howl in agony.

Mac whispered something in Cameron's ear, a final curse, and then Maria watched him drive the silver blade into Cameron's chest. Into his heart.

They'd have to leave in a moment. People would come to find the ninth body. But Maria, hesitating at first, just standing there, took a step toward the body, to where Mac was bent over it, laughing, licking.

And Maria joined her lover. ƒ

PRISONS

by Shane Hensley

This is the part I hate most. The scum's gonna open his briefcase and show me the shit, now I gotta open mine and show him the dough. Only I ain't got any. The department only had 500 and some change in the lock-up. It was hardly worth the effort, so I just dumped the locker room trash in my briefcase — for weight. This is the third time I've gone to a bust with an empty box of Dunkin' Donuts and couple of coffee cups instead of cash. It's the department's version of recycling, I suppose.

I give a quick look at the narc, Sam. He's the one that set me up with this goon. Hope he can read my vibes, 'cause it's that time. With my left hand I start spinning the case around — like I'm showing him the cash — with my right, I'm pulling my Beretta.

Damn! The punk's fast! Two shots whiz by my ear before I clear my holster. I've never seen anyone move like that. It's a good thing he's not a good shot as well, or Ma Barnes favorite son would come with air conditioning.

My turn. Double tap to the chest. . . creep must be wearing a vest, my rounds aren't even slowing him down. Sam's fired too, four more shots slam into the punk like me and Alice used to do in the back seat of the Chevy. He's a bleeder, but he ain't going down.

Two shots from the bad guy and Sam's spurting like one of those naked boys in the center of a fountain. He'll live, more than I can say for the punk — Slatter, I think is his name.

Hah! His gun jams! "Drop it, now! San Francisco PD." He laughs at me.

Jerk's got six slugs in him and he laughs at me. Now he's coming forward, baring his chops like that's gonna' scare me. Screw that, gumball! I empty the rest of the Beretta into his chest. He almost looks surprised he goes down. And then his lights go out.

"G' night, creep."

● ● ●

So now I'm sitting in this dirty alley waiting on back-up and an ambulance — which both should have been here 10 minutes ago. Sam's doing OK, he just feels like shit. Slatter ain't moving, of course. Jerk must've been on PCP or something. I ain't never put a whole clip into somebody. Internal Affairs is gonna tear me a new asshole.

There's a rain puddle in front of me. It's hard to see anything with the moon and a distant streetlight as the only illumination, but I can see the fuzzy edge of my chin doing the tango in the ripples. I never clean up before a bust like this. You always see cop movies where the locals look at some Joe and spot him as a cop right off. Well, not me. Cap'n says I look like a cop like his daughter looks like a girl — this is San Fran-Flamin'-Cisco, after all.

Still, I guess I could've at least run a comb through my hair. Maybe I'm just afraid I'll see more grays creeping into my browns. Guess that's why I wear this stupid hat all the time. Alice used to think it was cute. Before we split —

Cripes! Slatter's moving! I slam my knee down into the small of his back. There's a crunch, but who cares unless somebody's standing around with a video camera. "You're under arrest. You have the right to remain. . ."

Suddenly, Slatter swats me off him like a fly. Sam squeezes off a shot as the punk runs out of the alley and we both see his kneecap burst open like a microwaved melon. But he keeps on running!

"I'm too old for this crap." I say to Sam as I follow my perp out into the moonlit street. Slatter's looking around, like he don't know where to go. "Freeze or I'll. . ." Damn! Bolted again! Busted knee or not I've never seen anyone move like that. . . almost like he's floating and his good leg only needs to touch the ground to push him along. That's kind of creepy, but I know it's just a trick of the light and this damn rain.

I do the running bit for three blocks before I decide to fire a warning shot into the air — maybe more to remind the creep I'm wheezing along behind him than to actually scare him. Besides, I'm not really sure pumping more lead into him's gonna help. This poor sucker's dead and just doesn't know it yet.

Our marathon continues downhill — towards the beaches. I guess Sam didn't screw up his knee as bad as I thought 'cause this guy's sprinting like he just missed the trolley. Then I see him go down, he's tangled up in some poor schmuck and they both drop like a bag of Idahos. I'm on top of him before he gets free.

"Freeze, dammit! Or I'm gonna. . ." *Blam! Blam! Blam! Blam! Blam! Blam! Blam!*

They never seem to make it past the I'm gonna part. Truth is, I don't think I even know what I'd say after that. Anyway, this drug-crazed psycho is street-pizza now. I help the other guy to his feet, and watch as he looks at my handiwork. The color drains out of his face like the rain was washing it off.

"My God! You killed him!"

Great. A drug-dealing psycho slams into you, maybe breaks your nose by the looks of things, and now you're gonna yell at me for violating his civil rights.

"Cool. Just like on that show, ya' know? *Cops?*" Maybe it would have been better if he had yelled at me.

"They sure do bleed a lot."

Christ, he's right. Slatter's practically painting the town red, for real. I've never seen so much blood come out of one guy. I don't know why, but suddenly I can't help but think about the big, bloated ticks I used to pull off my dog's ear when me and Alice was still together. The things always gave me the shakes. They looked like, grapes or something. And you couldn't just pull 'em off. Every time you'd get a good grip they'd pop and the mutt's blood would bust out all over your hands. God, I hated that.

Slatter looks like that — like a popped grape. Maybe the drugs he was taking was bloating him up, filling him full of blood or something.

"Well, aren't you going to read him his rights now?"

I give the guy the idiot look. "He's dead. And the phone lines to Heaven have been down since the '40s."

"He's not dead."

I follow the guy's pointing finger to Slatter. I can't believe it, but he's getting up again. Like a cadet I clumsily reload my clip while Slatter lopes on down the alley. He's got this scared look in his eye, almost like I'm not supposed to be able to hurt him, but I did. I can see him trying to stop the blood with his hands, but two paws won't cover 13 holes.

I give Joe Citizen a shrug and chase after Slatter again. God knows how, but he's still going at a marathon clip. I gave up smoking a couple of years back, and now I remember why.

He's slipped into an alley, but you don't have to be a dog to follow the red trail he's leaving. But I ain't going in. It's too dark and this guy ain't right.

"Come on outta there, Slatter. You need a doc. Come out now and I won't kick the shit out of you."

I'm just about to change my mind when Slatter comes tearing out of the darkness. The sucker moves so fast he's knocked me flat on the pavement before I could squeeze off a round. Something in there must've scared him, but I don't see any. . . Oh, great. I see it now. Some big mutt's holed up in there. Slatter's afraid of a lousy dog. Of course, that is the biggest dog I've ever seen. Maybe I'll vamoose, too.

The dog growls as I start to get up, but somehow I get the weirdest feeling — like it wants Slatter for breakfast, but could care less about me. I've read animal's can sense fear before. Maybe Slatter's so messed up it can't tell I've just about wet my pants.

So before it changes its mind I'm out of there. I can see Slatter turning the corner at the bottom of the hill and I'm on him like a mayfly with a minute left to mate. We're in the marina district now. Slatter's heading right for the Alexandrian Club. Hmmm? Curiouser and curiouser, but that's a mighty expensive rabbit hole to fall into.

He makes it through the doors before I catch up — either their doorman was taking a leak or Slatter knows someone in there. Either way, narcotics detective Ignatius T. Barnes is about to get into one of the poshest joints in town.

• • •

Now I'm standing in the lobby of the Alexandrian Club, trying to figure out what the hell just happened. I came in after Slatter, and found him lying in the middle of the club. There was a gaggle standing around him. Some of 'em look like typical SF punks, but others are dressed in suits and ties. I can't help but feel I've stumbled onto something big here. Are these the leaders of the San Francisco gangs? It would make sense. This is a private club, and if I weren't in hot-pursuit, I'd've needed a warrant to get in myself.

I may have just stumbled into that big case I've always wanted. Course, I keep thinking about that old saying, "Be careful what you wish for. . . ."

"Kindly step away from the body, gents." Most of 'em do what I say, but not one guy. He's dressed in some sort of red-velvet suit, and long, black hair hangs down around his wide lapel. It's almost like he can't figure out whether he's a punk or a suit. His hair hangs down like a punk, but he's wearing an outfit that probably costs more than my whole wardrobe. Some of the other suit's have long hair too, but they've got it tied back in a ponytail. Maybe this guy's some sort of go-between.

"You too, buddy," I tell him.

"What seems to be the problem, officer?" he asks.

I give him the idiot look again. "The problem, pal, is that you've got a dead perpetrator laying smack in the middle of your club, and he seemed to think he was going to hide out in here. You know this creep?"

"No, sir. I've never seen him before in my, uh — life." It was Velvet again. He doesn't speak very clearly, when he stammered, it almost sounded like 'unlife.'"

Heh, heh. I'm gonna' have fun with this one. "So he just happened to run all the way through the district, through your doors, and then comes pawing all over you? Is that it?" I walk over and lift up his lapel, showing him the slick blood barely visible against the red velvet.

He looks down at it, and then gives me this almost excited look. "Ah, I see he's soiled my outfit. Yes, officer. . ."

"Barnes. Iggy Barnes."

"Officer Barnes. This young man did bump into me as he entered our parlor. But then he collapsed into the heap you see before you. He seems to have been shot. A lot."

It was obvious he was trying to put me on the defensive by pointing out the number of holes ventilating Slatter's corpse, but I wasn't falling for it. This guy was already pissing me off. Something about him just rubbed me the wrong way. As a matter of fact, all these grinning goons were starting to grind my gizzard.

"Whatever. Somebody gimme a phone. And nobody leave the room."

Velvet points at one of the goombahs and he brings me one of those little sissy phones. Velvet's getting a kick out of this, and I catch more than a few snickers in the crowd. But I grin and bear it and dial downtown.

"Central? This is Barnes. I've followed a perp down to the Alexandrian Club. I'm gonna need Forensics and an ambulance, but tell the meat wagon not to hurry. This guy needs a priest more than a doctor. Send me a couple of blue-bellies too, and see if you can, get a warrant for the club."

Soon as I hang up the phone, Velvet's in my face again. "I don't think there's any need for that, Detective Barnes."

Now I'm getting this drugged feeling. Velvet's staring me in the eyes and I feel like a rat looking right into the eyes of one mother of snake.

Hmm. He's probably right. There's no reason to search the rest of the club.

And then I'm snapping out of it. Guess all that adrenaline built up from the chase finally caught up with me. I got that feeling you get when you've got a cold and you stand up too fast — kind of dizzy and disoriented.

I drop their princess phone right on Velvet's foot and he backs off a little. He looks pissed, though. Like I should be caving in like the rest of his little toadies, but won't. Sorry pal. Now I'm on the offensive. "Hey, you." I whip out my notepad, sometimes it's more intimidating than my nine. "What's your name?"

"Giuseppe Renaldo."

"Renaldo, heh?" I jot down his name. That always scares 'em.

● ● ●

Fifteen minutes later there's a knock on the door. It's Forensics and a couple of boys from downtown. We go around the room a couple of times getting names and making these creeps generally nervous. Of course, nobody's seen anything, knows anything, or even knew who Slatter was. Then that damn silly phone tinkles. Renaldo answers it and looks over at me. "Detective Barnes. It's for you."

"Barnes here."

The voice on the other end is Lieutenant Coleson, night shift. He's a young prick right out of the academy, but he's usually smart enough to listen to us veterans.

"Barnes, I can't get a warrant for you."

"Why the hell not? I chased a perp right into this place. And it wasn't an accident, either. There were four or five other places on the way and the creep by-passed 'em all for the A-Club. Now what does that tell you, Lt.?"

"It tells me that his boss is in there somewhere, but word from on high is to leave them alone."

Halfway through this frustrating conversation I notice Renaldo grinning at me like a dog that's pissed behind the sofa, where he thinks no one will find out.

I want to stand here and bitch a while, but I've been playing this game long enough to know better. "Whatever you say, Lt."

I'm hanging up the phone when I notice one of the lab boys giving me a look. I walk out to the porch of the A-Club and he comes out behind me.

"Detective?"

"Yeah?"

"Did you put all those bullet holes in the body?"

Great. Now I'm gonna' get indicted by one of Mr. Wizards' graduates. "Yeah. I did. What about it?"

"Well, I don't suppose you, uh. . ."

"Spit it out kid. You wanna know why it took more than two clips to bring the jerk down?"

"No! No, detective. I want to know if you saw him break his neck."

The proverbial load of bricks crashes down on my noggin. "Broke his neck?"

"Yes. It wasn't obvious until we picked the body up, but there's no doubt about it."

"I guess it's possible. He fell a couple of times coming down the hill. Could that have done it?"

The kid looks away, out over the water. He's trying to place all the pieces into the puzzle, the big one that tells you exactly what's going on here. Hell, the way he's got his brow all scrunched up, he kind of looks like me. When I was younger.

"No. I don't think so." Then he gets some sort of idea and heads back over to the meat wagon. He crawls up inside and zips down Slatter's body bag. "It's hard to tell this soon, and with so much blood everywhere. . . but it looks like somebody's crushed his throat with a vice. . . or something. Something. . . really strong."

"Maybe somebody wrung his neck before I got in, to keep him from talkin'?"

"No. Beneath this jacket his neck's about the width of my wrist. I don't see any boot marks or anything. . . though these bullet holes have messed him up pretty badly."

"Bullet holes in the neck?"

"Yes, looks like at least two just below the right ear. Small entry wounds, actually." He turns Slatter's head around and I hear this disgusting squishy-crunching sound. "Hmm. And no exit wounds. Strange that both bullets would have deflected into the abdomen like that."

I didn't think I hit him in the neck at all to tell the truth, but it was dark and we were both running, so it was possible. But just on a hunch, "Hey kid. There any bullet holes in the collar, over the neck?"

"Actually. . ." Now I hear this sickening sucking sound, like the leather was sticking to the slimy flesh, ". . . no. Hmmm. How odd. Maybe they stuck a pistol down his collar when he stumbled in and popped him before you got there. The rounds could easily have broken the neck. The decompression and the lack of exit wounds is a little odd, but I've seen stranger things."

Suddenly, I see Renaldo standing on the porch of the A-Club. He's trying to figure out if I've noticed anything, and maybe trying to scare me off if I have. God, I wish I still smoked. This would be the perfect time to light a cigarette and ignore him. It's a lot harder to look nonchalant with a stick of Dentine.

"Okay, kid. Bag him back up. We'll get a full report from the coroner."

"And Renaldo," I turn around and fix him with my patented Bogart stare, "don't leave town."

But the last thing he says to me puts a shiver down my spine. It's not really what he says, more like how he says it. Like it was a whisper, though we're over 30 feet apart and the wind's blowing in off the bay. And I swear the mother's lips never moved.

"I wouldn't dream of it, Detective Barnes."

• • •

It's Friday. About 9:30, only five freaking hours since I left the bayfront. Busts are like that. You gotta go to the deal whether you've got the day off or not. Maybe that's why so many cops can't hold down a marriage. You get home from work, eat a TV dinner, go out and buy a couple of kilos of coke, throw some punks in jail, and then try to get home in time to watch Leno and pleasure the wife.

I've just sat down at my desk and poured my first cup of joe when the day lieutenant, a guy named Grange, walks up with one of those "your-work's-just-gone-to-shit" looks.

"There's been an accident, Barnes."

"Christ! Alice?" I'm about to pop a vein. She may be my ex-wife, but God knows I still love her. If anything's happened to her, I'll. . .

"No, Iggy. Calm down. Not Alice. Your stiff."

The world settles back down into a hazy shade of gray. "From last night? Slatter?"

"Yeah. Ambulance plunged off the Golden Gate Bridge about 30 minutes after it left the Alexandrian club, 4:23 AM to be exact. Driver must've fallen asleep at the wheel. It took City a while to pull up the wreck, what with the tremor and all, but they finally found it. I'm afraid it's been smashed into toothpicks and the bodies have been washed out."

"Then dredge the freaking bay!"

The lieutenant looks puzzled. He doesn't realize my evidence against Renaldo was wrapped around Slatter's throat. "I'm sure they will, Barnes, but the sharks've probably got them by now. What was so important?"

"Nothing. Nothing at all." I'm feeling pretty miserable now. I kind of liked the kid that spotted Slatter's broken neck. So I get back to the job at hand to get my mind off the fact that the kid probably never even got laid. "What'd you pull up on that name I gave Lt. Coleson?"

Grange opens the folder he's forgotten about carrying and hands me a print-out. "Uh, recent Italian immigrant, no known family in the States. Nothing much. Renaldo's got all the signs of a supplier, though. He's got no job but his bank accounts are full of zeroes. People on the street call him 'Virus.'"

"Virus. Nice name. Reminds me of something that lives in your colon."

"He's only been in the city for a couple of years, but he's already built up a loyal trafficking network. He's got a lot of flunkies but none of them have ever spilled anything. And even most of them have been clean. Slatter must be one of the exceptions. His rap sheet's a mile long. Unfortunately, there's nothing to connect him with Virus. Um, Renaldo."

"Okay, I'll keep on it. See what I can dig up."

Though Slatter's corpse is gone, things are still looking up. Internal Affairs wouldn't be able to touch me, and my buddy Sam made it through the night. But then the civvy shows up.

I see him sitting in the lieutenant's office with two other suits, probably IA. It was the guy Slatter had bumped into. A few minutes later, Grange calls me in.

I catch the guy's last statement as I walk in, ". . . everywhere. And then he got up again, kind of staggering, and the detective shot him at least 10 more times."

"Nine. My clip only holds nine."

The guy jumps when he sees it was me. He probably thinks we're going to gang up on him, cops protecting their own and all that. He doesn't know I'm the one that was about to get gang-banged.

One of the suits, a tall guy with glasses and a black crew-cut starts my 'trial.' "Detective Barnes, we would like to know why it took over 13 shots to stop the suspect. . ." he consults his fancy leather folder, "James Slatter."

They must've already talked to Sam. "PCP. Heroin. How the hell should I know? The creep was high as a kite and strong as an elephant. Ask this guy. He tackled him." I point out the civilian.

"That's true. He did run into — I mean, I tried to stop him. . . . Is there a reward involved?"

This is too much for me. I answer a few more questions, but without a body, there isn't much for them to yell at me for.

Now it's 5:04 PM. I'm on my way home to another TV dinner. Only there's no wife to play kiss-and-tickle with after Leno.

When I get home, there's something strange waiting for me at the door. Spot comes bounding out of the kitchen and jumps on my leg, but I notice he's sliding around in a puddle of piss. "Get down, Spot." Hey, I didn't name the mutt.

I bend down and smell the puddle, just to make sure. The only time Spot can't hold his water is when someone he doesn't know comes inside. I pull my nine and search the place, but it's empty. There ain't a hair out of whack in the apartment, but Spot's yellow alarm is all I need. Somebody's been poking around. At least they could have done the laundry.

Me and Spot share a meal and watch reruns of "The Night Stalker." I've eaten a thousand of these TV dinners, and it never ceases to amaze me how everything's in its own little pocket until you put it in the oven. Then, when you pull it out, the potatoes are partying with the carrots, and the Salisbury gravy has turned the brownie into pudding.

I'm licking out the last of the gravy when I see it. I keep a picture of Alice sitting on my Zenith. Right on her neck is this big thumbprint. It's just a little smudge in the dust, but it's there. I knock my brownie-pudding all over the couch as I grab for the phone. Spot's already licked it up when she answers.

"Hello?"

"Alice? It's Iggy. Is everything — are you, OK?"

"Yes, is something wrong?"

"No, I just thought. . . . Have you seen anything strange today?"

"No, I. . . no, not really."

"What do you mean 'not really?' That sounds an awful lot like 'sort of.'"

"Well, this guy called earlier. He asked if you were here and I said that you, well, that you didn't live at this number anymore."

"And?"

"Well, he said that he was worried about you. That'd he heard you'd picked up some sort of bacteria. I thought maybe the department was looking for you. Are you sick, Iggy?"

My skin goes as pale as Slatter's had been. I whisper a 'bye' and hang up the phone. The guy hadn't told her I'd picked up a bacteria. It was a Virus.

● ● ●

Virus was taking things personal, and he was sure as hell making it personal for me. I probably would've gone after him anyway, but now I had to.

So here I sit in my Chevy watching the Alexandrian Club. I haven't seen Virus yet, but there's plenty of other weirdness to check out. I've never seen so many punks and suits mixed together. Is this some new trend among the rich? Hanging out with the dregs of society?

Several hours pass. It's about 5:30 AM, and still no sign of Virus. I've fallen asleep several times. It'd be my luck to miss him. I remember one time. . . wait! There he is.

Three goons accompany him to a black Caddy and they head down to the warehouses. Fortunately, tailing cars is right up this detective's alley. They stop at one of the older buildings, and one of the goons gets out and unlocks the gate. They vanish into the darkness, and don't come out again for another 20 minutes. I should probably follow them home, but that'll be easy enough to do later on. Right now, I want to know what's in the warehouse.

When the Caddy's out of sight, I head to the gate. It's simple enough to pick the lock and I'm inside in less than 30 seconds. Down towards the water, I hear a groan. . . or something. I creep along the edge of the tin building and turn the corner. That's when the boundaries of my world started to collapse.

• • •

The warehouse is sitting on a pier, and the pier hangs out over a tiny section of the San Francisco Bay. Just on the edge of this pier is a little shack, probably a shipping and receiving office. Somebody's painted all the window's black, but I can see some light spilling out from under the door.

With my nine nestled in my hand, I push my ear up to the wall. There's some kind of heavy breathing coming out of there — like somebody's sick or something. I start thinking maybe Virus has killed a night watchman and left him for dead, and this might be my golden opportunity to get a warrant for his ass and all his other pink parts.

I throw open the door fast, just in case my breather's one of Virus' thugs with a bad case of asthma. It's one of Virus', all right. But asthma should have been the least of his worries.

It was Slatter.

• • •

He looks up at me, kind of like my kid, Alicia, used to do when she was sick. I get that father feeling for a second, and then I remember what kind of douche bag I'm dealing with. Still, there's something almost pathetic in those black eyes of his. Almost like he knows he should be dead, maybe even wanted to be, but something more powerful than him or me or all the ammo in my Beretta decided otherwise. He's been given a second chance at life, and it's scaring the hell out of him.

But there's more in that gaze. There's defiance there — defiance at whatever's pulled him out of the not-so-great beyond, and probably at me, too.

I break the mood. "I don't how you're still suckin' wind Slatter-boy, but as soon as I get a warrant and an ambulance, you're goin' with me.

He snarls like a dog, but I can tell he's a little relieved, too. Guess if I had 20 some holes in me I'd prefer to be handcuffed to a hospital bed than stuck out on some pier in a five-by-nine shack.

"Don't go anywhere." I smirk as I start for my car. But I haven't even cleared the door when I see headlights playing off the blacked-out windows. Damn! The Caddy's pulled up right in front of the shack! There's no way out. I've got to hide, but where? I look over at Slatter and hope the idea of young candy-stripers and a square meal's enough to buy a friend.

• • •

"Well, well, well. What's the matter, Jimmy? Have you had a visitor? I detect the most unpleasant odor of a human. It's difficult over your natural stench and that of the river, but it smells rather like. . . . Yes! Detective Barnes!"

So now I'm laying under Slatter's cot playing hide-and-go-seek with Virus. He's parked his ass on a seat right next to the bed in a lame attempt at the concerned father bit. His loafer's are about four inches from my ribs, but I don't think he knows I'm under here. Of course, he is scaring the be-Jesus out of me with all this sniffing me out crap, but maybe he just spotted my car and he's making a guess. At least Slatter's on my side. Before I dove under here it looked like he was more afraid of Virus than I was.

"So what should your punishment be, Jimmy? Should I simply leave you here for 15 or 20 years, barely giving you enough blood to survive until the next day?"

What? This guy's loonier than I thought.

"Or perhaps the punishment should better fit the crime. You led the police into our sanctuary. The mortal vermin were everywhere, crawling through our things like pathetic rats. Their foul odors have even permeated the Vampire Club, Jimmy. Perhaps I should summon the real rats that live on this pier and lock them in this shack with you. Then you would know what it feels like to be violated by something so despicable, so disgusting, that you feel you must shower thrice before retiring for the day. That would be a fitting punishment, would it not?"

Okay, something stinks more than Virus' Odor-Eaters here. He must know I'm under here and he's playing around — thinks he can scare me with all this Bela Lugosi action. Well, if he knows I'm here, I might as well come out with style.

My pistol's already in my hand — it's easy enough to slide it over to the bridge of his right foot and shatter it like a sand dollar. Virus is up and screaming like I've never heard anyone scream before. I roll out and point the Beretta up at his crotch. "Don't even get stiff, Vi —"

And that's all I get out before Virus grabs my weapon hand. His grip's like a freaking vice. . . he's crushing my fingers, pressing them into the ungiving metal. I want to yell at him but the pain's so bad I can't even cut wind. Christ! He's broken my fingers! I can feel the bones popping like bamboo stalks!

Then he drops the whole mess like the box a Big Mac comes in.

He's silent for a minute, or maybe I just can't hear him over my screaming nerve endings.

"Aaah. Well, that relieved a little tension."

Funny as a crutch. My hand's a bleeding mass of ruptured flesh and he's smiling like a Cheshire. A second ago he was raw fury — I've never seen anyone react like that. Now he's leaning back against the wall and watching me squirm, looking like he just got laid.

He looks down at his bloody shoe. I can hear something squishing around in there, like his toes were moving, though I doubt they're in any better shape than my hand. "That really hurt, Detective Barnes. It's the first time a mortal has wounded me in over 30 years. You should be proud."

"What ward did you escape from?"

"Hmm? Ah, yes. I suppose I would have had the same reaction when I was a mortal such as you."

Great. I'm bleeding to death with a certifiable lunatic standing over me, and he thinks he's immortal. If I can get my pistol back I'll show him otherwise.

"Let me tell you a story, Mr. Barnes. And then I will put my lips next to your ill-shaven throat, and drink of your blood until you die."

"There's nothing better than a story and a good-night kiss, V."

He gives me a strange look, an almost wishful look, then shakes his head and starts blabbing again. That's OK. While he's playing the gloating villain over the fallen hero bit, Iggy Barnes is gonna' figure a way out of this jam.

• • •

"I was born in Sicilia, the son of a carpenter. I was always a small child, and the other boys frequently abused me. It was a lonely childhood. But one day, at the age of 11 or so, one of the boys who had teased me the most, Angelino, fell into an old well. I happened upon him, and he demanded that I help him out. There was a rope and bucket hanging in the well, and it would have been an easy matter to turn the crank and help him out. Perhaps he would have thanked me, but I knew it was far more likely that he would only take out his humiliation on my frail form. So I ran away, leaving him there for the night.

"The next morning, all the adults were looking for Angelino, but I said nothing. After dinner, I went back to the well. He was still sitting there. I don't know whether I was excited or scared or both. I knew that if he was discovered he would tell the adults that I had visited him twice, and that my father would take the belt to me as never before. But I couldn't help watching him suffer down there. Suddenly it was beyond my mere desire for revenge, I simply enjoyed savoring his misery. I must have sat there for hours, leaning over the edge while delicious blood rushed to my head, Angelino cursing at me all the while. He was an insect in my petri dish of stone.

"For three more days I visited my 'experiment.' The well was far enough away from the city that no one had yet found it, and Angelino grew paler and weaker every day. The last time I visited him, he begged and pleaded. Perhaps if he had begged that first day, I would have helped.

"Perhaps.

"Anyway, there was a storm that night. It rained like I had never seen it rain before. All night long I listened to the torrent of the storm and dreamed delicious fantasies of Angelino wet and cold and miserable at the bottom of that beautiful well, my childish mind never realizing that the water was probably well over his head by midnight.

"The next morning, I eagerly ate my breakfast and ran as fast I could to the well. The field around it was muddy and I fell several times, but I barely noticed in my excitement to see what had become of my little insect. When I finally saw Angelino's bloated body floating in the murky water, I began to cry.

"And do you know why I cried, Mr. Barnes?"

"Because you realized what a little Eddie Munster creep you were?"

"No, Mr. Barnes. I cried because my experiment was over. And because I might never get a chance to enjoy human misery like this again. But that was where I was wrong."

This guy makes Jack the Ripper look like St. Bartholomew. But that's all right. Let him keep flapping his jaws. I've managed to grab the pistol again, with my off-hand of course. Slatter's seen me, but the only reaction he gives me is a nervous look up at Virus. Poor bastard probably can't move anything but his eyes anyway.

"Over the years, I was given several more opportunities to experience the angst of human tragedy. But it wasn't until the war that I realized my true destiny."

And that's when I go for it. I get off one, two, three shots. Only two of 'em hit, but it looks like they went center-mass, right in the chest. Virus is still leaning up against the wall but his head drops like a stone. Sicko must have died instantly.

Wrong! Crap! He's grabbed me by the neck and, *unghh. . . .*

•   •   •

When I come to, I'm lying in the bottom of a power boat out in the bay. Virus is driving and Slatter's nowhere in sight.

"Ah, welcome back, Mr. Barnes." He's giving me the scoping look, trying to figure out if I've got any fight left in me.

"Good. Good. I do so hate it when the rain comes." He smiles, hoping I've caught his meaning. I do. He's talking about that poor kid. When the rain came, the fight was over, and that's no fun for him.

"The rain ain't come yet, creep."

"Yes, but the skies are looking cloudy, Mr. Barnes."

Then he turns back around, piloting the boat out to the middle of the bay. I figure he's gonna dump me to the sharks or something.

"You didn't let me finish my story, Mr. Barnes."

There's a long silence. I can't tell if he wants me to encourage him or not, but I gotta admit this loonie's made up a pretty good yarn so far. So I bite. "I'm not going anywhere, V."

"True. True." He looks out over the water, trying his best to look like George Washington crossing the Delaware, but he's too short and scrawny for that, and he ain't got no powdered toupee, either. He'd be scrappy looking if not for his fancy duds. Of course, velvet went out of style before my tie.

"As I was saying, it was the war that revealed to me my true destiny. To many Sicilians, Mussolini was a blessing. He gave them a sense of pride, he improved our economy, and he gave us an enemy to fight — the communists. But there was a price. Anyone who spoke out against him would be dragged into the street and shot by his fascist armies.

"My father was one of those men. He believed that fascism was just a petty facade for a militaristic dictatorship, and made the mistake of voicing his opinions over a bottle of wine with an old friend. The friend turned my father in, and the next day my mother and I watched as he was taken into the street and beaten to death. We knew it would be only a matter of time before the brownshirts came for us.

"My mother and I decided to hide. But where? The betrayal of my father taught us that no one could be trusted. The only safe place would be one without people. So we fled to a ruined church on the shores of Sicilia."

We're getting close to Alcatraz. I thought maybe he was gonna dump me to the sharks, but now I could swim over to the Rock before those bloodsuckers got me. What's he up to?

"But the church wasn't deserted as we had thought. In the crypts below, Seraphis slept. The first night we sheltered there, I could feel his cold, immortal eyes washing over my mother and me with hungry desire. For several more days, the shadow of Seraphis loomed ever closer, until one night, he approached me as if in a dream.

"I was but 16, then. Far too young to understand the difference between raw sensuality and vulgar sex, but

Seraphis was so. . . beautiful, so mystical, that I could not scream out for my mother even though I was terrified beyond comprehension. And then the shadow swept past and descended on my mother like a ravenous wolf. I will never forget the shrill death screams he evoked from her, or how, in the last moments, her screams were as those I had sometimes heard her make with my father, behind the closed doors of their bedroom.

"When it was over, the only sound was an ominous wind rising from the beating surf below."

"You're a freakin' lunatic." I thought I'd try the direct approach. Maybe my timing was bad.

Virus reaches down and grabs my swollen hand just as the boat slams into Alcatraz Island. The pain is incredible, and I think he's jerked the whole arm out of its socket as he tosses me onto the rocks like a rag-doll. Slatter's strength had amazed me, but this is unnatural. Especially from such a scrawny little guy. Could he possibly be telling the truth? Nah, that's ridiculous.

Now he's dragging me up the rocks, towards the prison. I'm not exactly petite, and he's pulling me along like puppy that just shit on the rug. And he's still yapping the whole way.

"I remember little after that. Seraphis let me go, and I, with no mother or father, was quickly swept into the ranks of Italy's misguided legions. As with any other young man, I quickly became infused with the furor of nationalism. I rose quickly through the ranks, gaining a field promotion to lieutenant by '42. But I was hated even there.

"My punishments upon my men and my treatments of prisoners were considered far too. . . severe, for the tastes of my comrades. By '44, I had been sentenced to death by my superiors. I languished in the prisons for months awaiting my execution, all the while feeling some strange compulsion to return to Sicilia. But my prison was near Anzio, and the Americans were upon us before my execution."

Now Virus has pulled us up to the entrance, but I think he's screwed now. There's a big padlock on the door and even his strength ain't gonna pop that sucker. I'm just about to smart off again when he pulls a key out of his pocket.

"But to the Americans, there were only two things worse than Italians: Nazis and Italian criminals. They kept me in prison for a total of eight years. First in Anzio, then in Georgia, then France. I would have rotted there were it not for the French. You see, their battered country needed rebuilding, and the prisoners that remained were regarded as nothing more than cheap labor. I was put to work in a coal mine by a kindly old man named Gaston. Within three days, I had strangled him and was on my way back to Sicilia."

We're inside. Virus is giving me a major case of the creeps, but this place is a hundred times worse. They used to run tours out here, but that stopped a couple of years ago. Now I know why. The Rock has started to crumble everywhere, and it looks like the earthquake the other day tore it up even more.

"I wasn't sure that Seraphis would still be there. I wasn't even sure that the church would be there after you Americans had destroyed our beautiful island, but I had to try. Do you know what it's like to languish in prison when your love is calling for you? I do, Mr. Barnes! For eight long years I pined away for my beautiful Seraphis, but could not leave those infernal cells.

"I arrived in Sicilia shortly after midnight. My heart was racing, for the last time, and sickening sweat rolled down my mortal body as I tread ever closer to my destination. When I saw that the ruins still stood, I almost cried with delight."

We're at some kind of elevator shaft. What's he gonna do? Throw me down in there? I think he's totally. . . I'll be damned. The power's on. What the hell is going on here?

"There was a refugee family cowering in the shadows of the ruin, but I could not let them interfere. With my bare hands and a crazed frenzy I tore into them like shrapnel. Their blood oozed down through the weeded stone, and it was this that must have awakened my Sire. At last, after 13 long years, I had returned to Seraphis. He embraced me on the spot, and . . ."

"Look, fruitcake. I don't wanna hear about what you Eye-talian boys do to each other in the dark."

Bad move. He throws me into the elevator hard enough to make my skull crack, then he's on me before I can blink my eyes.

"*Fool!* Have you not yet realized that you have crossed into the realm of the immortals? Do you not understand that I am a *vampire!*"

He throws back his head and two of the longest teeth I've ever seen bust through the roof of his mouth. His eyes are filled with hate and lust and confusion and pain and a thousand other emotions. Suddenly, I believe in fairy tales and the boogie man and gremlins and all those things that lurk in your closet and under your bed when you turn off the light. And my world goes black.

● ● ●

When I come to, Virus is dragging me down by a row of cells. He's still yakking; going on about vampires and how he came to be, but my head's ringing and spinning and refusing to believe what I now know has to be true, so I don't catch a word of it.

My eyes are still adjusting to the darkness, but I'm starting to make out shapes in the cells. The first one is sitting in the darkness, not making a sound. It looks like a female by the shape of the hair and the ballerina outfit she wears, but she couldn't be more than six or seven years old by the size. Yet she looks up at me and her eyes gleam in the blackness, and I know the mind behind those orbs is far older. God! Is this what Virus is going to do to me? Lock me up in Alcatraz? It makes sense. His justice was running towards the poetic side with Slatter.

The next three cells are empty, I think, but the fourth makes me damn near wet myself. There's a guy standing in there, at least eight or nine feet tall, and the hairiest son-of-a-bitch I've ever seen. I know my noggin's cracked 'cause I'd swear that mother had a snout like a dog. Virus stops for a second, leaving me laying in front of the thing's cage. God, what if it reaches out for me? What if it touches m — Oh, God. Oh, God.

We're moving again. I hear a chuckle. I guess Virus is getting his kicks out of watching me squirm.

I feel like a scared kid again. Like when you're getting into bed and your feet are still on the ground, beneath the bed. Where the monsters are.

He drags me another 20 feet, my lips quivering like Jell-O and my spine feeling like Play-Doh. The last cell on the row is the weirdest. It's covered with hexes and pentagrams and chicken feet and all that shit you see in the movies; but there's nothing in there. At least, nothing I can see. I start to mumble something, but Virus kicks me to shut up. He wants me to listen. So I do.

There's a low, groaning sound in that dark place. It starts out like it's a million miles away, like it's coming over a pay phone with a bad connection. But then it starts getting clearer. Not stronger, not even louder, just. . . clearer. Like now that I'm listening I can hear it better, only I don't want to. Nothing on earth ever made sounds like these.

"They are screams of the dead, Mr. Barnes. Oh, yes. You can hear them. If you listen. And sometimes, they are far more delicious than the screams of the living."

"Then y–you won't be n–needin' me. . ." I whisper and try to stand.

He kicks me back down and I just lay there. I squint my eyes and try not to hear that sound anymore. I don't know why squinting my eyes helps me keep out sounds, but somehow it does, and the damn groaning becomes a distant echo somewhere in the back of my mind.

And then it hits me. He's gonna lock me up with that thing. I look over to the cell again, and I can feel the blood draining out of my face. Maybe it's just trying to get as far away as possible from Virus. The vampire.

Somehow, saying it made it real. As if, when Iggy Barnes finally admits that the guy who just dragged him into the dark heart of Alcatraz is a vampire, then it must be real.

Now I'm starting to convulse, probably going into shock. It's strange how the mind can detach itself and watch its miserable shell falling to shit.

Virus sees me staring at the thing in the cell. "Oh, you think I'm going to throw you in there? What a wonderful idea. You see? We are much alike, after all. But no. That is not my plan. I have one far better in mind.

"You see, we vampires are a very secretive, but very large population."

That idea never entered my mind. If Virus is really a. . . vampire, then there must be thousands of them out. . . oh my god.

"And as with any population, we too have our rules. One of our rules, Mr. Barnes, is that of the Elysium. You see, because there are so many rival factions within our society, we must occasionally find a safe place to meet, a place where no one is allowed to shed blood; an Elysium. Alcatraz is such a place."

Suddenly a sliver of light forces its way back into my world. "Then. . . y–you can't hurt me here?" I whisper.

"Correct. You are absolutely safe. Were I to, say, rip your head from your filthy neck, I would bring upon myself a world of pain. The prince and all those loyal to him would hunt me down and make me suffer. And I only like to watch suffering, Mr. Barnes. I have no taste for it myself."

Then I'm trying to stand, trying to regain a little dignity and play my last hand. "Then get the fuck out of here!"

I caught him off guard. Good.

"All I gotta do is wait for the sun to come up and I'm goin' home. T–take your scrawny immortal ass and get it out of my sight."

Virus grabs me by the throat. He's wanting to pop off my head but he can't, so I start giggling like a teen-aged girl. "You're the one that brought me here, moron. Now ya can't touch me."

Suddenly he regains his composure. I don't think I like that. "You're quite correct. You see, Mr. Barnes, I brought you out here to make you suffer the same fate I suffered for eight years, the same fate you make others suffer every single day of your life. I'm going to put you in a kind of prison for the rest of your life."

I can't help but look over at the groaner in cell 24 again.

"No, please. Nothing so mundane. Your prison will be the most frustrating kind of all, a prison without walls. While you remain here, you are safe. I, and others of my kind, cannot, and will not, harm you." Then he gets this evil look in his eyes, so evil I can feel the blackness trying to bust out like. . . a prisoner.

"But if you step more than two inches off this island, I will tear you into so many pieces the sharks won't even be able to smell your blood. And if you should make it to land, I will find you. We control your chief, your officials, your politicians; there isn't a place on earth that you can hide from me."

Then he drops me on the cold floor and starts walking away, like he's won. But I've reached the end of my rope. I start shouting and cursing and yelling everything I can think of.

"Someday I'm gonna get fed up, Virus. I'm gonna go crazy from the sound of that thing in there, or the hairy guy's gonna' scare my hair white, and I'm gonna leave. I'm gonna stand up on the highest wall I can find and dive right into the bay. And I'm just gonna wait for you to come and kill me because it won't matter anymore! You understand me, you blood-sucking freak? I'll be wantin' you to kill me and you'll just be doing me a favor! So come on! Do it now! Come and fight me like a man! Or have you been a ghoul so long you've forgotten what it's like to have a pair of nuts?"

Then he turns around and says one word to me. One word that makes me shut up and slink back into a little corner of my walless cell like a sulking child. The one word condemns me to an eternal prison with the screaming of the dead and the howling of what I'm now convinced is a werewolf. My life is over, and I won't even get a freaking funeral.

I wonder for a second about the word he said to me, how he knew, but then I remember that thumbprint on the picture in my apartment.

The picture of the word.
Of Alice.
I pray for rain. ☥

LEXICON

Common Parlance

These are the terms that are most commonly used among the Kindred.

Anarch: A rebel among the Kindred, one with no respect for the elders. Most fledglings are automatically assumed to be anarchs by the elders, and are despised as products of the 20th century.

Barrens, The: The areas of a city that are devoid of life — graveyards, abandoned buildings and parks.

Becoming, The: The moment one becomes a vampire; the metamorphosis from mortal to Kindred. Also called *The Change*.

Book of Nod: The "sacred" book of the Kindred, tracing the race's origins and early history. It has never been published in its entirety, although fragments are known to exist in various languages.

Beast, The: The drives and urges which prompt a vampire to become entirely a monster, forsaking all Humanity. Vide *Man* infra.

Blood: The vampire's heritage. That which makes a vampire a vampire, or simply the actual blood of the vampire.

Blood Kindred: The relationship between vampires of the same *lineage* and *clan*. The idea is much the same among mortals; only the means of transmission are different.

Blood Oath: The most potent bond which can exist between vampires; the receiving of blood in an acknowledgement of mastery. This grants a mystical power over the one who is bound. Vide *Blood Bond* infra.

Brood: A group of vampires gathered around a leader (usually their sire). A brood may in time become a *clan* (qv).

Caitiff: A vampire with no clan; frequently used in a derogatory fashion. To be clanless is not a virtue among the Kindred.

Camarilla, The: A global sect of vampires in which all Kindred may hold membership. Its rule is far from absolute, and it serves as a debating chamber more than a government.

Childe: A derogatory term for a young, inexperienced, or foolish vampire. The plural form is *Childer*.

Clan: A group of vampires who share certain mystic and physical characteristics. Vide *lineage*, *bloodline*.

Diablerie: The cannibalistic behavior common among Kindred, involving the consumption of the blood of another vampire. The elders do so out of need, whereas the anarchs do so out of desire for power.

Domain: The fiefdom claimed by a vampire, most often a prince. Invariably a city.

Elder: A vampire who is 300 years of age or older. Elders consider themselves the most powerful Kindred, and usually engage in their own Jyhad.

Elysium: The name given for the places where the elders meet and gather, commonly operas, theaters or other public places of high culture.

Embrace, The: The act of transforming a mortal into a vampire by draining the mortal's blood and replacing it with a small amount of the vampire's own blood.

Fledgling: A young, newly created vampire. Vide *Neonate, Whelp.*

Generation: The number of steps between a vampire and the mythical Caine. Caine's Get were the second generation, their brood the third, and so on.

Gehenna: The end of the Third Cycle; the impending Armageddon when the Antediluvians shall awaken and devour all vampires.

Ghoul: A servant created by allowing a mortal to drink Kindred blood without the draining that would give rise to a *progeny.*

Haven: The home of a vampire or the place where it sleeps during the day.

Hunger, The: As with mortals and other animals, the drive to feed. For vampires, though, it is much more intense, and takes the place of every other drive, urge and pleasure.

Inconnu: A sect of vampires, mostly Methuselahs, who have removed themselves from both mortal and Kindred affairs. They state that they have nothing to do with the Jyhad.

Jyhad, The: The secret war being waged between the few surviving vampires of the third generation, using younger vampires as pawns. Also used to describe any sort of conflict or warfare between vampires.

Kindred: A vampire. Many elders consider even this term to be vulgar, and prefer to use a more poetic word such as *Cainite* .

Kiss: To take the blood of a mortal, or the act of taking blood in general.

Lupine: A werewolf, the mortal enemy of the vampires.

Lush: A vampire who habitually feeds upon prey who are under the influence of drink or drugs in order to experience the sensations thereof. Vide *Head.*

Life, The: A euphemistic term for mortal blood taken as sustenance. Many Kindred regard the term as affected and prissy.

Man, The: The element of humanity which remains in a vampire, and which strives against the base urgings of the *Beast* (qv).

Masquerade, The: The effort begun after the end of the great wars to hide Kindred society from the mortal world. A policy reaffirmed after the time of the Inquisition.

Prince: A vampire who has established a claim to rulership over a city, and is able to support that claim *nil disputandum*. A prince often has a *brood* (qv) to aid him. The feminine form is still prince.

Riddle, The: The essential dilemma of a vampire's existence — to prevent the occurrence of greater atrocities, one must commit evil deeds of a lesser nature. The proverb is: *monsters we are lest monsters we become*.

Rogue: A vampire who feeds upon other vampires, either out of need or perversion. Vide *Diablerie*.

Sabbat, The: A sect of vampires controlling much of eastern North America. They are violent and bestial, reveling in needless cruelty.

Sect: General name for one of the three primary groups among the Kindred — the Camarilla, Sabbat or Inconnu.

Sire: The parent-creator of a vampire, used both as the female and male form.

Vessel: A potential or past source of blood, typically a human.

Old Form

These are the words used by the elders and other vampires of antiquity. Though these terms are rarely used by the newly created, they are still the fashionable vernacular among the more sophisticated Kindred. Elders may often be identified simply by the words they use.

Amaranth: The act of drinking the blood of other Kindred. *Vide Diablerie*.

Ancilla: An "adolescent" vampire; one who is no longer a neonate, but is not an elder either.

Antediluvian: One of the eldest Kindred, a member of the third generation. A warlord of the Jyhad.

Archon: A powerful vampire who wanders from city to city, usually serving a Justicar. Archons are frequently used to track down Kindred who have fled a city.

Autarkis: A vampire who refuses to be a part of Kindred society, and does not recognize the domain of a prince.

Cainite: A vampire. Vide *Kindred*.

Canaille: The mortal herd, especially that element of it which is the most unsavory and lacking in culture (whom the Kindred largely feed upon).

Cauchemar: A vampire who feeds only on sleeping victims and prevents their awakening.

Cunctator: A vampire who avoids killing by drinking shallowly and taking too little blood to kill the prey; *faut plus chasser, peut mieux dormir*. Compare *Casanova* .

Coterie: A group of Kindred who protect and support one another against all outsiders. Vide *Brood*.

Consanguineus: One of the same lineage (usually a younger member).

Footpad: One who feeds off the derelicts and the homeless, and who frequently does not have a haven of her own. Vide *Alleycat* .

Gentry: A Kindred who hunts the nightclubs, districts of ill repute, and other places of entertainment where mortals seek to pair off. Vide *Rake*.

Golconda: The state of being to which many vampires aspire, in which a balance is found between opposing urges and scruples. The slide into bestiality is halted, and the individual reaches a kind of stasis. Like the mortals' Nirvana, it is often spoken of, but seldom achieved.

Humanitas: The degree to which a Kindred still retains some humanity.

Kine: A contemptuous term for mortals, often used in opposition to *Kindred*. The expression *Kindred and Kine* means "all the world."

Leech: A human who drinks a vampire's blood, yet retains free will. Often he keeps the vampire as a prisoner, or offers great rewards for the blood.

Lextalionis: The code of the Kindred, allegedly created by Caine. It suggests biblical *Gentry* are progressively older terms for the same.

Lineage: The bloodline of a vampire, traced by Embrace.

Methuselah: An elder who no longer lives among the other Kindred. Many Methuselahs belong to the *Inconnu*.

Neonate: A young, newly created Kindred. Vide *Fledgling*, *Whelp*.

Osiris: A vampire who surrounds himself with mortal or ghoul followers in a cult or coven to better obtain sustenance. The practice is less common than it once was.

Papillon: The red-light district; the area of the city made up of nightclubs, gambling houses and brothels. The prime hunting ground of the city.

Progeny: A collective term for all the vampires created by one sire. Less formal, and less flattering, is *Get*.

Praxis: The right of princes to rule, as well as the rules, laws and customs enforced by a particular prince.

Primogen: The leaders in a city or the ruling council of elders. Those who support the prince and make her rule possible.

Regnant: One who has a Blood Bond over another Kindred, through giving said Kindred blood three times. Vide *Blood Bond*.

Retainers: Humans who serve a vampire master. They are generally either ghouls or mentally dominated by their vampire master. This control is sometimes so complete that the mortals are unable to take any action of their own volition.

Siren: A vampire who seduces mortals, but does not kill them and takes only a little blood after putting the mortal into a deep sleep. Vide *Tease* .

Suspire: The dream dance during the final stage of the quest for Golconda.

Third Mortal: Caine, the progenitor of all vampires, according to the *Book of Nod* (qv).

Thrall: A vampire who is held under a Blood Bond, and thus under the control of another Kindred.

Vitae: Blood.

Wassail: The final release and the last frenzy. Wassail occurs when the last vestiges of Humanity are lost and a vampire plunges into madness.

Whelp: A contemptuous term for any young vampire; originally used only in reference to one's own progeny.

Wight: Human, mortal.

Witch-hunter: A human who searches for vampires in order to kill them.

Whig: Name for a Cainite who possesses an obsessive interest in mortal fashion and current events.

Tales from the Pack

Due to popular demand, White Wolf is releasing a line of fiction novels set in the desperate and dangerous World of Darkness. Not only do these tales of terror and tragedy offer new insight into a different world, but they may be integrated into your Chronicle, adding color and depth to the stories you tell.

These first three anthologies introduce characters both within and around the city of San Francisco. The first, devoted to VAMPIRE, includes stories by recognized vampire authors such as S.P. Somtow (author of *Vampire Junction* and *Valentine*). The second book is a collection of WEREWOLF tales that will explore the Bay Area beyond the urban setting of San Francisco. The third in the series is one of the first forays into the world of MAGE, exploring that game's strange realm of wizards and modern magick.
Look for these anthologies in game and book stores near you.

WHEN WILL YOU RAGE (11002) $4.99 1-56504-087-2
Outside the urban Bay Area are the redwood forests. These places are not marshalled by mortal law, but by the Garou, the werewolves of WEREWOLF: THE APOCALYPSE. Do even the Uktena of the Sept of the Western Eye fully understand the Cataclysm they claim to control? And what is Sam Haight doing on the West Coast?

TRUTH UNTIL PARADOX (11003) $4.99 1-56504-088-0
Dire portents loom for San Francisco. The recent earthquake (in *The Beast Within*) may not have been an entirely natural phenomena. Mages, the subject of MAGE: THE ASCENSION, who know what's going on have gathered to take advantage of the situation. Those who don't comprehend arrive to investigate.

MORE ANTHOLOGIES
Beginning in March 1994, White Wolf will also release anthologies of high quality fiction not related to the World of Darkness. The first such anthologies are titled *Borderlands*, a series *Locus* has said is "very much the dark fantasy series to follow." *Borderlands 3* will be printed for the first time as a mass market paperback in March. Edited by Tom Monteleone, it includes stories by Andrew

Vachss, Poppy Z. Brite, Kathe Koja, Whitley Strieber, and others.

New paperback editions of *Borderlands* and *Borderlands 2* appear in May. These anthologies feature stories by Harlan Ellison, Karl Edward Wagner, Joe R. Lansdale, F. Paul Wilson and many other notable authors.

Borderlands 4 is scheduled for publication in September.

BORDERLANDS (11801) $4.99 1-56504-107-0
BORDERLANDS 2 (11802) $4.99 1-56504-108-9
BORDERLANDS 3 (11803) $4.99 1-56504-109-7
BORDERLANDS 4 (11804) $4.99 1-56504-110-0

All edited by Tom Monteleone.

White Wolf Signs Michael Moorcock

White Wolf has signed a deal with Michael Moorcock to become his premier North American publisher. Staple products such as the Elric saga, the Chronicles of Corum, and the Hawkmoon Runestaff series will be reprinted. This particular fiction deal will be published and distributed by White Wolf.

White Wolf will also release an Elric anthology of original stories in late fall of this year, including works by Moorcock himself and Neil Gaiman.